TERROR TALES
OF YORKSHIRE

Edited by Paul Finch

TERROR TALES OF YORKSHIRE

First published in 2014 by Gray Friar Press.
9 Abbey Terrace, Whitby,
North Yorkshire, YO21 3HQ, England.
Email: gary.fry@virgin.net
www.grayfriarpress.com

Typesetting and design by Paul Finch and Gary Fry

ISBN: 978-1-906331-47-4

TERROR TALES
OF YORKSHIRE

TABLE OF CONTENTS

IN OCTOBER WE BURIED
THE MONSTERS
Simon Avery

February

Emily decided that they'd unpacked enough boxes for the day. She took Jez's hand, led him out of the narrow little cottage his father had left in their care and out, up onto the hill. The lights of the little village of Holywell below them looked impossibly perfect from here. Emily kicked off her shoes and followed the lowering sun. The grass was still wet from the showers that had dogged the drive from London to this remote village some ten miles or so from Helmsley, on the edge of the North Yorkshire Moors. Now everything was so still, Emily felt sure that if she stopped and listened, she would only hear the blood in her veins and the hum of the earth beneath her feet.

She ran ahead of Jez. She felt light finally, full of optimism for whatever the future held for them. A new start perhaps. A new outlook. But when she turned, Jez was still in the same place, looking down at his feet, which seemed to say more than he'd intended it to.

"What is it?" she asked.

"This," he said, digging at the grass with the toe of his boots. "*This* is the labyrinth."

She returned to his side and saw what it was he meant. Holywell Hill was no normal hill; etched into its sides were a series of roughly symmetrical, yet well-worn terraces circling it from the base to the peak. "How is it a labyrinth?" she asked.

"It's not a labyrinth in the sense of a puzzle," Jez said, warming to his chosen subject. "Sometimes they're called turf mazes or Troy Towns, but most of them are relatively small in comparison to Holywell Hill. Glastonbury Tor is a better example, although its terraces are fairly well weathered now."

"But what are they for?"

"It was a ritual," Jez said. "Some kind of archaic ceremony tied into something that happened here centuries ago. This is where the song I've been trying to understand came from." He paused for a moment, glancing down at the village below them. They could hear the distant sound of the artesian well near the house, the trickling water. "On a certain day of the year, they'd all dress up in masks

1

and walk the labyrinth, singing that song my mother sang," he said. "I just about remember it when I was a kid."

"Why the hill? What's so special about it?"

He shrugged. "There are the usual legends of faeries, elves, goblins. From what I gather in this region they referred to them as the Pale Folk. But they weren't the pretty little winged faeries that the Victorians popularised. Some folklorists suggested that they were a conquered race living in hiding. Sometimes in stories they stole children and replaced them with changelings."

This was one of Jez's chosen subjects and although Emily found it fascinating, she was too tired to consider it any further. She didn't want him to think of his mother so soon. It was difficult enough that her memory was locked in the little cottage rooms: how she became a shadowy, sickly presence who'd been bedridden for months, and then when Jez was just six, had taken her own life. Jez had discovered her in the bath, her wrists opened up. These things were Emily's main argument against coming here. Jez didn't need these harsh memories making him any worse. She'd come to accept he was a distant man at the best of times, but he had the capacity for such warmth and tenderness; being surrounded by the memory of a mother who'd committed suicide and a father who'd gone mad just seemed too much.

But nonetheless, here they were. The sun had dipped below the other side of the hill and the light was leaving the day. Emily tugged Jez away from his stories and led him to the top of the hill, ignoring the ancient terraces, whether it was considered heresy or not. On the way, she let her dress fall from her shoulders and then she stepped out of it entirely. She turned and slapped a hand over her mouth to stifle a giggle as Jez began struggling with his shirt buttons and his belt. Soon they were naked and shivering beneath the stars. She'd never done this before. It made her feel like someone else entirely. When they finally lay down in the grass, the stars seemed to slide away into a glittering smear across the universe. When Jez pressed himself inside her, she felt a sudden longing to hold him there forever as if to ensure he didn't go away again. But when she held his face and covered it in kisses, she saw that even here, in this weightless moment on the hill, the haunted look in his eyes remained; whatever it was that sat like a stone inside him could not simply be relinquished by the act of hands and eyes and the soft pressing of skin upon skin.

She heard it then: the skeleton of the song he'd carried with him from this place to London and back, and hoped to understand here in the wild moors of his youth. Emily couldn't decide if the song was in him or her, or the earth they were lain upon. She encircled Jez in her arms, closed her eyes and held on.

March

"Dad?"

The old man hadn't even moved. He was sitting in the day room of the psychiatric unit with his hair awry and his dressing gown open. His feet were half in, half out of his slippers. Emily knew that the man Jez had grown up with wouldn't have been seen dead looking so unkempt.

"He's responding to the medication but it's a slow process," the doctor at his side said. She was a young Indian woman in a suit. "He was quite agitated initially," she said, looking at her notes. "I believe he was arrested after causing a disturbance at a gathering in his village."

"Yes," Jez said. "He was trying to stop them from performing an old village custom." The old man had smashed some village windows and attacked a couple of the people as they arrived on the hill. The police had been called when it became apparent that Jez's father would not be mollified. He hadn't responded well to the doctor who'd examined him so they'd arranged for involuntary commitment here in this unit. That had been in October, three months ago. Each time they arrived here at the unit, Emily hoped to find the man Jez remembered waiting for them, and each time they drove home with Jez feeling powerless, angry; hostile towards the people who only tried to make things better, Emily included.

After the doctor left, Jez and Emily sat down opposite the old man. He was staring out of the window at the flat square of the concrete car park. Jez seemed to be at a loss as to how to reach his father. "Dad," he began. "How are you feeling?"

Nothing.

"We've moved into the house. It's looking better. We've cleaned the place up. It'll be ready when you're well enough to come back." Jez stalled. They both knew that if the old man left here, he wouldn't be able to go back to Holywell.

"You shouldn't be there."

"What?" Jez leaned closer, putting an encouraging smile on his face.

But the old man wasn't smiling. He only had one more thing to say before he reverted back into himself: "The hill," he said. "You're a child of the hill. Leave. You're better off as far away from that place as possible."

3

April

The wind rushed down from the steep fells and across the grey sweep of moorland and down the narrow street of Holywell. It was a nondescript village with rows of unremarkable cottages built of local limestone and slate roofs. A grocer, a butcher, a pub and a general store that also acted as a post office. The dusty windows were filled with faded toys for children of a bygone age, and postcards and maps for the handful of fell walkers that passed through here.

"How's our mum-to-be doing today?" the woman at the post office asked, and came around the counter to place a warm hand on Emily's belly.

"Other than the morning sickness and feeling dead on my feet as soon as I wake up in the morning, I'm fine," Emily said. She reached for a packet of cornflakes so she could step away from the unwelcome hand without the woman taking offence. Initially the people of Holywell had been decidedly cool to the new additions to the village, but perhaps that had been purely in anticipation of a musician moving in and keeping them all up at night with his music. That and the fact that Jez's father had run amok during their last festival on the hill. But they'd thawed over the weeks, due in no small part Emily was sure, to the news of her pregnancy. The woman at the post office seemed to know almost as soon as Emily had.

And once she did, the rest of the village followed suit. They were even thawing towards Jez. Gradually.

It helped that the album he was working on was progressing well. It mellowed him a little. He had the bare bones of it recorded within a month. Emily heard the tune that he'd brought with him there in the new music. Those ten notes that he remembered his mother singing here in the cottage before she'd killed herself. He'd come back here to his father's home to discover the origin of that song. The secret, he was sure, was in these moors and hills and the people who called it their home, buried in the culture that he'd learned could be a basis for the music he wrote. Jez's father refused to speak about any of it. How many times had she heard Jez play those ten notes on a piano or a guitar, only to stall after a speculative eleventh or twelfth note?

But so far, despite the thaw, these people had been resistant to his queries. He'd spent time in the pub, cosying up to the older regulars who'd come in from the cold of the moors, subtly working the conversation around to the song that he remembered, but thus far, they were either genuinely ignorant of what he was asking after, or continued to harbour a quiet grudge against the son of the man on the hill who'd gone crazy. Emily could hardly blame them.

"Where's that husband of yours?" the woman asked. "I hope he's not neglecting the mother of his unborn child with all that rock and roll music he plays…"

Emily smiled. "He's in Leeds with a friend at the moment, researching some old music, but don't worry, he's looking after me. He'll be home later."

Although the bags would weigh her down, she'd been meaning to investigate the ruins of the church since they'd moved here, so she decided to do just that while Jez was away. She wondered what the reason was for a church to close its doors. Perhaps the pastor had moved on or died and the parish had somehow been overlooked, however unlikely that seemed. She wondered how the village worshipped, if they were that way inclined.

Emily placed her bags outside the ruin of the church and tied her hair back into a ponytail. Save for the skeleton of its shape, there was little to signify that the building had ever been a church. The lead and the slates of the roof had collapsed inward and left the joists bare to the elements. The stained glass windows were all but gone; only a few panes remained at the rear of the building where she assumed the pulpit to have been. In places the weathered stone of the church had collapsed entirely, and here the Yorkshire countryside had had its way and enveloped the interior with heather and gorse. She stepped through the archway and pushed aside the remains of the once stout oak door, peering inside. The interior still harboured some of the familiar objects but was transformed by dereliction and the encroaching trees and ferns tangled in the joists of the roof. Emily could smell the earth and the sweet corruption of hawthorn blossom. She heard the sudden rush of wind blowing through the shattered stained glass windows. There were several rows of rotted pews and the remains of a pulpit. A cross had fallen from its place between the windows and come to rest in the tangle of hawthorn; somehow it had wound itself around the wood of the cross, and it seemed to Emily to signify something else entirely.

Emily had stopped to study an inscription in the stone when she heard a noise that was neither nature nor weather. She froze and glanced around, studying the overgrown profusion and decay for movement. There was none. She relaxed a little and clambered carefully over a fallen beam to get closer to the altar.

She was half way over when a flock of starlings burst into the sky. The sudden sound was like stark applause rising into the

5

silence. When she glanced up she saw the long pale limbs of the man wrapped behind the cross.

But that was ridiculous. The cross was too narrow to hide anyone.

Emily, frozen, stared so hard at the cross that her eyes lost focus. She heard something that must surely have been wood cracking, but then she saw the hands, long and spindly like white spiders uncurling around the cross, and she fell backwards in her sudden panic to be away. The scene seemed to want to swallow her up into its madness. She couldn't move. Her legs felt as if they'd turned hollow. Something that was impossibly narrow and atrophied unpeeled itself from the underside of the cross and turned its pale, grub-like face to her. Its eyes and mouth were like soft, wet folds. Then it quickly crawled into the knots of hawthorn and through the shattered stained glass window. It took no more than seconds. Emily rose slowly, her eyes fixed where the pale thing had been, and backed away over the fallen joist and out of the church and home, where she checked all of the rooms and locked the doors until Jez came home.

May

One night Emily woke and reached over for Jez and found he wasn't there. She felt alarm spread throughout her bones. She'd had trouble sleeping since that day in the church and although Jez had been quietly dubious about what she had seen, he had promised to stay close at hand ever since.

She rose and slipped on her dressing gown and listened. Perhaps he was in the garage, working. Over these past few weeks, Jez had withdrawn gradually into the music he was composing. When they'd moved in, Jez had cleared the garage of all the junk that his father had accrued over the years and shifted the bare bones of his music equipment in there: a battered old Apple Mac, a keyboard, two guitars and a sixteen-channel analogue mixer. There was the usual mass of leads taped together, snaking from the cottage into the garage. Emily had grown used to trying to sleep with the sound of bass-lines and drumbeats vibrating through the walls. But it was important to Jez to make this record now. It had been years since his heyday with a major label behind him and a full diary of festival dates to fall back on. There had been some lean times, and he'd more than once on his bad days told her she should leave now there was nothing, but she hadn't ever wavered. It had never been about the money or the travel; it had always been about him; the man he was. She caught glimpses of it every now and then, like sunlight flashing through cloud, and she'd remained all these years for those moments, hoping he'd come back to her one day. Perhaps he'd never really been that man and the first flush of love had blinded her to that fact, but she sensed he would always be *attempting* to live up to her belief in him, and that was enough.

There was music playing in the garage but Jez was not there. The garage doors had been flung open and she heard that all too familiar melody buried beneath the music, that tune that his mother had sung all those years ago under this roof. It followed her up the hill to where she was relieved to find Jez standing. He was looking up at the stars.

"Jez," she said. "Baby, are you okay?"

He glanced down at her and smiled. "I'm fine," he said, but she knew he was not. His eyes were glazed with memories.

She took his hand and squeezed it. "You can tell me, you know. You know you can tell me anything."

He nodded and then said, "Did I ever tell you that my mother once drove me out onto the moors one night and left me there?"

"Christ," Emily said. She knew his mother had been unbalanced but Jez had never really told her the entire story.

"She drove me out into the moors, parked the car somewhere and walked me out over some stiles and beside a river. It was pitch black but she'd brought a torch with her. We walked for about half an hour. Then abruptly she stopped, turned off the torch and pushed me down. Then she walked away. I started crying, trying to keep up with her, but she turned and screamed at me: 'Stay the *fuck* away from me! You are *not* my son! You stay there or I'll *fucking kill* you!'"

"Jesus," Emily said. "What happened?"

Jez shrugged and smiled. The act of telling the story was a catharsis for him, in the same way the music had always been. "My old man came and found me a few hours later. My mum had gone home, saying 'I've got rid of him!' He made her drive him out to where she'd left me. It was starting to get light by then. He found me curled up under a tree by the river. He thought I was dead, I looked so still. He carried me back inside his coat. I sometimes think I can almost remember that."

"Why would your mother do that?" Emily asked. "I know she was sick, but she seemed to have something in her head that she fixated on…"

Jez nodded. "She burned my hand on the stove once." He pointed out the puckered skin on the back of his hand, but Emily had seen it, stroked it, and kissed it many times. "Sometimes she'd pull me close to her and I thought she was going to kiss me, but then she'd stare at me and smell me, and then push me away. I'd hear her arguing with my old man, saying, 'It's not *him*. It's not my Jeremy!'"

Jez accepted Emily into his arms and for a moment she felt that this was indeed the man she'd fallen in love with. She could ease this burden if he'd just *let her*.

"I always thought in the past that today just isn't my day. *Tomorrow* it will be. Tomorrow I'll turn a corner and things will change. But then I had music and I made money and I had a little bit of fame and still nothing changed. And then I met you and for a while I felt like I was almost whole. But then I realised I couldn't stay like that for good. This feeling in me, this depression, I suppose… I can't ever change. I'm the same person. I'm the little boy whose mother didn't love him enough to keep him. I might as well still be out there in the dark."

Emily touched his face. She thought there might be tears on his face, but there were none. There never were. He was not that kind of man. She clung to him on the hill and she listened to his mother's melody drifting up to meet them.

June

Emily went with Jez to Leeds in the second week of June. He'd finally tracked someone down who could tell him something about the tune that had haunted him all these years. They were quiet during the journey; Emily glanced from Jez to the view: gorse spilling down the side of a grey hill; factory chimneys half-erased by the morning fog. Their emotions seemed to have informed the landscape. She realised how important this was to Jez; she was glad to accompany him and glad to be away from the house, the hill, the village and the, by now, cloying attentions of its occupants.

Tom Finn was almost exactly the man Emily had expected to find nursing an encyclopaedic knowledge of folk music and a Midnight Bell Ale in the Victoria on Great George Street. His hair was fine and grey and pulled back in a pony tail; his horn-rimmed spectacles constantly fell forward to the tip of his nose, and his entire manner of amiable certainty seemed to have folded his lanky frame into a posture of permanent obeisance.

"I had a bugger of a time with this tune," he said, once Jez had bought a round of drinks for them all. His Huddersfield accent was as thick and blunt as his fingers.

8

"I told you, didn't I?" Jez said. "I've been looking into it for the last twenty years or so and made no headway." Emily was glad to see him animated by the prospect of solving the mystery at least.

"I had to go back and root through Percy Sharp and Nigel Huddleston's files and tapes, and even then, I had a game of it, as all I had to go on was your ten bloody notes of a tune."

"Who were Percy Sharp and Nigel Huddleston?" Emily felt bound to ask.

Tom shook his pony tail and pushed his spectacles back up his nose. "From 1958 to 1978 Percy and Nigel recorded nearly four-hundred Yorkshire folk songs, going back to the seventeenth century. They started with the repertoire of a school cleaner who was in her eighties at the time. *Old Matha Gummersal Had a Mule*, *I'm a Collier By Me Trade*, and the *Craven Churn-Supper Song* – all sung into their tape recorder, by singers, mostly now dead, in Todmorden and Whitby, Calderdale, Wensleydale, Eskdale... Songs of courting and seafaring and farming and hunting – and a fair bit of drinking. Bawdy songs. Accordion and fiddle tunes. And songs called 'mouth music', with no words as such, just 'Taroo-de-di-diddle-ee-dum's. And they were recorded by labourers and ploughboys and milkmaids in bars and homesteads and farmers' fields."

"And you found my song amongst all those tapes?" Jez was sat forward now, Emily noticed. He'd gripped her hand tightly under the table.

"With a bit of hunting, yes," Tom said, smiling. "From what I can gather it predates the Wars of the Roses and it's tied to Holywell Hill and its people. There are no other incidences of the song appearing anywhere else but in that village, which is why it was such a bugger to locate. But there's some evidence that it has antecedents hundreds of years before even that."

"What is it called?" Jez asked.

Tom reached down into his rucksack and produced some papers in a manila folder and a CD in a plain plastic sleeve. "Allowing for dialect and variants of the words over the centuries, the title is probably *In October We Buried the Monsters,* or *Faeries* or *Pale Folk*, or some variation thereof. They were definitely burying something. Because they were never written down, they were only sung and heard by descendants who copied them, like Chinese whispers. According to the notes with the song, the village was regularly plagued by these Pale Folk, which I assume bears some relation to faerie folklore: pookas, boggarts, changelings, will-o-the-wisps. Now the Pale Folk were believed to live inside Holywell

9

Hill, apart from when they came out to steal children or old folk, or Christ knows what else…"

Tom shrugged. "Whether there's any basis for truth here is entirely up to whether you still believe in the Tooth Fairy and Santa Claus or not. But the villagers sealed the hill by singing the song and marching through the terraces of the hill until they reached the peak. It's the words and the *belief* in those words that are magical, I think; the act itself is purely symbolic. Samhain, although it's primarily considered a Gaelic festival, was considered a time when the spirits or faeries could more easily come into our world, so that timing was considered efficacious. From what I understand, they still practice the ceremony at the end of every October."

"Over the years it's become a bit more extravagant," Jez said. "Masks for the children and offerings at the well in the weeks leading up to it. It's more of a bank holiday for the villagers."

"Except your old man took umbrage at it last year…" Tom hesitated; unsure if this last piece of information should be taken lightly.

Jez nodded. "Our family has issues," he said, squeezing Emily's hand again.

"Do you have a recording of the song?" Emily asked.

Tom slid the CD across to Jez. "It's all yours, mate," he said.

July

The villagers began to leave gifts at their door. They seemed like offerings: meadow buttercups and oxeye daisies, harebells and northern marsh orchids. For the first few days Emily and Jez gathered them up and put them in water around the cottage, thinking how they brightened the place now that summer had finally taken hold, and that perhaps the villagers were simply taking them to their bosom. Although Jez had found some consolation in the discovery of the song, it had also forced him deeper into finding something new in his own work, and that took him further away from Emily when she needed him the most. The baby was beginning to get into a pattern of sleeping and waking that was not in synch with Emily's. She'd noticed the first stretch marks begin to appear and she was starting to get hungry at the wrong time of the day. She wanted to talk to Jez more, but he was gone, even when he was there at the other side of the kitchen table.

After three more days of floral gifts, out of curiosity and the desire to talk to someone, Emily went down to the village and asked who to thank. As was her custom by now, the woman who ran the post office stepped out to embrace Emily and kiss her cheeks, which Emily accepted with as much courtesy as she could muster. Then she was enticed into the pub by several of the locals, purely to update them on the progress of the baby. There were three or four men inside, pints of ale in hand. They seemed pleasant enough, passing time with the usual niceties, but after ten minutes had passed, the proximity of these strange men, combined with the heat and smell of beer started making Emily uncomfortable and nauseous. She tried to make her apologies but realised that the landlord was suddenly behind her, florid-faced and grinning. He snaked an arm around her waist and placed his hand on her belly. She felt the baby kick, as if instinctively.

"I think it's time for me to be getting back to my husband," she began.

They laughed at this and pressed in closer. The landlord's hand crept lower and she felt the first bloom of fear inside her. She took the hand and tried to remove it, but it was rigid. The landlord pressed himself into the hollow of her back and she felt him swell against her backside. The moment seemed to stir out of reality. The faces around her became soft and leering and liquid; the voices narrowed to a whine in her ears. She was going to faint. She had to scream, otherwise who knew what might happen? She reached out blindly and grasped at a glass on the bar. Without thought, she threw it down on the floor where it shattered at her feet. The moment seemed to snap back into focus. The men stepped back. The hand withdrew. Emily could hear her breath coming in loud, quick gasps. She glanced around at the men's faces. They looked at her like scolded mischievous children. They turned away then.

She hurried out of the pub and back home, up the hill, to Jez.

She took all of the flowers and tossed them outside, let the breeze take them away.

August

She could hear breathing in the cottage.

It had hovered on the periphery of her awareness for several days. It was like a dog, following her around. It was so quiet, she couldn't decide if it was there or not. She held her breath and listened: *yes*, there it was; *no*, it had gone. She was beginning to doubt her sanity. Jez was always in the garage now. It seemed to be consuming him. He would get up before the sun, climb up the hill and watch it rise, spread across the Dales, the valleys and rivers, and then lock himself inside that little garage and work until the sun was gone and Emily was asleep.

She felt him get into bed next to her (for it seemed she could barely sleep anymore – there was simply no comfort to be had) and he put his arms around her. He clung to her until he was asleep. She listened to him. She could hear breath but it wasn't hers and it wasn't his. She pressed her ear to his chest and felt it rise and fall, could just make out the shallow breaths in his throat. It satisfied her for a while. He'd gone down to the village after the events in the pub last month. It seemed for a while to rouse him out of the torpor that the music was leaving him in. But after an hour, Jez had returned, stinking of booze.

"What happened?" she asked.

"You must have got the wrong end of the stick," he said, as gently as his inebriated state would allow.

She'd stared at him for a moment. "Fuck you," she said and walked away.

She'd considered packing her bags, and then she'd done just that. But who could she go to? The handful of friends she'd had when she was in her twenties were all married and had children and sensible jobs and sensible homes and sensible lives. She couldn't imagine arriving at one of their doors in this state. And her mother was in Australia now with a new husband. Her father was long gone. She had no one. Only Jez. And he was gone. Almost gone.

After listening to the breathing for an hour she rose finally, glad to be up and away from the discomfort the baby was causing her. She made a cup of tea and sat at the kitchen table, listening. The cottage was silent. She rose then and, her ears pricked, followed the sound. She had to. It was driving her insane.

It took her half an hour of pacing the handful of rooms, back and forth, upstairs and down. But then she smelled it too. The sound and the smell originated from the same place: the airing cupboard. As she moved the towels and sheets, the smell grew more unpleasant. It was an earthy smell, like mould growing behind wallpaper. With some effort she got down on her hands and knees and stared at the thing at the back of the airing cupboard. Whatever it was, it *was* breathing. She tensed herself, worried finally that it was a trapped or dying animal that might have one last attack in its bones.

But it wasn't an animal. It looked like a foetus. A foetus carved out of wood. It was lying on a bed of earth and flowers in the dark. It was no bigger than both of her hands pressed together. And it was breathing. She could hear it quite clearly.

Emily got to her feet and closed the door. She walked to the bedroom and watched Jez sleeping for a moment. After a moment

12

she went downstairs and out of the side door to the garage. The place was empty. There were no instruments here now, no tangle of leads, no synthesizers, no computers. At some point he'd cleared it all away. There was just a seat and a CD player, the speakers. When she pressed Play, she heard him singing *In October We Buried the Monsters*.

She sat down and began to cry.

September

"You shouldn't be in Holywell," Jez's father said. "You shouldn't have gone there in the first place."

Jez didn't know she had come to the hospital. She'd taken the car and driven away. She'd half expected the roads to be closed, for them to head her off, keep her from leaving, but there was nothing like that. Jez wasn't even there. She didn't know where he went anymore.

Jez's father was responding to the medication finally. He seemed more alert now amongst the other patients in the day room. He'd combed his hair, but his shirt and trousers were still creased. It made Emily want to mother him.

But he wasn't in any mood for that. "It's due isn't it?" he said, "The baby. Soon. Next month. October."

She knew what he was getting at even if she didn't understand the whys and wherefores. "Yes."

He nodded. "Of course."

"Why did you try to stop them last year?" she asked. "During their festival."

"They brought you here with it," he said. "You and Jeremy. They did away with me." He studied her for a moment with his arms folded. He was deciding what to say, she thought. Weighing up what would make him sound more insane with what seemed to be genuine concern for his daughter-in-law. Finally he said, "Once the people of Holywell used to keep the Pale Folk locked underground. Not anymore. They serve the hill, the Pale Folk. Every October. Sometimes the Pale Folk demand a sacrifice, which at the end of the festival they bury at the top of the hill. A child. They replace it with a changeling, or a fetch. They call them faeries, but they're. Not. Fucking. Faeries."

She thought of the pale thing in the ruins of the church. No, it certainly wasn't a faerie, but it did look like something that had crawled out of the earth.

"It demands," Jez's father said. "The village. It demands."

Emily took his hand. "Demands what?"

"That," he said, pointing to her belly. "It demands *that*."

*

Emily drove home and arrived at the cottage just as the last of the summer light fled the day. She'd decided to pack her things and go, whether Jez was there or not.

But he was home. There were lights on in the kitchen and the smell of food cooking in the stove. She saw him moving around through the windows as she locked the car doors. The scene was one of domestic order. It didn't *look right*. The normality of it was utterly alien to her. But she was tired now. It was too late in the day to be travelling. She couldn't decide which of these things was madness or the pregnancy, or isolation clouding her judgement. She had to talk to Jez. She was not someone who ran away. She still loved him and that meant not leaving him behind.

"Emily," he said. "Where have you been?" He came to her and he kissed her. He smelled of earth. Something was different. She couldn't decide what it was. He had changed, and it wasn't simply that his clothes were clean and his face was shaved. His eyes. His eyes were different. She felt the small hairs on the back of her neck and arms rise.

"Dinner's ready," the stranger with Jez's face said. "But I have something to show you first."

She didn't want to see. But Jez was tugging her away from the welcoming smells of the kitchen and into the front room. She didn't want to see. Whatever it was, she was sure *she didn't want to see*.

Jez was in there. *Her* Jez. The fetch. The changeling. He was in pieces on the floor. He'd been dismantled. His head removed from his neck, his legs from his torso. He seemed to be made of wood. There was earth spilling out of his wounds. His face stared vacantly at her.

Emily began to scream.

October

When she woke, the ceremony had begun. She rose after a while and, after she'd looked at the letter again, she looked out of the window. She saw the procession of the villagers in the streets of the village below. They were wearing masks of suns and moons. They had bells on their clothes. She heard children's exuberant laughter. They were scattering flowers in their wake. And they were singing the song. But it wasn't the song she knew. She listened, thinking she had it wrong, but then she realised that it made sense. Tom Finn had likened the songs to Chinese Whispers. Words got corrupted over time, changed to fit the people who sang them. They were not here to bury monsters anymore. They were singing *In October We Buried the Children.*

She'd given birth to their baby boy two nights ago. The Jez that had come back from inside the hill, the Jez who had killed *her* Jez, helped deliver him. The villagers had crowded into the small bedroom to watch as she pushed and strained and wept. She felt so utterly alone. Whenever she opened her eyes, there they all were – the butcher and the grocer, the woman from the post office, the landlord and the men from the pub, staring, cheering, laughing, leering, singing. She'd heard her baby begin to cry and waited for him to be placed on her breast. She pressed her head back into the pillow, panting, willing the pain to recede, waiting, waiting... She must have fallen asleep, because when she lifted her head again, the bedroom was empty and her baby was gone. She wept for a while. Jez came back and sat at the side of the bed. He'd kept her here after the night he'd killed her Jez. He'd dismantled the car and taken away her phone so she couldn't leave. How could the real Jez be this man? She didn't know this man. But how could her Jez have been nothing more than something enchanted out of wood and earth? He'd gone out to live in the world, knowing that something was amiss, that he would never feel whole, despite the things he'd brought with him: success and experience and love. They were never enough, no matter how hard he tried.

"Where is my baby?" she'd asked. "He'll need feeding."

"You want the child?"

He sounded surprised, but he left the room and returned soon after with her baby. Jez's baby. She felt a deep well of emotion open up as he placed him into her arms. She pushed him hungrily to her face and smelled him, tears dripping from her eyes.

But it was wrong. It dawned on her slowly. He didn't smell right. In fact he didn't smell of anything other than earth. She listened to him breathing and she realised what it was. She studied him. He looked like her baby should look. His skin was real skin. His face was the face she wanted to fill her life to the brim with.

But it was not her baby. She knew it in the same way that Jez's mother had known. But she'd seen it when it was no more than wood and earth, hidden behind the towels and sheets in the airing cupboard. A foetus carved out of wood. A replacement. A changeling. A fetch.

15

She lifted it and gave it to the man with Jez's face. "Take it away," she said.

She hadn't seen it since. Nor had she seen or heard her real baby. She remembered Jez's father saying, '*Sometimes the Pale Folk demand a sacrifice, which at the end of the festival they bury at the top of the hill…*

They replace it with a changeling, or a fetch.'

In October We Buried The Children. She stood at the window as the villagers snaked through the village and wound their way into the terraces of the hill. Her child was waiting at the top of the hill, buried in the earth with his changeling twin. His fetch.

They'd forgotten about her, it seemed. Her part in the ceremony was over and all that remained was to complete the ritual and make their sacrifice to the Pale Folk. She was still sore from the birth and her breasts felt uncomfortable. She hadn't had a child to breastfeed. She yearned to hold him. She felt abandoned. She had nothing left. What would happen when this was all over? Did they expect her to accept the changeling? The real Jez had told her he was only here to ease the transfer. Then he would return to the Pale Folk, to what was his own kind now. Emily was glad they didn't expect her to live with a fake family.

But she couldn't let that happen. She wouldn't.

She moved from room to room restlessly with the letter. She stared up at the peak of the hill where the Jez she didn't know waited. There was no way she could go up there and retrieve her child and escape. They wouldn't let her. The song seemed to fill the rooms as the villagers began to circle the cottage on the hill, traversing the sacred groves.

But she had found the letter. It was under her pillow, where none of them had looked. She'd subsequently found two more in other out-of-the-way places. Her Jez had wanted to be sure she got the note. Something about that kind of silly logic made her want to weep at his loss, but something was in her mind, itching to make itself clear since she'd read the note he had left. Something else Tom Finn had told them. Suddenly it came to her: '*It's the words and the belief in those words that are magical, I think; the act itself is purely symbolic.*'

And the note made sense: 'Play the song in the garage. You'll know when. Play it loud! Love J.'

She let herself into the garage through the kitchen door. Through the window she could see them traversing the labyrinth in the masks they'd made.

They were reaching the final revolution of the hill. The sound of the song was muffled as she slipped into the garage. The CD player and the speakers were still here.

But so was Jez. The pieces of him had been tossed into the garage and lay scattered across the concrete. Emily froze, felt a shard of grief explode inside her that she felt sure might be her undoing. She pressed the heel of her hand into her eyes and forced herself to step between what remained of the man she had loved for over half of her life. She cried out finally as she reached the CD player. It was too much. What could this do? She thought the grief would consume her. She wanted only to lie here with the remains of her life, pull them to her and sleep forever.

But no. Jez had seen that there might be a way out of this. He'd spent the last weeks of his life preparing for the worst so that she might have a chance. Emily pressed the Eject button and the tray opened to reveal that the CD was still in there. She pushed the tray back in. Before she began she locked the garage door with a heavy padlock and then found the key to the kitchen door. She locked herself in. She turned up the volume and then she pressed Play.

Jez began to sing. Emily sat on the floor and waited to see what would happen. It took several minutes before she heard them outside the garage door, and then the doors begin to rattle. She couldn't hear what they were saying, but she was sure they had stopped singing. There was conviction in Jez's voice, a conviction and sincerity that had been absent in him for too long. There was *magic* in that. He sang out and she began to cry for what she had lost. But he'd found what was absent in him for too long. *I can't ever change,* he had said on the hill. *I'm the little boy whose mother didn't love him enough to keep him. I might as well still be out there in the dark.*

By the time the Jez that wasn't her Jez had broken down the garage door, he'd been abandoned. The villagers had scattered. Whatever it was in the words of the song that Jez had imbued with magic had broken the sway that the hill held over these people. After a while the Jez that was not her Jez walked away too.

Emily gathered the pieces of her husband close to her and let the song play.

November

Later, after the villagers had stumbled, bewildered, back to their homes, and October turned to November, Emily climbed the hill and shifted the earth away from her baby. The sight of him made

17

her weep, but she gathered him up into her arms and cried until she was done. She was about to leave when she heard the other child cry out. She moved the earth aside and looked down at his face. The changeling. He held out his hands to her.

After a moment, Emily gathered him into her arms too and took her babies down the hill, and away.

THE DECAPITATION DEVICE

"**F**rom Hell, Hull and Halifax, good Lord deliver us."

So reads the infamous 'Beggar's Litany', penned by the poet John Taylor in 1622, in reference to three places, in his opinion, where thieves and vagabonds least wanted to be.

The torments of Hell speak for themselves.

The notorious Hull Gaol was one of the most feared houses of correction in the whole of northern England.

And Halifax, in the West Riding of Yorkshire, was home to the so-called Halifax Gibbet, a crudely constructed decapitation machine, which would serve as a prototype for the infamous French guillotine.

During the French Revolution, the fiendish device designed by Doctor Joseph-Ignace Guillotin is estimated to have severed 100,000 heads. But the earlier model utilised in Halifax between 1286 and 1650, while not nearly so greedy for blood – it is only known to have accounted for 100 lives – is in some ways a more horrific memento of our violent past because of the minuscule nature of the offences it punished. In Halifax, the theft of goods to the value of just over 13 pence carried a mandatory death sentence: an amazingly harsh law carried over from the days of the medieval Manor of Wakefield, for which the small wool town of Halifax was an essential part, and the lords of which held life-and-death control over their tenants by order of King Henry III (1207-1272).

Similar brutal rights were exercised by other great barons in the Middle Ages. A pipe-roll of 1278 claimed that 94 privately-owned gibbets were in use in England, though only in Chester and Halifax did everyday malefactors die by axe rather than rope. But another chilling aspect of the Halifax method was the way it continued its gory work for many centuries after the exercise of private justice had ceased everywhere else. Even Oliver Cromwell, a notorious disciplinarian, was appalled to hear about it, especially when he learned that its victims did not even receive a proper trial. All that was required to be proved against Halifax felons was their possession of stolen property, and the unimpressive value of such – 13 pence was a relatively paltry amount even in the 17th century. It was Cromwell, in his capacity of Lord Protector of England, who abolished the gruesome practise in 1650.

The site of the Halifax Gibbet was restored as a visitor attraction in 1974, a reconstructed device marking the spot, alongside a *plaque listing the 52 heads lopped off there that history has deigned to attach names to. But not everyone in the town had viewed its removal so lightly. Immediately after 1650, the good citizens of Halifax were outraged to have lost their gibbet, and continued punishing felons viciously – often to the point of death – by the pillory and ducking-stool.*

THE COAT OFF HIS BACK
Keris McDonald

"Hello Geoff," said Dr Archwin, and he watched the skin around her eyes wrinkle into lines of sympathy. "How are you?"

"I'm fine." Geoff Leighton had to say that. It was the correct social formula. He noted that she was still waiting with that warm concerned look, so after an awkward beat he added, "Thank you for asking, Joyce."

"Well, it's good to see you back."

"There's been a rush job on, has there?" That was a little in-joke, and he saw her relax a touch. Working here, deadlines were not something to worry about. Funding and manpower, yes – but not time. They were standing in the main materials conservation lab of the York Castle Museum and were surrounded by labelled boxes, all filled with artefacts and items of antique clothing scheduled for immediate inspection and possible remedial action. Behind this room was a humidity-controlled storage facility which Dr Archwin tended to refer to as The Backlog; it was full, always – so much so that parts of the collection had to be kept in warehouses out on the Clifton Moor industrial estate. And down the corridor from where they stood now was the public area where the actual displays began; glass cases full of gowns and breeches and shoes, masks and purses, combs and jewellery and hats – all dimly spot-lit in rooms sealed away from the natural light that would rot fabric and fade colour. The items that the Great Unwashed got to see counted for a tiny percentage of those within the museum collection.

"We've actually had a new donation in," Dr Archwin said. "It's over by your desk. I thought you'd find it interesting."

"What about that WRAF uniform I was working on?" Leighton asked as he followed her across the room. He could see that the white expanse of his desk had been cleared and it made him feel faintly anxious, as if his services had been dispensed with.

"I had Louise finish it off for you. Nice fresh start."

Leighton blinked. *It's not like I've been ill. It was compassionate leave, that's all.* "Thank you," he said again, without conviction. Then; "Is this the bequest?"

'This' was a chest about a metre long. One glance told him that it was a mass-produced object of little value to a museum: early Victorian, brass corners, with cheap leather cladding over the panels that was now torn and curling up. And he thought he could detect a musty smell.

21

Dr Archwin looked pleased. "It came out of a sealed attic in Heworth, when the owners had the roof re-tiled. They didn't even *know* they had an attic until then, apparently. But it's the contents we're interested in, not the box."

"I'm glad to hear that."

"Probably eighteenth century, most of them. Someone was a collector."

"*Probably*?" It wasn't like Dr Archwin to be vague on dating. If she'd accepted the bequest for the collection, it was because it was of historical value. As Textiles Curator, she was forever fending off worthless old clothes that the public tried to donate, telling them regretfully that their gifts were "not within the scope of our collections policy."

"You'll see. Not exactly fashion pieces."

Leighton was intrigued, despite himself. He put his case carefully on the desk, and leaned with palms flat down either side.

"You'll find the accessioning information all up on file. The items are in surprisingly good condition," Dr Archwin added cheerfully, "despite the old-lady-smell."

He thought of the hospice room with its pastel colours; his mother's hands, grey already, peeking over the edge of the duvet like trapdoor spiders waiting to pounce. And the smell of age, and disinfectant, and adult nappies.

"Oh –" said Dr Archwin. "I'm so sorry, Geoff! That was ..."

"That's okay." His voice was calm and emotionless. He was pleased with himself for that.

"I'm an idiot."

"Honestly, it's not a problem. We were never close. And she went peacefully in the end."

"If you need anything..." Dr Archwin was older than him, but like most English people of her class had no idea how to deal with bereavement. She put her hand awkwardly on the back of his and gave it a squeeze. It was the first time in eight years they'd ever touched.

He snatched that hand away as if her nervous warmth burnt him. Offence flared in her eyes.

"I'm sorry," he stuttered, half-aware that he was cradling his hand to his chest protectively. "I ... I just don't like being touched suddenly."

"Of course." She was, he saw, as flushed and dismayed as he was, but for her the clash was tainted with guilt and now the admixture was curdling to pity. "Geoff, whatever you ... Just take the time you need. And let us know if there's anything we can do ..."

"Thanks."

"I lost my own father, to cancer. I know how hard it is."

This was excruciating. Couldn't she just leave him alone? He shook his head, forcing a smile. "Like I said, we weren't close."

Dr Archwin's eyebrows rose slightly. She probably wasn't even aware of her expression of disapproval. "She was your mother," she said gently.

Just go away. "I'm fine. I'll get to work."

"Okay."

"Okay."

"Keep me up to date with the new acquisition," she said as she walked off.

*

Leighton slipped on clean cotton gloves after opening the chest. That was one of the things he really liked about this job: the need for care and cleanliness. In this lab, dirt was the enemy. A rust-stain, a grease-spot, the subtle acid etch of a fingerprint – any contamination could cause inexorable damage to delicate historical fabrics. Dirt abrades. It attracts moisture, and provides a base for fungus to grow on. Silk and cotton threads do not last forever, but neither does bone nor iron. Everything in nature decays. Everything is transmuted, molecule by molecule, in the slow-burning alchemical crucible of time.

The chest opened easily, releasing a wave of the musty scent he'd already noticed.

Not an old-lady-smell, he said to himself sourly. *More like ... Something agricultural. Earthy.* That wasn't a good sign; he braced himself for maggot-frass and mould.

The layer revealed in the open box wasn't dirty sheepskin or anything similar, though. It was a dark blue brocade, hand-embroidered with symbols of some sort. And on top was a small piece of paper upon which was written, in elegant Victorian copperplate:

> *From the house of Dr Marmaduke Palmes,*
> *surgeon of the City of York*
> *I will have none of it*
> *Lev 13:52*

Leighton took careful photos before touching anything. He opened the accessions file on his computer and added the page for conservation notes, prepped a new box and layers of acid-free tissue paper, and only then gently drew the garment out for inspection.

It was a robe with an open front: made from thin woollen cloth with an irregular weft that argued it had been hand-loomed. The base weave was rather fine. He was almost sure that it was a traditional Bedouin *bisht* – he'd have to look that up on their photographic database – but it had been customised with what looked like Hebrew letters on top, executed in much coarser style and thread by someone, he suspected, unused to wielding a needle. The garment was noticeably heavy, and when he laid it out for inspection Leighton realised that small lumpy objects of some kind had been sewn into the broad lower hem.

What they were would have to await further inspection.

In the meantime, what he needed to do was appraise the piece and remove surface dust. Using a small hand-held vacuum-cleaner with fine muslin stretched across the nozzle to catch loose objects such as beads, he hoovered the garment inside and out. Not much dirt came off, and there was little discolouration about the neckline where one might expect it. He suspected the robe was not often worn. He laid it within its new box and padded it with scrunched-up acid-free tissue to round out the arms and skirt; the ideal was to have no folds and no creases left in during storage.

Beneath the robe was a large square silk cloth that had started out black, he suspected, but was faded now to a mottled purple, the colour of old bruises. It was stitched with a red wool circle, more quasi-Hebrew letters, and some symbols that he tentatively identified as a chalice, a knife, a heart and an eye from which lines of light or possibly flame were streaming.

He took pictures and measurements of everything.

Beneath the altar-cloth, if that was what it was, were a pair of beaded man's slippers – definitely eighteenth century in style – a skullcap embroidered with more amateurish Hebrew, a shallow silver-edged bowl of yellow ivory, a dagger without a sheath, a plain wooden stick as long as Leighton's forearm with a leather grip at one end, and a lead cross scratched with sigils that he didn't recognise at all.

His area of conservation expertise was clothing, so he boxed up the hard artefacts and set them aside for Louise. Ritual kit for a magician, was his disdainfully amused surmise. He looked through the accession numbers on file, but only the date, donor and the barest of descriptions had been logged so far. Perhaps Dr Archwin found it faintly risible too, or wanted to avoid sensationalist statements. In every century magic lingered on as a kind of minority interest, sometimes vigorously condemned by the establishment and sometimes treated as a peculiar hobby for the not-quite-respectable. The eighteenth century was, after all, the era of the Hellfire Club. And the materials here – an imported Oriental robe, silk and ivory and gilding – suggested a well-to-do amateur. Perhaps even the Dr Palmes fingered by the Victorian collector.

Leighton was a conservator, not a curator. Only the structural integrity of the items mattered to him, not their purpose or history. Dr Archwin had been right about the state of preservation though: aside from some fading, which was to be expected from natural dyes, the fabric looked to be in good condition. He taped a clean layer of acid-free paper over his desktop before starting on the final garment. Cleanliness was king in this place.

The very bottom layer of the chest's contents proved to be the source of the smell. It was a riding coat, and as soon as he unfolded it upon his desk Leighton made an educated guess at the first decades of the 1700s, just from the style of the cut – those deep cuffs, that collarless neck, the ranks of buttonholes, the broad skirts. He was a little nonplussed by the material though. He'd expect to see a gentleman's coat made up in good cloth, not large patchwork pieces of leather.

Too thin to be a cavalry coat, he thought: *that's not armour.* Perhaps it was intended to afford some protection from rainfall or wind, but it had no lining or padding of any kind, nor any sign that any such had once been attached.

It didn't seem to fit with the rest of the box's contents at all. Instead of the near-fetishistic ornamentation of the ritual clothes, this was unadorned. It smelled strongly, but then a lot of leather did. Leighton wrinkled his nose. He was doubly glad for his gloves by now. Not just because they protected the coat from him, but because they kept his hands from unwanted contact with *it*.

He wasn't fond of leather, as a material. Too damp and it got clammy and unpleasantly soft; too dry and it went grotesquely crispy; exposure to the sulphur dioxide of gas-lighting could disintegrate it to powder. Leighton never wore leather gloves in his private life, and his winter coat was a heavy tweed.

But he was almost pleased to spot a faint white bloom on the beige panels of the coat-skirts. Fungal infestation would account for the musty smell, and that he could deal with. He got to work cleaning with dilute acetone on a cotton bud, rolling the wet head over an unobtrusive patch below a fold. The leather had a rich sheen once the matt layer of mould was removed.

That'll do nicely, he thought.

It was only when he happened to slip a hand into the square coat pocket that he found a second, smaller piece of paper. Unfolding it revealed another handwritten message:

John Palmer: his Innocent Coat

An innocent coat? Leighton wondered. *What's that then?* Then he noticed the coincidence in names, Palmes and Palmer, and wondered if he'd misread one or the other. A re-check did not clear up the question. The two notes did not look to be in the same hand, and neither thin, browning script was entirely clear. It was possible that they were meant to be the same name, but perhaps not.

"It's one thirty. Don't forget to have lunch," said Louise, passing behind him. Leighton glanced up, noticing for the first time the faint gnawing in his guts. It was so easy to forget to eat, he'd found over the last week. So easy to just get lost among his own thoughts. In that hospice room, time had seemed irrelevant. The murmur of distant voices, the faint rise and fall of the coverlet, the regular hiss of the plug-in air-freshener – those things were constant, all day and night.

He'd thought she'd never die.

It's not good for you, though. Going without food. He knew he'd lost weight, because he'd had to shave again for the first time this morning and he'd noticed the hollows of his own cheeks. And baggy, tired eyes, too.

He went out for a sandwich, walking past Clifford's Tower into the centre of town and casting a glance over the first yellow daffodil heads that were starting to dot the steep banks of the motte. Another spring on its way, he told himself. The daffodil display was always a pleasure.

When he returned twenty minutes later, he received an unpleasant shock. For just a moment, as he walked into the bright colourless space of the lab, he thought that someone was sitting at his desk, shoulders hunched and head down. Then he realised that it was the tan leather coat. It was supposed to be lying out on his work-desk, but someone had hung it over the back of his chair. Its broad skirts trailed on the linoleum.

Alarm washed through his veins. Fragile clothing could be damaged by hanging. Besides which, he'd left the coat spread out flat and no one should have altered that.

"Louise!" he snapped. "Did you move this?"

"Move what?" she asked, not looking up. She was bent over her own desk, painstakingly stitching a disintegrating Edwardian wedding dress to a net backing that would keep its shape.

"This coat!" Leighton couldn't help but find her irritating to look at. Why was it that she insisted on wearing a T-shirt to work instead of a proper long-sleeved blouse? Did she really have to have so much flesh on display? Her upper arms were plump and shapeless, and the sight of her flabby mole-speckled skin was not enticing.

"Nope," she said, through a mouthful of pins. "Not me."

"Well, did anyone else come in here?"

"Uh-uh."

Leighton narrowed his eyes. Interfering with a colleague's ongoing work was very bad form – and Louise was only a junior conservator. Clearly, allowing her to tackle that WRAF uniform last week had given her ideas above her station. He should really complain to Dr Archwin.

But he wasn't the sort of man who kicked up a fuss. He didn't like to complain.

Bottling up his irritation, he lifted the nasty antique coat very carefully from the padded back of the swivel-chair, laid it back on the worktop, vacuumed out the inside once again to remove foreign lint, and then got on with cleaning off the mouldy patches.

*

By the time five o'clock rolled around, the musty fungus smell had almost cleared under the sharp tang of the acetone and Leighton was pleased with his progress. He laid the coat out in a new box, to be finished off in the morning. Then he joined his colleagues for the farewell presentation to Yvonne from Accounts, who was going off on maternity leave – a bit of a pity he hadn't missed that while away himself, he couldn't help thinking, but there was no helping it – and slipped out forty minutes later, while most people were still chatting, to catch his bus home.

The rush-hour traffic was as bad as ever. Perhaps he should walk home now that the nights were getting lighter, he pondered; it could hardly take longer to cross the city on foot than to creep by bus round the outside of the medieval walls and then out along Bootham and Burton Stone Lane. The Council should do *something* about the traffic, for goodness sake. And why were the lights so slow to change each time?

As he descended from the bus he heard someone call out behind him.

"Scuse me mate, is this your –?"

The door wheezed shut. Leighton turned and looked up to see a man half-standing from the seat that must have been just behind his own, holding up a beige mac. They stared at each other through the window as the bus lurched away from the kerb. Leighton shook his head and lifted a hand to mime *Thanks, no, that's not mine*.

It was good to know that some people were still polite, he told himself as he walked home.

His house was a tiny end-terrace, two-up and two-down. The front room was full of the boxes he'd brought back from the hospice. Leighton looked at them coldly, and went through to the kitchen to make his tea, which consisted of a chicken fillet, peas from the freezer, and boiled potatoes. While he was paring the potatoes the peeler caught the tip of his left index finger and took a sliver of skin clean off. Leighton cursed and plunged the wound into cold water, watching the blood furl out like a tiny swatch of silk. He wadded a tea-towel around his fist and left it to staunch itself as he wandered back into the living room.

The silly accident had put him in a dark mood. The cardboard boxes full of junk – old-woman clothes, old-woman ornaments, yellowed paperbacks that no charity shop would want – seemed to stare at him in baleful reproach. He could imagine that his mother's smell still clung to them, that it was seeping into his home even now.

He remembered the day she'd turned up on his doorstep, asking to be let in, begging for the chance to talk. How he'd slammed the door in her face. The sense of relief then, as if he'd finally done something positive.

He remembered much further back; the way she used to gather him into her lap as a child when he was angry, when he was making too much noise, whenever they had a falling-out. Sometimes for no reason at all. The heaviness of her arm around his shoulders. The warm soft press of her palm against his face. The way she rested her cheek against the top of his head.

Rage burned in his guts – good, clean rage like the day he'd slammed the door – and he began to carry the boxes out the front, to the grey wheelie bin in the tiny front yard. There were too many to fit so he shook the contents out into the bin instead: underwear and cardigans and toiletries and shoes and photograph albums and over-the-counter medicines and all the tatty crap of a tatty crap life. He pressed it down and leaned in, creating layer after compacted layer of detritus. He was sweating by the time he smashed the last cardboard box flat with his tea-towelled fist and forced the bin lid down on top of it.

I will have none of it, he said to himself, triumphantly quoting the note in Dr Palmes' box.

The phrase had a rather satisfying ring to it. His finger stung, but he didn't care. He looked around as he turned back toward his front door, defying any of his neighbours to be watching, but nothing stirred in the dusk-stained street except for a half-glimpsed gingery flick of a cat disappearing over a wall.

Leighton took his dinner to his computer desk that night. Cradling his hurt fist in his lap and clicking to Google, he typed in *Marmaduke Palmes York* awkwardly with one finger of the other hand, his fork dancing over the keys.

It was an easy search; everything was on the first page. 'Palmes' turned out to be a very old Yorkshire name indeed, brought over from Normandy in William the Conqueror's retinue. The family had lived for centuries in Naburn Hall, just outside York. And a Marmaduke Palmes of the eighteenth century – Leighton rather doubted there could be many men with a name like that – showed up in the first volume of John Burke's 1834 tome, *A Genealogical and Heraldic History of the Commoners of Great Britain and Ireland enjoying territorial possessions or high official rank, but uninvested with heritable honours* – which was probably a thrilling best-seller in its day – wherein he and several siblings living in Naburn were listed tersely as having 'died unmarried'.

A gentleman surgeon of the city, confirmed bachelor, indulging in a little magical tinkering on the side. That didn't seem implausible.

Chewing a mouthful of chicken, Leighton reflected that historical research was ridiculously easy nowadays. He would have looked up the Biblical allusion, assuming that *Lev* stood for *Leviticus*, but he couldn't recall the relevant chapter and verse numbers.

*

That night Leighton slept badly. His cut finger had stopped bleeding, but it throbbed hotly with just enough insistence to keep him in the shallower waters of sleep. Which meant that he dreamed all night; exhausting, dreary dreams that made no sense and gave no satisfaction. The only one that he could really remember when he woke the next morning wasn't even a whole dream, just a scene. Two men were meeting in the dark corner of a pub. One of them was youngish and broad-set and looked like he really needed a shave and a bath. Under the stubble and the dirt his face was heavily pockmarked. The other was older, with smooth cheeks and grey hair and the air of someone who wanted to be elsewhere. This second man placed upon the wooden table a buff-coloured bundle, but kept his hands pressed down upon it.

"Is that it?" asked the first.

"Indeed it is," the old one told him.

"And will it do the trick?"

"I swear it will. You shall go blameless, though your sins be scarlet. Neither will any harm come to your life."

"You swear all this on my mother's name?"

The older man pursed his lips. "She would turn in her grave if she knew you had come to this."

With a grunt, the younger man reached inside his coat and pulled out a small leather pouch. "I think you would have occasioned her the greater shame, Uncle," he muttered, passing it over.

The recipient weighed the purse in his hand, but negligently as if the whole thing was too distasteful to care about, then pushed the folded bundle across the table top. "Be sure to wear it against your own skin," he answered. "Do not take it off."

"I am surprised that you do not wear one yourself," said the swarthy man.

"They are not so easily come by. Besides, there is a price to pay. There is always a price for such things, beyond the trouble that you have already put me to."

That was all the dream. It left a sour taste in Leighton's mouth and an itch in his brain, so that he couldn't help thinking about as he showered in the morning. But that was all of it he could recall.

No, there was one other dream, he realised – though it hadn't seemed to be connected to the first. It had kept looping round, like a clip from the worst home video in the world. He'd dreamed over and over that he got up out of his bed and went to the top of the stairs, waiting for someone who was ascending from below. Moonlight lay on the half-landing, and he'd stood and watched that square of carpet with a feeling of great discomfort, knowing that at any moment someone was going to climb into view. And then yes – there they were; lying flat on the stairs and crawling up, hand over hand over hand.

He never saw their face. The dream looped back and started again before that became clear. He wasn't even sure there was a face to see.

29

That recollection made him feel clammy despite the cascade of hot water.

When Leighton got to work, the Innocent Coat was missing.

*

At first he couldn't think where he'd left the coat. Its storage box lay open, ready to receive the padded garment, but the box contained only a few flat sheets of tissue paper. Had he replaced it in the surgeon's chest the night before – and if so, why?

Then he brought back to mind the events of the day, and he knew he'd definitely not shoved the garment away. He'd put it in its box there, just so. He knew he had. Someone else must have removed it.

Leighton ground his teeth and started a methodical search – not because he thought the coat would turn up in the wrong place, but because he had to be able to say "Yes, I checked there." He found the oriental robe and the altar cloth in their proper boxes, labelled up correctly. He found the magician's implements boxed on Louise's *pending* shelf where he'd left it; she looked up at him curiously as he glared at the contents, but went back to her wedding beads.

"You okay?"

"Fine." Beneath a flesh-coloured plaster, the cut on his finger burned.

He checked back in the bequest trunk. The slippers were still in there, along with the two pieces of paper and the hat. All was as it should be, except for the Innocent Coat. There wasn't even the lingering aroma of the old leather.

Slowly, Leighton sat down at his desk. For a moment he covered his face with his hands, but that unthinking action made him shudder and he sat up straighter. His stomach cramped, and he recalled dimly that he'd eaten no breakfast.

He had to tell Dr Archwin. He didn't want to – she would be furious, quite rightly, and the thought of incurring her blame made him feel physically sick. But he had to. Once formally accessioned, an object belonged to the museum in perpetuity, like it or not. They had no legal right to sell it, to throw it out or to give it away, even if it was deemed a waste of space and resources. It could not just *disappear*.

He had to flag up the loss.

Could someone have stolen it, he wondered? Louise was the only one with obvious access, but he had no reason whatsoever to suspect her. Or anyone else for that matter, he had to admit. By historical costume standards it had been a noisome, unattractive object. He'd disliked it, he had to admit, from the moment he'd lifted it out and laid it like a corpse upon his desk.

Did it have some hidden value he knew nothing about?

He logged onto the Web and did a search for *Innocent Coat*.

Nothing. He forced a deep breath, though his chest felt constricted.

"Louise ... Do you know what an Innocent Coat is?"

She stood upright, stretching her back. "What context?"

"Seventeen-hundreds."

She scrunched her face up in a doubtful grimace and started to shake her head.

Reluctantly, he added, "Possibly something to do with ritual magic or folklore."

"Oh – you've got something magicky, have you?" She brightened. "Let's have a look."

Well, that was the problem, wasn't it? He didn't have the coat to show her. He bent into the chest to retrieve the smaller slip of paper, simply to save face.

"If it is occultish, you probably want to e-mail the witchcraft museum at Boscastle," Louise said as she ambled over. "I can't remember the guy's name, but it'll be on file. He helped us out with that dead cat in the farmhouse wall at Pocklington, remember?"

The mummified cat had made the local papers, he recalled. He watched Louise take the piece of paper, and wished her fingers weren't so disgustingly plump.

She blinked, and then her eyebrows rose. "Dunno about the coat, but I know a John Palmer."

It was Leighton's turn to be surprised.

"Seventeen-thirties, say? That's Dick Turpin."

"I'm *sorry?*"

"The highwayman?"

"Yes – I know who Turpin is." Actually, Leighton's associations with that name were a lot of vague 'stand and deliver' jokes. And hadn't there been some rubbishy TV series back in the Seventies, all cheap sets and bad romance?

"Well, he fled to York when he was wanted for double murder in Essex. Lived in the East Riding for over a year under a false name – John Palmer – then got himself hanged on the Knavesmire for horse-stealing. And he's buried about two hundred yards that-a-way." She pointed toward the inner ring-road and looked pleased with herself. "I did a module on Turpin for my degree."

Leighton just frowned.

"Oh come on, Geoff – you must have seen his condemned cell in the museum?"

"Uh, yes. I suppose." The Castle Museum sprawled across several buildings including the old city prison, but he hadn't walked around it in years.

"The bloke was a total thug really; nothing like the legend. No Black Bess, no overnight ride from London, no chivalry. House-breaking and torture and sheep-rustling, more like. But he's a big

31

name." Her eyes widened. "If we've turned up his coat that's *fantastic* publicity."

"We haven't got his coat," Leighton said grimly. "We might have had it yesterday. But it's gone missing."

"Oh ... arse," said Louise. Then; "You need to tell Joyce."

*

The confrontation with Dr Archwin was horrible. Leighton could feel his shirt clinging to him in sweaty patches by the time he walked away, and the first thing he did was go to the gents and dry-heave into the sink.

It wasn't what she'd said. It was the way she'd looked at him.

The same way his mother had looked at him when she was angry, all those years ago. That cold disappointment that presaged colder punishment.

Leighton caught a glimpse of himself in the bathroom mirror as he splashed cold water across his face. His skin was pasty-white. He thought of his mother's grey face against the hospice pillows, and the tears crusting in the corners of her eyes.

You were always a horrible boy, but we've got to forgive and forget after all these years, she'd whispered. *Come here, Geoffrey. Give me a kiss.*

He remembered the papery feeling of her cheek against his fingers. Her skin already drying out to fine leather.

He washed his hands again, scrubbing with soap.

When he went back to the lab Louise looked up from her copy of the *Museums Journal*. "You alright?"

He nodded, though the movement brought back his nausea. "She says she's treating it as an internal matter at the moment. We have to double-check this whole place."

Dr Archwin had said – *Are you absolutely sure you never took it out of the lab, Geoff? At any point?* And she'd looked at him with narrowed eyes nested in lines of doubt. He could feel his throat closing up, just at the memory.

Louise gave him a cautious smile that looked sympathetic but meant nothing.

So they searched the lab for a misplaced coat, in every drawer and corner and box, all in vain. Then they went back to their respective desks. Leighton supposed he was meant to carry on working on the contents of the Palmes box, and he managed that for a time. But the coat was preying on his mind. He made a phone-call to an answer-machine in Boscastle, and in a fit of frustration went back online.

It was all there: the history of Dick Turpin. The trial proceedings had been taken down at the time and published in pamphlet form, along with a contemporary account of his final days and death on the gallows.

To Leighton's mind *The Trial of the Notorious Highwayman, Richard Turpin, at York Assizes, on the 22nd Day of March, 1739* was full of peculiarities. Turpin had taken the name Palmer when he fled north because he claimed it was his mother's maiden name. He'd lived in the manner of a gentleman, yet without visible income, for a year and more, and somehow that didn't rouse suspicion until he lost his temper one day, shot his landlord's cockerel in the street and then threatened to shoot the man who protested. At that point he could have walked away scot-free, yet he refused to be bound over to keep the peace. Only when in York prison did his true notorious identity come out by sheer fluke – someone recognised his handwriting – and even then he failed to make any serious attempt at defending himself. He didn't even take the opportunity to call on witnesses, which the judge himself found bizarre:

Prisoner: Several Persons who came to see me, assured me, that I should be removed to Essex, *for which reason I thought it needless to prepare Witnesses for my Defence.*

Court: Whoever told you so were highly to blame; and as our Country have found you guilty of a Crime worthy of Death, it is my Office to pronounce Sentence against you.

It was, Leighton thought, as if Turpin assumed he could get away with anything. As if he were immune to condemnation – to the point of recklessness – until it all went terribly wrong.

Even when he ascended the scaffold, Turpin had seemed to be possessed by what was described as an 'amazing Assurance' and 'undaunted Courage' that the situation hardly merited. He bantered insouciantly for half an hour with the hangman – *Half-an-hour?* Leighton thought. *What were they all waiting for?* – and only went to his fate when he jumped off under his own volition to die 'in about five Minutes'.

How long would *about five minutes* feel to a man strangling on a short noose, Leighton thought sickly? He felt worse when his eye fell on the name *Palmes*.

A few days after death, Turpin's body had been robbed out of its grave. Not an uncommon occurrence in those days when bodies for medical dissection were hard to come by; the city mob soon tracked it to the house of a local surgeon, Dr Marmaduke Palmes, where the corpse was discovered in a garden shed and carried back 'almost naked, being only laid on a Board, cover'd with some Straw,' and buried again, this time in slaked lime.

Despite the near-riot provoked by his theft, Dr Palmes seemed to have got away with his misdemeanour. Reading all this, Leighton felt clammy, as if something damp were pressed up against him.

He tried to bury the thought, but another search turned up a quote from a report in *The Gentleman's Magazine* of June 1737 that made things worse. In it a reward of £200 was offered for the discovery of Richard Turpin, murderer-at-large, who was described as 'broad about the Shoulders,' and 'very much mark'd with the Small Pox'. The coincidence with his dream made Leighton's throat feel as if his ribcage was heaving to draw in air.

"You alright?" Louise asked. "You look awful."

"Just a touch of asthma," he whispered.

"Go home if you're feeling sick. We weren't expecting you back this week anyway."

He went home early, as suggested, walking instead of taking the bus. But he made a detour first of all, to the tiny graveyard of St George, to see Turpin's plot. The stone was large and clearly marked:

John Palmer otherwise
RICHARD TURPIN
The notorious highwayman and horse stealer

Why had Palmes stolen the body? For illicit anatomical study, as everyone assumed? Or did family loyalty extend even to illegitimate and disgraced relatives? Why had Turpin been sent back for reburial naked, when it was recorded that he had specifically sent for a coat for his hanging?

The thin grass and grey stones offered no answers and the blustery spring wind seemed to cut right through his clothes to claw at his skin. Leighton couldn't bear to stand there long, so he headed back across the city. His route took him up High Petergate, and as he passed the small shops and pubs of that medieval street, the sign of the *Three-Legged Mare* caught his eye. The 'horse' in question was the tripod shape of the Tyburn-style gallows that had stood on the Knavesmire, and the painted sign depicted the crowd staring at the condemned men about to be hanged.

Pulling his coat tighter about him, Leighton passed under the thick walls of Bootham Bar and waited at the road crossing with the other pedestrians. Fatigue made him close his eyes momentarily.

"Why did you not wear it always, as I instructed you!" a man's voice hissed behind him. "See what a pass it has brought you to!"

"Stop your mouth, Uncle." The second man's voice was a good deal rougher, almost a bark. "The thing gave me evil dreams and I wanted respite. My head was a-pounding with their damnable voices. You never warned me of that!"

Leighton froze, shoulders hunched.

"I told you there would be a price, did I not? But you assured me you were man enough to pay it without fear. Now it all comes crashing down upon your head, braggart. You have no coat to keep off the winds

34

of ill-fortune, only a hempen scarf that is prepared for you in the morning. Tell me where you have left it."

Leighton cracked an eye open cautiously, but the traffic surged on before him and the voices went on behind.

"Why should I tell you?"

"Do you think that I made the thing, only to leave it hanging behind a door for any villain to pick up?"

"Any villain, Uncle? Do not concern yourself: I know where it is."

"Then tell me! It will do you no good now."

"Ah, that is where we disagree. Did you not tell me that the coat will save me from condemnation?"

"It is too late for that!"

"Is it? I think the Innocent Coat will save my neck, even at the last drop. They have told me so."

"Who has?"

"The ones who come and lie beside me at night, and whisper into my dreams. They promise me freedom. They tell me they need a strong fellow like me to wear the coat and walk them abroad. They tell me to trust them."

"Richard – *tell me where the coat is.*"

"I have sent for it. You might see it on the morrow, if you care to watch."

A foul smell of badly-tanned leather rolled over Leighton and he couldn't help it: he jerked around to face the men who had been conversing behind him, and nearly stepped backwards into the road in doing so.

There was no one there, of course. Only a young mother with a pushchair, looking at him gyrating on the pavement as if he were some kind of nutcase.

It's stress, he thought, with a sickly apologetic smile. *I should never have gone back to work this week.*

*

When he opened his front door, his first thought was that there was a body lying on the stairs just inside; stretched out flat, one arm crooked above its shoulders as if it had fallen face down while descending.

Then he realised it was worse than a body. It was the Innocent Coat.

In a moment he was inside, slamming the door and switching on the light. He didn't want the world to see that Dr Archwin had been right after all – that he had taken the coat home yesterday, just as she'd suspected. Well, he must have. Who could argue? He must have taken it home *without realising it* – because there it was. He had *stolen* it.

What was he supposed to do now?

What was wrong with him?

The unfairness of the situation made his heart hammer and his eyes blur over. He couldn't possibly take it back now that he'd declared it missing – "Here we are, sorry about that, it turns out I'd gone off with it after all, no hard feelings eh?" Could he smuggle it back into the lab and hide it in some dark forsaken corner where it could be found later?

That was hardly better. She'd still know he was to blame.

Wheezing a little, Leighton bent over the treads to pluck up the fallen coat. For a moment his tear-blurred eyes made the leather seem to quiver. Then it was in his hands, heavier than he remembered and a little clammy. The smell was faint but distinctive, and turned his stomach.

He carried the vile garment at arm's length, to keep it away from his body. Averting his twisted-up face, he stalked through into the living room, wondering how he was going to get rid of it – because he surely didn't want it in the house.

I will have none of it. The phrase sparked in his memory. Three strides took him to the desk where his laptop waited. *Leviticus 13:52* – he could remember the verse numbers now, since a second glance earlier today. Laying the coat across the top of his seat, he typed in the reference and picked an online version of the King James Bible.

The words were stark:

> *He shall therefore burn that garment, whether warp or woof, in woollen or in linen or any thing of skin wherein the plague is, for it is a fretting leprosy; it shall be burnt in the fire.*

A bitter laugh tore itself from Leighton's throat, leaving the flesh raw. Even the Web concurred with his desire to get rid of the thing! Burning it sounded like a great idea. Quickly he bundled the coat into a wodge that he stuffed into the open grate of his fireplace. He would need matches from the kitchen and logs from the lean-to out the back. He would burn the horrible object to ash, and Dr Archwin would never know of his guilt.

He was out of the room for perhaps three minutes. When he got back, the Innocent Coat was no longer there. Faint ash-marks on the hearth suggested that it had been dragged out onto the rug.

Leighton stood in the centre of the room and turned slowly on his heel, mouth agape. Where could it have gone? Had he suffered another blackout and stashed it somewhere? The shadows behind the furniture looked full of uncertainty, as if things were moving within them, and the hair crept on the back of his neck. He could not thrust away the uncanny mental image of the coat sliding flat behind the big bookcase, or creeping under the old-fashioned sofa. He found he didn't want to kneel down and check beneath. In fact he didn't want to breathe out, in case the sound masked the furtive approach of soft leather from behind or above.

A fretting leprosy, he thought.

When his cell phone rang he nearly jumped out of his skin. He did go as far as dropping all the logs on the carpet. "What?" he demanded as he retreated toward the kitchen where the light was so much better. "What is it?"

It was the man from the witchcraft museum, returning his call and wondering what he wanted to know about Innocent Coats.

"What are they?" Leighton asked, slamming the kitchen door and backing up toward the sink. "What do they do?"

"Um ... they're like ... have you heard of the Hand of Glory?"

Leighton scrunched up his eyes, trying to think straight. "That's some sort of candle made out of hand, or something?"

"It was a candle of human fat gripped in the severed hand of an executed criminal. A form of thieves' magic. It was supposed, when lit, to make the inhabitants of the house unable to wake or move, so that housebreakers could carry out their raid without raising an alarm. Well, an Innocent Coat was a similar idea – but rarer, and more potent. Anyone who wore one was supposedly immune to suspicion or the attention of the law. He could literally get away with murder, and no one would blame him."

Leighton tried to swallow. "What would it look like?"

"I've never seen one. If they ever did exist, I don't think there are any left – certainly not in museums, though maybe in a private collection somewhere. But I assume it would look like a leather coat. It had to be made from the skins of hanged men, you see. And they had to be murderers."

John Palmer: his Innocent Coat.

Leighton ended the call without another word. Then he simply stood, and stared at the kitchen door. The clock ticked. Behind him, the light faded out of the afternoon.

That coat was out there, somewhere in the house. On top of a wardrobe, perhaps, or behind a chest of drawers, or under the bed. Somewhere, waiting. He knew that now. It had waited decades in that sealed attic, and now it could afford to be patient, he supposed. It would wait for him to fall asleep, or to shrug the whole affair off and convince himself that nothing had really happened. Then it would make its move.

He wondered briefly what it would look like. Would it slide, like a snake? No ... he rather thought it would crawl arm over arm, like in his dream; that thin cold leather malignantly inexorable.

He could escape now, out the back. Escape to ... he could not think where. But he suspected it would just keep following. It wanted him. When he was off-guard, then it would appear. Its soft sleeves would brush over him, groping for his face ... just like his mother used to. She'd gather him into her lap when he was small, and press her hand over his mouth and under his nose, cutting off all air. He'd squirm and struggle as his lungs started to ache, but she was so much stronger than him, then. Fear would become panic, discomfort would become agony. He'd even try to bite, but it never worked. Darkness would flood in around the corners of his vision as consciousness faded, and his stillborn shrieks were muffled in her implacable palm.

That memory was enough to send sweat running down his back and thighs.

It was years before he was big enough to resist her choking embrace. Years before he stood up to her. Even now, the recollection of her face in the hospice bed made him shake. Her gummy saliva had smeared the flat of his palm as she'd tried in vain to fight him off, spasming weakly. Her eyes had opened wide and bloodshot and she'd pissed herself under the duvet.

His regret that day was that he hadn't had the foresight to bring gloves. The texture of her skin had very nearly been enough to make the task impossible. Skin against skin – just unbearable. And it had taken *so long*.

Why had she taken so long to die?

The Innocent Coat would be the same, he knew. That thin leather would feel like his mother's crêpey hide as it piled onto his face and throat. As it slithered its sleeves over his arms, and spread its skirts over his legs, and clung to him like a second skin.

He couldn't stand that: the feeling of skin against skin. The soft and intimate smothering. The *touch*. That thought was simply … unbearable.

So he would not bear it.

Shaking, Leighton took the potato peeler out of the kitchen drawer, and began the long hard task of stripping himself of the terrible stuff.

HAUNTING MEMORIES OF THE PAST

The underground mines of old industrial Britain have been a rich source of spooky stories for many generations. Even now, with scarcely a pit-wheel turning from Kent to Clydeside, remnants of these tales linger, with overgrown spoil-heaps and abandoned colliery buildings the alleged location of multiple eerie presences. Though of course, when the pits were actually in operation, the rumours were vastly rifer.

From the tin mines of Cornwall to the coal fields of South Wales, the Midlands, Lancashire, the Northeast and nearly all the corners of Yorkshire, those deep, dark warrens of tunnels were regarded as hotspots of ghostly activity even when they were teeming with able-bodied men. And it's hardly surprising. The potential for untimely death was an ever-present throughout the history of deep-level mining. Terrible disasters involving mass fatalities occurred with alarming frequency in locations as far apart as Caerphilly, Bilsthorpe and Wigan. If one accepts the concept of the supernatural, it's difficult to believe that such catastrophes – often occurring in cramped, enclosed spaces with limited opportunity for escape (which must have led to scenes of unimaginable horror at the time) – could not have generated mysterious after-effects.

Britain's most notorious haunted pit was Silverwood Colliery, near Ravenfield in South Yorkshire – not so much for the preponderance of ghost stories emerging there, but for the vivid details attached to them and for their air of authenticity. Several men's reputations as tough underground workers were badly tarnished by their accounts of experiences down Silverwood Pit, but the witnesses stuck to their guns through all the ridicule. Even more impressively, the majority of these reports come to us not from the dim, candle-lit years when superstition was commonplace, but from the modern age, the period between the 1950s and 1980s. Some of them describe formless lights following lone miners along darkened galleries. Others refer to fully materialised apparitions, the shadowy forms of men in old-fashioned clothes, wielding outdated equipment. On occasion, it was even more frightening: one employee left Silverwood Colliery vowing never to work underground again after an encounter with a hulking figure in an otherwise empty tunnel; apparently the shape was standing with its back turned, but when it looked around, it only had half a face.

Bone-chilling tales like this travelled so widely and were taken so seriously that, in 1985, Arthur C. Clarke featured the mine in an episode of his paranormal investigation programme, *World of Strange Powers*, but he was unable to reach firm conclusions.

Like most collieries, Silverwood suffered more than its fair share of accidents and mishaps, but though it was first opened in 1900, it was spared any major disaster until 1966, when the underground railway – or *Paddy Mail* – crashed, claiming the lives of ten men. However, given that several ghostly sightings had been reported at Silverwood before this date, this calamity offers no ready-made supernatural explanation.

Underground operations finally ceased at Silverwood in 1994, and the site is now occupied by new housing estates, where no disturbances have been reported. The Silverwood phantoms are still remembered, but now with an air of poignancy, as though they are symbolic of the British coal mining industry itself, which died before its time and of which only shadows remain.

THEY WALK AS MEN
Mark Morris

"Um... Angela?" Ben says.

But as soon as her green eyes fasten on him his carefully rehearsed words take flight, like a flock of startled birds. Her friends snigger as his face reddens, but Angela merely looks at him quizzically.

"Yes?"

"Can I..." Ben tries to mask the fact that by breathing in he's gathering his courage. "Can I have a word?"

"You're having one now, aren't you?" one of Angela's friends sneers.

His eyes flicker towards the girl, then skitter away.

"I mean in private," he mutters.

But he's spent almost all of lunchtime plucking up the courage, and now it's too late. The afternoon bell shrills with what he imagines is gleeful spite. And worse, here comes old Blanchford, his paunch trying to outwobble his chins and the sun reflected in miniature on the shiny pate that divides the bristly tufts of greying hair above his ears.

"Come along," he booms, "don't dawdle," even though the air is still shuddering from the aftermath of the now-silent bell.

"Never mind, see you later," Ben mumbles, turning away so abruptly he almost stumbles.

More giggling, and one of the girls replies, "Not if we see you first."

"Did you ask her?" says his best friend, Colin, who's waiting off to one side of the main doors, the strap of his Liverpool FC sports bag a red diagonal stripe from his left shoulder to his right hip.

"Couldn't, could I?" Ben grunts. "Bell went."

Colin, who is small and darting, with fox-red hair and pastry-white skin beneath too many freckles, rolls his eyes. "You've gotta ask her, you div. What if she goes home on her own and gets got?"

"She won't get got."

"Yeah, but what if she does? It'll be your fault."

"Shut up," Ben says.

*

41

Ben's having his tea in front of the telly. Fish fingers, chips and peas. *Tops of the Pops* is on.

"What's this bloody racket?" Ben's dad says, coming in with his mug of coffee and sinking into the chair with the frayed arm where his metal watchstrap snags the material.

"It's not a racket," says Ben. "It's the Adverts. It's brilliant."

Ben's dad snorts. "Bloody hell, look at the state of 'em. What are they wearing? Is that one a girl?"

"They're punks, Dad. They're supposed to look like that."

"Punks." Ben's dad shakes his head. "Why can't they dress like normal people?"

"'Cos that'd be boring," says Ben.

When the song finishes and Tony Blackburn comes back on, Ben's dad says, "So what did you learn in school today?"

Ben shrugs. Instead of answering the question he says, "A policeman came to talk to us in assembly."

"Oh aye. Has there been some bother?"

"No, it was about that woman that got killed by the Yorkshire Ripper. That Helen somebody."

Ben's dad seems to tense. "Oh aye?"

"The policeman said we had to watch out. We had to be vigilant. And he said none of the girls should walk home on their own. Not on these dark nights."

"Quite right too," Ben's mum says, stepping from the kitchen into the front room, drying a plate on a tea towel printed with pictures of British Wild Flowers. "If you were a lass, Ben, I wouldn't let you out the house. They found this latest one on Great Northern Street, Geoff. Imagine! Makes you shudder to think of it!"

Great Northern Street is just up from Huddersfield Sports Centre, where Ben sometimes goes swimming. It makes his skin crawl to think he's been close to where it happened. He wonders whether murder leaves something behind on a place. An atmosphere. A stain. He wonders how far it spreads, and whether the badness of it affects people, seeping invisibly into their bones like radiation.

"Decent girls are all right," Ben's dad says, scowling. "He only goes for... you know."

"Prostitutes," says Ben.

"Ben!" his mum says, shocked.

"That's enough, Ben," his dad says, raising a finger to point at him.

Now it's Ben who's scowling. "It's only a word. Anyway, it was you who said it."

"No I didn't. I only said the girls weren't decent."

"Yeah, well, that's not true, is it? He killed that other girl in Leeds. She was only sixteen. She wasn't –"

"Don't say it," his mum says, brandishing the plate as if she'll hit him with it if he disobeys.

"Well, she wasn't," Ben says.

"Aye, but what was she doing walking round Chapeltown at night?" Ben's dad says.

"Walking round isn't a crime, Dad."

"Late at night? In a red light district?"

"So what are you saying? That she deserved what she got?"

Ben's dad looks furious. "That's enough from you, lad. You're not too old for a good hiding, you know."

"Stop it, you two," Ben's mum says, looking upset. She stares at the telly, where Althea and Donna are singing *Up Town, Top Ranking* which is number one. Distractedly she says, "How many's that he's killed now?"

"Too bloody many," says Ben's dad.

"Eight," says Ben. "That's what the policeman said. But he's attacked other girls too. Some that survived."

"Bloody animal," Ben's dad mutters.

*

"Someone's farted, I can smell it," Colin announces loudly, turning round in his seat to address the class.

The other kids laugh – Ben sometimes thinks if Colin didn't make them laugh, some of the bigger lads would pick on him – and he's about to protest his innocence (he's the one sitting next to Colin, after all) when Blanchford walks into the room.

Colin doesn't see him, though. He's got his back to the door. He doesn't even register that the other kids have suddenly fallen silent and are now rooting in their bags, pulling out their maths books.

"Stinks of monkey's bollocks and dead hamsters," Colin continues. "Though on second thoughts it might just be old Blanchford's breath –"

The end of the word becomes a squeal as Blanchford marches up behind Colin, grabs his ear and twists it. Colin bends double, his face going as red as his hair, as Blanchford forces his head down on to the desk.

"Ow!" Colin yells. "Fuck off, Burnsey. I know it's you."

Blanchford looks like an enraged warthog. He gives Colin's ear another twist, forcing his head down further so that his forehead hits the desk's wooden surface with a clunk.

"Sorry, sir!" Blanchford roars, and even though Colin's face is twisted in agony, Ben sees his skinny body stiffen as he realizes who his assailant is.

"Sorry, sir!" Blanchford snarls again, and it suddenly strikes Ben that Blanchford wants Colin to repeat it.

"Say it," he hisses, barely registering the pink blur of Blanchford's fat hand before it delivers a stinging slap across the back of his head.

Colin's weeping now, his tears pooling on the desk beneath him and smearing all over his face.

"Silence, Preston," Blanchford snaps at Ben. "Freele doesn't need your help."

Finally Colin twigs and gasps it out. "Sorry, sir, sorry, sir."

With a final twist, eliciting another squeal from Colin, Blanchford releases him. Colin's hand goes to his ear, which looks mangled and beetroot-red. He's crying but trying not to, making little whoopy gasps as he breathes in and out, his body shaking, chest heaving.

Everyone's appalled, but they stay silent, eyes down. Ben sneaks a look at Blanchford, who's straightening up now, tugging down his waistcoat, which has got rumpled beneath his tweed jacket. The maths teacher is sweating, his eyes a flat, black glare beneath his spectacles. He looks at Ben and his plump lips curl back over yellow teeth.

"Is there something you want to say, Mr Preston?"

"No, sir," Ben says quietly.

Blanchford marches to his desk and turns to face the class. Flicking a dismissive glance at a still-weeping Colin he says, "Freele, you will report for detention this evening and every day next week. The rest of you turn to page thirty."

*

Ben's lying on his bed reading one of his dad's James Herriot books when his mum calls up the stairs.

"Ben! Someone here to see you!"

Angela! he thinks, his heart leaping, but he knows she has no reason to seek him out. Even though he thinks about her all the time with a fierceness that almost hurts, he doubts she even knows his name or what class he's in. As it's Friday, and today was his last chance to see her before the weekend, he hung around the lockers after school, hoping to catch her alone, hoping to offer to walk her home like the policeman said the boys should do. But she didn't show, and he feels he's let her down again, put her in danger for the second day running, though he knows that's stupid.

I'll definitely speak to her on Monday, he thinks as he turns the corner of the page to mark his place and drops the book on the bed. Stepping out of his bedroom, he looks over the banister. Colin is in the hallway, wearing his jacket with the big red checks and the woolly collar. His face looks pinched and white, though the tip of his nose is red. It's a cold, raw February night.

"Awright?" Ben calls, and Colin looks up.

"You lekkin' out?"

From the living room Ben can hear *The Pink Panther Show* music. He shrugs.

"Yeah, all right. But I wanna get back for *The Professionals* at nine."

*

"I think it's him," Colin says.

"Who?"

"Blanchford. I think he's the Ripper."

Ben and Colin are sitting on a low wall in front of the petrol station before the big roundabout. The petrol station is on New Hey Road, which connects Huddersfield town centre to the M62 that leads to Leeds and Bradford. Colin's brother Nick, who's doing his 'A' levels, works in the petrol station three nights a week. The boys hang around there because there's nowhere else to go at night in the winter, and because sometimes, when it's quiet, Nick brings them Mars Bars and polystyrene cups of oxtail soup out of the machine. The boys watch the cars going back and forth along the stretch of road in front of them, and they blow out breath, which the cold air converts to orange steam under the street lamps. The concrete wall is cold, and Ben worries about getting piles, even though he doesn't really know what piles are.

He looks at Colin now, who, like him, is hunched forward in his thick jacket to keep warm, his hands encased in woolly gloves.

"Don't be daft," he says.

"I'm not being daft."

Ben snorts so loudly that his body rocks backwards. "You're only saying that 'cos he gave you detention."

"No I'm not."

"Yes you are. Where's your bloody evidence?"

Colin gives him a knowing look. "You didn't see Angela at the lockers after school today, did you?"

Ben looks at him sharply. "How do you know?"

"'Coz I know where she was."

"Where?"

"In detention with me."

Ben's eyes widen. "Angela? No way! What for?"

Colin shrugs. "Nothing probably."

"You don't get detention for nothing."

"All right, put it this way. She was in detention because Blanchford wanted her there. You should have seen him. Perving all over her."

Ben feels sick, anxious. "What do you mean?"

"He was watching her the whole time. Couldn't take his eyes off her. Then when detention was over, I was going to tell her I'd walk her home –"

Ben jerks as if stung. "You weren't!"

"Calm down. It was dark. I couldn't let her go home on her own, could I? I was gonna put in a good word for you."

Ben dreads to think what Colin would class as a 'good word'. Even so he's curious to know what Angela might really think of him. "So what happened?" he asks. "Why didn't you?"

"Blanchford got there first, didn't he? Soon as detention was over he came sliming up and offered Angela a lift. I could tell she weren't keen, but he said even though she'd been bad he couldn't let her go home in the dark, said it was his *duty* to take her." Colin shrugs. "I think that's why he gave her detention. I think that was his plan all along. He just wanted to have her to himself."

Ben jumps up. "We've got to do something! We've got to save her!"

"She'll be all right," says Colin.

"What do you mean, she'll be all right? You just said you thought he was the Ripper."

"Yeah, but he's not gonna be this stupid, is he? If owt happens to Angela everyone'll know it's him."

Ben scowls. "Make your mind up. So do you think he *is* the Ripper or not?"

"Yeah, but I think he's cunning. I think he's playing a game."

"What game?"

For a moment Colin looks stumped. Then he says, "He's laying false trails. If he doesn't kill Angela this time, then people won't suspect him, will they?"

Ben frowns, confused. Colin's logic sounds skewy. "You're talking shite," he decides and sits down again. "Blanchford's not the Ripper."

Colin counts off pointers on his fingers. "He's weird. He's violent. He's a perv. He lives on his own."

Ben jerks his head towards the lighted window of the petrol station, behind which they can see Nick moving about. "Nick said the police think the Ripper lives in Leeds or Bradford. That's why they were asking about the customers who stopped for petrol after that prozzie was killed."

"They're just guessing," Colin says dismissively. "They don't know anything."

"Neither do you."

Colin looks sly. "So don't you *wanna* come to Blanchford's house with me then?"

"What?" Ben says, startled.

*

"This is stupid," Ben whispers. "What are we even doing here?"

They're standing across the street from Blanchford's house, trying to keep to the shadows between a pair of streetlamps. It's a quiet street, a cul-de-sac, the neat, mostly white-painted houses set back from the pavement behind hedges, stone walls and front lawns.

Colin takes something out of his jacket pocket, something that crackles. "We're here to deliver this."

Between the forefinger and second finger of his gloved hand is a folded piece of paper.

"What is it?" Ben asks.

"A note."

"What does it say?"

Ben thinks Colin isn't going to tell him, but then he hands the note over with a smirk.

Ben unfolds it. Written in black felt tip in block capitals are the words:

WE KNOW WHAT YOU ARE

Ben feels a thrill of horror and excitement go through him. "You can't give him this."

"I'm not gonna give it to him, I'm gonna put it through his letter box."

"But you *can't*!"

"Why not?"

Ben thrusts the note back at Colin, as if he's incriminating himself by holding it. "Because if he finds out it's you, he'll call the police and you'll get done."

"Yeah, but he won't find out it's me, will he?" says Colin.

"How do you know?"

"How can he? I've not signed the note, have I? And I've not written it in my own handwriting. And there's no fingerprints on it 'cos I'm wearing gloves."

"Yeah, but what if he sees you?"

"I'll run."

"What if he recognizes you?"

"He won't. I've got a hat, and a scarf to put over my face. I've got one for you as well."

Ben blinks. "*Me?*"

"Yeah. We're in this together, aren't we?"

"Fuck off," Ben says, glancing at the house across the road, half-hidden behind the high hedge bordering the garden. "I'm not going."

"Not even to help Angela?"

"What do you mean?"

Colin sighs and rolls his eyes as if Ben is being thick. "Think about it. If Blanchford's after Angela and he reads the note he'll know we're on to him, so he'll leave her alone."

"He'll know *someone's* on to him, you mean," says Ben.

"Exactly."

Ben's silent for a moment, his brow furrowed. "Why don't you just tell the police what you think and let them deal with it?"

"They won't listen. I'm just a kid. They'll think I'm doing it to get back at Blanchford for giving me detention."

Ben thinks so too, but he says, "So what happens when we've delivered the note?"

"We watch. And wait."

"For what?"

"For Blanchford to get twitchy. To start making mistakes."

It all sounds a bit vague to Ben. "And what if he's innocent?"

"He isn't."

Ben sighs. "Yeah, but what if he *is*?"

Colin shrugs. "Then he'll just think the note's a joke, won't he, and throw it away?"

There's the soft roar of an approaching car at the end of the street. Colin and Ben tense, but the car drives past.

"Look, let's stop arguing and just post the note and see what happens," Colin hisses. "We'll work out the rest later when we see what Blanchford does."

Ben sighs. He knows he won't hear the end of it if he refuses. And there's a small part of him that wonders whether Colin *is* right and Blanchford *is* the Ripper. If he is, and if he ends up getting caught because of Colin's note, Ben imagines how Angela might feel if she were to find out he had a hand in Blanchford's capture.

She'd think of him as a hero, wouldn't she? Maybe even as her personal saviour?

He knows it's daft. He knows he's living in cloud cuckoo land.

But then again…

He has a sudden image of Angela sidling up to him in the playground, looking at him shyly, asking, "Aren't you one of the boys who caught the Ripper?"

And it's only a silly note. They only have to push it through the letterbox, then scarper.

"All right then," he says. "Let's get it over with."

*

They wait until they're in Blanchford's garden, out of sight of the street and pressed up against the inside of the tall, prickly hedge, before they pull on their black bobble hats and tie their scarves around their faces. Blanchford's car – a brown Hillman Imp – is parked on the drive, and there's a faint glow coming from behind the closed curtains of the ground floor room to the right of the front door.

Ben's scared. His mouth's dry and his heart's going nineteen to the dozen. There's hardly any cover between the hedge and the front door, and he knows if Blanchford parts the curtains as they're sneaking across the lawn he'll see them for sure. He might not recognize them, he might only see their dark shapes, but that makes no difference; it doesn't reassure Ben one bit.

Because the thing is, if Blanchford *is* the Ripper, Ben can't help but think that somehow, despite their scarves and hats, the maths teacher will still somehow *know* it's them. Worse, that he'll *mark* them in some way; stain them with his evil; take something indefinable from them – their scent, their essence – that will enable him to track them down.

He knows it's daft. He knows the Ripper's just a man, not a bloodhound, or a wolf, or a monster.

And yet he can't stop the doubts from circling in his mind. He can't help wondering whether the Ripper *is* just a man. Can't help thinking that to do what the Ripper's done, you surely have to be something else; something inhuman; something ferocious; something like a demon or a devil. Something like pure darkness and madness and evil all rolled into one.

Because you can't do what the Ripper's done and just be *normal*, can you? You can't just be a *man*?

"Ready?" Colin whispers.

Ben nods, even though he's not ready, and doesn't know whether he ever will be.

They sneak across the lawn, on tiptoes, like robbers in a film. Their feet make the softest sound on the grass, barely a sound at all – but Ben imagines Blanchford sitting motionless in the dark, his eyes open and staring behind his spectacles, his hearing as sharp as a bat's, his head snapping round and his wide, staring eyes drilling through the night, fastening on to them like hooks.

The house looms closer, black and silent, crouching, ready to pounce. Someone at school said they'd heard the Ripper uses something long and sharp on his victims, something like a screwdriver, and that he stabs them and stabs them and stabs them… that he even stabs out their eyes.

Ben feels sick. His bowels are churning, heavy, dragging him down. He wonders whether Colin is feeling the same, whether to suggest they just forget this and go, run and run until they're home, until they're safe.

But his throat's too dry, too clogged with his own fear. He licks his lips, but it doesn't help. They're almost at the door now, stepping off the grass and onto the concrete flags in front of it.

And there's no letterbox. Ben stares, thinking he must be mistaken, that there must be one somewhere. But there isn't. The front door is a panel of dark, stained wood with a half-moon of wobbly glass at head height, which you can't see through properly.

But there's not a letterbox to be seen – *and that,* Ben thinks suddenly, *is because Blanchford is the Ripper, and the Ripper doesn't need one. Because he's not normal, he's not human. He only pretends to be, in order to fit in, but he's not really. Because he's camouflaged, he's disguised.*

Daft, he tells himself. *Daft, daft, daft.* But he can't dislodge the idea from his head. He imagines Blanchford in an empty house with no furniture, no telly, no carpets. Imagines him standing in the middle of the room, silent as a statue. Waiting for the next time he has to pretend to be normal. For the next time the urge comes upon him to kill.

"Shit," Colin whispers, his voice muffled through the scarf.

"Let's go," Ben says, but he can barely squeeze the words through the tightness in his throat.

"We'll have to go round the back," Colin says, ignoring him. "It's like my gran's house, this."

"What?" Ben says, and this time his voice emerges as a breathy squeak.

Colin doesn't seem to notice how horrified Ben is by his suggestion, though. "My gran's letterbox," he explains. "It's in the back door, not the front. It's to stop kids putting stuff through it. Fireworks and that."

Ben's terrified that by going round the back they'll be cutting off their escape route, but before he can say anything Colin turns away from the front door and slips into the narrow wedge of shadow between the side of the house and the hedge that separates Blanchford's property from his neighbour's.

Ben stays where he is, wondering what to do. Should he follow Colin or wait here? Stick with his friend or stand on guard in case Blanchford comes out of the front door?

But the thought makes Ben step back. If Blanchford opens the door now he'll be able to lunge out and grab Ben. Ben's fast and Blanchford's fat and old, but if Blanchford *is* the Ripper that won't matter. Because Blanchford won't really be what he seems. Because if he wants to, the Ripper will get him no matter what.

Ben takes another step back. He's on the lawn again now, amidst shadows and silence. But suddenly he wonders what's *in* the shadows, what might even now be sliding soundlessly through the blackness in his direction, homing in on him like a shark.

He turns, looks. The tall hedge around Blanchford's property is a wall of solid black that seems to be gathering yet more blackness to it. Even as Ben watches, it seems to be expanding, creeping slowly towards him.

Daft, he thinks, *daft, daft, daft. It's just your stupid eyes.*

Then a sound cuts through the silence.

"Psst."

It's Colin. His friend is a bobbing shadow in the oily darkness at the side of the house. He looks as though he's trying to pull himself out of the darkness, as though he's trapped in it.

"What are you doing?" Colin hisses.

"Nothing," says Ben.

"Come on then," Colin says, jerking his hand in a beckoning gesture.

Even as he walks towards Colin, Ben wonders why he's doing it. Colin's not his boss, nor even his only friend. So is he doing it for Angela? Is she worth the risk he's taking?

He doesn't know. All he knows is that he wishes he wasn't here. He plunges after Colin and the darkness envelops him like cold, black water. For a moment it's like being blind, and he waves his hands in front of him as his fear inflates like a balloon, pushing its way into his throat. Then his gloved hand bumps against something that's both hard and soft, and there's a grunt of pain and Colin hisses, "What you doing, you div? That was my face."

51

Ben halts. His heart's beating so hard he hears the rhythmic crackle of it in his ears.

"Sorry," he says. "I couldn't see."

"Let's take it slow."

They creep along the path at the side of the house. Ahead of them, where they might expect to see a flash of green back lawn in the daytime, is only blackness.

"What if Blanchford comes?" Ben asks. "What if he traps us?"

"We go over the back fence," Colin replies. "Blanchford's a fat fucker. He'll never catch us."

If he's just a man, Ben thinks, but he doesn't say so. He sticks close to Colin, and half a dozen steps later they reach the end of the path, and then they're round the back of the house.

There are scraps of light bleeding in from here and there – a few glimmers from surrounding houses, a faint bleed of orange from the lamps in an adjoining street – but they provide the boys with only the sketchiest layout of their surroundings.

What Ben can see is the house – of course – then a flat bit of concrete with bins on it, then a black area that looks like grass, and then beyond that... he feels a tingle of fear sweep through him as he realizes there is no opening – or at least, none that he can see – in the six-feet tall hedge that surrounds the back of the property.

What this means is that if Blanchford came round the side of the house, they'd be trapped. Ben thinks again of the screwdriver, wonders what it would feel like if someone rammed a screwdriver through his skin and into his insides. All at once he feels flimsy and vulnerable. He feels full of soft wetness.

He stares at the hedge, hoping to spot a darker arch, a way out, hoping a gate will magically appear out of the gloom. There's something in the back corner of the garden, a more solid block of darkness. A bush? A tree? No, it's squatter than a tree, and with a more defined shape. He takes a hesitant step towards it, and then he realizes. It's a shed. It could be something to hide behind, he thinks, or something to climb on to in order to scale the hedge. And then he wonders whether Blanchford keeps his tools in there. The tools he kills with.

"Bingo," hisses Colin.

He's moved away from Ben and is crouching down beyond the bins. Ben takes a couple of tentative steps towards him, wincing at the crackle of damp grit between the bottom of his trainers and the concrete slabs.

"What is it?" Ben whispers.

"Letterbox."

Ben sees a glimmer of white as Colin takes the note from his pocket. Next moment he slips it through the letterbox, but as he does so there's a creak, which causes Colin to scuffle backwards like a crab and Ben to freeze in shock.

"Shit," Colin breathes.

"What?"

"Back door's open – like, properly open, not just unlocked."

"Come on, let's go," says Ben.

But before Colin can move they hear a rustle of movement from somewhere near the shed.

Ben spins so fast towards the sound that the heel of his trainer squeaks on the concrete. Out of the corner of his eye he's vaguely aware of Colin scrambling to his feet.

Blanchford! he thinks, and the horror of it is like a great white bird spreading its wings inside him. *He was in his shed all the time. Maybe spying on us. Maybe getting his tools.*

He braces himself to run, and then he freezes as a new thought hits him:

What if he's got Angela in there?

Ben glares into the darkness by the shed, anguished and terrified, his body motionless even though every instinct screams at him to run.

There's more rustling, more movement. Something breaks away from the dark block of the shed and begins to shamble or slide or creak across the lawn towards him. It doesn't sound like a man, that's the weird thing. It sounds like part of the dense, prickly hedge has detached itself and is moving in his direction. There's a spiky, dark shimmer in the air, a sense of something shapeless. He hears the rattling of dry leaves, the scraping of what sound like tiny branches rubbing together. And then there's a crack, and another, followed by several more. Like sticks breaking. Or bones.

And *still* Ben doesn't run, because terrified as he is, he has to see, he has to *know* what's coming. There's a paleness emerging from the rustling dark, a blur of white where a head should be. But *is* it a head? It looks like less than a head. He blinks, looks again.

But no, it *must* be a head. Because now Ben can see a face, or at least the crude approximation of one. Dark, mismatched hollows for eyes, a gaping black gash of a mouth. But the flesh of the face doesn't look like flesh; it's gnarled, whorled; the edges of it are rough, jagged, asymmetrical.

It's wood, he suddenly realizes. This shambling thing is wearing a wooden mask.

Is this Blanchford's disguise? Is this what he wears so no one can identify him?

Or could it be that Blanchford is the disguise? That this thing —
Then Colin, running past in a whirlwind of limbs, grabs his arm.
"Scarper!"

*

When Ben wakes next morning he's under his covers curled into a
ball. He can hear the radio downstairs and the occasional rumble of
a car going past outside. He can tell from the crackly whoosh each
car makes as it sweeps by that the road is wet, and sure enough
when he finally crawls out of bed and opens his curtains he sees rain
slithering down the window, the world beyond grey and shiny and
colourless as wet clay, squashed beneath a sky like a huge dirty
thumbprint.

He shivers as he plods downstairs in his dressing gown,
although it's not only from the cold. He hears his mum in the
kitchen singing along to a song that goes 'Do Wah Diddy Diddy
Dum Diddy Do'. It's daft and normally he'd smile, but today he
doesn't feel like it. He's still seeing that horrible face in his mind.
He saw it for hours last night in the darkness of his bedroom, before
exhaustion finally dragged him into sleep, and at the moment it feels
not only like he'll see it forever, but that now that he *has* seen it
he'll never feel safe or happy again.

He wonders if Colin feels the same as he does, or whether he's
just over-reacting. Colin was definitely as scared as he was last
night. When they finally stopped running, streets and streets away
from Blanchford's house, they were both shaking so badly it looked
like they were suffering from exposure. Ben had a tight knot in the
pit of his stomach, and even though he felt sure they hadn't been
followed, his eyes still darted into every shadow, every scrap of
darkness, half-expecting to see that horrible, yawning face rising out
of the black like a corpse breaking the surface of a muddy river.

"What *was* that thing?" Colin gasped, almost sobbed, bending
double and clasping his knees with his gloved hands.

"It was a mask," Ben said, the scarf having slipped down to his
chin, his panting breath white and jagged in the air. He looked at
Ben and his voice grew plaintive, as if he needed both of them to
believe it. "Just someone wearing a mask, that's all."

His mum looks round now as he enters the kitchen. She's
making meat and potato pie for tea. As stewing steak bubbles in a
pan with carrots and onions and stock, she's rolling out the pastry,
her hands all floury.

"Here you are at last!" she cries, and stops what she's doing. She wipes her hands on a tea towel, bustles over to him and presses a palm against his forehead.

"How are you feeling, love? You don't seem to have a temperature."

"I'm all right," Ben says, pulling away.

"You weren't all right last night. You looked terrible when you came in. Straight to bed without even watching your favourite programme. I thought: he *must* be ill."

"I'm all right now," Ben assures her. "What time is it?"

"Nearly eleven. I thought it'd be best to let you sleep. Do you want some breakfast?"

Ben doesn't, but he roots in the pantry for Golden Nuggets, knowing his mum'll only fuss if he doesn't eat anything. "I'll get it. Where's Dad?"

"At work. They've got a big job on. Should be back at lunchtime. Said he'd call at the chippy on his way home."

"Ace," Ben says, trying to sound enthusiastic.

He takes his Golden Nuggets through to the living room and watches *Swap Shop* for a bit. Or rather, he stares at it, but he doesn't really see it. All he sees is that twisted wooden face with the gaping holes for eyes and mouth. There's something about it he doesn't want to focus on, something he's trying to deny, though it's niggling away at the back of his mind. He tells himself he didn't really see the face settle and change, become more human, as it surged from the darkness. That was nothing but a trick of the light, simply his eyes trying to make sense of what he was seeing.

Something scratches at the big picture window that looks out over the front lawn and he jerks round. There's a dark, rustling shape creeping inwards from the top left hand corner of the frame. It's the ivy, which his mum is always nagging at his dad to cut, made restless by the wind that's accompanying the rain. As Ben rises to his feet, intending to immerse himself in the soothing embrace of a hot bath, the telephone rings.

He hears the kitchen door open and his mum bustle along the landing to answer it. Her voice is too muffled and the telly too loud for him to hear what she's saying, but he can tell from the way her tone immediately becomes shrill and jagged that something's wrong. Hunching up his shoulders, he sits down again, and when he hears the clattering ting of the phone, followed by her approaching footsteps, he braces himself, certain she's about to tell him that something bad has happened to Colin.

The door opens and her stricken face makes him feel as though he's shriveling inside.

"It's your dad," she says. "He's been arrested!"

*

"For the last bloody time, I wasn't arrested!" Ben's dad snaps.

They're sitting at the kitchen table. It's gone two in the afternoon. Ben's dad didn't get to the chippy, so they're having sardines on toast instead. He's telling them what happened that morning at the depot, how the police turned up and asked to speak to everybody.

Ben's mum looks contrite, but she says, "They made you go to the station to give your fingerprints, though, didn't they? They didn't exactly give you a choice."

Ben's dad shrugs. "I suppose I could've said no if I'd wanted to, but why bother? I've got nowt to hide."

"Well, I don't think it's right. Accusing innocent folk."

"No one was accused of 'owt, love. It were just a routine enquiry. Police've got to be thorough about these things. I were glad to help, and so were the rest o' the lads."

Ben listens and munches his way stolidly through his sardines on toast. His dad doesn't know for sure, but he says the rumour was a van like the ones they use at work was seen driving away from the scene of the murder the other night.

Ben thinks about Blanchford. He has a Hillman Imp, not a van – unless he keeps it somewhere else. Then again, the van might not have anything to do with the Ripper. Like his dad says, the police have to follow up every lead, however slim.

Ben's mum shakes her head. "I just wish they'd catch this devil. He's making everyone's life a misery."

"They will, love," Ben's dad reassures her. "He's only one bloke and he's got the whole of the police force after him. He's bound to make a cock up eventually."

Ben says nothing.

*

By the time Ben goes to bed the rain is hissing and clattering, and blowing in angry pebbledash gusts against his window. He hasn't seen Colin, because he's stayed inside all day, reading and pretending he's not feeling very well. He hears his dad shout downstairs, but only because he's watching *Match of the Day*. Ben burrows under his covers with his torch, hoping to block out the sound of rustling from somewhere above his ceiling, which he knows is only rain running down the roof into the gutter, and the shrill, intermittent creak of what he assures himself is the TV aerial buffeted by the wind.

He doesn't realize he's fallen asleep until he snaps awake with the crawling certainty that something is in the room with him. He's still under the covers and the torch is still on, though its light is feebler now because its battery has run down. Ben's face is hot and flushed, and the first thing he hears is slow, gravelly breathing. However, even when he realizes the breathing is his own it doesn't change his opinion that he's not alone. He clamps his mouth shut and swallows, his dry throat clicking like a cracked knuckle. Switching off the torch, he lies as motionless as he can and listens.

The first thing he's aware of is that the rain has stopped. He hears soft-edged plinks and plops as the world drips. But that's not in his room, that's outside, beyond the four walls between which black silence is waiting for him to emerge from beneath his covers. It's a silence so profound it seems as dense as oil.

His body is rigid, almost aching with the effort to remain still. He keeps his breathing shallow, thinking of the other presence, if there is one, as a snake poised to strike at the slightest movement. Oddly he feels that sleep is his ally; feels as if his fear is giving strength to whatever's in the room with him, and that if he can block it the intruder's threat will dissipate. He closes his eyes and wills unconscious to creep over him.

But before it can begin to, something on the far side of the room moves with a dry rustling sound.

Ben responds instinctively, hurling the covers away and sitting bolt upright, his knees coming up and his heels digging into the mattress and pushing down with enough force to piston his body back against the headboard. His bed is in the corner of the room, the wall on his right-hand side. The darkness that fills the rest of the room is like a black, icy sea full of murky shapes. It's not a particularly large room, and most of the shapes he recognizes despite their lack of definition. Here's his wardrobe, there his desk and chair, there his record player, and over there his bookcase. The window, on the far side of the room, maybe ten steps from the bed, is a dim, greyish square.

But as he stares at it, the left side of the window is slowly obliterated by a creeping stain of darkness as a black shape, accompanied by the rustling scrape of dry twigs and old leaves, moves across it.

Ben screams – he can't help it – and scrabbles for the torch, which is tangled in the covers at his feet. He spends an agonizing few seconds trying to tug it from the crumpled folds of bedclothes, and another second or two fumbling with it, turning it the right way round, trying to locate the switch.

Then he *does* find it, a serrated square of sliding plastic, and snaps it from 'off' to 'on'. An insipid, mustard-coloured light flounders across the room as Ben points the torch like a weapon at the thing by the window. Before the light can separate the shape from the blackness around it, his door flies open, and with the snap of a switch the room is saturated with light so bright that the pain of it is like thumbs pressing hard against his eyeballs. Ben squeezes his eyes shut, then immediately starts blinking as they begin to water.

"Ben, love, what's the matter? What's happened?"

It's his mum's voice, full of ragged, just-woken-up alarm.

Ben blinks and blinks, and eventually his vision clears, the glare of the light subsides.

He looks across the room at the window, his muscles tightening as his body braces itself for what he might see.

But there's nothing there.

*

"Have you heard?"

Ben turns. Colin's running up behind him, his bag bouncing on his hip.

"Heard what?"

Colin's eyes are shining with fearful excitement. "Blanchford's done a runner."

Ben stumbles to a halt. Around him his schoolmates continue to flow towards the main doors, heading for cloakrooms and lockers prior to the morning bell.

"What do you mean?" he says, staring at Colin.

Colin looks pleased at the impact his news has made. "No one knows where he is. He's disappeared."

"How do you know?"

"Everyone's talking about it."

"Who's everyone?"

Now Colin frowns, as if Ben is being pernickety. "My mum knows Mrs Havers who works in the office, and she says Blanchford was supposed to be at school on Saturday to run some club or something. But he didn't turn up, and no one's been able to get in touch with him since."

Ben starts walking again, Colin falling into step beside him. "Has anyone been round to his house?"

Colin shrugs. "Dunno."

Ben thinks of Blanchford's open back door and, before he can prevent himself, of the shambling, creaking figure beside the shed. "Maybe he just forgot. Maybe he's ill."

"He's not turned up at school today either."

"How do you know?"

"Well… he's not here, is he? He's always in the playground before the bell, hassling people to hurry up."

Ben looks around. It's true. Blanchford's nowhere to be seen. And he can't see his brown Hillman Imp in the teacher's car park either.

"Yeah, well, like I said, maybe he's ill." Then a thought strikes him. "What about Angela? Is she here? Have you seen her?"

Instead of replying, Colin nudges Ben with his elbow and nods his head. Ben looks in the direction of the nod and sees Angela cutting diagonally across the playground, approaching the school from the opposite direction, having presumably entered via the far gate. She's with another girl from her class, who Ben thinks is called Beverley something, whose white-blonde hair and pale skin makes her look like an over-exposed photograph. Ben feels a flood of relief to see that Angela's safe, although it's combined with the other things he always feels when he sees her: a desperate, stomach-curling, primal desire, and a longing to speak to her, to be noticed by her, which is nevertheless tempered by a stew of churning emotions in which embarrassment, fear, frustration, unworthiness and a sense of inadequacy are the key ingredients.

Lovesick. That's what he is. He's so crazy about Angela that seeing her and thinking about her makes him feel literally nauseous with passion.

Pathetic, he thinks. *Bloody daft.*

Colin nudges him again. "Why don't you talk to her now?"

"I…" Ben's about to say 'can't' – but then he thinks of what happened on Friday night at Blanchford's, and on Saturday night in his room, and of how terrified he was, and he thinks that nothing could be as scary as that, that talking to Angela would be a breeze by comparison.

And so he says, "All right then, I will."

And before he can change his mind or think about it further, he changes course, marching across the playground towards her.

She becomes aware of him converging on her when he's still half a dozen paces away. She looks up and the expression on her face is one of bemused acceptance, almost as if she's been expecting this.

"Hi, Angela," Ben says, trying to sound casual, trying not to stutter over his words, "it's me again. Can I talk to you for a minute?"

Angela and her friend stop. Ben stops too. Angela gives a little sigh, though it's not a *mean* sigh. She says to her friend, "I'll see you inside, okay?"

The friend glances at Ben, then leaves without a word. Now it's just Ben and Angela standing there. To Ben it seems as if everyone and everything else is fading into the background.

Angela turns her green eyes on him and raises her eyebrows expectantly.

Ben clears his throat, and then, trying not to babble, he says, "Well, it's just that, you know last week when the policeman came, and he told us about the murder, and he said that the boys should walk the girls home? Well, I was wondering if I could do that? Walk you home, I mean?"

Angela is silent for a minute. She gives a little half-smile, and Ben feels warm and melty inside at the knowledge that the smile is directed at him.

"Why would you want to do that?" Angela murmurs.

"Well, um, because the policeman said – "

"No, I mean, why would you want to walk *me* home? It's not like we're in the same class or anything."

To Ben her voice is like honey or caramel or warm chocolate sauce. His own seems coarse and blunt and stupid in comparison.

"Well, 'cos I... I like you," he mumbles, and feels himself blushing.

"Like me? You don't even know me," she says.

He can tell she's not being mean, because her voice is soft and she's still half-smiling at him. It gives him the courage to say, "No, but I'd like to. Get to know you better, I mean."

She's silent for a moment. She looks away from Ben, gazing off to one side as if she's thinking of something, perhaps even considering his offer. But Ben's a bit puzzled because her green eyes look almost sad.

Finally she says, "It's really nice of you, and I'm sure you're a very sweet boy, but I can't."

Ben feels a fist inside him, squeezing and twisting his guts. All he can think of to say is, "Why not?"

She smiles again, and it's a warm smile, but a sad one. "I just... can't, that's all. I'm sorry."

"Have you... already got a boyfriend?" he mumbles.

She regards him for a moment, and then she nods. "Yes. That's it. I've already got a boyfriend. But thank you for your offer. I really appreciate it."

She reaches out and briefly touches his hand, and the brush of her fingers is like delicious electricity on his skin.

"It's all right," he mumbles, but there's a pulse in his ears, which is pounding so hard he's not even sure he made any sound at all. And the next moment, with a final smile and a shimmering swish of her mahogany-coloured hair, Angela is moving away from him, leaving him standing alone amid the tide of bodies flowing into the school.

*

"We should follow her," whispers Colin.

They're in Chemistry. Mr Parkes is droning on and on at the front of the class.

Ben looks at Colin. "What do you mean?"

"After school. We should follow her. See where she goes, who she meets."

"Why should we?"

"Well… then we can see if she's telling the truth."

"Why *wouldn't* she be telling the truth?" says Ben irritably.

Colin shrugs, an expression on his face that makes Ben want to slap him.

Ben faces front again. Colin is silent for a moment, playing with his ruler.

Then he says, "What if she's meeting Blanchford?"

Ben's head snaps round. "Are you *mad?*"

He hisses so loudly that a few people turn to look at him, but Parkes doesn't notice.

Slyly Colin says, "Wouldn't you like to know for sure?"

Ben scowls. "No I wouldn't. I'm *not* following Angela. No way."

*

"There she is," says Colin.

The boys melt back behind the bus queue as Angela approaches on the opposite side of the road, her satchel over her shoulder. She's alone, which is something at least. If she was with her friends they would have more chance of being spotted. On the other hand, Ben doesn't like the thought of her walking home on her own after what the policeman said last week – but neither does he like the thought

61

of seeing her meeting a boyfriend either. He's been torturing himself all day with an idea of what her boyfriend will be like. In Ben's mind he's eighteen, tall, good-looking and confident, and he drives a red sports car.

When Angela passes by the boys slip out of hiding and follow her. Ben still feels it's weird and pervy to be doing this, but Colin has been on and on at him all day, and in the end Ben has agreed to go along with the plan just to shut Colin up. Ben doesn't even know why Colin *wants* to follow Angela, and in fact he doubts that Colin himself would be able to give a proper reason. The thing about Colin is that he often gets stupid ideas in his head and refuses to let them go. Although the boys have been best friends since they met at primary school when they were five, Ben finds Colin a real pain in the arse sometimes.

Angela is easy to follow at first, because there are loads of other kids around and it's no problem blending into the crowd. After a while, though, the other kids start to filter off in different directions, and Ben begins to worry that Angela might turn round and spot them.

What will he say if she does? That he just wanted to make sure she was safe? Or would it be better to pretend he hasn't seen her until she confronts him, and then say that he and Colin are going to see a friend whose house must be close to where Angela lives?

After a while the lie about the friend becomes less likely because Angela turns off the main road and goes down a lane where the houses become sparser and more spread out. There's a row of cottages, then a park, then a few bigger houses, and then the road gets narrower and becomes enclosed first by high hedges on both sides and then by dry stone walls which enclose farmer's fields.

It's at this point that Ben stops and grabs Colin's sleeve. Colin looks surprised.

"What's the matter?" he asks.

"I think we should go back."

"Why?"

"'Cos we've walked about two miles, and we're heading in the opposite direction to where we live, and what will we say if Angela sees us?"

Colin looks unconcerned. "We'll ask her why she lied about her boyfriend."

Ben frowns. "What makes you think she did?"

"Didn't she say her boyfriend would walk her home?"

Ben narrows his eyes, trying to remember. "No, she just said that she *had* a boyfriend."

"Right, but he's not here, is he? So how come she wouldn't let *you* walk her home just to make sure she was safe? I mean, it's not like that means she has to marry you or anything, is it?"

Ben scowls, but Colin's right in a way. Pressing home his advantage, Colin continues, "Look, we've come this far, and we're in the middle of nowhere, which is even more reason to make sure Angela gets home okay."

"Why do you even care?" Ben says.

Colin shrugs, his nose wrinkling. "It's just fun. It's something to do."

Suddenly Ben realizes that to Colin this whole Ripper thing is little more than an exciting game.

"Was it fun on Friday round at Blanchford's?" he asks angrily.

Colin looks momentarily troubled; his eyes slide away from Ben's. But he says, "I'm not saying I wasn't shit-scared, but we got away, didn't we?"

"And what about that thing we saw? That thing with the wooden mask?"

Ben's sure he sees Colin shudder. Quickly he says, "Look, let's talk about this later. If we don't hurry up we'll lose her."

It's true that while they've been talking Angela has rounded a bend in the road and they can't see her any more. There's a part of Ben that wishes they *would* lose her, because then that would give them a reason to go home, and at first when they hurry around the long bend, keeping close to the dry stone wall on their left, and see the road stretching downhill in front of them, it seems his wish has been granted. The stretch of road ahead, undulating between a patchwork of brown and yellow fields, looking drab and dead under the grim winter sky, is empty.

"Where's she gone?" Colin asks, bewildered. And then he points, and answers his own question. "There she is!"

Angela has taken a left a little way ahead and is now walking down a narrow track between two muddy fields, her mahogany hair shimmering and bouncing with each step. Ben can see that the track leads into a dense clump of woodland beyond the fields.

"Where's she going?" he murmurs.

"Probably to meet her secret lover," Colin grins. "Wish I'd brought my camera with me."

"Don't be a perv," Ben scowls, but he can't help feeling a tingling thrill at the prospect, however unlikely, of seeing Angela naked. He and Colin hurry along the road until they come to the turning, whereupon they follow Angela down the track.

She's some way ahead of them now, and the narrow track, like a thread which connects the road to the woods in the shape of a stretched out S, is enclosed by shoulder-high stone walls, which are entwined with fibrous vines and other foliage. For this reason it's difficult to keep Angela in sight without getting too close, as a result of which she's nowhere to be seen by the time they reach the border of the woods.

"Fuck," Colin mutters, standing between two trees as though they constitute a doorway and looking around. "Where's she gone?"

Ben has a different concern. "Why is she even here? She can't live in the woods."

Colin smirks. "I've already told you – secret lover."

"Shut up, Col. It's not funny."

Colin's smile fades. "Maybe she's led us on a wild goose chase on purpose."

"You mean she knew we were following her?"

"Dunno. Maybe."

Ben steps forward, elbowing past Colin. Already the sky is taking on a pre-twilight flatness, which thickens the shadows between the trees and makes everything look dull and dead.

Peering left and right, all Ben can see are a random mass of tree trunks clustered like a motionless, endlessly receding crowd, each connected to the next by clumps of tangled foliage.

"Angela!" he yells, causing a flock of birds to take to the air in a flapping mass.

Colin grabs his arm. "What are you doing?"

Ben shakes off his grip and rounds on him angrily. "I'm sick of this. I should never have listened to you. All I want to do is find Angela and say sorry for following her and make sure she's all right."

"All right," Colin says sulkily. "Don't throw a wobbly."

Ben scowls and peers into the trees once more. "Angela," he shouts again. "It's me, Ben, from school. Are you there?" There's no reply, and he hesitates, wondering what to do. "We should go look for her."

"She could be anywhere," says Colin.

"Yeah, but we can't just go off and leave her, can we?"

"Why not? It's not like we made her come here, is it?"

Ben glares at Colin. "You fuck off then if you want to, but I'm staying."

Colin sighs. "All right, I'll stay too. But we should leave before it gets dark, otherwise we'll be the ones who end up getting lost."

"These woods aren't that big," Ben says.

"Big enough when it's dark."

"What's up? Scared of the Ripper, are you?"

"Oh yeah," says Colin with heavy irony. "'Coz he's bound to be looking for prozzies in a deserted wood."

As far as the boys can tell there are two paths, one going left, the other right. On a whim they follow the left-hand path, which meanders between the trees and undergrowth for a while, until eventually it becomes so overgrown that it hardly looks like a path at all.

The light continues to drain from the sky as they walk, so that eventually the woods around them begin to lose definition. Bushes become brambly masses of ragged-edged darkness lurking between the trees, whilst the tree trunks themselves seem to smooth out as blackness slowly fills in their gnarls and pits and wrinkles, obliterating detail and texture.

"We should go back," whispers Colin, who seems nervous of the various bird cries, which have accompanied them for a while, but which suddenly seem to have adopted a more sinister, threatening tone now that the daylight is fading.

Ben knows his friend is right, but he tries calling Angela's name once more. When no one answers, he points to the darkening path ahead.

"Two more minutes and then we'll go."

Colin sighs but nods in agreement and the boys trudge on. A minute later they come to a small clearing, on the opposite side of which, at the base of a tree, is a dark, hunched shape.

"Look there," Ben whispers to Colin.

Colin looks, and Ben knows from the gasp he makes that he has seen it too. The shape appears to be a figure, squatting utterly motionless in front of the tree, staring at them. They both see the pale glimmer of what appears to be a face, indented with a vague triangle of dark blotches, which may be two eyes and a mouth.

"Is it her?" Colin whispers, his voice wavering with nerves.

Ben hesitates. He has to fight a sudden urge to turn and flee. "Let's see, shall we?" he hears himself replying.

The boys creep across the clearing, each tentative step bringing them closer to the crouching shape. Although it doesn't move it appears to watch them. As he gets closer to it, Ben stares so hard in an attempt to penetrate the fog-like gloom that it makes his eyes sting. Is he seeing details rise from the murk – a dark, V-neck jumper over a white shirt, the strap of a school satchel across one shoulder, a shiny sweep of mahogany-coloured hair – or are the details purely a mirage of what he *wants* to see, conjured from his imagination? He steps closer, and suddenly he's sure.

"It *is* her! It's Angela!" he cries.

He breaks into a run, rushes across, and only when he's a few steps away from the figure does he realize his mistake.

It's not her at all. It's not even a person. And yet for a second or two the illusion was extraordinary. Even now, if he looks away and glances back, he sees Angela clearly for a split-second – and it's unmistakably her, squatting by the tree, looking up at him.

But when his vision settles he sees that her face is nothing but an upturned clump of white fungus clinging to the tree bark, with vague indentations that suggest features, and her body is a combination of foliage and shadows arranged just so.

"It's weird," Colin breathes, standing now at Ben's shoulder. "I blink and I see her, clear as day. Then I look again – and it's nothing like her."

As they stare down at the weird conglomeration of matter and darkness, which both resembles and does not resemble Angela, something rustles behind them. Ben whirls, as Colin clutches his arm in fear.

"What was that?"

"Just an animal in the bushes," Ben whispers. "A rabbit or something."

But there's something in the gloom on the other side of the clearing that is considerably larger than a rabbit. It oozes from the darkness; no, more than that, it *forms* from the darkness, gathering itself together from available materials, rustling and creaking as it does so.

They both watch as the shape solidifies, and then, with a series of sharp bone-like cracks, begins to shamble towards them. Is it becoming sleeker, more upright as they watch? Is its 'face', a gnarled lump of bark like a crude wooden mask, becoming smoother, more rounded, more human?

Suddenly they're surrounded by rustling, by the sense that more of the creatures are coming out of hiding, creating forms for themselves out of their environment.

Ben thinks of how Angela sweetly rebuffed him, and realizes now that she was being kind, that she was trying to protect him.

"Oh God," Colin moans, his voice reedy and high-pitched, "I've just realized what she is."

Ben and Colin are squeezing together now for mutual protection as the creaking, rustling shapes close in on them. Ben glances at his friend.

"What she is? What do you mean? What is she?"

Colin looks at Ben, and the terror and hopelessness in his eyes is appalling to see.

"She's bait," he whispers.

THE YORKSHIRE WITCHES

There are few darker chapters in England's history than the witch-hunting era of the 16th and 17th centuries. Though the cruel and irrational nature of this so-called 'moral panic' has been exaggerated – researchers estimate that over two thirds of all witch trials in England resulted in acquittals, often with magistrates denouncing prosecutors and their witnesses as scoundrels and fools – several hundred innocent victims still paid with their lives, so it was hardly a triumph of reason.

Yorkshire, like most English counties, played its part in the tragedy, but two of the most fascinating tales of Yorkshire witchcraft are not concerned with ignorance and injustice, but, on one hand, with bizarre instances of apparent genuine magic, and on the other with a ruthless pretense of paranormal power and two subsequent gruesome deaths.

In the first case, Ursula Southill was born in a cave at Knaresborough, North Yorkshire, in 1488. Throughout her childhood she was allegedly attended by spirits and invisible imps who protected her zealously, even attacking those seeking to help and befriend her. As an adult, she was said to be ugly and irascible, but still found herself a husband, a certain Toby Shipton, who she married in 1512. Shortly after this, she adopted the nickname 'Mother Shipton', and commenced a lucrative career as a fortune-teller. Several of her prophecies are still taken seriously today: she appeared to foretell the Civil War, and the arrival of motor vehicles and iron-clad battleships; while erroneous predictions credited to her – such as the end of the world occurring in 1881 – were discovered to be Victorian-era forgeries. Local folk consulted Mother Shipton on a range of issues, and though wild rumours held that she punished her enemies by unleashing hordes of goblins upon them or cursing them with unstoppable laughter, on the whole she emerges through the prism of history as a woman of wisdom and probity. She certainly gave no-one any cause to investigate or execute her, dying peacefully in her bed in 1566.

Not so Mary Bateman, who lived much later but was known simply as 'the Yorkshire Witch'. A thoroughly wicked individual, who came to prominence long after the Witchcraft Act of 1735 reduced sorcery in England from a potential capital offence to a minor felony, she still managed to finish up on the gallows.

Bateman was basically a con-artist who left her native Thirsk, in North Yorkshire, to set up home in Leeds. She told fortunes as well, *but caused more of a stir by selling 'defences against the dark arts' in the way of potions and spells, most of which she had fabricated on the spot. She came unstuck in 1806, when she attached herself to a young couple, the Perigos, who believed themselves hexed. Charging them continually for her services, Batemen didn't just deceive them, but actively tried to kill them and secure the remainder of their wealth by feeding them poisoned pies and puddings.*

When Rebecca Perigo finally expired, the authorities became suspicious. Bateman was subsequently arrested and convicted.

She died by hanging in 1809, at the age of 41 – not for the crime of witchcraft, but as an everyday fraudster and murderess. As a gruesome footnote to the tale, and perhaps as evidence that science had not yet overtaken men's minds, ghoulish souvenir-hunters descended on the gibbet after her death and stripped the flesh from her corpse, selling the individual pieces in local markets as magical charms.

ON ILKLEY MOOR
Alison Littlewood

It wasn't until I turned off the main road and up towards the moors that it really struck me that this had been my home. There was that old sound, the wind billowing its way across the tops and down into the valley, a sound out of memory; but the way it buffeted the car was real enough. I reached out and turned the radio up, but in my mind it was another tune I heard, different lyrics:

Wheear 'ast tha bin since ah saw thee?

I smiled. Where indeed? I hadn't felt the need to come back here since Dad had died, and that was years ago. I had my own place now, my own job; my training was done, my school days long behind me. I'd never thought to see Inchy – Warren Hinchliffe – again. I jabbed at the radio, turning it off, and listened to the sound of the wind coming over the tops. Up there were swathes of green, patched with the lighter shades of dead grass and the darker growth of heather, the purple flowers darkened to grey under a cloudy sky. And grey paths wound through it all, leading nowhere, or so it had seemed when we were small.

I remembered what Inchy had said on the phone: *It'd be just what I need.* I had the impression that he'd been prepared for my rejection. He'd just lost his job, he said, nothing special, just helping out on a farm, but now it had ended: *I need summat to help me start ower.* And he'd waited in silence, and the old guilt had crept from his end of the line to mine.

Wheear 'ast tha bin since ah saw thee?

I'd been miles away, while he had stayed, along with the memory of what had passed between us, the thing we had done. I pushed the thought away. I'd started again long ago; the least I could do was help Inchy do the same. I dropped down the slope and saw the pub – *The Cow and Calf* – named for the giant outcrops of millstone grit that could just be seen at the edge of the moor, and I slowed, and pulled into the car park.

*

Inchy was propping up the bar. I recognised him at once, though he wasn't so much taller than me as I'd remembered, and he'd been working on a beer gut in the time I'd been away. He didn't smile when he saw me, didn't act surprised, didn't say "How've you been?"; he just nodded to where a pint stood at his elbow.

"I was going to have a Coke –"

"You might as well 'ave it. Get it dahn thee neck, Andy." And then, belatedly: "All right, mate?"

"Not bad." I grinned at him before taking a drink. It was cold, but more welcome than I'd expected.

He grinned back and drained what was left of his own pint. "Lad's day out, and all that. Get you out o' t' city furra bit. God's own country."

I tried not to let him see how the beer was going straight to my head. "My dad always called it that."

"Aye, well, 's changed a bit round 'ere since them days. 'S all posh folk in Ilkley now – more accountants and bankers than you can shek a stick at."

I kept quiet, taking another sip. He knew what I did for a living, didn't he? I was already wondering if this had been a good idea.

"Not locals. Not like us. Remember 'ow we'd go off looking for frogspawn an' that, in t' streams?"

I smiled. I did remember.

"They don't do that these days. Now it's all off to ballet in their fancy Land Rovers, or walking their labra-fucking-doodles. They sink a hundred quid on designer wellies, and chuck a hissy fit if they get 'em mucky. Well, we'd best go, mate."

He pulled on an army surplus jacket and nodded at my padded coat. "Cragface, eh?"

"Craghoppers." I shrugged and bent to tighten the laces on my hiking boots, only then realising how clean they were. They'd been more than a hundred quid, but they were guaranteed comfy out of the box, and I hadn't been walking in a long time. When I straightened I expected Inchy to narrow his eyes or make some comment, but he didn't; he only nodded.

"We'd best get off then," he said.

*

Once we got walking, it was just like the old days. Inchy had always led the way then too; he was a few months older than me but he'd always been taller, and he seemed more so now, since he was higher up the hillside. The wind barrelled off the slope, flattening the grass, and we leaned into it. The path led steadily upward past the side of the old quarry and it felt as if I was fifteen again, playing hooky from school, led astray by "that boy," as my mum used to call him. She'd even correct me if I said his nickname – *Hinchy*, she'd insist

– but he was never called that; no one ever said their aitches, not round here, not then.

The old song started to run through my mind as we climbed higher:

On Ilkla Moor baht 'at . . .

We used to sing it for a joke and it seemed more than ever like one now, with the wind raging around us. How on earth could anyone have kept a hat on their head? The wind was cold too, chilling my ears and the nape of my neck. *Tha's bahn to catch thy deeath o' cowd*, we'd sung. I paused and pulled up my hood, holding it in place, the fabric buffeting about my head. It was loud, and at first I didn't realise that Inchy had spoken.

"Cow n' calf."

He pointed down at the quarry, towards the two huge boulders. The calf stood away on its own, the cow jutting from a longer crag. Beyond them was more moor and fields and little villages and all the long grey sky watching over it all.

"Bet you never knew t' legend," he said. "There was this giant, see. Rombald. He ran off from 'is wife – dunno what 'ed done – an' 'e stamped on them rocks and split t' calf off from t' cow. Course, it never looked like no bloody cow n' calf to me."

I laughed. "Me neither. I could never work out why they called it that."

"Aye, well." Another pause. "'E split summat up, anyroad."

I stared after him as he started to walk, seeing only his back, the dull green of his coat blending into the landscape. I wasn't sure he'd said what I thought I'd heard. I blinked the idea away. He hadn't meant anything; it was only the rocks he'd been speaking of. I shrugged and started after him, climbing higher, away from the quarry and the pub and the view behind it.

*

As we laughed over the old days, I started to remember them in a way I hadn't for a long time. The further I'd gone, the hazier the memories had become; now Inchy brought them back. I remembered trying to smoke a cig he'd nicked from his old man's pocket; unscrewing people's gates on Mischief Night; and coming up here, to the moor. That, most of all; and I remember the way it felt, as if anyone in the world could look up and see us and know what we were up to, and yet hidden too, as if we were a hundred miles from anything.

71

We fell quiet. There was only the sound of the wind and the rustle of our coats, and I started to drift, and I heard the old song once more in my mind:

Tha's been a cooartin' Mary Jane
On Ilkla Moor baht 'at ...

I pulled a face. There were things I wanted to remember and things I didn't, and this was one of the things I didn't.

It was Inchy who'd got a girlfriend first. Of course it was; he was taller than me, and harder, and he always seemed so much older, even though the difference between us was small. And Joan was the best of them, the one all the lads fancied. It wasn't long before they started going out, and Inchy suddenly didn't have so much time for fishing or wandering or anything else.

She was pretty, Joan Chapman. Her long dark hair was never tied back and she had a pale oval face and, what all the lads thought but wouldn't say in front of Inchy, the best pair of tits in school. She had a laugh like a drain and sparkles – it sounded corny even now, but she did – she had sparkles in her eyes. She looked like she was going somewhere, but of course she never did; she hadn't gone anywhere, had never even become any older than we were then. But I hadn't had to think about that, or not too much, because by then I'd been leaving. I was wondering how far that was true of Inchy when he said, "'Ere: I wanted to do summat. For *'er*."

"You what?"

He turned and I saw that his face was white. It came as a shock to see the way he kept blinking, as if he was trying to hold something back.

He pulled something from his pocket. I stared at it. It was a candle. I didn't know what on earth he was thinking: it wasn't something I wanted to remember, and anyway, a *candle* for God's sake, just as if the wind wasn't howling over the tops like the very devil. And it was daylight, even if it was thin and mean, the clouds heavy and grey.

"I thought we could," he said. "Old time's sake. Finish it, you know? Just summat to ..."

Start ower, I thought. I felt suddenly sick, the beer uneasy in my belly. I didn't want to agree, but I found myself saying: "All right."

"Serious?" He brightened at once and I suddenly felt as if I was the older one. I nodded and he went on, towards another grey rock, this one overhanging the hillside as if at any moment it would tumble to the valley below.

*

72

The pancake stone was balanced on a small grey outcrop, its position precarious, and yet it had stood there for years. Its name had never seemed quite right; it was flat on top but it looked to me more like an anvil, pointing out over the empty air. Ancient markings were carved into it, cup and ring formations, some almost joining so they looked like part of some larger pattern that had long since been lost.

"Here," he said.

"Inch, I'm not sure –"

The look he sent me was so hurt I didn't say anything else.

Anger I could have understood, but this, from him, was worse. He took the candle and set it into one of the cups, but it wouldn't hold. He jammed it instead into a crack in the rock and pulled a matchbox from his pocket. The wind almost took it from him. He struck a match and it blew out at once. He swore under his breath; the wind whipped the curse away.

"Ne'er mind," he said. "I brought summat else."

He fiddled in his pockets and took out a small plastic bottle. Carefully, he tipped some of the liquid it held into one of the cups. "'S what they were for, they reckon," he said. "Lighting fires."

I looked at the rock. I wasn't sure anyone knew what the patterns were for, not really, but I somehow felt there must be more to it than that.

This time he threw the match down as soon as it sparked and the liquid caught, flaring, and he jerked away from it. The flame became invisible almost at once.

"I 'eard," he said, "this place behind t' rock – Green Crag – they used t' call it land o' the dead. They did rites, an' that."

I pulled a face. I didn't know where he was getting this stuff. For all I knew, he was making it up. This trip was a mistake, I knew that now.

Tha's been a cooartin' my lass Joan ...

I shook my head, trying to clear it. I felt my guilt stirring, rising into the air with the flame that was already dying, dead and gone like ...

"This is wheear she did it," he said.

I whipped around to face him. "What?"

"Oppened a vein. Right 'ere. Laid 'ersel' down on t' rock, an'–"

"No. She *didn't*."

He half turned to stare at the stone, just as if he could still see the fire burning there, as if anybody could.

I took deep breaths. He had to be lying. I'd heard she'd killed herself – of course I did, everybody knew, everybody knew everything in a place like this – but I'd imagined her doing it in the bath, lying down, putting her wrist under the water before she sliced.

But I *hadn't* known, had I? Because I'd left. I'd gone away to college because I couldn't wait to turn my back on it; I hadn't *wanted* to know.

And now he'd brought me here. Inchy had brought me back.

Tha's been a cooartin' my lass Joan (baht thee trahsers on) ...

The voice in my head had become mocking. No: accusing.

It hadn't been my fault. I'd told myself that so many times. I may have gone after her, *set my cap at her* as my mum would have put it, but it was Joan who'd decided: it was her choice. And when she realised it was a mistake, when we'd split and she tried to go back to Inchy and he wouldn't have her – that wasn't my fault either, was it? He'd been happy enough to have me back, as a friend. I'd often wondered how he could bring himself to forgive me but not her, but friendship was like that, wasn't it? It was for keeps. It was for *ever*.

Now I looked into his face and I found myself wondering who the hell he was; who he had ever been.

"I would've bought her a ring," he said, his voice distant. "If she 'adn't – I mean, I know we was young. But I would 'ave. Eventually."

I went on staring. I realised my mouth had fallen open; I closed it again. When he didn't say anything else I tried to find words, but there were none. All I could think was, *he said he didn't care*. He'd said she was just a lass and she didn't matter, not really. He'd laughed at her when she tried to win him back. He told folk she'd let anyone lift her skirt and he called her a slag, even when she cried to his face. If he hadn't told me he wasn't bothered, if I'd known –

But I looked at him now and I *did* know. Of course he couldn't forgive her. He hadn't been able to forgive her because of how deep the hurt went, and I saw now that time hadn't eased it, only weathered it, carving the grooves deeper.

When he turned, it didn't come as a surprise to see that he was crying.

"Inchy. I – I'm going back to the pub," I said, and I backed away.

"'Ang on." He looked startled.

"I didn't ask for this. Look, I said I was sorry. I *am* sorry. But this –" I raised my hands and let them fall again.

"Look, I din't mean nowt. But this is why we came, in't it? We did that to 'er, thee an' me, and it seemed right, tha's all. It's done now. I've said wha' I want to say, an' tha's it. No more, all right? It's ower."

74

"Is it, Inchy?"

He rubbed a hand over his eyes and he smiled. If it hadn't been for that smile, I would have turned and gone back then and there, but I didn't; I looked at him for a long time, neither of us wavering, and then I nodded and I stayed.

*

"Rombald's missus dropped that," Inchy said.

I looked at the odd cairn set into the wiry grass. It was made of grey stones of similar sizes, forming a low, rough circle. It reminded me of a plate with an indentation in the middle.

"Skirtful o' stones," he added. "She were runnin' after 'im, see, when 'e put 'is size nines through t' cow n' calf. And then she dropped all t' stones she were carryin' and med this circle. Dun't know 'er name. Nubody did."

I gave him a sharp look, but there didn't seem to be any hidden meaning in what he said. He seemed to have put Joan out of his mind; he'd been striding out with new energy, his cheeks reddened by the continual assault of the wind. It was me that couldn't stop thinking about her. I opened my mouth to ask why the giant's wife was running after him, but realised I didn't want to know. I had an image in my mind; me and Inchy heading off up Curly Hill on one of our expeditions, and Joan catching up with us; the look she'd had on her face when she pulled on Inchy's arm. The look on her face after he'd brushed her off. She hadn't been angry. If she'd been carrying something then, a skirtful of stones, I imagine she'd have just dropped everything too; she'd have let it all go.

I started walking, pulling my hood tighter. The wind was full in my face, chilling my eyes and my skin. It felt like little knives. I walked faster. I probably deserved it.

But Inchy had deserved it too. I felt a stab of anger. He was the one who'd let her go, wasn't he?

I was leading the way, though I hadn't asked where we were headed. I didn't suppose it mattered. I wasn't even looking at the moor, not really; I was looking into the past, and I could see Joan's face as clear as anything. It struck me now she had always been a little like the moor, half ordinary, something that was just *there*, but half wild too; her hair always flying and in knots, something unfathomable in her eyes.

I wondered if it was still there when she died.

I almost felt I could hear that lilting song again, and the words crept across the moor:

Then we shall 'ave to bury thee ...

I shook my head, spoke without turning. "Inchy, did you hear something?"

He didn't reply.

"Inchy?"

His voice, when it came, was gruff. "Nowt but the wind. And you know what, mate? Me name's *Warren*."

I was only half listening. He was right, it *was* only the wind, but it sounded as if there were voices in it. I was sure, at some point in the past, I'd heard it called a devil wind; now I thought I knew why, only it sounded less like a devil than a host of demons crying together.

Bury thee, bury thee ...

I shook my head. I was tired and wishing I was a hundred miles away, back in my old life – no, my *new* life – and that bloody wind just wouldn't ease up. I was allowing the past and other people's mistakes and yes, my own, to get to me. It was only then that Inchy's words sank in.

Me name's Warren ...

I whirled around. He wasn't there.

I scanned the hillside, knowing how the dull green of his jacket would have faded into it. It wasn't any use. Inchy had gone.

Bastard.

I took a few steps back the way I had come, watching for any sign of another living being, and I saw none. Despite the wind, I felt hot all over. He'd lured me out here and then ditched me, an act of petty revenge, and why – because he'd lost his job, was jealous all over again?

I squinted into the cold air. He surely couldn't have passed out of sight so quickly. But it occurred to me that maybe he wasn't out of sight. He might be crouching in the grass, hiding in his green coat; but somehow it didn't feel like that. The place felt empty. He'd already scarpered, heading back to the warm pub and leaving me to freeze. No doubt, when I got there, I'd find he'd let my tyres down too. Well, good luck to him. He was going nowhere, someone who hadn't even had the nous to grab the girl he'd cared about and hold onto her.

The sky was heavier than ever and everything had darkened, taking on the colours of a storm. In the distance the space between earth and sky was streaked black with rain. It seemed to echo something inside of me.

I could try and blame Inchy all I liked, but the knowledge squirmed in my gut: *it was my fault.* It had always been my fault, not because I went after her, because I fancied her, but because the reason I'd gone after her was that Inchy had had her first.

76

He had always been taller than me. He'd was always tougher. He was the one who smoked without chucking his guts up, back when smoking was something cool. I pictured him in the pub, clutching his pint glass with his yellowing fingers, and I imagined the rot creeping inside him.

But I'd been the one who set out to destroy something. I was the one who'd *thought* about it, something Inchy never seemed to do, not back then. Now it seemed that had changed. I could hardly blame him.

It didn't matter. All I had to do was retrace my steps and get out of here, leave it all behind, just as I had before. I turned a full circle. All around me was purple heather, long grass bowing in the wind, and bared grey earth. It looked as if there were paths everywhere, radiating like the spokes of a wheel. My belly contracted as I realised I was no longer sure which way I'd come. But it should be easy, shouldn't it? All I had to do was head downhill. Except now I appeared to be standing at the summit of a crag. That couldn't be right, could it? *Everywhere* was downhill.

My mouth felt dry. I cursed Inchy for the alcohol I'd had earlier. It was confusing my mind, clouding my judgement. Still, I couldn't stay here; I'd pick a direction and get moving. I'd soon know if I was going the wrong way. Scowling at the moor, wondering if Inchy was still out there, watching, I started to walk.

*

As I went, the old tune became the background to my steps, the refrain to my thoughts. I remembered us singing it, the story of comic cannibalism where the man caught his deeath o' cowd, was buried and eaten by worms, which were eaten by ducks, which were eaten by the people. I never knew who the 'we' in the song was supposed to be, the singers or someone else, and now I wondered.

Then t'worms'll come an eyt thee up . . .

That had seemed the funniest line of all. It wasn't so funny now.

Then we shall all 'ave etten thee. On Ilkla Moor baht 'at . . .

I stopped walking and frowned. I didn't think this could be the right way. The moor all looked the same, flat and bleak and with nothing to relieve the monotony, and across everything, that merciless scouring wind.

I remembered I should be walking away from it, the wind behind me, but it seemed to be coming from all directions; whichever way I turned it blustered and spat in my face. My cheeks were numb, all feeling long since faded. I turned and started to walk back the way I had just come. As I did, it started to rain.

77

*

I'd forgotten how bloody miserable the moor could be. Even the air seemed grey and it was hard to keep my eyes open; I squinted against the rain. It lashed my hood, drowning everything in a loud patter. *Fuck this.* The sooner I got off the moor the better. I tried to move quicker and my boots slid on the wet, slicked-down grass. I landed on my arse, pushed myself up, went on again. I could hardly see at all. I found I was muttering the words of the song, over and over:

Tha's bahn to catch thy death ...

I realised what I was saying and shut my mouth. I'd be off this hill soon, then I could dry off in the pub before heading home. I've have the heater on full blast. I'd be too hot then, and I wouldn't bloody care.

It was then that I saw the light.

It hung there on the other side of the rain, a faint yellow glow, and I realised: it was *her* light, it was the pancake stone, and I was back after all. It had to be. It had somehow kept burning and soon I'd be there; I'd see all the lights of Ilkley and Ben Rhydding shining out from the valley, calling me back. I hunched myself against the rain and hurried towards it.

*

The light flickered in and out of existence. One moment I'd think I was getting closer and then there it was, in the distance again. I must be going in a circle. Or I was seeing things. Whatever it was, I couldn't seem to find it. And all the time the rain kept coming down and the sky was growing darker.

I tilted my head, allowing my hood to fall back and let the rain find my face. It was dead cold, and I cursed, pulling my hood back up, though it wasn't any use; the rain was inside it. I shivered and turned. The light was still there, but it was behind me now. I didn't know how I'd got turned around but I started off again, unable to tell if I was going up a rise or moving slightly downhill. The light kept moving. It bobbed and wavered, confusing my eyes. I had to reach it soon. The moor couldn't be that big. If I just kept going in a straight line, sooner or later, I had to reach its edge.

*

It was Inchy, it had to be. He'd hidden a lamp out here and he was taunting me with it, and I had to give it to him; he was *fast*. One minute it was off to the left, the next, away to my right. I'd tried to keep straight but somehow I'd found myself following anyway, being drawn this way and that. Well, enough; I wasn't playing any longer. I was cold and wet and tired.

There was a large boulder in front of me and I leaned against it, slicking water from my coat. The rain was easing off at last. I knew I couldn't stay here for long: cold was spreading from the rock, finding its way inside my skin. Still, I couldn't quite bring myself to move. I stayed while the rain reduced to a light patter and then I felt something, almost as if the rock at my back had trembled, and a moment later I heard it; a dull, hollow boom ringing out across the moor. I reached out and touched the rock, and thought I could still feel it; a faint resonance that took a while to fade.

A few seconds later, the sound came again. I froze, listening. It had to be thunder, didn't it? It could take on all sorts of odd sounds, out here. It's just that, for a moment, it had made me think of footsteps; the footsteps of a giant, echoing in my ears.

Damn Inchy. It was his stories, playing on my mind. Stones and giants, old legends that wouldn't die. The cow and calf, where were they now? And something flashed across my mind, something I'd heard long ago, that there had been a bull once too; a rock bigger than any of them that was broken up and carried off for building. No one ever seemed sure if it was true or not and it was odd to think that something so large could simply disappear, out here, and no one could even agree if it had ever existed.

Just as the rain was letting up at last, the wind was rising again. Its voice moaned across the hills, and my head began to throb with it, aching behind my eyes.

I forced myself to my feet, my wet jeans sticking to my skin, and set my face to the darkness. It wasn't the rain now, robbing everything of light; soon night would fall. I would be out here all alone, and no one would come to help.

But it wasn't entirely dark. Somewhere ahead and a little to my left was the gentle glow of a light. No: *two* lights, now.

Tha's been a cooartin' my lass Joan ...

I must be seeing things, that was all. But it was easy, with night hailing at the edges of the world, to believe that both of them were out here with me: Inchy and Joan, walking hand in hand maybe, together again ...

I shook my head, trying to dispel the image. It was nonsense, of course. I started walking again, pulling my coat tight around me. I'd be off this moor in no time; I would soon be warm.

Except there seemed to be no end to this place. It was as if I'd walked into some giant land that went on and on. Everywhere I looked was the moor, dark and smudged with shadows that could have been rocks, could have been anything. *The land of the dead*, he'd called it.

It was suddenly easy to imagine the way Joan might have felt when she came up here all alone. The way she would have sat down on an ancient stone, perhaps smoothing a hand over the things that were carved there. And she'd opened a vein, over those cup markings perhaps, the hollows ready to receive what she gave …

And what had the old gods offered in return? What had she asked for as she lay there dying – *me?*

A slow chill spread through my chest.

Then we shall 'ave to bury thee …

Something struck me then, something that had never made any sense before. The last verse of the song, the very last – it was about revenge, wasn't it? Only I'd never understood why. Yes, that was it:

That's wheear we get us ooan back …

The 'we' had had their revenge because they'd eaten him, the man who'd courted the girl and caught the cold and been buried and eaten by the worms – but why *our ooan back?* The song never explained what he'd done to them.

But the song was a part of this place. No one even knew who'd written it; it had been sung down the ages. Now, with the light failing and no one in sight and nothing around for miles, it almost felt as if it had been intended for this moment. It repeated itself inside my mind, but the intonation was different:

That's wheear we get us ooan back. On Ilkla Moor baht 'at …

I shuddered. *Here*, that's where it would be. This was where Joan would come to me, to thank me properly for what I'd done. She'd come with the rain and the wind in her hair, her eyes all a-sparkle in the dark.

I let out an odd sound and started to hurry onward, stumbling in my haste. I realised I was singing as I went, and I knew it was crazy but I couldn't stop. I sang the words faster and faster, no inflection in them now at all, not thinking about what they meant or where they had come from, and I stumbled and slipped and for a time, everything was dark.

*

When I woke, the cold was bone-deep. I was lying on something hard and I touched it, felt the whorls and dips beneath my fingers, and I pushed myself up. My head swam. I was lying on a grey rock, partially hidden in the ground, and I must have hit my head on it because there was something dark there that looked like blood. I looked at the cups and the rings, delineated more clearly than any I had yet seen. I thought of Joan, her blood. How much had she given? Perhaps this would help. It was an offering, a libation; *something*. Perhaps it would be enough.

I lay back, not caring that the ground was hard. It wasn't dark any longer, I realised. It wasn't dark and the wind had fallen still, its voices silenced. I was still on the moor but now it was beautiful. The moon had risen and stars were sprinkled across the sky, sparkling like eyes, watching me. I imagined staying here forever, just looking up at them and letting everything slip away.

Then the sound came again, a long, ringing echo as of giant footsteps, and the earth shook beneath me.

I think I smiled. And I remembered a line that we used to add to the song when we were small:

On Ilkla Moor baht 'at
Wheear's that?

The words seemed to whisper in my mind now: *Wheear's that?* And I looked into the sky with its infinite stars and I realised I was no longer sure.

THE BLACK MONK OF PONTEFRACT

I t is a strangely English tradition that ghosts don't just walk in ruined castles and big country mansions, but on quiet suburban housing estates as well.

During the 1970s in particular there were accounts of poltergeists plaguing semi-detached homes as far apart as Swindon (1973), Newcastle (1975), Dartford (1977) and most famously of all, Enfield in North London in 1976, in which latter case the viewing public watched agog as young children were apparently possessed on live television, and eerie voices emanated from nowhere.

By the time screenwriter Stephen Volk penned his compelling drama, Ghostwatch, aired by the BBC on Halloween Night 1992 and purporting to be a real-time investigation into a genuine suburban haunting, the nation ought to have been well prepared for spooky events on quiet, tree-lined avenues. But in actual fact they were terrified, and the BBC was deluged with complaints afterwards. The reality is that it's been bred into us by centuries of social and psychological conditioning to look for ghosts in run-down buildings or on former battlefields. Whatever we say, we do not expect to meet spectres in the suburbs. Perhaps this is why famed occult investigator Colin Wilson described the case of the 'Black Monk of Pontefract' – which occurred on the Chequerfield housing estate, Pontefract, in West Yorkshire – as one of the most frightening of his career.

Pontefract is a pleasant market town, which has long enjoyed an enviable standard of living. This made the events of the late 1960s/early 1970s, in the Chequerfield home of the Pritchard family, all the more shocking. They included prolonged, destructive poltergeist activity in which persons were damaged as well as inanimate objects – the family's eldest daughter was dragged upstairs by unseen hands, which gripped her so viciously that visible claw-marks were left behind – and one especially disturbing incident when an attempt to bless the house with holy water resulted in the painting of black inverted crosses on doors and walls. If all this sounds suspiciously similar to the events said to have engulfed the Amityville house on Long Island, New York, also in the 1970s, it is important to remember that the alleged 'Amityville Horror' occurred well after the Pontefract case, in 1975, and that news of it only reached the wider world much later via the book, published in

1977. Incidentally, the case of the Black Monk was so named because one especially weird series of events reportedly culminated in the manifestation of a robed and hooded figure (another detail similar to the later largely discredited Amityville case).

Colin Wilson for one was so impressed by the Pontefract incident that he later said it had transformed his opinions about the possible existence of the spirit world, and became a key component in his scholarly 1981 study of violent house-hauntings, Poltergeist.

Ironically, given the mundane environment of a modern housing estate, the case of the Black Monk may have its roots in ancient atrocity. The Chequerfield estate is not far from Pontefract Castle, which witnessed some tumultuous historical events, including the murder by starvation of the deposed Richard II in 1400, and several brutal assaults by Cromwellian troops during the Civil War, one of which cost the lives of many townsfolk. The figure of the suburban Black Monk has also been associated with a black-clad ghost said to roam the castle and believed by locals to be the shade of a Cluniac monk who was hanged during the Dissolution of the Monasteries in 1539.

The house is still occupied today, but though a recent movie has renewed interest in the case, and subsequent sightseers have been described as a nuisance, no disturbances of the ghostly kind have been reported of late.

THE CRAWL
Stephen Laws

The days are bad, but the nights are always worse.

Since it all happened and I lost my job, it seems as if the front door is always the focus of my attention, no matter what I'm doing. I try to keep myself occupied, try to read, try to listen to music. But all of these things make it much worse. You see, if I really *do* become preoccupied in what I'm doing, then I might not hear it if ... If he ... if it ... comes.

I've recently had all my mail redirected to a post office box where I can go and collect it, since the clatter of the letterbox in the morning and afternoon became just too much to bear. I had to nail it up against junk mail and free newspapers. The house has become a terrible, terrible place since I lost Gill. God, how I miss her.

And in the nights, I lie awake and listen.

The sound of a car passing on the sidestreet is probably the worst.

I hear it coming in my sleep. It wakes me instantly, and I'm never sure whether I've screamed or not, but I lie there praying first that the car will pass quickly and that the engine won't cough and falter. Then, in the first seconds after it's moved on I pray again that I won't hear those familiar, staggering footsteps on the gravel path outside; that I won't hear that hellish hammering on the front door. I listen for the sounds of that hideous, hoarse breathing. Most nights I'm soaked in sweat waiting for the sound of the door panels splintering apart. Sometimes I dream that I'm down there in the hall, with my hands braced against the wood of that front door, screaming for help as the pounding comes from the other side.

Sometimes I dream that I'm in bed, that he's got in and he's coming up the stairs.

That same slow, methodical tread.

I run to the door, trying to slam it shut as he reaches the landing. In slow motion, I turn and scream at Gill to get out quickly through the bedroom window as I heave the bedside cabinet across the floor to the door. But as I turn, Gill isn't there. She's in the bathroom at the top of the landing, so now I'm frantically tearing the cabinet away from the door as he ascends, but Gill doesn't hear him because the shower's running and I slowly pull open the door screaming her name just as the shadow reaches the landing and Gill turns from the wash basin and ...

If I started by telling you that the whole thing began on the A1 just a half-mile from Boroughbridge, you might suppose that it has some kind of relevance for the horror that came afterwards. If it does, then that relevance has eluded me. Believe me, I've been over the whole thing many times in my mind, trying to make sense of it all. No, like all bad nightmares, it defied any logic. It seemed that we were just in the wrong place at the wrong time; like a traffic accident. Thirty seconds earlier or thirty seconds later, and maybe I'd be able to sleep at night a little better than I do these days. But since all stories start somewhere, the A1 turn-off half-a-mile from Boroughbridge was our somewhere.

*

The day had started badly.

We had spent Easter weekend with my wife's parents, and on the trip home Gill and I weren't speaking. There had been a party at her folks' house on the Sunday evening (we'd been there since Thursday), and that bloody personnel manager friend of theirs had been invited. I'd been made redundant from an engineering firm three years previously, and it was two years before I found another job. Not easy, but things were going fine again at last. Nevertheless, the use of my previous firm's psychometric testing to 'reduce staffing levels' was a bug-bear of mine. ("What is the capital of Upper Twatland? You don't know? Then sorry, you're sacked.")

We were driving home on Easter Monday, and I had promised not to drink during the evening so that we could take turns behind the wheel. But this bastard personnel man (who I'd never met before, but whose profession didn't endear himself to me) was standing there all night, spouting off his in-house philosophy about big fish eating little fish, and only-the-strongest-will-prevail. My anger had begun as a slow-burn, and I'd had a drink to dampen the fuse. But then a second had begun to light it again. And by the third, I was just about ready for an intervention. By my fourth, I'd burned it out of my system, was having a chat with Stuart and Ann and their light-hearted banter was making everything okay again. Then, the personnel man was left on his own and, having bored his companion to tears, decided to move over to us. If he'd kept off the subject, everything would have been okay. (But then again, if we hadn't been on the A1 half-a mile out of Boroughbridge, none of this would have happened either).

Disregarding anything we were talking about, he started again where he'd left off.

And I'm afraid that was it. All bets off. Fuse not only rekindled, but powder-keg ignited. I could probably go on for three pages about our conversation, but since this tale is about the worst thing that ever happened to me, and not one of the best, it seems a little pointless if I do. Just let's say that without giving in to the urge for actual bodily harm, I kept a cold fury inside. I dispensed with any social airs and graces or the rules of polite party-conversation, and kept at his throat while he tried to impress us with his superior 'if-they-can't-hack-it, out-they-go' credo. Like a terrier, I kept hanging at his wattles, shaking him down and finishing with a 'who-lives-by-the-sword-dies-by-the-sword'. Sounds obvious, but believe me; as a put-down it wasn't half bad. Maybe you had to be there to appreciate it. He left our company, and kept to other less-impolite partygoers. Stuart and Ann were pleased too, and that made me feel good.

However, I could tell by Gill's face that I wasn't going to get any good conduct medals. At first, I thought that maybe I'd overstepped the mark; been too loud, let the booze kid me that I was being subtle when in fact I was acting like Attila the Hun. But no, her tight-lips and cold demeanour were related to more practical matters than that. I'd seen off at least a half-bottle of scotch, and we had that long drive tomorrow. Remember? Well, no I hadn't. My anger had seen to that.

So by next morning we were in a non-speaking to each other situation.

I tried to hide the hang-over, but when you've been living with someone for ten years it's a little difficult to hide the signs. The two fizzing Solpadeine in the glass were the final insult. I stressed that I would take care of the second half of the journey, but this didn't seem to hold water. Did I mention that she'd lost a baby, was still getting over it physically and psychologically, that she was feeling very tired all the time? No? Well, just sign out the Bastard Club form and I would willingly have signed.

Tight-lipped farewells to the In-laws.

And a wife's face that says she's just waiting for the open road before she lets rip.

Well, she let rip. But I probably don't have to draw you a map.

I let it go, knowing that I'd been a little selfish. But Gill always did have a habit of taking things a little too far. My temper snapped, and seconds later it had developed into the knock-down, drag-out verbal fight that I'd been trying to avoid.

BOROUGHBRIDGE, said the motorway sign. HALF MILE.

"That's the last time we spend any time together down here at Easter," said Gill.

"Fine by me. I've got more important things I could be doing."

"Let's not stop at Easter. How about spending our Christmases and Bank Holidays apart, too?"

"Great. I might be able to enjoy myself for a change."

"Maybe we should make it more permanent? Why stop at holidays? Let's just ..."

"... spend all of our time apart? That suits me fine."

There was a man up ahead, standing beside the barrier on the central reservation. Just a shadow, looking as if he was waiting for a break in the traffic so that he could make a dangerous run across the two lanes to the other side.

"God, you can be such a bastard!"

"You're forgetting an important point, Gill. It was people like that Personnel bastard who got me the sack. You should be sticking up for me, not ..."

"So what makes you think we need *your* money? Are you trying to say that what I earn isn't enough to ..."

"For Christ's sake, Gill!"

The shadow stepped out from the roadway barrier, directly in front of us.

Gill had turned to look at me, her face a mask of anger.

"For Christ's *sake!*" I yelled, and it must have seemed to her then that I'd lost my mind when I suddenly lunged for the steering wheel. She yelled in anger and shock, swatted at me but held fast.

And in the next minute, something exploded through the windscreen.

Gill's instincts were superb. Despite the fact that the car was suddenly filled with an exploding, hissing shrapnel of fine glass, she didn't lose control. She braked firmly, hanging onto the wheel while I threw my hands instinctively up to protect my face. The car slewed and hit the barrier, and I could feel the front of the car on Gill's side crumple. The impact was horrifying and shocking. In that split-second I expected the body of that idiot to come hurtling through into our laps, smashing us back against our seats. But nothing came through the windscreen as the car slewed to a halt on the hard-shoulder, right next to the metal barrier, and with its nose pointed out into the nearside lane.

There were fine tracings of red-spiderweb blood all over my hands as I reached instinctively for Gill. Her hands were clenched tight to the wheel, her head was down and her long dark hair full of fine glass shards. I could see that her hands were also flayed by the glass and with a sickening roll in the stomach I thought she might be blinded.

"God, Gill! Are you alright?"

87

I pulled up her face with both hands so that she was staring directly ahead through the shattered windscreen. Her eyes were wide and glassy, she was breathing heavily. Obviously in shock, and hanging onto that wheel as if she was hanging onto her self-control.

"Are you alright?"

She nodded, a slight gesture which seemed to take great effort.

Twisting in my seat, making the imploded glass all around me crackle and grind, I looked back.

We hadn't hit the stupid bastard.

He was still standing, about thirty or forty feet behind us on the hard-shoulder. Standing there, unconcerned, watching us.

I kicked open the passenger door and climbed out. Slamming it, I leaned on the roof to get my breath and then looked back at him. He was a big man, but in the dusk it was impossible to see any real details other than he seemed to be shabbily dressed and unsteady on his feet. The sleeves of his jacket seemed torn, his hair awry. A tramp, perhaps. He was just standing there, with his hands hanging limply at his sides, staring in our direction.

"You stupid *bastard*!" I yelled back at him when my breath returned. "You could have killed my wife."

The man said nothing. He just stood and looked. His head was slightly down, as if he was looking at us from under his brows. There was something strange about his face, but I couldn't make it out.

"You stupid *fuck*!"

Then I saw that he was holding something in one hand, something long and curved in a half-moon shape. I squinted, rubbing my shredded hands over my face and seeing that there was also blood on the palms, too. The sight of more blood enraged me. Fists bunched at my side, I began striding back along the hard shoulder towards the silently waiting figure.

After ten or fifteen feet, I stopped.

There *was* something wrong with this character's face. The eyes were too dark, too large. The mouth was fixed in a permanent grin. I couldn't see a nose.

And then I realised what it was.

The man was wearing a mask.

A stupid, scarecrow mask.

It was made from sacking of some sort, tied around the neck with string. From where I was standing, I couldn't tell whether he'd drawn big, round black eyes with peep holes in the centre, or whether they were simply ragged holes in the sacking. I could see no eyes in there, only darkness. Ragged stitchwork from ear to ear gave the mask its permanent grin. Bunches of straw hair poked from under the brim of the ragged fishing hat which had been jammed down hard on the head. That same straw was also poking out between the buttons of the ragged jacket. More string served as a belt holding up equally ragged trousers. The sole had come away from the upper on each boot.

As I stood frozen, taking in this ridiculous sight and perhaps looking just as stupid, the figure raised the long curved thing in its hand.

It was a hand scythe.

This one was black and rusted, but when the scarecrow raised it before its mask-face it seemed as if the edge of that blade had been honed and sharpened. Then I realised that it was this that had smashed our car windscreen. The bastard had waited for us to pass, had stepped out and slammed the damned thing across the glass like an axe.

And then the man began to stride towards me.

There was nothing hurried in his approach. It was a steady methodical pace, holding that scythe casually down at his side. His idiot, grinning scarecrow's face was fixed on me as he moved. There was no doubt in my mind as he came on.

He meant to kill me.

He meant to knock me down and pin me to the ground with one foot, while he raised that hook, and brought it straight down through the top of my skull. Then he would kick me to one side, walk up to the car and drag Gill out of the driving seat ...

I turned and ran back to the car. As I wrenched open the passenger door, I glanced back to see that the figure hadn't hurried his pace to catch up. He was coming at the same remorseless pace; a brisk, but unhurried walk. Inside the car, Gill was still hunched in the driving seat, clutching the wheel.

"Drive, Gill!" I yelled. "For God's sake, *drive!*"

"What ...?"

I tried to shove her out of the driving seat then, away from the wheel and into the passenger seat. Still in shock, she couldn't understand what the hell was wrong with me. She clung tight to that wheel with one hand and started clawing at my face with the other. I looked back as we struggled. In seconds, that maniac would reach the car. He was already hefting that hook in his hand, ready to use it.

"Look!" I practically screamed in Gill's face, and dragged her head around to see.

At the same moment, the rear windscreen imploded with shocking impact.

Everything happened so fast after that, I can't really put it together in my head. I suppose that the scarecrow-man had shattered the glass with the hand scythe. There was a blurred jumble of movement in the ragged gap through the rear windscreen. And I suppose that Gill must have realised what was happening then, because the next thing I heard was the engine roaring into life.

"*Go!*" someone yelled, and I suppose it must have been me. Because the next thing I remember after that was me sitting in the back of the car, swatting powdered glass off the seat. Then I heard another impact, and looked up to see that the scarecrow was scrabbling on the boot of the car. The scythe was embedded in the metalwork, and the scarecrow was clinging on tight to it. I thrust out through the broken window and tore at the man's ragged gloves, pounding with my fists. The car bounced and jolted, something seemed to screech under the chassis, and I prayed to God that it was the madman's legs being crushed. We were moving again, but Gill was yelling and cursing, slamming her hands on the wheel. The engine sounded tortured; the car was juddering and shaking, as if Gill was missing the clutch bite-point and 'donkeying' all the time.

The scythe came free from its ragged hole and the madman fell back from the boot. There was a scraping, rending sound as the hook screeched over the bodywork. To my horror, I saw that he had managed to snag the damned thing in the fender and now we were pulling him along the hard-shoulder as he clung to its handle. With his free hand, he clawed at the fender; trying to get a proper grip and pull himself upright again. His legs thrashed and raised dust clouds as we moved. Somehow, I couldn't move as I watched him being dragged along behind us. The car juddered again and I almost fell between the seats. Lunging up, I seemed to get a grip on myself.

The madman had lost his hold on the fender. We were pulling away from where he lay. I saw one arm flop through the air as he tried to turn over. Perhaps he was badly hurt? Good.

We were still on the hard shoulder, near to the barrier, as traffic flashed past us. But something had happened to the car when it hit that roadside barrier. Something had torn beneath the chassis, and Gill was yanking hard at the gear lever.

"It's stuck!" she shouted, nearly hysterically. "I can't get it out of first gear."

"Let me try ..." I tried to climb over into the passenger seat, but in that moment I caught sight of what was happening in the rear view mirror. The scarecrow was rising to his knees, perhaps fifty feet behind us now. I lost sight of him in the bouncing mirror, twisted around to look out of the window again, just in time to see him stand. There was something slow and measured in that movement, as if he hadn't been hurt at all. He had retrieved the scythe.

And he was coming after us again.

Not running, just the same methodical stride. As if he had all the time in the world to catch up with us.

I faced front again. Gill was still struggling with the gears, and the speedometer was wavering at five miles an hour. As we juddered along on the hard shoulder, it seemed as if we were travelling at exactly the same pace as the man behind us.

"Hit the clutch!" I yelled, lunging forward again as Gill depressed the pedal. I yanked at the gearstick, trying to drag it back into second gear. The best I could do was get it into the neutral position, and that meant we were coasting to a halt. Behind us, the man started to gain. Gill could see him now, slapped my hand away and shoved the gearstick into first again.

"Who *is* he?" she sobbed. "What does he want?"

I thought about jumping out of the car and taking over from Gill in the driving seat. But by the time we did that, the madman would be on us again, and anyway, Gill was a damn sight better driver than me. There seemed only one thing we could do.

"Steer out onto the motorway," I hissed.

"We're travelling too slowly. There's too much traffic. We'll be hit."

"Maybe he'll get hit first."

"Oh *Christ* ..."

Gill yanked hard on the wheel and the car slewed out across the motorway.

A traffic horn screamed at us and a car passed so close that we heard the screech of its tyres and felt the blast of air through the shattered windscreen as it swerved to avoid us. I looked at the speedo again. We were still crawling.

I moved back to the rear window.

The radiator grille of a lorry filled my line of vision. The damned thing was less than six feet from us, just about to ram into our rear; crushing the boot right through the car. I yelled something, I don't know what; convinced that the lorry was going to smash into us, ram us both up into the engine block in a mangled, bloody mess. Perhaps it was the shock of my yell, but Gill suddenly yanked hard at the steering wheel again and we slewed to the left. I could feel the car rocking on its suspension as the lorry passed within inches, the blaring of its horn ringing in our ears. But we weren't out of danger yet. I reared towards the dash as another car swerved from behind us, around to the right, tyres screeching.

"You were travelling too *fast*, you bastard!" I yelled after it. "Too bloody *fast!*"

More horns were blaring and when I flashed a glance back at Gill I could see that she was hunched forward over the wheel. Her face was too white, like a dead person. There were beaded droplets of sweat on her forehead. In the next moment, she had swung the wheel hard over to the left again. Off balance, I fell across my seat, my head bouncing from her shoulder. I clawed at the seat rest, trying to sit up straight again. Suddenly, Gill began clawing at me with one hand. I realise now that my attempts to sit were hampering her ability to pull the wheel hard over. To my shame, I began clawing back at her; not understanding and in a total funk. She yelled that I was a stupid bastard. I yelled that she was a mad bitch. And then I was up in my seat again as Gill began spinning the wheel furiously back, hand over hand. Glancing out of the window, I could see that she had taken us right across the motorway and was taking a slip road. The sign said: Boroughbridge.

She had done it. She had taken us right across those multiple lanes without hitting another vehicle. We were still crawling along, but at least we had got away from the madman behind us. I knew then that everything was okay. When we found the first emergency telephone, we would stop and ring for the police.

"Okay," I breathed. "It's okay ... you've done it, Gill ... we're okay now."

Until I turned in my seat and looked back to see that everything was far from okay.

The man in the fancy-dress costume was walking across the highway towards us, perhaps fifty yards back. His steps were measured, still as if he had all the time in the world, the scythe hanging from one hand. Grinning face fixed on us. Even as I looked, and felt the sickening nausea of fear again, a car swerved around him, tyres screeching. Its passage made his ragged clothes whip and ruffle. Straw flew from his shoulders and his ragged trousers. By rights, it should have rammed right into him, throwing him up and over its roof. But just as luck had been with us, crossing that busy motorway, it was also with him.

Our car began its ascent of the slip road, engine coughing and straining. Gill fumbled with the gears, trying without success to wrench them into second. The engine began to race and complain.

"He's there ..." I began.

"I *know* he's fucking *there!*" yelled Gill, eyes still fixed ahead. "But we *can't go any faster!*"

The speedo was wobbling around fifteen miles an hour; even now as we ascended the slip road, the gradual slope was having an effect on our progress. The needle began to drop ... to fourteen ... to thirteen.

When I looked back, I could see that nevertheless, we were putting a little distance between us and the madman. When a car flashed past, between the scarecrow and the entrance to the slip road, I could see that fate wasn't completely on his side, after all. He wasn't invulnerable. He had waited while the car had crossed his path, and that slight wait had given us a little time. Not to mention a certain relief. The man might be mad, but he was human and not some supernatural creature out of a bad horror movie. As the car passed, he came on, the scythe swinging in his hand as he moved.

It came to me then.

There was a tool kit in the boot. If Gill pulled over, I could jump out and yank the boot open, grab a screwdriver or something. Threaten him, scare him away. Show him that I meant business.

"Pull over," I said.

"Are you joking, or what?" asked Gill.

When I looked at her again, something happened to me. It had to do with everything that had occurred over the last forty-eight hours. It had to do with the stupid fights, with my stupid behaviour. But more than anything, it had to do with the expression on Gill's face. This was the woman I loved. She was, quite literally, in shock. And I'd just lashed out at her when she'd been acting on my instruction and taken us across the motorway, away from the maniac and – against all the odds – avoided colliding with another vehicle. I'd let her down badly. It was time to sort this thing out.

"Pull over!" I snapped again.

"He's still coming," she said. Her voice was too calm. Too matter of fact.

Then I realised. At this speed, I could open the door and just hop out.

Angrily, that's what I did.

I slammed the door hard as I turned to face our pursuer; just the way that people do when there's been a minor traffic 'shunt' and both parties try to faze out the other by a show of aggression, using body language to establish guilt before any heated conversation begins. Inside the car, I heard Gill give a startled cry as the car shuddered to a halt.

The scarecrow was still approaching up the ramp.

I stood for a moment, praying that he might at least pause in his stride.

He didn't.

I lunged at the boot, slamming my hand on it and pointing hard at him; as if some zig-zag lightning bolt of pure anger would zap out of my finger and fry him on the spot.

"You're fucking *mad* and I'm fucking telling *you*! You want some *aggro*, eh? You want some fucking *aggro*? I'll show you what fucking *aggro* is all *about!*" If the 'fuck' word could kill, he should be dead already.

But he was still coming.

I swept the remaining frosting of broken glass from the boot and snapped it open. There was a tyre-wrench in there. I leaned in for it, without taking my eyes off the clown, and my hand bumped against the suitcase. In that moment, I knew that the wrench must be at the bottom of the boot and that all our weekend luggage was on top of it. I whirled around, clawing at the suitcase, trying to yank it aside. But I'd packed that boot as tight as it's possible to get. The only way I was going to get that wrench was by yanking everything out of there onto the tarmac.

And the scarecrow was only fifty feet from us.

I looked back to see that he was smacking the scythe in the palm of one hand, eager to use it.

"*Shit!*" I slammed the boot again and hurried back around the car.

The scarecrow remained implacable. From this distance, I could see how tall he was. Perhaps six feet-seven. Broad-shouldered. Completely uncaring of my show of bravado. And, Good Christ, I could hear him now.

He was *giggling*.

It was a forced, manic sound. Without a trace of humour. It was an insane sound of anticipation. He was looking forward to what he was going to do when he reached us. As I dragged open the passenger door, I had no illusions then. If I engaged in a hand-to-hand physical confrontation with this lunatic, he would kill me. There was no doubt about it. Not only that, but he would tear me limb from limb, before he turned his attentions to Gill. I stooped to yell at her, but she was already yanking at the gear-stick and the car was moving again; the engine making grinding, gasping sounds.

The scarecrow's pace remained unaltered.

There was a car coming up the slip road behind him.

Some mad and overwhelming darkness inside myself made me *will* that car to swerve as it came up behind the scarecrow. I wanted to see it ram him up on the hood and toss him over the fence into the high grass. But then I knew what I had to do. I skipped around the front of our own car and into the road as the car swerved around the scarecrow and came up the slip road towards us. I ran in front of it, waving my arms, flagging it down. I can still hardly believe what happened next.

The driver – male, female, it was impossible to tell – jammed their hand on the horn as the car roared straight at me. I just managed to get out of the way, felt the front fender snag and tear my trouser leg as it passed. I whirled in the middle of the road, unbelieving. The car vanished over the rise and was gone from sight. I turned back.

The scarecrow was still coming.

"For Christ's sake!" snapped Gill. "Get in."

I stumbled back into the car and we began our juddering crawl again. I wasn't in a sane world anymore. This couldn't possibly be happening to us. Where was everyone? Why wouldn't anyone help as we crawled on and on with that madman behind us? I turned to say something to Gill, studied her marble-white face, eyes staring dead ahead; but I couldn't find a thing to say. The scarecrow behind us was still coming at his even stride. If he wanted to, he could move faster, and then he'd overtake us. But he seemed content to match his speed with our own. At the moment, he was keeping an even distance between us. If our car failed or slowed, he would catch up. It was as simple as that.

We reached the rise. Down below, we could see that the road led deep into countryside. I'd lost all track of where the hell Boroughbridge might be, if it had ever existed at all. On either side of the road were fields of bright yellow wheat.

At last, God seemed to have remembered we were here and wasn't so pissed off with us, after all. As our car crested the ridge and began to move down towards the fields, it began to pick up speed.

"Oh thank God ..." Gill began to weep then. The car's gearbox was still straining and grinding, but we *were* gathering speed.

Leaning back over the seat I watched as the lip of the hill receded behind us. When the scarecrow suddenly reappeared on the top of the rise, silhouetted against the skyline, he must surely see that we were picking up speed. But he didn't suddenly alter his pace, didn't begin to run down after us. He kept at his even march, right in the middle of the road, straight down in our direction. Following the Fucking Yellow Brick Road. Soon, we'd leave him far behind.

I swung around to the front again, to see that we were doing thirty, the engine straining and gasping. I gritted my teeth, praying that it wouldn't cut out altogether. But it was still keeping us moving. When I looked back again, the silhouette of our attacker was a small blur. Another vehicle was cresting the rise behind him. I heard its own horn blare at the strange figure in the middle of the road, watched the small truck swerve around him. It seemed to me that someone was leaning out of the truck window, and the driver was giving the idiot a piece of his mind. The vehicle came on towards us, picking up speed. Should I chance our luck again? Slow the car, jump out and try to flag down help?

"No you're not," said Gill, without taking her eyes from the road. She had been reading my mind. "I'm not slowing this car down again. I'm keeping my foot down and we're getting out of here ..."

When I looked at the speedo, I felt as if I was going to throw up, there-and-then.

" ... and we're never, *ever* coming back to this fucking hellhole of a place," continued Gill, her voice cracking and tears streaming down her face, "As long as I ever live. Do you hear me, Paul? Not never, *ever*!"

"I've got to stop that truck before it passes us."

"You're not listening! I'm not stopping. Not for anything!"

"We *are* stopping, Gill! Look at the speedo! We got extra speed on the incline, that's all. Now we're slowing down on the straight. Look."

Gill shook her head, refusing to look.

The needle had fallen from thirty to twenty and was still descending.

"Will you just *look*?"

"*No!*"

I lunged around. The truck was less than two hundred yards behind us, and soon to overtake.

"Gill, look! It's a *tow-truck*! From a breakdown service. It's stencilled on the side. Look!"

"*NO!*"

With the needle wavering at ten miles an hour, I did what I had to do. I kicked open the passenger door. Gill refused to take her eyes from the road, but clawed at my hair with one hand, screaming and trying to drag me back into the car. I batted her off and hopped out into the middle of the sun-baked dirt road. A cloud of dust enveloped me. I just made it in time. Five seconds later, and the tow truck would have overtaken us and been gone. But now the driver could see my intent. He slowed, and then as I walked back towards him, the truck trundled on up behind us, matching an even time at ten miles an hour as I hopped up onto the standing-board.

The man inside had a big grin. He was about sixty, maybe even ready for retirement. Something about my action seemed to amuse him.

"Don't tell me," he said, without me having to make any opening conversation. "You're in trouble?"

Something about his manner, his friendliness, made that fear begin to melt inside me. Now it seemed that the world wasn't such a hostile and alien place as I thought it had suddenly become. I was grinning now too, like a great big kid.

"How could you tell?"

"My line of business. Been doing this for thirty-five years. People always come to me. I never go looking for them. How can I help you?"

Suddenly, looking back at the scarecrow, now perhaps two or three hundred yards away and still coming down that dirt road towards us, I didn't know what to say.

"Well ... the car. We had a bash and ... and it's stuck in first gear. Can't get it any faster than five, six miles an hour. Got some speed on the incline there, but it won't last."

"Okay," said the old man with the lined face and the rolled up sleeves. "Just pull her over and I'll take a look."

If my smile faltered, the old man either didn't notice or failed to make anything of it. I hopped down from the board and, realising that I was trying to move too nonchalantly, moved quickly back to the car. Running around the front, I leaned on the window-edge, jogging alongside where Gill was still hunched over the driving wheel, still staring ahead with glassy eyes.

"We're in luck. It is a tow-truck. He says he'll help us."

Gill said nothing. The car trundled along at seven miles an hour.

"Gill, I said he'll help us."

Somewhere, a crow squawked, as it to remind us that the scarecrow was still there and was still coming.

"Come on, stop the car."

Gill wiped tears from her eyes, and returned her white-knuckled, two handed grip to the steering wheel.

"Stop the car!"

This time, I reached in and tried to take the keys. Gill clawed at me, her fingernails raking my forehead. I recoiled in shock.

"I ... am ... not ... stopping the car. Not for you. Not for anybody. He's still coming. If we stop, he'll come. And he'll kill us."

I thought about making another grab, then saw that the old man was leaning out of his window behind us, watching. He wasn't smiling that big smile anymore. I made a helpless, 'everything's fine' gesture and stood back to let our car pass and the tow truck catch up. Then I jumped up on the standing-board again as we trundled along. Behind us, I could see that the scarecrow had gained on us. The silhouette was bigger than before. Had he suddenly decided to change the rules of the game and put on a burst of speed to overtake us? The possibility made me break out into another sweat. The old man seemed to see the change in me.

"Got a problem?" His voice was much warier this time.

"Well, my wife. She ... she won't ... that is, she won't stop the car."

"Why not?"

"She's frightened."

"Of you?"

"Me? God, no!" I wiped a hand across my forehead, thinking I was wiping away sweat, only to see that it was covered in blood. Gill's nails had gouged me. The old man was only too aware of that blood.

"Well if she won't stop the car I can't inspect it, can I? What's she want me to do? Run alongside with the hood opened?"

"No, of course not. It's just that ..."

"So what's she frightened of?"

"Look, there's a man. Can you see him? Back there, behind us?"

The old man leaned forward reluctantly, now suddenly wary of taking his eyes off me, and adjusted his rear view mirror so that he could see the ragged figure approaching fast from behind.

"Yeah, what about him?"

"He ..." My throat was full of dust then. My heart was beating too fast. "He's trying to kill us."

"To kill *you*?"

"That's right. That's why the car's damaged. And he just keeps coming and won't stop and ..." I was going to lose it, I knew. I was babbling. The old man's eyes had clouded; the sparkle and the welcoming smile were gone.

In a flat and measured voice, he said: "I don't want any trouble, mister."

"Trouble? No, no. Look, we need your help. If you just ... well, just stop the truck here. And stand in the road with me. Maybe when he sees that there're two of us, he'll back off. Maybe we can scare him away. Then you can give us a tow. We'll pay. Double your usual rate. How's that sound?"

"Look, I just wanted to help out. I could see your car was in trouble from way off. Steam coming out from under the hood. Oil all the way back down the road. But I don't want to get involved in no domestic dispute."

"*Domestic* dispute?"

"Anything that's happening between you and the lady in the car and the fella behind has nothing to do with me. So why don't you hop down and sort your differences out like civilised people?"

"Please, you've got it all wrong. It's not like that, at all. Look, have you got a mobile phone?"

"Get off my truck."

"Please, the man's *mad*! He's going to kill us. At least telephone for the police, tell them what's happening here ..."

"I said, *get off*!"

The flat of the old man's calloused hand came down heavy where I was gripping the window-edge, breaking my grip. In the next moment, he lunged sideways and jabbed a skinny elbow into my chest. The pain was sharp, knocking the breath out of my lungs; the impact hurling me from the standing-board and into the road. I lay there, engulfed in a cloud of choking dust, coughing my guts out and unable to see anything. All I could hear was the sound of the truck overtaking our car as it roared on ahead down the country road, leaving us far behind. When I tried to rise, pain stabbed in my hip where I had fallen. I staggered and flailed, yelling obscenities after the old man.

The dust cloud swirled and cleared.

The tow-truck was gone from sight.

Behind me, the scarecrow was alarmingly close; now perhaps only a hundred yards away and still coming with that measured tread. Despite my fears, he didn't seem to have put on that burst of speed. Relentless, he came on.

Gill hadn't stopped for me. The car had moved on ahead, itself about fifty yards further down the road. Perhaps she hadn't seen what had happened between the old man and myself, didn't realise my plight. So it was hardly fair of me to react the way that I did. But I reacted anyway. I screamed at her, just as I'd screamed at the departing old man. I screeched my rage and blundered after the car, the pain in my hip stabbing like fire. Even with my staggering gait, it didn't take long to catch up with the car, making the evil mockery of the scarecrow's relentless approach all the more horrifying. If he just put on that extra spurt of speed, he could catch up with us whenever he liked. I threw open the back door of the car and all but fell inside. I tried to yell my rage, but the dust and the exhaustion and the pain all took their toll on my throat and lungs. When I stopped hacking and spitting, I tried to keep my voice calm but it came out icy cold.

"You didn't stop, Gill. You didn't stop the car for me. You were going to leave me there."

Gill was a white-faced automaton behind the wheel. She neither looked at me nor acknowledged my presence. In her shock I had no way now of knowing whether she could even hear what I was saying. I wiped more blood from my forehead, and struggled to contain the crazy feeling that I knew was an over-reaction to outright fear.

There was someone up ahead on our side of the road, walking away from us. He was a young man, his body stooped as if he had been walking a long while; with some kind of holdall over his shoulder. He didn't seem to hear us at first; his gaze concentrated downwards, putting one foot in front of the other. I moved towards Gill but before I could say anything, she said:

"Don't!"

"But we should..."

"No, Paul. We're not stopping."

I had no energy. Fear and that fall from the tow-truck had robbed me of strength. But as I leaned back, I saw the young man ahead suddenly turn and look at us. Quickly, he dropped his holdall to the ground and fumbled for something inside his jacket. We were close enough to see the hope in his eyes when he pulled out a battered cardboard sign and held it up for us to read: HEADING WEST.

I looked at the back of Gill's head. She never moved as the car drew level and began to pass the young man. The hope in his eyes began to fade as we trundled past. Did he think we were travelling at that speed just to taunt him? I looked back over my shoulder to see that the scarecrow was still closing the gap, still coming. The fact that I was looking back seemed to give the young man some encouragement. Grabbing his holdall, he sprinted after us. I wound down the side window as he drew level.

"Come on, man." His voice was thin and reedy. He jogged steadily at the side of the car as we moved. "Give me a lift. I've been walking for hours."

"That man ... back there ..."

The young man looked, but didn't see anything worth following up in conversation.

"I'm heading for Slaly, but if you're going anywhere West that's good enough for me. How about it?"

"That man ... he's mad. Do you hear me? He tried to kill us."

Now, it seemed that he was seeing all the evidence that there was something wrong about this situation. The quiet woman with the white face and the staring eyes. The broken windows and the sugar-frosted glass all over the seats. The dents and scratches on the car as it lurched and trembled along the road, engine rumbling. And me, lying in the back as if I'd been beaten up and thrown in there, blood all over my forehead.

"You and me. If we square up to him, we can frighten him off. I'll pay you. Anything you want. And then we'll drive you where you want to go."

"I don't think so," said the young man. He stopped and let us pass him by. I struggled to the window and leaned out to look back at him. He waved his hand in a 'Not for me' gesture.

"Yeah?" I shouted. "Well, thanks for fucking nothing. But I'm not joking. That guy back there is a *psycho*. So before he catches up, I'd head off over those fields or something. Keep out of his way. When he gets to you, you're in big trouble."

The young man was looking away, hands on hips as if deciding on a new direction.

"I'm telling you, you stupid bastard! Get out of here before he catches up!"

I fell back into the car, needing a drink more than I've ever done in my life. Up in front, Gill might have been a shop mannequin, propped in the driving seat. She was utterly alien to me now, hardly human at all.

"You've killed him," I said at last. Perhaps my voice was too low to be heard. "You know that, don't you? The guy back there is as good as dead."

When I turned to look back again, I could see that the young man was still walking in our direction. The scarecrow was close behind him. But still in the middle of the road. Perhaps something in the tone of my voice had registered with him, because he kept looking over his shoulder as he moved and the scarecrow got closer and closer. I couldn't take my eyes away from the rear window. There was a horrifying sense of inevitability. When it seemed that the scarecrow was almost level with him, I saw the young man pause. He seemed to speak to the scarecrow. Then he stopped, just staring. Perhaps he had seen the scarecrow's face properly for the first time.

I gritted my teeth.

The young man shrank back on the grass verge.

I could see it all in my mind's eye. The sudden lunge of the scarecrow, wielding that scythe high above his head. The young man would shriek, hold up his hands to ward off the blow. But then the scarecrow would knock him on his back, grab him by the throat and bring the scythe down into his chest. The young man would writhe and thrash and twist as the scarecrow ripped that scythe down, gutting him. Then it would begin ripping his insides out while he was still alive, the man's arms and legs twitching feebly, and then he would lie still forever as the scarecrow scattered what it found into the surrounding fields.

101

Except that it wasn't happening like that at all.

The man was shrinking back on the verge, but the scarecrow was still walking.

And now the scarecrow had walked straight past the young man without so much as a sideways glance. He was coming on, after us, at the same relentless pace. Now, the young man was hurrying back in the opposite direction; stumbling and fumbling at first, as if he didn't want to take his eyes off this figure in case it suddenly changed its mind and came lunging back at him. The man began to run, then was heading full pelt back in the opposite direction.

The scarecrow was coming on.

It only wanted *us*.

"You bastard!" I yelled through the shattered windscreen. "You fucking, fucking *bastard*! What was the matter with *him*, then? What do you want from us? What the hell do you want us for?" I think I began to weep then. Maybe I just went over the edge and became insane. But I seemed to lose some time. And I only came out of it when I realised that I could still hear weeping, and realised that it wasn't mine. When my vision focussed, it was on the back of Gill's head again. She was sobbing. I could see the rise and fall of her shoulders. Looking back through the rear window, I could see that the man had continued to gain on us. He was less than fifty yards behind, and the engine was making a different sound. I pulled myself forward, and it was as if the tow-truck driver was whispering in my ear at the same time that my gaze fell on the petrol gauge.

I could see you were in trouble. Oil all the way back down the road.

The gauge was at 'empty'. We'd been leaking petrol all the way back to the motorway. Soon we'd be empty and the car would roll to a stop.

Fear and rage again. Both erupting inside to overcome the inertia and engulfing me in an insane, animal outburst. I kicked open the door, snarling. My hip hurt like hell as I staggered into the middle of the road. I tried to find something else to yell back at the approaching figure. Something that could encompass all that rage and fear. But even though I raised my fists to the sky and shook like I was having a fit, I couldn't find any way of letting it out. I collapsed to my knees, shuddering and growling like an animal.

And then, crystal clear, something came to me.

I don't know how or where. It was as if the damned idea was planted by someone else, it felt so utterly *outside*. Maybe even in that moment of pure animal hate, a cold reasoning part of me was still able to reach inside and come up with a plan. Had I had time to think about it, I would have found dozens of reasons not to do what

I did. But instead, I acted. I clambered to my feet again. The scarecrow was thirty yards away; close enough for me to see that idiot, grinning face and the black-hollowed eyes. I hobbled after the car, braced my hands on the metalwork as I felt my way along it to the driver's door. I knew what would happen if I spoke to Gill, knew what she would do if I tried to stop her.

So instead, I pulled open the door, lunged in and yanked both her hands off the steering wheel. She screamed. High-pitched and completely out of control. The violent act had broken her out of that rigid stance. She began to scream and twist and thrash like a wild animal as I dragged her bodily out of the car, hanging onto her wrists. When she hit the rough road, she tried to get purchase, tried to kick at me. She was yelling mindless obscenities when I threw her at the verge. She fell badly and cried out. Twisting around, she saw the scarecrow – and could no longer move. In that split-second as I dived into the car, already slewing towards the verge and a dead-stop, I didn't recognise her face. The eyes belonged to someone else. They were made of glass.

I jammed on the brakes, felt so weak that I was afraid I couldn't do what I was going to do. My hand trembled on the gearstick.

Yelling, I rammed the gear into reverse. It went in smooth. I revved up the engine and knew that if it coughed and died from lack of petrol I'd go quite mad.

Then I let up the clutch, and this time the car shot backwards. Maybe it was twenty, thirty miles an hour. Not so fast maybe, but three or four times faster than we'd been travelling on this Crawl. And it felt like the vehicle was moving like a fucking bullet. I was still yelling as I leaned back over the seat, twisting with the wheel to get my bearings right – and the scarecrow began to loom large in my sight-line, right smack centre in the rear window. Dust and gravel spurted and hissed around me.

The scarecrow just came on.

Filling the ragged frame of that rear window.

I just kept yelling and yelling as the scarecrow vanished in the dust cloud the car was making. It gushed into the car, making me choke and gag.

And then there was a heavy *crunching* thud, jarring the frame of the car. It snapped me back and then sharp-forward in the seat. The engine coughed and died. The car slewed to a stop.

I had hit the bastard – and I had hit him hard.

The car was filled with dust. I couldn't see a thing. I threw the door open and leapt out, feeling that stab of pain in my hip but not giving one flying fart about it. I dodged and weaved in the cloud, crouching and peering to see where he had been thrown. I wanted to see blood in that dry dust. I wanted to see brains and shit. I wanted to see that he'd coughed up part of his intestine on impact and that he was lying there in utter agony. I wanted to see his legs crushed; his head split apart, his scythe shattered into hundreds of little bits.

The dust cloud settled.

I warily walked around the side of the car, looking for the first sign of a boot or an outstretched hand. I strained hard to listen in the silence for any kind of sound. I wanted to hear him moaning or weeping with pain.

But there was no sound.

Because there was no one lying behind the car.

I hobbled to the grass verge. The car was still in the centre of the road, so there was a chance that it had thrown him clear into one of the fields at either side. But there was no one in the grass at the left side, and when I skipped across the road to the other field, there was no sign of a body there either. I knew I had hit that bastard with killing force. But at that speed, surely he couldn't have been thrown the two hundred feet or so into the stalks of wheat out there. It couldn't be possible, unless ... unless ...

Unless he wasn't very heavy.

Unless he hardly weighed anything at all.

Like, maybe, he weighed no more than your average scarecrow.

The thought was more than unnerving. I cursed myself aloud. He'd had real hands, hadn't he? I'd seen them up close. But then a little voice inside was asking me: *Are you sure you saw them properly? Wasn't he wearing gloves?*

On a sudden impulse, I ducked down and looked under the car.

There was nothing there.

When I straightened up, I could see that Gill was staggering down the road towards me. She looked drunk as she weaved her way towards the car. I leaned against the dented framework, holding my arms wide, imploring.

"I know I hit him," I said. "I *know* I did. I felt the car hit him. He must be dead, Gill. I didn't want to do it, but it was the only way. Wasn't it? I'm sorry for what I did to you, just then. I shouldn't have. But I had to at least try and ..."

She was almost at the car now; face blank, rubbing her eyes as if she might just have woken up. I felt the temptation to retreat into that safe fantasy. To pretend that none of this had happened. Lost for words, I shook my head.

I was just about to take Gill into my arms when she screamed, right into my face.

I don't know whether the shock made me react instinctively. But suddenly, I was facing in the opposite direction, looking back to the rear of the car.

And the scarecrow was right there.

Standing on the same side of the car, right in front of me, about six feet away. Grinning his stitched and ragged grin. Straw flying around his head. That head was cocked to one side again, in that half-bemused expression that was at the same time so horribly malevolent. Something moved in one of the ragged eye sockets of his 'mask', but I don't think it was the winking of an eye. I think it was something alive in there; something that was using the warm straw for a nest.

The scythe jerked up alongside my face.

I felt no pain. But I heard the *crack!* when the handle connected with my jaw.

In the next moment, I was pinned back against the car. Instinctively, I'd seized the scarecrow's wrist as it bent me backwards. My shoulders and head were on the roof, my feet kicking in space as I tried to keep that scythe out of my face. He was incredibly strong, and I tried to scream when I saw that scythe turn in and down towards my right eye. But no sound would come, and I couldn't move. Somewhere behind, I could hear Gill screaming. Then I saw her behind the scarecrow, tearing at its jacket and yanking handfuls of straw away.

I slid, the impetus yanking me from the thing's grip as I fell to the road. Stunned, dazed, I saw one of the car wheels looming large; then turned awkwardly on one elbow as the scarecrow stepped into vision again. The sun was behind him, making him into a gigantic silhouette as he lifted the scythe just the way I'd envisaged he'd do it for the hitch-hiker. This wasn't real anymore. I couldn't react. I couldn't move. It wasn't happening. Somewhere, a long way away, Gill was screaming over and over again; as if someone was bearing her away across the fields.

Then the car horn rang, loud and shocking.

It snapped me out of that inertia, and everything was real again.

Somehow, the scarecrow's arm was stayed.

It just stood there, a black shape against the sun, the weapon raised high.

And then the horn rang again. This time, a gruff man's voice demanded: "You put that down, now!"

Someone had grabbed my arm and was tugging hard. I grabbed back, and allowed myself to be pulled out of the way and around to the rear of the car. Everything focussed again, out of the sun's brilliance.

Gill had pulled me to my feet, and clung tight to me as we both leaned against the battered bodywork. Neither of us seemed able to breathe now.

A car had pulled up on the other side of the road. Only fifteen or twenty feet separating the vehicles. A man was climbing out, maybe in his forties. Thick, curly grey hair. Good looking. Checked shirt and short sleeves. Perhaps he was a farmer. He looked as if he could handle himself. His attention remained fixed on what stood by the side of our own car as he slammed the door with careful force.

"I don't know what's happening here. But I know you're going to drop that."

The scarecrow had its back to us now. Its head was lowered, the scythe still raised; as if I was still lying down there on the ground, about to be impaled.

"You alright, back there?" asked the farmer.

All we could do was nod.

"Drop the scythe, or whatever it is," continued the farmer slowly. "And everything will be okay. Okay?" He moved towards our car, one hand held out gentle and soothing, the other balled into a fist just out of sight behind his back. "And you take off the fright mask, alright? Then we'll calm down and sort everything out."

The scarecrow looked up at him as he approached.

The man halted.

"Take it ..." he began.

The scarecrow turned around to face him.

"... easy," finished the farmer. Suddenly, his expression didn't seem as confident as it had before. He strained forward, as if studying the 'mask'.

The scarecrow stepped towards him.

"Oh Christ Jesus," he said, and now he didn't sound at all like the commanding presence he'd been a moment before. He backed off to his own car, groping for the door handle without wanting to turn his back on what stood before him. He looked wildly at us. "Look, mister," the farmer said to me. "If we both rush him. Maybe we can take him. Come on, that's all it needs ..."

I moved forward, but Gill held me tight and pinned me back against the car.

The scarecrow took another step towards the farmer.

"Come on!" implored the farmer, fumbling with the handle.

I tried to say something. But what would happen if I opened my mouth, and the scarecrow should turn away from him and look back at me again?

"Please," said the man. "Help .... help ... me ..."

The scarecrow held out the scythe to the farmer, a hideous invitation.

I wasn't going to speak, but Gill put a hand over my mouth anyway.

The man yelped and dodged aside as the scarecrow lunged forward, sweeping the scythe in a wide circle. The tip shrieked across the bodywork of the car, where the farmer had been standing a moment before. Flakes of paint glittered in the air. The man edged to the rear of his car as the scarecrow jammed the scythe down hard onto the roof the vehicle. With a slow and horrible malice, the scarecrow walked towards him. As it moved, it dragged the screeching scythe over the roof with it.

"Please help me!" shouted the man. "Please!"

The scarecrow walked steadily towards him.

We saw the man run around the back of his car.

We saw him look up and down the road, trying to decide which direction. He held both arms wide to us in a further appeal.

"For God's sake, please help!"

We clutched each other, trembling.

And then the man ran off into the nearest field of wheat. He was soon swallowed by the high stalks. We watched them wave and thrash as he ran.

The scarecrow followed at its steady pace.

It descended into the high stalks, but didn't pause. It did not, thank God, turn to look back at us. It just kept on walking, straight into where the farmer had vanished, cutting a swathe ahead with its scythe. Soon, it too was swallowed up in the wheat. We watched the grass weave and sway where it followed.

Soon, the wheat was still.

There were no more sounds.

*

After a while, we took his car. The keys were in the dash. I drove us back to the nearest town and we rang for the police. We told the voice on the other end that we'd been attacked, and that our attacker had subsequently gone after the man who had ultimately been our rescuer. We were both given hospital treatment, endured the rigorous police investigations and gave an identical description of the man who had pursued us in his Hallowe'en costume. The police did not like the story. It didn't have, as one of the plain-clothes men had it, the 'ring of truth'. The fella in the tow-truck was never traced, neither was the hitchhiker. They could have given the same description, if nothing else.

But the man who stopped to help us – Walter Scharf, a local farmer, well liked – was never seen again. And he's still missing, to this day. Despite every avenue of enquiry, the police still couldn't link us to anything.

*

That's what they began to think at the end, you see? That Scharf was somehow the attacker (maybe some sort of love-triangle gone wrong), that he was responsible for the damage to the car and/or us. And that we had killed him, and hidden him. I got a lot of hate mail from his wife. But they couldn't link us to anything.

So we got out of it alive, Gill and I.

But there was something neither of us told the police.

Something that neither of us discussed afterwards.

We never talked about the fact that when the first person to stop and volunteer to help, asked us ... *begged* us ... to help him: we kept quiet. We said nothing, and did nothing. And because of it, the thing went after him instead of us.

And we were *glad*.

But the darkness of that gladness brought something else into our lives.

Shame. Deep and utter shame. So deep, so profound and so soul-rotting that we couldn't live with ourselves anymore. Gill and I split up. We couldn't talk about it. We live in different cities, and neither of us drives a car anymore.

I know that she'll be having the same nights as me.

The days are bad, but the nights are always worse.

The front door is always the focus of attention, no matter what I'm doing. I'll try to keep myself occupied, try to read, try to listen to music. But all of these things make it much worse. You see, if I really *do* become preoccupied in what I'm doing, then I might not hear it if ... If he ... it ... comes.

And in the nights, I'll lie awake and listen.

The sound of a car passing on the sidestreet is probably the worst.

I'll hear it coming in my sleep. It wakes me instantly, and I'm never sure whether I've screamed or not, but I lie there praying first that the car will pass quickly and that the engine won't cough and falter. Then, in the first seconds after it's moved on I'll pray again that I won't hear those familiar, staggering footsteps on the gravel coming up the path; that I won't hear that hellish hammering on the front door. I listen for the sounds of that hideous, hoarse breathing.

Sometimes, I'll wonder if I can hear Walter Scharf distantly screaming as he runs through the dark fields of our dreams, the scarecrow close behind. Perhaps those screams aren't his; they're the screams of the next person who crossed its path. They'll fade and die ... and the quiet of those dreams is sometimes more horrible than the noise.

And to this day, there are two things that terrify me even more than the sounds of a car, or someone walking up the drive, or the noise of that letterbox before I nailed it down.

The first is the sight and the sound of children playing 'tag'.

The second is a noise that keeps me out of the countryside, away from fields and wooded areas. A simple, everyday sound.

It's the sound of crows, cawing and squawking.

Perhaps frightened from their roosts by something down below and unseen, thrashing through the long grass.

Now, this crow stays home.

And waits.

And listens.

And crawls from one room to the next, making as little noise as possible.

The days are bad, but the nights are always worse ...

THE WOMAN IN THE RAIN

It was mid-winter sometime in the late 1970s, and a young district nurse, having been out on call until the early hours of the morning, was driving tiredly home along a little used road that crossed the bleak, empty countryside between Leeds and Tadcaster. It was a bitterly cold night and heavy rain was falling, so the nurse was amazed when she saw an old lady standing by herself at the roadside. Though wearing extensive waterproofs, the old lady was clearly getting drenched and had to be frozen to the bones.

Knowing there was no town within walking distance, the nurse stopped the car and offered to give the old lady a lift. The lady nodded and climbed in. They drove away together, but the passenger did not speak much. In fact, her non-communicative state slowly became a source of concern to the nurse. The old lady's refusal to answer questions about who she was or how she had found herself out there alone verged on rudeness; in fact it was vaguely menacing. And then, quite suddenly – without asking permission – the old lady lit herself a cigarette. In the spurt of light from the match, her hands were revealed to be gnarled, knotty, and covered in warts and tufts of thick, black hair.

Completely bewildered as to who or what she was in the presence of, and now terrified as well, the nurse slowed the car to a halt and asked the old lady if she would climb out to check the headlights were working properly. When the passenger asked why the nurse couldn't do this herself, the nurse lied that she wanted to ensure the engine kept running as it had recently been cutting out. Very reluctantly, the old lady climbed from the car, and the nurse immediately drove away without her.

Initially relieved, she hurried on to Leeds, but gradually, as she returned to civilisation, she started to wonder if she might have overreacted. Soon she was feeling guilty, thinking she'd abandoned someone vulnerable in the worst possible place, and all for the rather pathetic reason that she had offensively hairy hands. When the nurse noticed a handbag still sitting in the foot-well of the passenger seat, she really became agitated. Might the old lady think that she'd done all this just to steal from her?

The nurse headed to the nearest police station, where the desk sergeant told her to relax and made her a cup of tea. He said he'd send a patrol out to bring the old lady to safety, and in the meantime they'd try to discover who she was. He opened the handbag, expecting to find personal effects and identification.

But all the bag contained was a large meat cleaver.

Needless to say, the police searched but no trace of this mysterious person was ever discovered.

Disappointingly, this story is almost certainly untrue. It is, in fact, a classic example of the urban legend. Similar and identical tales have been told all across the western world, and in no known case have any facts been ascertained to suggest it really happened: the name of the woman driving the car, the name of the police officer who assisted her, and so on. There are even prototype stories in regional folklore, wherein thieves and murderers would inveigle their way into lone country houses by disguising themselves as old beggar women.

However, in Yorkshire in the early 1980s this apocryphal tale took on a genuine life of its own – to such an extent that police officers heard numerous reports from frightened members of the public, who assured them it had happened to a friend of a friend or an in-law of an in-law, or such. Of course, at the time, the county was in a grip of terror thanks to the activities of two serial killers: Mark Rowntree, a paranoid schizophrenic who stabbed four people to death at random in Bingley, West Yorkshire, and later finished up incarcerated in a secure hospital; and Peter Sutcliffe, the Yorkshire Ripper, who murdered and mutilated 13 women in Leeds, Bradford and Huddersfield, and was eventually sentenced to a full-life tariff.

Unfortunately, these tragic tales are all too true, their memory alone haunting the good people of Yorkshire to this day. It was surely no surprise that a population besieged by the gruesome deeds of two seemingly unstoppable murderers would have reached the state where even the most outlandish rumours only fuelled their panic.

To this date, it is probably the only occasion in British history when a modern myth has been attributed by many, many people to a real time and a real place.

RAGGED
Gary McMahon

Tha' used to say t' pigeons flew backwards ower Putham Park to stop t' dirt gettin' in tha eyes."

Wes twisted around on the park bench and stared at the old man sitting next to him. He hadn't even been aware of someone joining him there until now. "I'm sorry?"

"Back in t' old days…y' know, textile mills 'n' that."

"Oh. Yes. I see." But he didn't; not really. He simply wanted the old man to shut up, or piss off and leave him alone. Either one would do.

The old man seemed to get the message. He muttered something under his breath and adjusted his position on the bench so that he was facing slightly away from Wes, in the direction of the children's play park. He crossed his legs and stared into the middle distance.

Wes closed his eyes, trying to blot out the day. He felt tired, but his mind was racing. It was over a year since Anne's death but still he couldn't seem to shake off his grief. It covered him like a thin blanket, one whose corners he couldn't quite get hold of so that he might discard it.

He opened his eyes and got to his feet, being careful not to glance at the old man; there was always the possibility that eye contact might make him try to start up another conversation, and that was the last thing Wes wanted.

He walked slowly through the park, towards the boating lake. The waning sunlight shimmered like a layer of grease on the surface of the water. A few children and their parents were feeding ducks beside the boat shed; a man was lifting a squealing toddler off her feet, pretending to throw her in; a sad-faced woman dressed entirely in denim was standing by the side of the lake, staring down at the water.

When he reached the lake, Wes stopped and mirrored the denim woman's pose. He wondered what she could see there, reflected in the grey surface. For his own part, he could see nothing: just a glimmer of dying light. He didn't feel sad or depressed. He was lonely but it wasn't anything that he couldn't handle. There was just a sense of melancholy at his core, a feeling that he knew would never leave him. He had changed; things were different. Anne's death had dimmed some light within him, casting a part of his inner self into perpetual shade.

He took a couple of backward steps, knowing that there was another park bench immediately behind him – he'd seen it on his approach. The backs of his knees made contact with the edge of the bench, and when he turned his head to the side, went into a slight squat, and used his hands to locate the seat, he was aware of a fluttering movement to his right, as if someone was moving quickly past him.

He sat, and turned. There was nobody there.

The denim woman was still standing at the edge of the lake. Between them, still fluttering gently to the ground, was what looked like a used handkerchief; a sad thing, all grubby and creased. Had someone dropped it as they raced by on some errand?

On impulse, Wes stood and walked over. He bent down and picked up the rag between the tips of his forefinger and thumb. It wasn't a handkerchief at all, just a small square of material with frayed edges. It was old and filthy, but there was something vaguely interesting about the rag: it had something embroidered on one side. It looked like words, a phrase or slogan, but the language wasn't English. Latin … was it Latin?

Wes had studied a little Latin during his school days – enough to recognise the written language but not to translate its meaning. Without thinking, he crushed the rag in his fist and slipped it into his jacket pocket. He wasn't sure why he did it, other than the fact that he hated to see people drop litter in public places. He could dispose of it in the bin by the gate when he left.

By the time he sat back down on the bench, Wes had forgotten completely about the piece of cloth in his pocket. He stayed there for a while, for some reason waiting until the denim woman had departed. He often did this, fixating on strangers, making their actions important to his own, reacting to what they did in a completely unrelated way.

He got up from the bench and walked past the lake, across the grass, and towards the exit. The sun was fading. The park was emptying fast. Families were returning home for a late Sunday dinner, or perhaps a spot of tea after exercising in the park.

Wes crossed the road outside the park gates and walked east. The footpath was taken up by three women in dark robes and with burkas covering their faces, so he stepped into the road to avoid colliding with them. It didn't take him long to get to his house, the one he'd shared with Anne. He unlocked the door and went inside. There was no one to greet him. He didn't even have a cat. He threw down his keys on the dining table and began to prepare dinner. The beef was already roasting in the oven; he'd put it there before going out to the park. He cut the vegetables and put them on to boil, laid the table, and by the time a knock came at the door everything was almost ready.

He opened the door.

"Hi," said Jane, smiling. The last of the day's sunlight at her back made her hair glow golden.

"Good to see you," he said, leaning over to kiss her cheek. He backed away, letting her in. She followed him inside and shut the door behind her.

"Need any help?"

"You could open the wine."

The meat was overcooked but Jane didn't complain. She never did. She wasn't like Anne, who had always voiced her criticisms.

"How was your day?"

"Okay," she said, putting down her knife and fork. "I'm sick of working all this overtime. It's not as if I'm getting paid for it."

He nodded.

"What about you?"

"I slept late, went for a walk in the park."

"Just your typical action-packed Sunday, eh?" When she grinned, the bridge of her nose creased. It was cute, but Wes could see himself growing annoyed by the affectation at some point in the future.

"This old geezer tried talking to me when I was sitting on a bench."

"Poor him … I know how you are with strangers."

He smiled, despite himself. "Yeah … yeah. He said something weird. Something about pigeons flying backwards … I have no fucking idea what he meant, but it stuck in my head. I think he might have been insulting me." He took a sip of the wine; it was good.

"Was it about the pigeons flying backwards over the park to stop the soot getting in their eyes?"

He paused. "Something like that, yes."

She laughed. Her teeth were white and straight. Anne's two front teeth had been slightly crooked and stained by nicotine. "Oh, that's just an old saying, from back when textile mills were all over this area. It's an old textile town – you know that, don't you? Pretty affluent in it's time. Not like now. That's why we have such a nice park. The Victorians used to show off their wealth by building parks." She leaned back in her seat and patted her belly. "That was a good feed." She grinned. The bridge of her nose creased.

114

"Textiles …" He remembered the rag he'd picked up. What had he done with it?

Jane stood and started loading the plates and pans into the dishwasher. "There's a good drama on telly tonight. How about we relax and watch that?"

"Yes, that's fine. Sounds good."

"You take the wine through and I'll finish up here. You can rub my feet if you're lucky."

After the drama – something about a dishonest policeman that Wes was too distracted to take in properly – they retired upstairs to bed. The curtains were open. Jane undressed in the streetlight through the window. Her body was thin and pale; Anne's had been heavier, more athletic because she liked to keep fit. Jane's breasts were large and heavy; Anne's had been small and hard. When Jane climbed into bed and he went down on her, he resisted the temptation to compare how the women smelled.

They made love, and it was good. It was never going to be great, but that wasn't really a requirement of their relationship. Sometimes just good was good enough. He lay on his back and listened to her breathing. She moaned in her sleep. He glanced at the window; the curtains were still open and he could see moonlight through the glass.

It wasn't long before he started to drift. Sleep was still a distance away, but from where he was he could see its darkening shore.

His eyelids flickered. His breathing became shallow. He twitched. When he opened his eyes he saw a shape at the side of the window, against the curtain. It was long and slim; he thought it looked like a denuded mannequin. He remembered the women in burkas from that afternoon. There was movement near the top of the shape – where the mannequin's head would be: a soft, delicate flapping, like an oversized moth's wing. He blinked and the shape was gone. It was just shadow-play and weariness.

There was nothing there.

Jane had left by the time he woke up. She'd left a note on the pillow, but he'd crumpled and dribbled on it in his sleep. He smoothed out the damp paper and read the message: *Missing you.*

She was a good woman. She deserved better than him and his inability to let go of his dead wife's ghost. He felt groggy, as if he had a hangover, but last night's wine had not been enough to cause one. He looked at the bedside clock and saw that he was running late for work. It took all his energy to get out of bed, shower, and put on his clothes. He drove to work on autopilot. When he got out of the car, he could remember nothing of the journey.

115

His shift seemed to last forever. The machines kept breaking down and he was constantly running across the factory floor to fix them. The machine operators seemed to mock his southern accent more than usual – but that could have been an overreaction on his part because he was tired. By the end of the day his hands were filthy and aching and he was experiencing a peculiar sullen rage. His headache had cleared, but his body ached so much that he felt as if he'd been beaten up and left for dead.

He drove home slowly and carefully, trying to be aware of every turn in the road. When it started to rain he slowed down even further, terrified that his tiredness would cause him to hit a child or a pensioner trying to cross the road. He got home late. His vision was blurred. Jane wasn't coming round until late this evening, so he could have a restful few hours before she did. Read a book. Listen to some music. Maybe work on one of his illustrations – the one he'd been commissioned to do for a book cover.

He put his hand in his pocket for his keys and his fingers wrapped around a loose rag. He drew it out of his pocket and remembered picking it up in the park. His keys were in his other pocket. He opened the door and went inside, switched on the light. Reading the Latin inscription, he noticed how filthy the rag was – mouldy, frayed at the edges, almost falling apart. If there was a pattern on there, it was occluded by the grime.

He balled up the rag and threw it in the kitchen bin, then went upstairs for a shower.

He worked on the book illustration for an hour or so but couldn't settle into a rhythm. He kept sensing that someone was standing silently behind him, peering over his shoulder. He resisted the urge to turn around for a long time, and when he did succumb to his paranoia the room was empty. Rain spattered against the window. The streetlights spewed sodium brightness into the night.

Jane arrived later than usual. She looked exhausted.

"Fucking overtime," she said as she stumbled through the door.

"You need to tell them no. This is going to make you ill."

"We're short staffed. There's no one else. If I don't cover, then who'll look after the residents? That'll be us, you know, when we're old and frail and unable to do anything for ourselves. We might even end up in the same nursing home. Wouldn't that be fun?" She grinned. The nose-crease appeared. He shook his head and stroked her face, feeling inexplicably tender towards her.

When they went into the living room the rag was on the floor, by the sofa.

"What the hell's this doing here?" He bent down and picked it up.

"What is it?" She switched on the television.

"I found it in the park ... just an old rag. But there's writing on it."

"Give me a look?" She snatched it from his hands, and for a moment his fingers twitched, began to curl into fists. He felt a vague anger that she'd taken it from him, but it faded quickly.

"Oooh ... stinky."

"Latin," he said. "It's in Latin."

"Let's see what it says."

"How?"

"Google is your friend." She crossed the room and took her mini iPad from her handbag – the one she'd bought herself with her Christmas bonus. She switched it on, waited for it to boot up, and then located the search engine. She checked the wording on the rag, tapped the screen a few times, and then smiled in quiet triumph.

"I cover your grief."

"What?" He felt cold for a second – or a fraction of a second – and then it was gone.

"That's what it means. The phrase ... I think I might know what this is."

"What?"

She dropped the tablet onto the sofa and sat down. "Back in the Victorian era, when the textile market was at its height, the mill in Putham became well-known for a certain speciality item." She paused. "They used to make mourning veils – or, as the locals used to call them, 'mourning rags'. These were worn by grieving widows over their faces.

"Usually a mourning veil would be made of something thin enough that the wearer could see through the weave. But in this area of Yorkshire they were made of a much coarser material. The widows couldn't see through the rags. They were effectively blind, so they had to be guided by family and friends to the graveside. I suppose it was a Putham spin on a familiar tradition: something that became a local ritual. Seems a bit weird now, but, hey, those Victorians were a queer lot."

Wes sat down in the chair opposite. His hands wrestled in his lap. He felt a sense of dislocation, as if he shouldn't really be here. "Is this true?"

"Oh, yes. We learned about it at school – a bit of local history. You weren't born here, so being a southerner you wouldn't know about such esoteric northern ways." She kicked off her shoes, bent to massage her feet with her short, thin fingers. "As far as I can recall, the tradition stated that the mourning rags should be burnt after the funeral. It was supposed to destroy the ill-effects of the

117

grief, to stop the remaining family being cursed by it. Something like that, anyway. It's all very Hammer Horror if you ask me …" She yawned. The history lesson was over. "Where's the rest of that wine?"

They were both too tired to cook so Wes ordered in pizza. When the delivery man came, he was wearing a scarf pulled up over the lower part of his face. Wes felt uneasy; he was seeing hints of Jane's story everywhere. He stood on the doorstep and watched as the man rode away on his scooter, a figure masked by rain.

Jane went to bed first and he followed half an hour later. She was already in a deep sleep, wrapped up in the bedclothes like a giant larva in a cocoon. Her face was covered. He sat down on the edge of the bed, reached out a hand and stroked her thigh. She moaned in her sleep and pressed her body against him. He realised that he hadn't thought about Anne all night. Maybe he was getting somewhere close to acceptance after all.

He could barely keep his eyes open. His head began to nod. He stood and took off his clothes, walked to the window in his underwear, and reached out to close the curtains. The rain had eased off to a light drizzle. The roads were slick and black. As he looked down at the street, a tall, thin figure stepped away from the bushes on the other side of the road. Its face was covered; its body was draped in a long, black dress with a hem that trailed on the ground. The figure raised a hand, as if in greeting, and slowly it began to wave. Before he even realised what he was doing, Wes waved back. The figure stepped back into the shadows, was gone.

Wes shut the curtains and climbed into bed. He held onto Jane, feeling the warmth of her body, and wondered if he should make an appointment with the doctor. He knew that depression could cause hallucinations, and that the human mind looked for patterns everywhere. Perhaps he needed some kind of medication.

As he stared over Jane's sheet-wrapped shoulder, at a spot on the floor near the window, he saw something flutter there, like the bottom edge of the curtain as if it were caught in a breeze. He closed his eyes. When he slept, he dreamed of open graves and women with their faces covered. One of those figures was Anne, come back to him. He couldn't see her face, but he recognised the way she carried herself, despite the fact that she was so thin, so very frail.

*

118

He didn't see Jane for a few days, until the weekend.

In that short space of time, a sense of dread began to leak into his life.

They met in the park, by the boating lake. The day was fine; the clouds held no threat of rain. Families played on the grass, drank coffee from flasks, ate from cardboard cones filled with chips from the burger van on the corner.

"You look like you haven't been sleeping."

He looked at her face, imagined it covered by a cloth. "I'm not … I haven't been. I'm shattered."

She held his hand. Her fingers were warm. "What's wrong?"

"I think I might be ill. He put a hand in his pocket and took out the rag. "It's this … I … I can't get rid of it."

She squeezed his hand. "What are you talking about?"

He took a deep breath, held it, and then let it out again. "Every time I throw this rag away, it comes back. I find it in different places around the house." He said nothing of the figure. He hadn't seen it since the night it had waved at him from the street, but he felt its lingering presence. He decided to keep quiet about its nocturnal visits. Jane might think he was losing his mind.

"I don't understand. What are you trying to say?" She kept her hand on his. It seemed like she was doing everything she could to keep her hand still, to make sure it didn't even twitch.

"I don't know. I have no idea what's happening to me. All I do know is, I can't get rid of this thing. On my way here I threw it in a public bin along the street, near the pub, but here it is again. It doesn't make any sense."

She shook her head. "I don't know what I'm supposed to say. You do realise this all sounds a bit … well odd?"

He nodded, pursed his lips.

"Perhaps you *are* ill, like you say. My mother suffered from stress, years ago. She kept having these paranoid fantasies about people standing in cupboards, always with their backs to her. It got pretty scary." She glanced away from him. "It might be that. You might be stressed. I know you've not got over Anne's death, not yet"

"I'm sorry," he said. "I shouldn't put you through crap like this."

She laughed, but it sounded slightly bitter. "Don't be daft. We'll get through this. You'll start to feel better about things – you'll always miss her, but you'll learn to manage it." She squeezed his hand again, but this time he detected a hint of desperation. "I'm happy to wait until that happens."

They walked back to his house through the park. Nothing else was said about the rag. He'd left it on the bench when they'd stood up, but now it was back in his pocket. He took it out and wrapped the rag around his knuckles, toying with it. Jane walked at his side, her stride falling in step with his own.

"Give me the rag."

He stood in the hallway, staring at her. Reaching behind him, he shut the front door. "Why?"

"I have an idea."

He handed it over, but reluctantly. He couldn't understand why he wanted so badly to keep hold of it, but he did.

"Follow me." She walked into the kitchen and turned on the gas hob, lit it. The flame burned blue. "This is purely symbolic. But it might help." She held the rag between her fingers and let it drape across the flame. It caught light quickly, the old, dry weave inviting the flame.

Wes felt a tugging sensation in his chest; he started to panic. He didn't want to see the rag burn. It was his. It had always been his.

But it did burn, and he watched it.

Before long, he felt calmer, more relaxed. Whatever strange psychological hold the mourning rag had over him was gone. It was just a mouldy piece of cloth, or rather the ashes left behind when the cloth had burned.

Jane brushed her hands together. "See? It's gone." The black ashes scattered over the top of the cooker and the adjacent work surface. Jane dampened a dishcloth at the sink and mopped them up, then rinsed the cloth clean.

"Gone. For good." She moved towards him and put her arms around him. He paused for a moment and then returned her embrace.

"Feel better?"

He nodded, but wasn't sure if he did.

That night their lovemaking was better than it ever had been before. There was a sort of desperation in the act that bound them together; they reached out to each other across a vast, empty space, seeking comfort and finding something that was a rough approximation. When it was over they lay on their backs holding hands, breathing in unison. Jane went to sleep first, and then Wes felt himself following her down.

The room was dark apart from the meagre light bleeding through the gap in the curtains. There were only the sounds of the house settling: the soft creaking of timbers; water moving through the pipes in the walls. Wes turned his head to look at the side of Jane's face, and beyond her he saw the figure sitting on the floor at the side of the bed. He was paralysed; he tried to move but he couldn't. He gripped Jane's hand and wished that this moment would pass. The figure bent slightly forward and lifted a hand. The mourning rag fluttered, caught in a draft, or the breeze summoned by the movement. Fingers that were more bone than flesh slid out of the end of the dress sleeve and the hand dipped deftly towards Jane's sleeping face.

The figure caressed Jane's cheek, its rag-covered face tilted at an angle that suggested it was looking at her. Wes opened his mouth and tried to scream but the sound was lodged in his throat. His nostrils filled with the odour of decay. He strained and stared at the mourning rag. He could make out the shape of the embroidered inscription, and for a brief moment he felt that he was close to understanding what it meant.

Giving one final massive effort, he managed to lift his body an inch or so off the mattress, and as he turned the figure seemed to float backwards into the room, towards the wall. Then it was gone. The lights of a passing car painted a diagonal stripe on the carpet. There was nobody in the room but Wes and Jane, and Jane was still sleeping.

Wes raised a hand to his face and realised that he was crying.

Morning came slowly, in stages. Graduations of light filtered through the gap in the curtains, building up until the room was almost filled with daylight. Wes got up and opened the curtains fully, letting in the rest of the light. He looked out at the street, the houses, the parked cars, and realised that beneath this fragile skin was another world waiting to be discovered.

Anne was there, in that world, and she was waiting for him.

When Jane woke up he said nothing of his experience the night before. They showered together, got dressed, and ate breakfast. If Jane suspected that anything was wrong, she said nothing. But she looked tired, as if something – some essential energy – had been leeched from her as she slept.

"Don't bother coming round tonight," he said. "You look exhausted. I could do with working on that illustration. The deadline's coming up and it isn't even half done."

She was so tired that she agreed without questioning his request.

They kissed and went their separate ways to work. If Wes's kiss had lasted longer, and been deeper, than usual, he didn't think she'd noticed. When he thought it was safe, he turned back and let himself into the house. When he rang in sick, his boss barely said a word; just told him to rest up and drink plenty of fluids.

"Thanks," he said. "I will." His fingers played with the mourning rag as he spoke. A decision had been made and he was unsure if he'd had any part in it, or if events had taken on their own momentum.

Whatever the case, something had to be done.

He spent the day putting things in order, trying not to think about what he was going to do. He assembled all the paperwork he could find – his will, insurance policies, and the pension forms – and made sure that they were stacked neatly on the table for whoever found him. He'd changed his will months ago and left the house to Jane, but he doubted she'd want to live in it after he was gone. She probably wouldn't feel comfortable. Too many memories; too much emotional residue left behind to remind her of him. He knew exactly how that felt.

He made a few phone calls and said goodbye to people he hadn't seen in years, since long before Anne had died. Most of them were surprised by his sudden call; a few of them barely remembered him but pretended otherwise.

It was early evening before he realised the day was almost done.

Every day was done. This, he thought, was his last.

"This is it," he said, and laid out the rag flat on the dining table. It felt course under his fingers, but the cloth looked cleaner. The embroidery stood out more than it had before, almost like new.

He wasn't sure how long he stared at the rag, but it comforted him to do so.

When it was dark he went upstairs and sat on the bed. He felt as if he should perform some kind of ritual, perhaps strip naked and wash his body clean, purify his flesh. But he resisted the urge. That would be absurd, making too much of the situation. So he just sat there, waiting for his cue.

When the cue came, it was subtle. The rag twitched in his hand, as if someone had tugged it. Following the old Yorkshire tradition, he raised it and covered his face. The rag seemed to mould itself around his features, taking on the contours of his skull. The weight of history pressed against him. He was part of this now. He had taken his place in line. He imagined the rows and rows of yellow Yorkshire stone houses as they had been decades ago, when they were first built. Textile workers struggling to survive between the walls; widows grieving lost fathers, sons and husbands; small families gathered around the kitchen stove and seeking warmth from the grate.

There was a slight odour but he couldn't detect what it was. Mildew, perhaps; certainly something damp.

He waited. They came.

He heard the soft swishing of their funereal dresses, the soft tread of their feet on the boards. They took him by the hand and helped him to stand. Their fingers were hard and sharp, with barely any flesh left to cover the bones. Their teeth chattered in their skulls, the joints of their limbs clicked and rattled beneath their heavy, tattered clothing. Their smell was the odour of decay, oddly sweet and overpowering.

They led him downstairs in silence. The door was already open. He could breathe easily beneath the mourning rag but he could not see a thing. He trusted them to guide him, to take him where he needed to be.

Time passed, but he had no idea how long they walked, and finally they came to a place where he was forced gently down onto his knees. The night air was still. He felt cold but it was not unpleasant. The ground was soft and spongy beneath his knees. The rag was slowly, carefully lifted. He kept his eyes closed. They waited until he opened them, applying no pressure, just allowing him to make his own choices.

If this was a ritual, it was a polite one. Nobody was forcing him into anything. He was his own man, and had arrived here under his own steam, guided by a sense of history and the knowledge that this had been done so many times before.

For perhaps the first time since Anne had died, he felt in control of what was left of his life.

Looking down, he saw that he was kneeling at the side of an open grave. The dark earth at the sides and bottom of the grave was damp. The smell of the wet soil made him feel dizzy. When he looked around it was too dark to see clearly, but he was surrounded by silent figures. Each one of them seemed to have their face covered, but he couldn't be entirely certain if that were the case. Perhaps some of them simply had no flesh left on their skulls.

The figures were so thin that they could not possibly be alive. There was the suggestion of clothes hanging on narrow frames, flesh drooping on bone, eyeless sockets beneath the mourning rags. Air hissed dryly through grizzled throats. Rotten feet shuffled on the soft ground. They moved their arms in the air, making signs whose meaning he did not understand.

Wes looked back into the grave, wondering who it might be for. This felt like it was the death of everything – this place, this entire region, was claiming his life, extinguishing his flame. He was being absorbed into the fabric of something much deeper, richer, and more meaningful than his own limited existence. He rubbed the soil between his fingers and saw that it contained tiny pieces of fabric: shreds of shrouds, scraps of mourning apparel, the material that had clothed people so long ago at the height of their grief.

A cold, almost weightless hand came to rest on his shoulder. When he glanced at it he saw only beauty: a flash of bright white bone, a frill of dry, ragged flesh, the torn, grubby lace cuff of a black dress. The ring the hand was wearing looked like the wedding ring he had given to Anne.

When he heard the voice behind him, he almost recognised it, but it sounded clogged with dirt and ruined to the point that it was barely even human. It was a hundred voices speaking as one, but softly, so softly:

"I cover your grief."

He was so close to realisation that he thought he could reach out and touch it. The dead waited for him to respond, but he had nothing to say. If he could find the right words, perhaps it might change things. If only he knew what to say … then he might be saved.

But the words wouldn't come. He was empty. He placed the rag back across his face. It was much safer behind the veil. He could pretend that none of this was happening.

The thin, ragged hand on his shoulder shifted, and then repositioned itself against his shoulder blade before gently pushing him forward into the waiting darkness.

THE HOBMAN

A recurring character in English folklore is the 'hobman' or 'hobthrust'. A friendly imp inclined to benign trickery but also given to assist those farmers whose homes he inhabited, particularly if they were struggling, he appears throughout the homespun rural mythology of the 16th, 17th and 18th centuries as a happy-go-lucky, elfin figure about whom there are few actual tales of terror.

However, there is one story from Spaldington, in East Yorkshire, which suggests a more sinister origin to this fairy tale being.

Spaldington Hall, an Elizabethan manor house, once dominated Spaldington village, and according to gossips of the 1690s and 1700s, played host to one such interloper whose name was Robin Roundcap, though by all accounts this mysterious trickster was more of a hindrance than a help. Constant childish pranks – the mingling of wheat with chaff, milk with water, etc – drove the occupying family to distraction, so much that three local parsons were finally summoned. Together, they commanded a meeting with the hobman, and somehow persuaded him to decamp to the nearby well, there to remain in hibernation for an unspecified number of years, leaving his host family in peace.

You can almost hear the phrase 'and they all lived happily ever after'.

It's a charming piece of village hokum. However, a later version of events, circulating in the 19th century, gives a very different account.

Spaldington Hall was demolished in 1800, and a new farmhouse built on the site. According to its owners, the 18th century exorcism of Robin Roundcap had indeed taken place, but only one minister had been involved and he had found himself grappling with a much darker entity, which claimed to be the vengeful soul of a murdered man. Apparently, Robin Roundcap had been a jester, who was employed at the hall during the reign of James I (1603-1625). Having reached above his station one day, he was brutally beaten and thrown down the main stairway, suffering injuries from which he never recovered. In this second version of events, the encounter with Roundcap was not nearly so friendly, and the officiating clergyman almost died. However, as in the first tale, the spirit was finally banished into a local well, though – in a macabre twist worthy of MR James – the family also felt it necessary to exhume the jester's corpse and then re-bury it with a stake through the *heart, the uppermost section of which would remain visible above ground for many years to come.*

This seemed to do the trick temporarily, though by the late 19th century neither the well nor the jester's grave were visible, having either been ploughed up or covered over by new buildings. Whether or not this released the angry spirit is a matter for debate, but the farm was said to be haunted until well into the 20th century.

A TRUE YORKSHIREMAN
Christopher Harman

Again, something perplexing in the gloom under the third arch, like a thick cluster of mist moving high up in the scaffolding.

Even though the great sprawl of the car park separated City Hall from the viaduct, Lime felt exposed, alone under the bright strip-lighting of the open-plan office. He took several steps back from the tall iron-framed tripartite windows just as two of his Human Resources colleagues entered with Monday morning faces. They were moaning about traffic hold-ups on the viaduct due to maintenance work.

"I've been avoiding it," he said, striding to his desk.

Shortly before midday, he stood, ostensibly to stretch his cramped limbs. The car park was a multi-coloured bubble wrap of vehicles. A small queue at one of the ticket machines. The entrance and exit barriers saluted vehicles entering and exiting. Shoppers headed to the retail outlets that ran off at an angle from the far end of the viaduct. A mundane scene under the heights of Hackfast, the hills with their high rises, the sandstone former mills like gargantuan steps, the flourishes of flyovers. A woman and child threw bread to ducks in Hislop Beck which flowed sluggishly under the third arch.

By five past five, Lime's colleagues had gone, their abandoned beige computer monitors like neat headstones. The sun was behind the hills and lights speckled the city. The viaduct was like twenty bridges strung together.

The man was under the arch again. The first time Lime had thought it was a site supervisor or clerk of works assessing progress but with no hard hat and no florescent green band across the shoulders he'd abandoned that theory. This time the man had a camera and was aiming it up at the curve. Lime stared hard. The thick blot of mist suspended within the scaffolding early that morning was back, and appeared to have taken on a greater solidity. He was reminded of the inflatable Santa clinging to a pillar of Scarborough Pier the previous spring when he and Tracy had visited for the day.

The man had gone – maybe through to the other side of the arch. Nothing but gloom now within the straight lines of the scaffolding – and Lime was glad of that.

He had his car key ready as soon as he stepped out of the building. His car was on the near edge of the staff car park which was a few steps up from the public space behind; in the gloom the key hole in the driver's door winked in and out of existence like a bit of eye debris. Safely inside he activated the central locking.

He drove around the Record Office, a couple of office blocks and tawdry terraced housing to the lightshow of the intersection. He still felt the pull to the left turn which led onto the viaduct. Before commencement of the maintenance work you were over it in seconds and onto Avian Way which soared over the muddle of the city centre. He wasn't going to risk being trapped on the viaduct, so again the ground level frustrations of one-way streets, double parking and shadowy zipping cyclists.

*

He took the polite-voiced lift to their fourth floor apartment. A sweet scent lingered in the vestibule, odours of spice and herbs in the kitchen where Tracy had left half a stir-fry for him on the granite worktop. She had four appointments that evening but Lime still felt furtive getting out the unmarked folder from the tightly packed *His Stuff* drawer of the filing cabinet.

The booklet was dog-eared and faded white at the thin stapled spine. FFFF on the cover in big letters, smaller ones depending from each F reminded him of the thick pillars of the viaduct; *Firthford Fantastic Film Festival: Crossways Hotel*. Inside, photos of guests of honour with big eighties hair and wearing jeans-jackets and black-framed glasses. His name was listed amongst the attendees. There was a page of Firthford's amenities and places of interest – not many of either. Nothing remotely fantastical about the place other than Troll Bridge a mile outside which merited a back-cover photo.

*

Dusk, a mile outside Firthford. Cold porridge clouds against papery dark blue; eggy smears and the sun, a burst tomato on the limestone paving the horizon.

Other conventioneers that day had taken a break from the panels and cozying up to familiar faces to take a look at the bridge. Lime thinks he might be the last.

The shape looms as Lime gets out of his car. "F – " Not the initial letter of FFFF people had been lisping and stuttering all weekend, the other word. He keeps his hand on the door handle.

128

Not a troll. The man is close to six feet in height, broad and with a dense, neat coal-black beard. He's burdened with an opened OS map and a camera, a large professional-looking model.

"Supposed to be a bridge here." Frown lines deepen as he looks back and forth between Lime and his silver Lotus 91. He can't believe Lime owns it, or doesn't believe he should.

"Troll Bridge?"

"If you say so. Just says 'bridge' on this map."

"I'm here to see it. It's hidden away but near. Over the river."

"I'd guessed it was over something."

Lime decides not to interpret that as sarcasm. The man scratches his beard in which his mouth is pinched small. "Yours?" he says, incredulous.

"Yep," Lime says. He dresses like he's still at university and hasn't told anyone the car is a twenty-first birthday present.

It seems man-made more than natural, the steep slope of bare earth. It's littered with long sheaves of grass and dock leaves, and scored through by a narrow rising rabbit-run of a path. A couple gingerly make their way down. Lime has seen them at the hotel and would have preferred their company now. Greetings are exchanged while the bearded man slinks to one side. There are shrugs when Lime asks if the bridge is worth seeing.

"You lot have taken over the town," the man says when they've gone. "That series is set there, isn't it. Preposterous – I only saw one episode."

"Preposterous? Wasn't called that! *Holmwich Fears*. And nobody has to watch it," Lime says, setting off up the slope. Mumbling to himself, the man follows.

At the top of the rise, the bridge is in view. It crosses a narrow gully in which the river is in spate. The bridge comprises an arch of big limestone blocks with a central keystone. It looks quaint and forbidding, though that might be as much due to the high wire enclosure blocking access. There is a notice: 'Danger: Bridge Unsafe'. A devils' dance imprinted in the mud where people have peered through the diamond mesh.

At the Question and Answer session earlier he'd asked the producer-director Bert Urqwuat why the bridge appeared here and there in the six episodes but was never identified as Troll Bridge, and had they considered a troll-themed episode? Bert said he hadn't wanted Holmwich too closely associated with the real Firthford, and residents of the small market town had made representations to the same effect. The advisor on the show, Martha Hobshaw, chipped in to say someone should write a troll story, "though we'd have to film in daylight". Knowing murmurs at that while Urqwuat's face remained studiedly neutral, maybe at the use of "we". Martha, a self-styled white witch, was a walking advert for her shop in the village *The Magic Cell*; she'd worn a white blouse with huge baggy sleeves, and a necklace of shiny grey pebbles; paper bows were tied into her straggly hair. A small woman with apparently no waist. A questioner asked if the character Mother Gornall was based on her. Frost in her round face until Urqwuat said, "Of course Mother Gornall is a couple of generations older." Someone asked for directions to the bridge and Martha began with, "Here's what you must do," to a scatter of laughter; it was a running refrain in the series prior to Mother Gornall advising the elderly lead characters on some means of righting a supernatural wrong.

*

Lime took the DVD out of the folder and watched the special episode shot in the spring following the convention and shown in that year's Christmas schedule. He opened a can of lager and began to drink; that always helped.

The story concerned a local radio DJ who has moved into the manor house where he leads a brood of vampires. Lime no longer took in the dialogue, the shaky sets in over-lit studio interiors, the broad brush acting, the coarse-grained colours, the occasionally slap-dash editing. He looked out for that single stray shot of the bridge, far in the background. From it, an anomalous figure watches the characters. Backlit by the low red sun it's like a massive cairn. A hiker would never bulk so large. An obese resident from the village? Whoever it is, their interest seems to extend past the scene being shot and into the camera lens, as if detecting the viewers, even now twenty-five years on.

Lime had finished the can when Tracy's key scratched in the front door ten minutes before the credits. He ejected the DVD, shoved it under a cushion and listened as she took her large portable mirror and portmanteau containing her hairdressing kit through into her office.

She came back in with a mug of tea.

"Wasn't expecting to see you." His irritation, hard to conceal, hadn't prompted hers. She told him her first client of the evening had cancelled. "She rang from her office just as I was knocking on her house door. What have you been watching?"

"Nothing yet."

"What have you been drinking?" With an Ugg booted foot she tapped the can, bent in half on the coffee table. She could see it was lager.

"Must piss you off when they do that."

"She re-booked. I have to be very understanding with my clients."

"Yes, but the petrol money. You should get premises."

"We've been through all that. The rent's astronomical anywhere decent." She got up and went into the bedroom and closed the door. Lime secreted the DVD into the filing cabinet.

*

The job got Lime down the next day. There were murmurings about redundancies, moans about workloads. To get a break from his crew, late in the afternoon he took a piece of paper and hiked hundreds of yards of corridor. The place had an air of being on the point of shutting down; blurred voices behind closed doors; a hollow melancholy whistling he guessed was coming from a ventilation shaft or along antediluvian pipe work; he traced it to the door of Committee Room 16. He opened the door a crack, then fully; nobody inside.

Underneath the Arches proved a persistent 'earworm' throughout the remainder of the day. Just after five, he avoided looking towards the arch as he headed for his car.

He was inside, the door nearly pulled to, when he heard the rhythmic creaking. A glance in his mirror and he was shrinking in his seat. He pulled the door so it was touching the frame; a slam and the man would have spied him. The long coat looked half empty. Lime was certain it was the man he'd seen the previous morning by the viaduct. A camera hanging on a strap around his neck confirmed it. In the seconds before he'd passed by and onto the steps leading up to the service road before City Hall, Lime glimpsed his face and knew of whom it reminded him.

He heard the plastic sounding creaks again over the next few days, but rounding corners fast, rushing out of meetings, to colleagues' consternation and amusement, he was always too late to catch the fellow.

*

A week later he was in City Hall early again, surprised that he wouldn't be the first to enter the stationery office. He heard the photocopier before noting that no light was visible within the open door. Hearing a squeak of plastic he thought, *Got you*, with more apprehension than triumph. He switched on the light.

Nobody inside, so he can't have heard anything, let alone a creak. He had HR's senior team meeting agenda to photocopy and lifted the lid. A sheet had been left on the glass plate.

It was a photograph. The arch filled it and in the height of the curve something whose outline was feathered to indistinctness. Lime had the overall impression of a shape reminiscent of a great bell.

*

The photographer crouches and pulls up violently the lower edge of the wire barrier by the door, then feeds himself through. He says he's working for a company buying properties and he needs some pictures of Firthford from the knoll on the other side. It's backed by dense thorny vegetation. The bridge leads nowhere.

Lime crawls through after him and wishes he'd visited earlier with other FFFF attendees. Colours are like film stock of an old episode of Holmwich Fears. There's a scratchy vintage quality to the light. A blood-stained citadel of cloud looms. The limestone of the bridge faintly glows.

He tries to relish this disobedience. Ale-brained and running along hotel corridors last night with other fans wailing and wrapped in bed sheets didn't count. He feels tiny, a negligible phenomenon before the ancient stones. The river's din condemns their impertinence as they are about to step onto the sugary stone. And this is the moment when Lime thinks things are about to go wrong.

It's no policeman, or other official, but clearly someone intent on intercepting them. The descent on the other side of the bridge doesn't look deep enough to have concealed the enormous man prior to his emergence at the apex.

*

The staff restaurant on the top floor was well-lit and had the biggest windows. Free from computer screens and the perennial lie of paperless offices, there was animated chatter, even laughter. It seemed to die a little, Lime's hearing shutting out everything other than what the man might have to say. The fact that he wore his long dark coat indoors might ordinarily keep his table free of company, but Lime sensed it was more than that. He ignored the small voice in his head advising him to go to *Brenda's Butties* and eat at his desk.

Lime placed down his tray. He wouldn't have sat in the place directly opposite even had the photo prints not been spread over both sides. The man's plate and cup had already been removed or he'd yet to eat. With his right hand he placed down two final pictures while his other arm hung below the table.

All the photographs were of the arches and the upper surface of the viaduct.

"Missing this one?" Lime handed over the photo and the noise of diners sank away as eyes, grey and bright and cold as pebbles in a stream, considered him. Lime explained it had been left in the stationery office photocopier. The turned-down mouth corners removed any doubt.

"Halfpenny, isn't it? I never forget a face."

"Even this one? Changed, hasn't it. Yours hasn't." And that clearly rankled; the thin skin around his eyes tightened.

"Round the middle I have. You ask my other half." An edgy laugh.

"Your other half?" As if he didn't know the expression.

"Yes ... Tracy."

Halfpenny's drastic loss of weight widened his bony shoulders. Hollows at the sides of his forehead looked capacious enough for another pair of eyes. Clean shaven, these days, his five o'clock shadow resembled the painted kind on puppets. Lime squirmed under the pebble-hard gaze.

*

Satisfied he's achieved the appropriate setting on his camera, the photographer sets foot onto the bridge, making no acknowledgment of the gargantuan bloke descending to meet them.

Is this a hippy gone bad? A kaftan-like garment, a kind of tent the colour and texture of the stones of the bridge, hangs from his stooped posture. Leggings are tight around massive calves. Sour milk dreadlocks conceal all but a column of face in which one eye is as white and round as the moon rising in the east.

The photographer climbs the slope of the bridge, right up to the pale bulbous arm with its granulated skin which blocks him. The sausage fingers of the other limb crook under an enormous wrinkled satchel at the hulk's flank and jangle the contents, surely coins.

His request confirms it. "*It costs to cross.*" Little stray echoes flit around deep notes. Lime desperately wants to return to his car.

The photographer looks up river and down river. "*What?*" His voice is bodiless in comparison, as from a snide teacher. He can't bring himself to look at this adversary; Lime can't look anywhere else.

133

"To cross me *bridge*." Flat northern vowels, but nothing else normal. A stamp of a sandaled foot shakes the tonnage of rock.

Lime glances for other cameras. Is this a stunt by the makers of the series? Is there someone recognisably human under the fat suit, the grotesque makeup, the gear?

"Listen," the photographer says. "I don't know what you're game is but I'm not with these film geeks. And according to that notice, nobody's supposed to be on this bridge anyway." He steps forward, and the bloke hunches lower, arms out at his sides, blocking the way. "*Ten sovereigns*." The voice buffets them like a wind.

The photographer laughs. "What's that in real money? Sounds like an arm and a leg to me. I'll give you fifty pence and we'll shake hands on it."

Lime thinks the photographer's hand will disappear in the other's should his terms be accepted. The figure transfers his weight from one foot to the other, like a child working up to a tantrum though his face is as immobile as stone. Lime feels shudders through the ground. The lump's skin doesn't seem of a markedly different texture to his clothing, or the stones of the bridge itself come to that. Nobody and nothing exists outside this confrontation, so Lime speaks to the strengthening wind when he says, "I'm heading back."

The rushing whispering crowd of the river mocks his stiff slow flight. He lifts the flap of wire netting and squeezes through.

He descends the earth wall and it seems a fortification from which military types would repel anyone trying to get to the bridge, were anyone foolish enough to make the attempt.

He waits. He knows in his singing blood that the photographer isn't going to appear, murmuring obscenities and imprecations. He feels there's nobody but him in a wide radius.

He climbs the path again, a bundle of dread inside him.

At the top of the earth wall the crosshatching of wire makes one shape, still as a sculpture, on the highest point of the bridge.

The photographer is clasped at shoulder and hip. The moon-round white eye of his captor holds Lime. Halfpenny stares at him, too. He's become a delicate beast held fast by a predator, nothing in his eyes but an expressionless acceptance of what is to be. As Lime stands frozen, overwhelmed by the futility of attempting any rescue, the massive fellow jumps easily onto the parapet taking his captive with him, another back step and they both fall out of sight.

The splash unfreezes Lime's limbs. He groans, even before he breaks skin forcing himself under the wire flap. On the bridge he looks over the side.

A marbling of red, then nothing but the water tumbling onwards, chasing what has gone. On the bridge the camera, lens smashed, the strap torn. He picks it up and its casing. Block capitals inside written in felt tip – 'Halfpenny' with no initial.

*

"What happened? You survived, I see. I went to the police. They said they'd search the next morning, took my name and I left. That was the last I heard about it." A forkful of lasagna waited at Lime's lips.

"I was found." Spoken as if it hadn't been a cause for celebration then, nor was it now.

"Christ, they might have let me know." Diners at the next table stared. He lowered his voice. "Sorry I couldn't do any more at the time."

He recalled the peevish Halfpenny before the attack on the bridge. The same expression now but attenuated.

"He was a psycho. Never saw him again after we hit the water. I was carried a mile downstream. I was concussed, covered in bruises, freezing cold and in shock when this riverside resident fished me out. That was hours later. The police were called, and a doctor. The *lady* who found me – well, I stayed. I rang relatives and told them not to come looking. Days turned into weeks and we were, you know …" Lime guessed pretty well. "Been with her ever since. We moved here not so long ago. Her shop in Firthford was on the skids and I wasn't making anything from photography, so I took the 'King's shilling' and started working in this place." As unenthusiastically as Lime by the look of him. "She's sick now, and a car smash did for my arm and leg. But we cope."

"These …" Lime said, gesturing at the pictures.

"I'm in Highways, as low down as you can get. I take photographs of progress on the viaduct amongst my other duties which I'd better return to if you don't mind." He stood, intensely dark against the diners, active and murmuring like bees in a hive.

Incurious to hear Lime's story, Halfpenny moved away. The creak, Lime now understood, was from the prosthetic limb around which his trouser leg flapped.

*

He walks the rise of the bridge and down to the far end. He's in shock even before the shout shakes the stones of the bridge and his bones. Fear like a foul liquid in his blood, his heart wants to crawl

135

out of his mouth. He turns, raises his face to the bulk of fabric and grey flesh on the hump of the bridge.

"Pay me!" The white eye nails him. The man scoops a bunch of fingers under his bulging satchel and hefts it up and down, making the contents jangle. In his other hand he clutches a wand, pink like a bent stick of Scarborough rock. He gnaws it briefly then stamps forward and Lime feels the immoveable solidity of the stone vibrate. The mouth gapes open and the teeth look like thumbs with blood on them.

Lime charges off the bridge, runs up the knoll of smooth slippery grass to the thicket at the top. He battles through it, hands cut, clothes ripping. The ground shakes under massive impacts or it's his heart battering down to his feet.

An outraged bellow, as from an instrument of brass and stone makes Lime's ears ring.

He bursts out into flat pasture. Sheep flee, prancing in time to the audible thumps of the footfall. A premonition in his bones that they will be joining the pale vertebrae of limestone pavement stretching into the distance.

He runs on the unstable floor under the slow crash of sunset-painted clouds. Heather flickers afire.

A hedge feels like metal tracery as he forces his way through it. Blacktop on the other side. It's like he's burst out of a picture in an old book of fairy tales. He sits on a milepost, eyes closed, his body shaking as if it's being passed roughly between river banks by successive pairs of cold hands.

*

Two days after the encounter in the staff restaurant, Lime was alone at the window of deserted HR. Vehicles were leaving the staff car park. Blackness under the arch that tonight not even the sodium lamplight could penetrate.

"I mentioned you to *my* other half last night."

Lime spun around. He'd been so intent on the arch he hadn't heard Halfpenny's creeping, presumably creaking, approach.

"She'd like to meet you." A slump of his shoulders as if he'd relayed a message for which he'd no great enthusiasm. Neither did Lime.

"She's housebound. We'll go now if it suits. It's a few miles. Burnsop."

Burnsop made the prospect of a visit even less appealing. "Now?" Lime finding speech at last.

"Yes. She insists. And you'll recognise her." Halfpenny refused to reveal more and Lime relented. "What's your address – I've got satnav."

"I'll direct you," Halfpenny said, having things his own way. Lime realised he'd be taking him home.

*

Inside the car, Halfpenny ran spindly fingers over the walnut dashboard. He sat high in his seat as if he weighed next to nothing. Five minutes after they'd driven off he reached his right arm across his body to indicate the left turn at the intersection, onto the viaduct, but Lime drove straight on and complained about queues. Sometime later, after Lime had swerved to avoid the hole under a road bridge, Halfpenny said, "I see you have a thing about bridges."

"Don't you?" Lime said.

*

An isolated house in a space defined by boarded shops and the blister of a mini-roundabout at a gathering of pointless roads. Close by, a house-high wall nobody had bothered to deface descended to a hollow, like a cartoon mouse-hole in skirting board. The lights of a train flashed over it as Halfpenny, his false leg no hindrance, manoeuvred himself out of the car and onto the crumbling tarmac. Feeding his key into the door, he said, "Don't believe everything she says."

Inside, a phantom pattern in the wallpaper. The linoleum took Lime's weight like teeth cracking boiled sweets. He flicked his embarrassed glance away from the sight in the front room. A woman sitting up in a double bed ended a conversation on a big cream-white cell-phone circa 1990 and placed it on the bedside table. She wore a fluffy pink nightdress. The round face, caved in at the cheeks, looked familiar.

After Halfpenny had ushered him inside, Lime accepted the woman's offer of tea.

"Wife not expecting you?"

"Partner," he corrected. The waiting silence of the pair encouraged his lips to flap banalities. "No, she's out tonight. She's a mobile hairdresser."

"You're right – mine needs doing." He'd been staring at her straggly grey hair, partly tamed into a bun. Illness had aged her though she might not be more than fifteen years or so older than him. "Have you a number?"

In his pocket, Lime had some business cards Tracy had asked him to leave in the staffrooms at City Hall. The woman took one. With any luck, she was expressing polite interest and wouldn't take things any further. If she did, Tracy, aiming for an up-market clientele, wouldn't thank him.

"Are you going to make the tea or just stand there like a lemon?" Her face was a cruel mask as Halfpenny, his face closed and unreadable, left with a violent swing of his false leg.

"Close the door would you," she said to Lime.

The water in her glass trembled. "That's the railway bridge," she said, adding, "It's close by – but not too close." Her large weary eyes peered at the card. "Tracy shouldn't be driving around alone at night."

'Tracy' from the card – too familiar. Lime wished he hadn't given the woman that toe hold into his life.

"If it can't get at you, it might get her. Have you warned her about bridges?"

Lime was shocked into taking in what was actually depicted in the photographs Blu-tacked to the walls. The viaduct, one of the arches; distortions and odd shadings in the brickwork.

"You must have gone over without paying. If you'd just gone back the way you came …" She shook her head, sadly.

Lime yellowed her hair, put little ribbons and bows in it, plumped out her face. Paste emeralds in the numerous rings – and probably the same ones as at the convention. "Martha …"

"… Hobshaw. Recognise me now do you?' She put a finger to her lips, hissed, "He's coming back."

Halfpenny came in with a tray. Lime took a mug and drank quickly. He wanted to get away. He wanted to think.

"Of course," she said, "I lived in Firthford all my life until we came to Hackfast. Small world, isn't it? Did you go in my shop, *The Magic Cell*?"

"That's 'cell' spelt s.e double-l," Halfpenny said, like a sullen teenager.

"A lot of the folks at the convention dropped by. Magic was just up their street. And I helped out on *Holmfirth Fears*. Got mentioned in the credits." With a shrug of her bony shoulders she examined the chipped green varnish on her fingernails.

"Under catering," Halfpenny said, not a scrap of teasing in his face.

"Oh, shut up,' she said, not deigning to give Halfpenny a glance.

"They based Mother Gornall on me – should have used a younger actress." Her fluttering eyelids lacked the luxuriant false lashes on display on the panel that day.

"You look more like her now," Halfpenny said.

Lime felt their dislike of each other; he and Tracy were lovebirds in comparison.

He said to the jumble of grey net-curtains, "I should be getting back. Thanks for the tea."

Halfpenny hadn't even got to sit down and he was showing Lime out. In the hallway, with the bedroom door closed, Halfpenny said, "Talk about trolls and stuff, did she? I did warn you."

"Trolls? Not exactly. So *she* fished you out of the river?"

Halfpenny sighed. "A mixed blessing." A smirk under his stony gaze, then he glanced at the closed door, alert, on guard. "She'll get suspicious if we talk for much longer. I'll speak to you again." Virtually bundled out into the street, Lime turned and the door closed in his face.

In the liquorice black hole of the railway bridge a shaking of metal fragments he couldn't easily equate with the approach of a train above.

*

Tracy was doing her accounts on her iPad in the flat. "Late for you, isn't it?"

"Gave a colleague a lift. Doesn't drive. He's disabled but he could manage an automatic."

She ceased tapping in figures and looked at him.

"Yeah, car crash. Lives with this woman." Lime shook his head forbearingly. "I was invited in. She's ill. Medication she's on has sent her off with the fairies. I mentioned you and ended up giving her your card. Sorry."

Tracy surprised him. "Don't be. Hope she makes a booking. I'd be happy to go round."

"No, don't. She's no go-getter." The kind of business women Tracy had set her sights on were only free in the evenings. "Anything she's got is going fast. On her last legs. Halfpenny's got his work cut out."

"A bit of pampering'll cheer her up."

"During the day, please, if you go. She thinks it's unwise for you to be driving around the city at night – and I agree."

"We need the money, especially with all the jobs going at City Hall. Could be you next."

"Being so cheerful –"

"Beats being stuck in here every night."

"We go out occasionally."

"Yeah, but you hate it these days – and your eccentric route finding drives me mad."

*

Entering the kitchen of the flat the following evening after working late, Lime was met by a pan on the hob, its lid panting steam, new potatoes peeping over the rim. A tuna-bake demurely turned in the microwave.

Voices from behind the closed door to the dining room. With his ear to the keyhole Lime heard Halfpenny. He tried to create the maximum shock in his vicious turn of the door handle.

Sparkle drained out of Tracy's enlivened eyes as if Lime had cast a shadow onto them. Halfpenny spoke first, his false leg stretched out under the table between Tracy's denim clad ones. "Came round to carry on where we left off."

"He won't stay to eat," Tracy said, admiring his refusal. "He's on a micro-diet – and I think it's working." 'Tell me more' in the blink of her large eyes, her fingers interlocked under her chin, mouth in a pout-smile. Lime thought the car accident had given Halfpenny a head start losing weight.

"I run too," Halfpenny told Tracy, in a for-what-it's-worth tone that patently sought admiration.

"No!" Tracy said, her delighted astonishment a bit much. His cold pebble-grey gaze should have made her shudder rather than flush. "What I mean is – that's great."

"It is," Lime said in the smallest voice he could produce short of inaudibility. Halfpenny drank in their patronising pretense of admiration; when he slapped his right thigh with his right hand it collapsed hollowly. He addressed Lime.

"Time for a drink in *The Crowsfoot*? We can compare and contrast our other halves." A wink at Tracy who said, "Don't mind me," enjoying the novelty of Lime going out to the pub with another male.

"In about an hour?" Halfpenny said, tightening the noose.

Lime made a noise in his throat which Tracy and Halfpenny interpreted as assent.

As Halfpenny was leaving she touched his empty left sleeve. "Don't forget – if Martha wants me to I can pop round, no trouble. Mates rates."

After Halfpenny had gone, Lime said, "Mate? Hope she lives up to that." Tracy didn't respond, her face slackening from former animation. Lime said, ruminatively, "So he just turns up. No invite."

"He rang the *Hair Options* number on the card. I said you'd be back before six but then you weren't. I couldn't leave him in the foyer."

"That wasn't sensible. You know him less than I do. And I know too much. He could have dropped in at HR, or rang me there. Hasn't he heard of email?"

"Oh, for God's sake. Look what he does for Martha. You'd be off like a shot if *I* lost the plot."

"Yes, admirable," Lime said tightly. "And he runs! I'd like to see that."

"I can believe it. Anyway what about those Olympians who run on blades. And I like that scruffy-chic long coat. He's like a soldier returned from the wars."

"Praise him to your clients, not to me," Lime said, wishing he had an evening paper to shake out and hide behind.

*

Lime would have rather stood at the bar in *The Crowsfoot* but Halfpenny manoeuvred him to a round table away from the mass of voices and brighter light.

Halfpenny said, sharp-eyed, "You've got a jewel, I've got Martha. Was there a fairy at your christening?" He might have a back catalogue of misfortunes, but it seemed grossly unfair to Martha, addled and sick as she was. "I mean, I'm grateful for what she did." He looked and sounded anything but. "That white-witch nonsense – well, there's bits in it that work. Me sitting here's proof of that. Actually her daft notions predate her illness. Not long after the incident she said it was a troll that got me. She said it had gone back to sleep under the bridge and she never said another word until we were here in Hackfast. Said she saw it on the viaduct when she was being taken home by ambulance one evening. She figured someone who crossed Troll Bridge without paying was living or working nearby. She demanded I bring home photographs of the viaduct for her to study. Well, anything to keep her happy. Then when I let slip I'd seen you in City Hall she put two and two together and insisted on being introduced. I bet you think we're a right pair."

Halfpenny got up, creaking like the lid of an old chest. "I'll get back. She doesn't trust me. Thinks I've got a roving eye. Well, who could blame me?"

Lime drank several shorts to get Halfpenny out of his head. Outside, he couldn't keep a straight course on the pavement. Aysgarth Shopping Centre occupied massive tiled blocks on both sides of the road. An umbilical joined them, a segmented glass tube, three floors up. No shoppers crossed now. Underneath, one person was drunker than Lime, standing in the middle of the road like that. Lime stopped, swayed, and the road seesawed, finally tipping downwards to him, at which point the overweight inebriate began a heavy tramping descent. Lime backed away from the outline growing massively until it was thirty yards nearer to him than the glass bridge. It stopped, a pale bulky shadow stained a jaundice yellow by the sodium street lighting.

"Come on, if you think you're hard enough," Lime shouted. "Hard as limestone, eh?" He laughed as it strained to come forward, but couldn't, then he turned and found another route home.

*

In bed that night Lime said, "Halfpenny never shut up about Martha. No love lost there."

"Oh *Halfpenny*," Tracy said through a great sigh. Weary of the name, not captivated by it, Lime insisted to himself.

"He left after five minutes. We never even got drinks in."

"You made up for it afterwards, though."

She faced away, like the great earth barrier before the bridge. He laid a hand on her hip and she shook it off like a cow's shudder to displace a fly.

He turned over to face the digital alarm clock, and the bed creaked like Halfpenny's leg. A padding sound. A finger on a keypad, a faint green light.

"Texting?" he said.

"Just confirming an appointment."

*

The following evening Tracy went to the gym. She'd been twice since January when they'd both joined, twice as many times as Lime. The evening after, Lime stopped by the bedroom door. Inside she was before the dressing table mirror thickening up her lashes, teasing her black hair into shape. She'd told him she was off with some friends to see a "girly movie".

Minutes later, Lime looked down to a black cab waiting at the kerb. As she was leaving he asked if she'd got her phone and she said that was a "silly question".

Once she was in the taxi, Lime watched it until it was out of sight. From the opposite end of the street someone came running, owning the road, a wide and empty thoroughfare at this time of evening – running up the centre white line. Not a jogger, not dressed for it in that long coat. A fit guy, nevertheless, gathering speed; a long striding run of ease and power.

At a dawning recognition Lime backed away then was up against the window glass to ascertain if it really was Halfpenny. When the figure turned at the junction in the direction the taxi had gone, Lime rang Tracy's mobile. He identified himself and told her to check-out the road behind.

"Just cars –"

"Anyone running?"

"No – and what if there were?"

"– I don't know. Sorry, forget it. Enjoy your evening."

"Rob –" He cut her off. The flat was three or four miles from Burnsop – and whatever Halfpenny's boast, Lime doubted he could achieve that even and potent locomotion.

Lime watched the Christmas episode of *Holmwich Fears* and froze the picture when the bridge was briefly and distantly visible. He went up close to the screen. Someone else on the bridge he hadn't noticed before, a narrow shadow in the air next to the hulking figure.

Tracy's phone had rung for most of the credits before she answered in an impatient stifled voice. "It's me," he hissed back, as if he were next to her on the cinema row.

"Damn it Rob, it's the middle of the film. What's this about?"

"You tell me, *you're* watching it." Her phone must have been on 'vibrate' otherwise she wouldn't have let it ring so long. He lied that he just wanted to apologise for earlier.

"I thought it was Halfpenny pelting along after your taxi like a para-Olympian."

"That's insane."

"Agreed." He realised he'd heard nothing but Tracy's voice. "Silent film is it?"

"Right now, yeah. I'll have to go, someone's shushing me." If they had, Lime hadn't heard it, though the next second he did hear a seat creak – if it had been a seat.

"I hope you're taking notes – I'll be asking questions later."

"Bye Rob," she said, ending the call as he began to ask her for the title of the film.

*

He left work as early as he could the next evening, a dense hot smoke of confusion and suspicion and fear filled his thoughts. Stray sights jogged his memory and guided him tentatively but surely: an alignment of mills on a hillside, a succession of factory chimneys leading to a smudged diagram of streets without road markings or paths. Hell down here in the soot and weather stains; above, on the sweeping curves of flyovers, angelic vehicles flew to the neat houses and manicured gardens of the suburbs where devoted wives put the finishing touches to evening meals.

That day he'd gone to 'Highways' to interrogate Halfpenny about his whereabouts last night. A string-tied fellow with shaving nicks clearly hadn't recognised the name and a moment later Lime had been given to understand that nobody else had. Further checks revealed Halfpenny wasn't listed in the global email address book, nor on HR's complete staff establishment.

Lime banged hard on the door until a light appeared in the fanlight. Sweet as a strawberry bonbon in her pink nightie until you clocked her face, cheekbones like babies' fists under the hollows of her eyes. She stood within a zimmer frame like a frail conductor on a podium.

"I want to speak to Halfpenny."

"Me too – you'd better come in."

An interminable time to get into the bedroom where Martha sat in a high-backed chair.

"I've discovered he doesn't work for the council in any department –"

"Course he doesn't. He works for me, monitoring the troll, taking photos."

"So he gets past Security in the mornings and wanders around and nobody notices?"

"That's right. You must have cottoned on there's something different about him?"

"What … his disability?"

Martha shook her head impatiently. "No, no. The troll took more than his arm and leg –"

"Hang on, he said he'd been in a car crash."

As Lime told her Halfpenny's version of events since the bridge, Martha shook her head, clicked her tongue, disappointed but hardly surprised at her errant partner. "The troll took his soul and put something nasty and greedy in its place, I've suspected as much for a good while now. When he was washed up outside my cottage there was more river than blood in his veins. I got him going again – no doctor could've. And he knows it. Resents the fact he owes me. Hates the fact he's a collection of body parts and bits and pieces from my box of tricks. He's not strictly alive at all: you only see him 'cos you're like a tuning fork for the unnatural after your run-in with the troll. And he's jealous. He's right to be – you've got the luck of the devil. Oh yes. Hates you for getting across that bridge scot free. I've heard him muttering about your fancy car, your lovely wife."

Lime didn't bother to correct her. "Halfpenny's right – you are out of your mind. You're both crazies. When you see him, tell him to keep away from Tracy and me or I'll call the police."

"You leave Halfpenny to me. He'll be back. He's nothing without me. It's the troll we need to concern ourselves with – and I have a solution."

"Troll? What troll?" Outside the Aysgarth Shopping Centre he'd encountered a drunk who'd tip the scales. Everything else was the residue of that trauma on the bridge.

He left her and drove home.

*

The next day he spent more time wandering around City Hall in search of Halfpenny than working. In the canteen at lunchtime, harsh winter light was a fog around everyone. A name drifted to him from scattered conversations – not "Halfpenny" but "Shilling" – in whispers and asides. Someone was "for it" in Treasurers since auditors had discovered a "Shilling" on the payroll who couldn't be traced to any specific department. Thousands had gone into his bank account which had since been "cleaned out" according to the police.

Rain that evening in racing gold droplets on the windows of HR. The viaduct looked made from tyre smoke.

Mad women, trolls and half-made men in his head as he drove away from City Hall. Horns sounded and headlights flashed around the dark circles of the failed traffic lights at the intersection. After a moment of hold-up, Lime's line moved at the behest of a beckoning policeman, hardly visible in the downpour. Lime was thinking Shilling represented a greater value than Halfpenny when he was abruptly aware of the arm sweeping his car leftwards. Towards the viaduct, he realised with a jolt. Too late to alter course now with the white van tailgating him and what Martha had said was still nonsense. In the rear view mirror he could no longer make out the figure who had waved traffic leftwards. Three quarters of the way across the viaduct he had to stop for the red light, six cars away.

A policeman in a florescent jacket was at the front of the queue looking into a driver's window, shining a slim torch. A day of strong tea in Lime's system, no alcohol or drugs. *Sitting pretty*. The forces of law and order had nothing on him. His car had passed its MOT and was fully insured.

The officer was closer. At some point he'd cast off his florescent jacket. Light duties for the heavy plod. He wouldn't be for chasing down dank alleys, tripping along rooftops. You're in a *bell* of a shape, Lime thought, a fingernail tracing down his spine. The copper had abandoned his torch, with sufficient amber light to see drivers' faces.

And this was no copper. Instantly, Lime was as damp as the bodywork of his car in the pelting rain.

An immense gleaming waterproof, a veritable tent. Rain had combed the fellow's hair into long rat-tails which dangled before his face. Getting nearer, this piece of *human* dross, this overfed tramp. Single steps took him from car to car; Lime felt each transmitted through the chassis and up his spine.

The lights were stubbornly remaining red. Heavier rain was fogging the air, grey shoots sprouting on car roofs, red taillights bleeding into it.

Three cars behind, a driver began to execute a three-point turn, exploiting a hiatus in the flow of traffic in the opposite direction. The figure straightened its back and swept back long strings of pale hair so the eye could look out, round as a moon, pale as one. Under it, the mouth stretched the length of Lime's hands pressed together, not that he had the leisure to pray. Like brass instruments distorted electronically, the cry; recognition and rage in it shook droplets down the windscreen.

Lime reversed, the over-revved engine the sound of his distress. He tapped the bumper of the car behind, which blared its horn warningly. Forward again in a wide curve into the screaming brakes of an oncoming car. One more jerk backwards, as the stamping feet shook his hands on the wheel – and he was away, whooping and laughing. To the end of the bridge he felt the impacts that would surely entail weeks more of reconstruction.

Lime drove to Burnsop. He told Martha about the thing on the viaduct, his suspicion that Halfpenny had directed him there. No apology for last night. "You said you had a solution."

"Yes, and I'd sort things myself if I could. You see it's my fault, I encouraged all those fans of the telly series to check out the bridge – I think they woke the troll. You and Halfpenny getting onto the bridge were the icing on the cake. Now he's getting stronger. Soon he won't be confined to bridges. Then you'll be in big trouble – and not just you. You must hurry. The council wants the bridge demolished. I've told them they mustn't, not yet anyway. Once the troll is safely asleep under it, where he belongs, then they can knock it to pieces and he'll sleep forever. He's a true Yorkshireman – he wants what's owed him and you have to make him an offer he can't refuse." She opened the bedside cabinet and took out a Yale key. With the utmost gravity she said, "Here's what you must do." She would have made a great Mother Gornall.

As he was leaving Lime said, "Halfpenny, can he run?"

"Like the wind for what it's worth."

*

Lime spent the next day wondering how to broach the subject of a trip to Firthford. At dinner that evening, Tracy mentioned her Mazda Sport had been serviced and the mechanic had given her some guff about it needing a good fast run to "clean out the pipes".

"How about a long drive tomorrow?"

"Yeah, okay.'" Not taking her eyes off him she picked something up from the chair beside her. "Wouldn't be thinking of Firthford would you?"

She held the FFFF booklet by a corner between finger and thumb as if it were a piece of litter off the street, but she was smiling too. "Found this under the sofa. Didn't know you were into this kind of thing."

"A long time ago. I was just sorting through stuff to chuck," Lime said, carefully enunciating the words.

"Let's do it." He hadn't seen her look this excited in months.

*

They left the city late Saturday morning. The fast A road took them along the edge of the Dales, passed small towns wedged into clefts and clinging to slopes. Dairy herds gave way to sheep, reddish millstone to limestone like dirty ice.

Lime recognised little of Firthford other than the limestone crag that overlooked it. In a genteel café Tracy giggled at the other customers, all ladies over sixty and wearing hats and speaking like they'd been displaced from the Home Counties. Oppressed by what lay ahead, Lime's smiles and attempts at conversation were forced but Tracy showed no signs of noticing.

Outside, in a maze of quaint alleys and courtyards Lime said, "I've left my wallet in my rucksack, dammit. Can you give me your car key – I won't be a tick."

The Magic Cell was in a stone flagged covered precinct. Letters were missing from the shop sign and there was a spectral whitewash in the window.

In the dusty, musty atmosphere inside he trod warily. After the troll, how could he not believe in the house spirit Martha had mentioned, set to guard the shop's secret hoard from the avaricious Halfpenny?

The white shelves were empty. Elaborately patterned carpet stuck out from the neck of a black plastic bag. His shadow slunk around him curiously as he shifted a stand with clean lozenge shapes where books must have stood on end.

He moved the loose floorboard and reached down. The metallic jangle from the cotton bag reminded him of the thing's loaded satchel on the bridge and sent a trickle of cold water down his spine. He opened it, pulled out a handful of coins.

Several hundred quid the gold sovereigns had cost her, she'd said, insurance for if she ever found herself in need of them on Troll Bridge. Genuine, if Queen Victoria's worn-down profile was anything to go by. He'd thought his dense shadow stood over him in the moment before he fled the shop, the coins stashed in his rucksack weighing like nonsense in physical form.

Tracy looked disrespectful, her Louis Vuitton bucket bag placed on a ledge of the war memorial as she spoke into her phone. Seeing him, she rang off and said, "Just business."

Lime suggested that before the clouds erased every bit of blue they go for a walk by the river.

It was slow moving and wide after the turmoil of its upper reaches. Tracy's enjoyment of the fresh air and exercise was as suspect as his own. By some tatty cottage yards backing onto the river path he stopped, brought his wristwatch to eye-level, said he wouldn't have minded seeing Troll Bridge. "Didn't get a chance the last time I was here." In two minds about seeing it now, his tone suggested. "It's getting a bit late though. Looks like rain soon – and you wanted to do some shopping."

Tracy suggested he take the car and meet her back in the village.

*

Time had stretched the distance. At unexpected junctions and forks he drove to higher ground. Shortly after a glimpse of tumbling white water he parked by the steep slope of weed-coated earth; in memory it towered higher and his lead-filled legs and lungs like old bellows thought it still did by the time he'd climbed to the top. The sight before him didn't aid his recovery.

The high wire enclosure had gone – and so had the bridge. He was in the right place; the massive coping stones at each end were still present. The river was quieter in its narrow channel. The distant line of limestone pavement looked as drab as concrete. Soporific, the turning blades of the copse of turbines that had been erected since he'd last been here.

He keyed in Martha's number, recalled what she'd said while the ringtone sounded like another river in his ear. ("Stand on the end of the bridge and rattle the sovereigns. He'll appear. He'll have to accept them. He'll sleep again under the bridge.")

Martha wasn't answering. Again nothing, after carefully dialing again. As he made his way to the lip of the earth wall the river chuckled at this back and the coins tinkled uselessly.

*

In a window of *The Crossways Hotel* Tracy was talking into her phone – or rather listening. He went inside. Noticing him, annoyance – before a smile brightened her face. "A jewel"; Halfpenny's recollected voice in Lime's ear, reminding him of what he had – a lucky devil indeed.

She slouched back, loose-limbed, as if she'd been drinking vodkas and not the half-finished lemonade before her.

"Worth seeing?"

"It's gone. Demolished."

"Poor troll. Can you have a troll without a bridge?"

He felt a crushing sensation, as if a stone was leaning against his chest.

"Never mind, Rob." Did he look as defeated as he felt? Tracy was rummaging in her bucket bag. "Got you something."

A vague regret that he hadn't thought to do the same for her was curtailed.

A knitted thing – a child's toy? "It's a troll," she said. Amusement and a look in her eyes as if observing him from a hidden place.

"I can see that," Lime said, with heavy good humour.

She showed him other things she'd bought in tiny up-market shops until he interrupted to ask if she'd like a real drink and then he'd drive them home.

She shook her head. "Let's buy a bottle on the way back – to have at the flat."

He rubbed some life into his face. "All that fresh air – I need a coffee."

At the bar he ordered a latte. When it arrived, he asked about the bridge, his voice anguished, as if at the death of loved and respected resident.

"It's a scandal, most are agreed on that." A sense of the barman wheeling out others' outrage. "Police are investigating now. There

149

have been resignations from the parish council and *English Heritage* is involved. Anyone could see a bridge like that wasn't going to fall over in a hurry. There's a rumour engineers have cooked up structural faults that aren't there. There's been talk of –" He glanced, lowered his voice. "Bribery. The name Halfpenny's been mentioned. What anyone would have to gain by knocking an old bridge down is beyond me."

"Halfpenny? Martha Hobshaw's other half? You've heard of her?"

"Martha? Course I have. But there's never been another half. Nobody could put up with her for long. I've heard the poor woman's about to pop her clogs. You'd think she'd want to end her days here, not in Hackfast."

*

Tracy drove. Stray streaks of paleness in the sky were reflected in blocks of limestone like icebergs. Would Halfpenny have ensured the bridge was destroyed for any other reason than to keep the troll active and dangerous elsewhere?

Lime sensed she was at ease with the silence that nagged at him.

"Another booking was it? Saw you on the phone in *The Crossways*."

"Should have brought my diary. Said I'd ring back from home." Recalling her animated smile, Lime assumed the client was as much a friend.

Starless black over the Dales. Smudges of limestone were like distant galaxies. Lit windows of farms floated like satellites. The interior of the car was warm; its excellent engine purred him to sleep.

The moon woke him, peeping between two vertical drapes of clouds. Ahead a cluster of lights, in which a straight-sided lump on the lit apron divided into petrol pumps.

A slow sweep into the forecourt, indicator light flashing. Habit, Lime supposed; no cars behind, and none approaching on the straight length of blacktop before a wall of hillside like an escarpment, its crest sharpened to a blade by moonshine.

She parked alongside a pump and got out. "There's a shop. See if there's a bottle of something decent. For the end to a perfect day."

It had seemed far from that to Lime, even allowing for the shock of the absent bridge. The disparity in their perceptions bothered him.

Just inside the doorway there was a glass fronted area with a circular glass grill, like in a bank. Whoever was meant to be at the till was shifting boxes in a back room.

Two free-standing shelf units running the length of the shop faced the forecourt. Lime wandered to the back where he picked up a bottle of *Pinot Grigio*.

Someone else came in, not Tracy, he could see her from around the far end of the shelf unit, still filling the big tank. A good time to try Martha's number again. *The bridge is gone, tell me this isn't the disaster it feels like.* Her number entered on his phone, he was startled to hear the ringing of a phone close to the door of the shop. Whoever held it let it ring and ring. Martha wasn't answering either. As Lime rang off, the other phone's ring ended too.

He'd been able to brush aside one coincidence, not this second; his phone was on the point of slipping out of his suddenly clammy fingers.

He looked around the corner of the shelf end again. Tracy had finished filling up and was sitting in the car, and not on the shadowed driver's side.

Not only would he be driving the remainder of the journey, she was expecting him to pay for the fuel too.

The shop door clattered and a shoe scraped on the poured concrete floor outside. Steps headed away, alternate ones creaking.

The deep breath Lime took made his head swim, and liquefied Halfpenny. Tracy didn't look and see that it wasn't Lime heading around to the driver's door.

He rushed to the front of the shop and tore outside as the car moved slowly off. He shouted, but Tracy was looking the other way – at the intruder? And too shocked to scream? Something pale flew out from the driver's window and clattered to the ground.

Lime ran and scooped up the phone. White and brick-sized – like Martha's. Faint red lines, like watermarks, stained the plastic.

The car accelerated then maintained a speed only marginally faster than Lime's as he ran. He was on the straight stretch of road now, his shouts shaken from his mouth.

Too dark to make them out inside. If there was a struggle taking place, it was having no visible effect on the straight trajectory of the vehicle.

Half way along the road, Lime, wheezing and stumbling, was catching up. Halfpenny taking pity or preparing to zoom off and gloat? Lime was almost upon the car when the engine blared and it surged forward, its demonic red taillights taunting against the immense black wall of hillside ahead. Lime ran on, flesh loose on his bones. No screams or cries. A knife held to her side?

He slowed, hands to knees. As the grating of his breaths lessened, a rattle like congested lungs. Only a door, not one of the car's, whose lights were distant and dim but not shrinking – the garage shop door.

Lime gasped a bitter laugh. The wine bottle was in his hand, unpaid for. Life went on. The garage assistant was justifiably irate on a further count with petrol unpaid for too. *Deal with this*, Lime thought wretchedly.

Hearing more now – a lapping of water. He looked over the metal barrier bounding the road. Gleams, a flowing stream, streaks of milk-white luminescence reflected the bright moon.

A bridge, I'm on a bridge. The moon stared, a single white eye, before a closing lid of cloud occluded it.

The garage assistant was an enormous bloke, the darkness made him seem to partially float though his stamping was an indication of his true weight, as well as his fury. The bridge responded, buzzing under Lime's shoes.

"*Y'owe me!*" A rock-fall of words at Lime's heels. He dropped the bottle and it smashed like a dash of laughter. He thought of the coins, in the rucksack, in the boot of the car, whose taillights watched for what was about to unfold. Would *sovereigns* have assuaged that anger? To judge from the rhythmic jangling, as of numerous tambourines, his pursuer was already loaded with coins.

Lime ran on, his shoes meeting the tarmac in a drunken rhythm, untidy faltering echoes of the larger, regular and relentless impacts which approached. He flung down some loose change in his wake, then his credit cards like the final useless hand in a game.

That he was many yards from the end of the bridge was indicated by the faint blood specks of the taillights. They disappeared completely, shortly before Lime realised that the man, his elephantine stamping closing in, must have come way past his offerings.

THE TOWN WHERE DARKNESS
WAS BORN

Whitby, at the mouth of the River Esk on Yorkshire's east coast, is one of Britain's best preserved seaside towns. In an era when most British coastal resorts are notable for how badly they've declined, Whitby is still a handsome and popular destination. And it isn't just down to the pleasing nautical architecture and pretty red-tiled roofs; Whitby is also of great historical significance.

First established as a fishing port in the early Dark Ages, it withstood numerous Viking attacks (including at least one led by the terrifying Ivar the Boneless), diversified into shipbuilding during the Middle Ages, and in later centuries became a vital cog in Britain's herring and whaling industries, memorials to which are visible all over the town. Despite that, Whitby is no anachronism. It's as popular now as it ever was, visited by an estimated one million tourists each year.

And yet the quaintness of Whitby, its timeless aura, the golden-sand beach, the mouth-watering tang of salt and vinegar wafting up from the seafront, these aren't the only things that have put the town on the map. There are also sinister undertones to life in this peaceful place – and they are not secrets. Traditions of full-blooded horror, both literary and mythical, have connections with Whitby, and the townsfolk have been happy to exploit them for many generations.

First of all, Whitby wouldn't be Whitby without its vampire connection.

The town has long played host to fêtes, conventions and guided tours organised both by and for British and overseas vampire societies, some claiming themselves to be actual Nosferatu, some content just to read about these undead entities, and others who are involved purely for the Goth-chic fashions. This all stems from a holiday held in Whitby in the year 1890, when Irish author, Bram Stoker, was making notes for a new novel, which, on its publication would make a lasting cultural impact, not just in Britain but all over the world.

That novel, of course, was Dracula.

Though this wasn't the first time a fanged blood-drinker with a penchant for predating on nubile young women had made it into print, it was certainly the most carefully written and thoroughly researched. It also introduced the prototype 'modern' vampire; the crazed beast of Balkan legend transformed into a nocturnal aristocrat, a dangerous but sensual nobleman of impeccable breeding.

Stoker took plenty of inspiration from the Yorkshire seaside town. The ruins of the Norman abbey, which overlook Whitby harbour from the East Cliff and are frequently encircled by fluttering bats, impressed him no end. The ruins feature prominently in the novel, while Count Dracula's ship is wrecked just off the coast here.

But the connection between the book and the town might actually run a lot deeper than that. It's highly likely Stoker was holidaying in Whitby when he established the name of his main protagonist and the title for his book. Stoker is known to have been inspired by the reputation of Vlad 'the Impaler' Dracula, Prince of Wallachia in the 15th century, a man given to spiking his enemies alive on sharp pieces of wood. There is no reference in written history to Vlad ever being suspected a vampire, but the Eastern European angle clearly fitted the picture in Stoker's mind, as did the notion of a feared tyrant living alone in his ghostly castle high in the Transylvanian peaks. And yet there is only one reference in any of Stoker's surviving writings to indicate that Vlad Dracula was the model for Count Dracula – when the author refers to 'An Account of the Principalities of Wallachia and Moldavia', by William Wilkinson, which he found in Whitby Library.

So there you have it, Count Dracula, the most feared and probably most desired of all literary and movie monsters, was born in a picture postcard Yorkshire town where the gentle pace of life hardly ever changes.

And yet Whitby's dreams aren't just disturbed by fictional terrors.

The town's museum contains the only known Hand of Glory in existence. Much written about in olden times, and believed to have been in use up until the early 20th century, Hands of Glory were cut from the bodies of executed murderers as they dangled from the gallows. When pickled in certain herbs and incanted over in the correct fashion, these gruesome relics were believed to possess mystical powers, not least the ability to induce unending sleep (in other words coma and death). The normal form would be for a criminal gang to secrete such an item in a lone country house, often by smuggling an accomplice indoors. The hand was set alight when the household were sleeping and its poisonous fumes would gradually engulf them, at which point the rest of the thieves would be admitted so they could pillage the property at their leisure.

154

Though historical data holds that many hanged felons were noted to be missing one of their hands when finally cut down from the gibbet, few official records mention use of these grim artefacts in the actual commission of crime, though folklore insists they were.

The full provenance of Whitby's Hand of Glory is unknown. It was donated to the museum in 1935, having been found hidden in an old cottage wall. Beyond that, nothing is known of it – whether it was ever used in the commission of black magic or commonplace murder cannot be ascertained. But it is further proof that the blood of both the innocent and the not-so-innocent has enriched Whitby's coffers.

ALL THINGS CONSIDERED,
I'D RATHER BE IN HELL
Mark Chadbourn

We are all haunted. By memories, mostly; guilt, embarrassment, white faces that loom out of the night while we lay in our beds. The vengeful revenants that drive us on to a just end. Psychologists say it is better to confront them; out of their wooden boxes so we can watch them dissolve in the bright sunlight. They're wrong. Sometimes the best you can hope for is containment. Let them out and develop a life of their own beyond your control; the repercussions are unguessable.

Kinsella had coped with it the worst. It was evident in his eyes, the tics on his face, the wild movements off his hands.

"How ya doin', Doug?" he said as if it had only been a few days since we had seen each other. "I'm coping just fine. Don't you worry about me."

He was American, but only nominally, having been sent to England by his parents to 'get an education' when he was eight. They saw him intermittently over the next eight years and then their visits stopped completely. I've followed his work in the glossies over the years, and I've always wondered if it was his family background which explained the bitterness in his writing, or if it was another little punishment inflicted by that night so long ago.

The rest of us, with our English reserve, seemed to contain the demons more effectively, but it was all a matter of degree. Sometimes, in quiet moments, you'd see our eyes glaze over, then widen and stare at inner images, or there would be laughter that went on too long, too loud.

We'd all aged. Naturally; it had been fifteen years. Kinsella's lean face had grown hollow. Carole, in contrast, had put on weight and her hair seemed like straw from too many years of peroxide. Braden was completely grey and balding on top, his skin almost bloodless. I never looked in the mirror any more.

The few drinkers in the bar of the Sheffield hotel had moved away from us long ago as if sensing our secret lives. We had a table in the centre of the room, which was already beginning to fill with empty beer bottles and drained gin glasses. Carole was smoking heavily, occasionally meeting my eye when we remembered what we had together the last time we met, then looking away in the knowledge that all those feelings had amounted to nothing. She'd made a name for herself in the women's weekly mags. *I slept with my sister's husband*, that sort of thing. She was an editor these days. Braden had headed out to the States for a white-knuckle journalistic ride with *The National Enquirer* and *The Star*. He was back in Blighty for good now and it was at his insistence that we had all got together.

"So how's the gutter press then, Doug?" When he grinned, Kinsella always showed his teeth like a model, although he looked more like a weasel.

"I'm getting too old for it now. All those late nights sitting on someone's doorstep. Hanging around seedy hotel rooms, then making my excuses and leaving. It's a young man's game." That was true. I felt more like a hundred than thirty-six.

"We've all done pretty well for ourselves, haven't we?" Carole said. I waited for the *despite*. She sucked on her cigarette, then washed it down with a grin. "Despite everything." There it was.

"We've done well in our careers, certainly. But privately? I haven't, and I bet you lot haven't either." Braden always did look gloomy, but at that moment he seemed on the verge of suicide. Nobody else met his eyes so I suppose he was right.

Out of the office, my own experience had been one long succession of misery: a failed marriage, affairs that burnt out in weeks if not days, a sea of booze and an eternity of maudlin mornings after. A life defined by the words *sad* and *pathetic*.

"How could we do such a thing?" Carole said suddenly, stabbing her cigarette out with venom.

"I don't want to talk about it now!" Kinsella snapped. He looked over my shoulder to the windows. "Can't you see? It's nearly night!"

"Maybe we should call it a day," Braden ventured. "We could go up there a first light."

"Why are we putting ourselves through all this?" I thought Carole was going to cry.

"Do you think this will be any worse than what we've all gone through over the last fifteen years?" Braden replied sourly. "We've got to do something. I don't know, find some kind of closure."

"Do you really think we'll be allowed to?" I said. Outside, the night seemed to sweep in with my words.

*

We'd never really talked about what we were going through, but we all seemed to know our experiences were the same, as if that terrible day had instilled in us some strange telepathic bond. When we had met on a calm May day at Richmond College in Sheffield, the four of us had banded together instantly, recognising something that we felt set us apart from the others on the course. In our youthful arrogance, we considered it a greater ability, perhaps, or a stronger motivation. With hindsight, I'm convinced that what we recognised was something peculiarly unpleasant in all our natures.

We were on a ten-week block release course from our various provincial papers, there to study the fundamentals of the journalist art we had chosen as a career: law, public administration, shorthand, interviewing technique, story structure. I suppose honesty and integrity were on the curriculum too, but we paid little attention to those; there was no obvious gain to our ambitions. And that was our little group's defining word: ambition. The thought of spending our days on some dreary, small-minded rag in the sticks filled us with dread. We were on the road to *big things*.

*

The knock on the door came not long before midnight, just as I had expected. It was Carole. She looked as if she had been ransacking the mini-bar, but when she spoke she didn't sound drunk.

"Mind if I come in?" She ran her hand through her hair uncomfortably. "If you'd rather be alone, I don't mind. It's no big deal. I …"

I swung the door wide and returned to the bed. She looked much older than I imagined. We all think it's time that ages the face, but the truth is it's what goes on inside the head. People can stay young for fifty years and then a bereavement turns them ancient overnight, each sour or sad thought a wrinkle, a fractional sag of muscle.

"How have you been?" I asked with honest tenderness.

"I get through each day." She sat on the edge of the bed and eyed me curiously. "Fifteen years, huh?"

"Fifteen years."

"Before that fucking horrible day, I thought we'd never be apart."

"Me too." I felt a rushing sense of the immensity of what had been lost and had to swallow hard to control my emotions. "It's funny … People spend all that time struggling to find a life-partner, all those dates, all those conversations into the night, and then suddenly you see someone and you know instantly …" My voice trailed off when I saw the tears in her eyes.

Carole crawled up the bed and nestled in close so I could hold her more as a child than a lover. "Do you think we've been cursed?" she mumbled.

"I'm in two minds. Sometimes I think that, sometimes I think we cursed ourselves. Maybe somewhere in our brain there's a centre devoted purely to morality. When it's triggered by some immoral act, it sends out a slow-acting self-destruct mechanism that ensures you can no longer be a threat."

"To what?"

"Yourself. Society. God's will. I think of it as a cancer of the soul."

"That's depressing."

"Then again, maybe she did curse us. God knows, we deserve it."

In the silence that followed, there were too many terrible thoughts buzzing around like meat flies, but neither of us could bring ourselves to give voice to them."

*

In the dark, we tried to make love, but it wasn't very effective; it felt more pathetic than erotic, two weak people clinging on to each other for support. Afterwards, Carole cried and I thought how nothing in life had ever matched up to the feelings I felt back then. I wondered how Kinsella and Braden were getting on, alone in their rooms with their own rotten thoughts.

We both drifted off uneasily; there were no dreams. I hadn't dreamt since that time. I suppose it was some kind of self-preservation mechanism. I was woken some time later by a wild thrashing in the bed beside me. A first I thought Carole was having a nightmare, but the concerned animal frenzy of her movements went far beyond that.

Somehow I managed to grip her wrists and pin her down, although she continued to heave and buck beneath me.

"Carole. Calm down. It's Doug."

I became aware of strange sounds strangled behind her clamped lips, grunts and gasps buried deep in her throat, and in a flash of insight I realised she must be choking, having some kind of fit. I crawled off her, swung her up so she was leaning against me, and tried to force her mouth open. Her teeth were ground so tight, they seemed to be welded.

Just as I was starting to panic, she suddenly yawned open her mouth and sucked in several gulping breaths that racked her body and eventually turned to juddering sobs.

"My God, what was wrong?" I asked when she had recovered enough to speak.

"Nothing's wrong with me," she replied bitterly. "I'm just coming out in sympathy. In the night, always in the night. I wake up and instantly I … empathise."

"You're saying she's doing that to you? It sounds like a psychological reaction go me," I said, attempting to comfort her.

"It was intermittent for most of the time, just enough to remind me," she continued. "But recently it's been getting more frequent. I wonder what she's trying to tell me?" And then, almost fatalistically, "I wonder where it will end."

*

The hotel reception at 5.30am had the eerie atmosphere of a cheap seaside town in the close season. A bleary-eyed young man with a sallow complexion sat behind the desk, struggling with the *Telegraph* quick crossword. Carole was already smoking anxiously; the stink of cigarettes made me feel queasy at that time of day, but I couldn't bring myself to tell her to stop. Kinsella emerged first, and then Braden a couple of minutes later; both of them looked as if they hadn't slept a wink.

"You all set?" Kinsella asked. I nodded; Carole looked away. "Who's driving? I have to admit, I don't feel up to it myself."

"I will," Braden said. "After all, this little reunion was my idea. And I suppose it has a certain symmetry."

"Do you remember where it is?" Carole asked, then bit her lip; it was a stupid question.

Braden's BMW was brand new and top-of-the-range. Fifteen years ago he was driving a light-green Vauxhall Viva splattered with primer and filler. We eased out into the deserted streets and made our way through the city centre up the steep hills on the south of the city.

"There's a chance it might not still be there. Have you thought of that?" Carole ventured. "They could have plumped a multi-storey down on top of it, or something."

"It doesn't matter," Braden said. "We can still go to the site. We can still experience feelings. We can only try to put the damn thing to rest."

"So you weren't thinking about digging her up?" I said. He gave me a steely look in the rear-view mirror.

"You know, I've been thinking," Kinsella began tentatively. "I don't want to point the finger or anything … I mean, this isn't about blame, is it? … but I wondered who had the idea. Originally." He took a deep breath. "Who set it all in motion? I've tried to remember, but that part of it's a blur."

160

"I remember being in class when the lecturers set the exercise," Carole said, staring out of the window. "There'd been a lot in the news about the homeless, and that was going to be our topic for our first field exercise. We'd already split into groups, hadn't we? We were so sure we were going to come back with the best story ..."

"And we did, didn't we?" Braden said. "Only we couldn't write it."

The car slid smoothly on to the brow of the hill and behind us Sheffield was spread out in the chill morning sun. It all looked so bright and modern and optimistic.

"You know when that lecturer held out that waste bin with all the pieces of paper in it, I thought, boy, we've really reached the pits of our career now," Kinsella laughed. "I thought we should be out exposing cheating politicians. I didn't have any time for stupid exercises." He paused thoughtfully." That was why we tried to make it into something bigger."

"I wonder how it would have turned out if we'd picked another name out of the bin," Carole mused. "If we'd had to find an interview with a social worker who dealt with the homeless, or a housing officer at the local council, like Bushey and his team did."

"Yeah, and look how boring their stories turned out," Kinsella snorted.

"We'd have found some way to twist it," Braden said. "It's in our nature."

We fell silent as we drove to the outskirts of town. A milk float trundled to a halt ahead of us, the milkman casting a suspicious glance as we rolled by, four gray faces behind glass. A teenage girl returning from some party in a short skirt and night make-up sat wearily on a front wall and smoked a cigarette. Soon the city would be waking.

"How has it affected you?" I asked them all out of the blue. Inexplicably, I felt an urgent need to know, although it hadn't seemed important before.

"Bad luck, little disasters," Kinsella muttered.

"Not that. The physical manifestation."

"You know about me," Carole said, resting a hand on my thigh. "The choking."

"Braden?"

"The smell. It comes in waves, whenever I'm on the verge of feeling happy or doing something important. You remember it? That foul odour of sour wine, dirt, vomit and urine. Sometimes it's a struggle not to be sick." I watched his knuckles grow white on the steering wheel.

"Kinsella."

At first I thought he wasn't going to answer. Then: "I see her. Out of the corner of my eye. Just a glimpse, you know. She's never there when I look full on, but it's enough to eat away at me, never let me rest. Sometimes she's slumped in the corner like that first time we saw her in the city centre. Other times she's just standing. Watching me."

"How about you, Doug?" Braden asked.

"Nothing much," I lied. They didn't pursue it; I suppose it wasn't important after all.

*

We found the place without any trouble. It hadn't changed in the slightest since the last time we had seen it, as if our actions had frozen it in time for all eternity. There had been other developments nearby – a new housing estate across the way, monotonous design for aspiring executives, and a row of insipid shops further down the road – but that prime site for builders was still a collapsing, boarded-up, double-fronted house with an enormous garden to the sides and back. It didn't make any sense; not by any rational yardstick, anyway.

We stood at the front for ten minutes, looking up at the house, not talking. Forcing ourselves to dig up all those memories we had struggled to keep buried for so long. Memories of Carole trying not to gag from the smell of her. Kinsella, taking her hand, leading her drunken legs from the car around the back of the house. Braden grinning and whispering, "Yes indeed. This will make our names."

"Do you think this will work?" Carole asked as she took the last cigarette, scrunched up the packet and threw it over the wall.

"It has to," Braden said quietly. "I don't think I'll be able to go on if I can't put it all behind me." That comment surprised me. Braden always seemed implacable, the strongest of us all.

"I can't believe we kept such a big secret for so long," Carole said. "That alone has been eating me up. I never told a soul. Did you?"

"No," I replied. "Not even my wife."

"I didn't know you'd been married?" There was a spark of passion to the question, but the thought was lost almost instantly as she looked back at the house.

"Well, we can't stand here all day." Braden led the way, retracing ancient footsteps.

We had to fight our way through self-set elders and brambles to get to the rampantly overgrown rear garden; no-one had been in there for years. Carole started to cry, silently, as if she was simply

162

expelling tears and not emotions. I didn't know what thoughts were going through her head; we were all aliens to each other as well as the rest of humanity.

"It wasn't my idea," Kinsella said. "It wasn't, you know."

We crashed through the last thicket of thistles and then stood tentatively on the rubble where the back wall of the house had collapsed. I had expected some kind of disturbing atmosphere, a creeping sense of menace, of fear and despair, but all I felt was simple desolation, magnified by the wind rustling the undergrowth and the birds in the trees.

We found the spot easily enough. It was overgrown, of course, but the mound in the relatively flat surroundings stuck out jarringly. Looking at it, the memories began to burst thick and fast, like fireworks; it was almost more than I could bear.

"What do we do now? Say a prayer?" I said bitterly.

Carole moved in close and fumbled for my fingers. "Things could have been so different. Think how lucky we were not to get caught. We didn't think it through at all. We were too wrapped up in getting a big story that would make our name. Launch us into great careers. And look at us. We got the careers anyway. All of this was for nothing."

"We weren't lucky, we were just good at being cowards." Braden squatted down and began to pull the weeds and yellowing grass from around the mound. "We couldn't face the responsibilities of our action so we covered it up. The reason we got on in our careers is the reason we did this in the first place and the same reason we've been suffering for fifteen years. Our nature. We're deceitful, underhand, mendacious, self-obsessed, arrogant, envious. Despicable."

"What's the matter with you? Did you find God out in the States?" I said with contempt.

"That's the last thing I found."

With anger fuelled by self-loathing, I watched Braden clear the mound, oblivious to Kinsella who was muttering to himself on the edge of my vision. Suddenly he lurched forward, knocking Braden out of the way, and then he began to scrabble at the solid earth of the mound like a dog digging for a bone.

"Adam! Don't!" Carole screamed. We both moved forward together and tried to haul Kinsella up, but he thrashed madly until we were driven back.

"Jesus, he's lost it," I muttered. I slumped back on a pile of bricks, terrified that Kinsella would unearth our dirty little secret, yet perversely hoping that finally it would be brought out into the open. Then a curious thing happened. For several long seconds,

163

Kinsella stopped and looked fearfully past me to the rubbled area where he had sat her down and poured the remainder of the bottle of vodka down her throat. It made the hairs on the back of my neck prickle and for an instant I almost looked round.

Carole took a few steps forward to the foot of the mound, her face wet with tears. "We're sorry. We're so, so sorry." Her voice had the strained timbre of a tired little girl. "We were stupid little kids." *A lie, I thought. Twenty-two does not qualify as childhood. That's not the best way to begin.* "It started with a newspaper cutting about some boys setting fire to an old man sleeping rough in London. All we wanted to do was bring attention to how terribly everyone treated the homeless. We wanted to make the point that if people saw them as less than human, they could inflict any atrocity on them. We thought, how could we shock people into seeing the truth? Really, we had the best intentions. But then, everything got out of hand. Someone had vandalised the phone box we were going to use to call the police to come and save you. And we'd only checked it out a few hours earlier. Then, when we drove off looking for another one, we got caught up in some disturbance, some protest on a dirty, run-down housing estate. There were riot police, people throwing stones and bottles. None of the police would listen to what we had to say. They thought we were wasting their time. But we tried, we really did. And then we drove back as fast as we could, but it was too late. Too late. We never expected it to end up the way it did. I mean, we shouldn't have done it in the first place. We just wanted ..." A sob. She composed herself and then continued with her ... prayer? Plea? Spoilt brat outburst? "Please, we just want to be forgiven. We want to forget. We've suffered enough."

I winced at that.

It was at that point that Kinsella hit something. I couldn't see what it was, just the look of horror that came over his face as the last spark of rationality fizzed out in the darkness of his head. He mumbled something, stared wide-eyed, then attempted to burrow into the mound with her.

Where was the absolution Braden had hoped for? I wondered what he was thinking, but strangely he seemed too obsessed with his nose, rubbing it, pinching it, cupping his hand over his mouth. Then he doubled up at the waist, coughing and spluttering, before turning to one side to vomit into a patch of thistles. When he looked back at me, there was panic in his eyes.

"She won't let us go," he said in a terrible creaking voice. "We shouldn't have come back. She's going to make us pay."

He clutched his mouth again and then shook his head in a futile attempt to drive away the stink of what was filling him up. As another gout of vomit bubbled out onto his chin and shirt, he looked around madly for an escape route and then launched himself into the bushes and trees.

Carole was already turning blue by the time I reached her; there was nothing I could do. I left her sprawled across Kinsella, still twitching, her eyes bulging, hands clutched to her throat.

Braden was right – we should never have come back. What did we expect? I left them there, in that forsaken acre, and made my way back to the car, remembering in agonising detail every sight and smell and sound of that awful night. The big story: concocting the why, knowing the when, choosing the who, discovering the where, the brainstorming session that came up with the what. Cold facts, no emotions. Kinsella digging the hole, chuckling, trying to second-guess the headlines.

I stumbled against a wall, raised my hands, gouged chunks out of the side of my head. It wouldn't stop.

Carole laughing. "We're just putting you to bed, sweetie. Don't worry." Braden, Kinsella and me shoveling the soil as quick as we could. Seeing a flicker of awareness surface through the drunkenness in her eyes. Kinsella saying, "I'll give it ten minutes, then I'll call."

Me, settling back on the rubble to wait, and slowly becoming aware of the terrible, terrible sounds. Snorts, snuffles, choking, then those stifled screams turning to coughs as the soil filled her mouth. Checking my watch. Worrying if the neighbours would hear. Cold sweating. Checking my watch. Hearing the sounds grow less and less. Feeling the rising panic. Pacing about. Checking my watch. And then the silence, even worse than what I had heard before.

My head is filled to bursting, my thoughts like radio static in the night. Somehow I find the car, lean against it, pull myself inside. I try to compose myself.

The final scene is frozen in my mind for all time, however long that will be. The four of us, standing in the moonlit garden, staring at the silent mound, thinking we should have been heroes, the team that rescued a homeless woman from sick local bastards who had buried her alive for sport. Thinking how we would get out of this mess. Thinking of our careers hanging by a thread. Thinking of everything apart from that poor woman.

If we had dug down then, we might have saved her. That's the worst thing. She still might be alive, and we might have escaped the torment of the last fifteen years. Instead, we drove away and after the course was over never spoke of it again.

But I couldn't forget what we did; she wouldn't let me. Those dirt-choked final cries filled my head when I was making love, when I was walking up the aisle, every time a little bit of happiness threatened to squeeze into my life. Yet somehow there was just enough respite from the harrowing to muddle through my days. Now, instead of Braden's absolution, she has released the full weight of punishment for our crime.

Was she waiting for us, I wonder? In the full knowledge we would be unable to resist returning for some relief from our pain? I didn't think it could get any worse, didn't think I could feel any more guilt. But now her screams are with me constantly, just on the edge of my hearing, trapping me in that moment of horror and despair for the rest of my days. I see a bird on a wall, its beak open in morning song. I hear screaming. I see a businessman shouting a cheery goodbye to his wife as he sets off for the day. I hear suffering.

I will never experience a quiet, peaceful moment again.

Unlike the others, I still have my life and sanity. I suppose I could attempt to carry on in some way, but I can't take the guilt. All things considered, I think I'm better off dead, better off with whatever damnation faces me in the afterlife than this agonising suffering here.

Finally. After all this time. All things considered.

A FEAST FOR CROWS

The North of England has witnessed some of the most savage battles in British history, many fought to resist invasion by enemy powers and thus shedding blood on an unparalleled scale. Yorkshire played host to at least two of these. In 1066, at Stamford Bridge in the East Riding, King Harold Godwinson destroyed the marauding Viking army of Harald Hardrada, killing an estimated 10,000 Norsemen on the day and losing 6,000 warriors of his own. In 1138, at the Battle of the Standard in the North Riding, English forces repelled David I of Scotland, 12,000 of whose troops were slaughtered on the battlefield.

But even these massacres pale to insignificance compared to a Yorkshire affray fought on March 29, 1461 – Palm Sunday, of all holy days – between rival factions of Englishmen.

It was the height of that prolonged conflict, the Wars of the Roses, and though it was an unseasonably cold March morning, with driving snow, it saw two vast armies – the Lancastrians under the Duke of Somerset, the Yorkists under Edward, Earl of March – square up to each other on a desolate moor near the village of Towton, in the North Riding. There were about 80,000 participants in total, both sides equally matched, fielding even numbers of footmen, heavy horse and archers, the latter group equipped with longbows and the all-penetrating bodkin-tipped arrows.

What followed was a bloodbath worthy of any fictional horror story.

The details of the actual combat are complex, consisting of repeated cavalry and infantry charges, feints and counter-feints, but basically boil down to a relentless clash of blades as knights and men-at-arms engaged for the whole of that day in the most bitter hand-to-hand fighting imaginable, while the bowmen of both sides rained death on each other until they were out of arrows. Aside from longbows, other terrible weapons were used: long-swords, poll-axes, maces, flails, falchions, war-hammers and billhooks. Eyewitnesses described the most horrendous and protracted combat waged amid rivers of blood and heaps of butchered corpses. Only by late evening, after an approximate ten hours of nose-to-nose fighting, and with the Lancastrians on the verge of victory, did Yorkist reinforcements arrive under the Duke of Norfolk and alter the balance of power. The Lancastrian left collapsed, and the Yorkists took full advantage, turning the ensuing retreat into a one-sided rout. Countless Lancastrians were ridden down from behind as they fled, while entire companies drowned attempting to cross the freezing Cock Beck in their armour. Even then it went on; prisoners who fell into Yorkist hands were summarily executed – either by having their heads cut off or their skulls split down the middle.

Towton was such a frenzied affair that tragic accounts of brothers unknowingly killing each other, fathers killing sons and vice-versa, seem entirely plausible. The ultimate victory went to the Earl of March, who was so galvanised by success that he drove on to dethrone the Lancastrian king, Henry VI, and have himself crowned as England's first Yorkist monarch, Edward IV. But the cost of his triumph staggered even the war-scarred world of the Middle Ages.

According to poets of the time, it was "a true feast for the crows of Yorkshire".

Never in the written canon of English history had so many been slain in one day. Even modern estimates put the death-toll at an astounding 40,000 – many more than the British Army's losses at Waterloo, and almost twice as many as the British servicemen killed on the first day of the Somme. But it doesn't end there, because official casualty lists compiled in medieval times often failed to take account of common soldiers: squires, serjeants, yeomen and the like. So when some contemporary chroniclers claimed the death-toll was at least 70,000, even they may have been underestimating the true extent of the calamity. Of course, even if the lower estimate is more accurate, it is still too horrible to contemplate given that most died in the melee of close-quarter battle, in other words were hacked, slashed and dismembered where they stood.

Towton field is an eerie place even now, windswept and neglected, crows and ravens still playing unhealthy attention to its wild, wind-blasted grass. Despite the presence of ominous grave-mounds near the river and local names like 'Bloody Meadow', only a single stone cross, thick with moss, marks the spot. It is a mystifying fact that most passers-by are completely unaware of the gruesome events that once occurred here on the most violent day in English history.

THE DEMON OF FLOWERS
Chico Kidd

W hat does 'Yorkshire' make you think of? Men in flat caps, sheep, tea, cricket, Nora Batty? Whatever it is I'm pretty sure it's not the reason I moved to the other side of the world to avoid ever having to go back again. Not that there's much chance of that, although given a choice I'd have dropped a bomb on the place. Probably wouldn't have done any good. That thing is inexorable.

But I'm getting ahead of myself.

My family is not huge, but it's spread around a lot. (I'm talking continents here.) I'm no exception. A while back, when I was living in San Francisco, I had an email from a firm of solicitors in Leeds.

It looked like spam and I nearly deleted it unseen. That would have solved a lot of problems, but no, I read the damn thing, because the subject was Re: Estate of Theodora Esther Dickinson. Theodora isn't a name you see very often, and it was the real mod moniker of my Aunt Teddy. She'd been an eccentric presence in my childhood, but had been ostracized by the family for some reason when I was about ten or eleven years old.

Turned out that the reason the family had disowned Aunt Teddy was because she'd found herself a Daddy Warbucks type to get spliced to and inherited squillions when he kicked the bucket. And now I seemed to be the only one in the family who hadn't done the 'Go and never darken my door again' thing, she'd left me a bunch of cash. Her own sprogs (my cousins!) and their families got most of it, of course, but Auntie's bequest was enough to come in really handy.

She didn't request my presence at the funeral, but I decided to go anyway. Curiosity may have killed the cat, but let me tell you one thing – never respond to anything that looks like spam, because even if it's for real, there's never a good ending.

After a fifteen-hour flight to Heathrow I needed a rest, so I took a room in a fairly awful airport hotel and tried to phone my cousin David, to no avail. I left a voicemail and went to bed. It took me most of the next day to get to Leeds, without any response from David. The solicitor's office was closed when I arrived, and I ended up in the little town that housed my long-lost relatives far too late to make myself known.

I expected a picturesque hamlet, but the little town appeared to have been built in the sixties and was comprised of a few former farmhouses, a couple of pubs, and rows upon rows of identical houses. Its only claim to fame was a ruined and mostly-brambled pile of stones and tumbled vaults, which I was to learn rejoiced in the name of Flowers Abbey. Well, they have a Fountains Abbey; why not Flowers? Nearby stood a small mediæval church and a hall of the same vintage as the town of little boxes.

In the morning I was soon overwhelmed with cousins and/or second cousins and various other relatives some times removed, all of whom sounded like Sean Bean, including sixteen-year-old Josh. I'm one of those people who finds it hard to resist echoing other people's accents, but I made a gallant effort to refrain from doing my 'It's grim oop north' voice.

Truth to tell, it wasn't all that grim oop north. The sun was shining and the breeze was balmy. Daffodils bobbed their yellow heads, and the hedgerows were full of primroses' charming pale little faces. The trees were acquiring a mist of green, and the boxy houses mostly seemed to be inhabited by a green-fingered tribe. Seemed appropriate, for the Abbey of Flowers.

Aunt Teddy, it appeared, was not to be buried in the ancient churchyard, since the church had recently been deconsecrated. Sneaking a glimpse, after the cremation, under the dusty ancient yews, I couldn't see a single inch that wasn't full of sloping gravestones, mossy mausoleums or wonky crosses, so there probably wasn't any room anyway.

We were milling about in that aimless way that people do between funeral and finger sandwiches, nobody really wanting to eat at eleven in the morning.

"Dora said you like ghost stories." I turned to see which Sean Bean soundalike was addressing me, and found young Josh. Still a little strange to hear all these Yorkshire accents calling Aunt Teddy 'Dora'.

"Well, I *write* 'em," I replied.

"You know M. R. James?"

"Couldn't call myself a fan if I didn't."

He nodded. "So you know the one about the church with the haunted tomb. *Incident of Cathedral History.*"

The pedant in me made me say "Episode."

"Yeah, whatever. We got our own haunted tomb, in t' church."

"Really?" I said, interest piqued.

"Come on." He headed into the overgrown graveyard. Seen up close, the little church was unimpressive, a kind of tick-the-boxes mediæval structure. It hadn't yet acquired the forlorn air that most deconsecrated churches have, but it already seemed a little wistful.

Inside it proved to be a veritable jewellery box. On that sunny day the stained glass let in a vivid riot that spattered the pews and grey stone floor with colour. Extravagant carvings filled the interior, pillars turned into trees with all manner of birds and beasts peeping out from behind their leaves, not to mention more than one Green Man. It was clean and smelled of furniture polish.

"Yorkshire Heritage's taking care of it now," said Josh. "And that's our haunted tomb."

It stood at the back of the church, a monolithic slab of a thing. It wasn't simply a contrast to all that exuberant decoration – it sucked the joy out of it. Looking at it made me feel as if the colour yellow had been abolished.

"Jesus." I sidled closer to read the inscription on the tomb, somehow reluctant to approach it openly. It was, of course, in Latin, and my knowledge of Latin is vanishingly small. It's a long time since O-levels. "What's the story?"

Josh shrugged. "Just supposed to have a demon inside. Not really a ghost story."

The tomb was surrounded by a small fence comprised of two-foot-high posts linked by chains. The iron posts were quite plain, but the chains looked like they were made of thorns. I suddenly, urgently, wanted to be elsewhere, so I turned away from the horrible tomb and walked quickly out into the sunshine. The day was utterly still, and the warmth had turned a little oppressive.

"Better go and stuff ourselves with sausage rolls," I said, and headed toward the church hall. As we approached, a wind came out of nowhere, a ridiculously strong wind that tugged at my hair and clothes.

"Whoa!" exclaimed Josh. "Let's get indoors."

"Wait." I've no idea why I stopped him, but we stood there in a kind of limbo for a second looking in at the windows of the church hall. I saw my cousin David approach the left-hand one and lean forward, suddenly still. Had time to see that his face and upper torso had somehow penetrated the glass while the rest of the people in the room were milling around in panic behind the right-hand window. The next second the glass turned to dust and so did the people, blown away on the gale.

David and his window followed suit a moment later.

That sudden stillness before everything went to hell transfixed me: I had witnessed the moment of his death. Then I just turned and ran, stumbling out of control, forward momentum keeping me just one step ahead of falling flat on my face. I am a runner with a few

171

marathons under my belt, but this was no long-haul race, it was a full-scale panic-driven flight.

I staggered to a breathless halt within the ruins of the old abbey, and leaned against a rough pile of stones that was all time and ruin had left of a wall. Josh pitched up a little later, while I was getting my breath back.

"What was the story on the demon?" I yelled at him. He looked blankly at me, scarlet in the face and panting.

"You run like bloody Usain Bolt," he gasped. I cast around wildly, not sure what the hell I was looking for. Something that turns people to dust? What does that look like? I wanted to duck down behind the remains of the wall. I wanted a weapon that would take it down, whatever it was. Ideally, I'd never have left San Fran and was looking at the Golden Gate flying in the fog.

"The demon, Josh!"

"I don't know! Dora was the one knew all the stories. Summat about wanting kids…" That made no sense. The church hall had been filled with adults. "They tricked it onto hallowed ground and sealed it up in t' tomb."

And the church had just been deconsecrated. Josh was running his hands through his hair. I thought he was going to tear it out.

"Josh. Josh! Stay with me. Focus."

"Jesus, cuz. I'm freaking out here! I just saw Dave *die!*"

"I know, mate," I said. "I did too. I'm having a hard time believing it. You think we might find something in Ted – Dora's stuff?"

"Yeah, I guess so."

The bigger question was whether we could summon up to nerve to actually go and find it. We crept nervously along the wall and peered round the corner. Josh was still breathing like Darth Vader. Both of us jumped like jackrabbits when someone called our names.

If I'd actually had that big honking anti-demon gun there would have been one less clergyperson in the county of Yorkshire. Not being of a religious nature, I'd shaken the vicar's hand after the funeral and noticed only the fact that she was a she. Now she was visibly rattled, but unlike me, she was toting a shotgun.

"Sam Thorne, in case you didn't catch my name earlier," she said.

"You got silver shot in that thing?" I asked, a little hysterically.

"Insurgents are insurgents." She smiled grimly. "I assume you've heard our local ghost story."

"Parts of it," I replied, glaring at Josh. "We were just going to see if my aunt had anything that would help."

"You might be better off closer to home," the Rev said. "Did you see the inscription on the tomb?"

"My Latin's not up to much."

"Me neither." She stuck a hand in her pocket and brought out a page torn from a spiral-bound notebook. "This is supposed to be a translation."

It said: "Look to your children when men turn to dust. / Bind it with thorns and the bones of the just./ Seal it on hallowed ground, with holy water all around."

"Bones of the just?" I muttered. "Not exactly Wordsworth."

Rev Sam looked at us as if she wanted to knock our heads together. "Theodora's ashes. Come on, people, work it out. This thing, whatever it is, demon is a useful enough name for it, escaped because the church was deconsecrated. Here we have a recipe to put it back in jail."

"Where's the nearest hallowed ground?"

"Anywhere you like, Josh. I'm the vicar, remember?" She gave another of her fierce grins. "In fact, let's do the show right here!"

Amongst the brambles we marked out a grave-shaped space using fallen white stones that had once been the walls of an abbey, an exercise that left us running with sweat and scraped of hand. Josh joined in without complaint. Perhaps he hadn't realized that he was going to be bait. I wondered why the demon preyed on children. Probably better not to speculate on that. Better to bind the thing before it got rid of any more adults.

"Any idea what we do next?" I asked the Rev, who had just finished blessing the ground, or whatever it was she did to hallow it.

"No clue," she replied. "We're not officially supposed to believe in demons, let alone try to catch one."

Helpful.

"Well, I've got an idea," ventured Josh. We both looked at him, and he flushed. "I'm not an idiot. I know it's me that t' demon's after, so why don't I just, you know, call it?"

"Don't we have to know its name?" I said.

"How many demons do you think there are running about Yorkshire?" snapped Rev Sam. "Go get your aunt's ashes and a bottle of water. Josh, stay here with me."

"The urn's in the church hall." I was not at all anxious to revisit that particular building, but she shot me such a withering glance that I trotted off obediently. Speed seemed to be a good idea.

Far from being deserted, the church hall was surrounded by police, sundry busybodies and rubberneckers, and a Do Not Cross tape. I managed to avoid attention, which wasn't difficult as nobody seemed to have a clue what they were doing, and snuck in the back. Grabbed Aunt Teddy and ran back to the others.

I was almost too late. As soon as I got within earshot I heard Rev Sam yelling something in Latin, and ran round the corner to find poor Josh writhing on the ground and making an awful noise, something between choking and screaming. His jeans were covered in blood. The Rev was holding his hands, but he was thrashing around so much that she couldn't hold him. One hand came loose and clouted her hard on the side of her head.

"Hold on!" I called, stupidly, and charged towards them. Only to meet some invisible obstacle painfully hard and bounce back. I lost the bottle of water, and the urn flew out of my grasp and crashed to the ground, I watched in horror as the lid came off. I've never had occasion to wonder why urns are that shape, but turns out when they roll around on the ground they are bottom-heavy. The ashes stayed put. The Rev loosed her grip on Josh and seized the bottle of water, doing some on-the-fly hallowing over it before tipping holy Evian over Josh.

He went still. The air above him distorted into a disturbed, shivering maelstrom. Rev Sam shouted more Latin at it. I tried again to get to them, succeeded this time and ran to Josh. He was breathing, but cold as ice. I hastily stripped off my jacket and put it over him. The Rev finished speaking and the air calmed.

"I have no idea whether that worked," she panted, "but throw the ashes onto the grave."

I did so, despite hearing a voice that she seemed unaware of. The ashes curved in a great arc over the plot, and something said in my head *I know you, and I know your kin.*

It follows me, around the world, and children suffer. I've been living on a remote island in New Zealand for a while, but last time I went to the mainland for supplies people told me there had been an "unexplained incident" with a local boy.

Time to move, again.

CITY OF THE DEAD

York is one of the great cities of Northern England, and long has it held that status. It is two millennia old, was the administrative centre of a powerful Roman state and the armed capital of two different kingdoms. It has witnessed major political events throughout the history of Britain, and is today regarded as a site of significant social and cultural importance.

But like all major cities, there were grim episodes in its past.

From the Viking wars of the Dark Ages to the anti-Jewish pogroms of the 12th century, from the tit-for-tat slaughters of the Saxon revolt against the Normans to the Parliamentarian siege in 1644, which ultimately led to massive loss of life at the battle of Marston Moor some six miles away, this grand old metropolis has stood in the midst of bloodshed for generations.

Little wonder it is regarded by many as the most haunted city in Europe.

York's ghost stories are, to be frank, innumerable – far more than could be recounted here – and appear to date from all the ages of England's past. Some are very well known – the Roman legion allegedly seen marching through the basement of York Minster for instance, or the 'Grey Lady', the mournful shade of a bricked-up nun said to visit various theatres in the city.

Others are less famous, but no less mysterious. The ghostly child who regularly appears at funerals hosted by All Saints Church, or the unknown teenage girl said to gaze from mirrors in the different buildings along Stonegate. Inevitably, some possess the air of tragedy – the Jewish blood that manifests on the floors at Clifford's Tower, where the 1190 massacre took place, or the form of Mad Alice, a mentally ill woman who was hanged in 1825 and who supposedly still weeps in Lund's Court (formerly known as Mad Alice Lane). York also boasts some of the eeriest spirits. The decapitated shape of Thomas Percy, executed for treason in 1572, has been spotted in the yard of Holy Trinity Church, allegedly hunting for his severed head, while a popular city centre pub has been disturbed by terrible screams from its cellars, which date back to the 1640s, at which time they didn't just house wounded Civil War troops but were used as the 'amputation rooms'. Even the terrifying barguest – or 'hill-ghost' – a ghastly dog/man hybrid of weird pagan tradition, has been seen prowling the precincts around the Minster late at night.

It is little wonder that York's many ghost-tours are among the liveliest and best subscribed in the UK. But one doesn't need to see a ghost to experience the supernatural in this place. With its ancient walls, antique buildings and its warren of narrow, medieval alleys and courts – known locally as 'snickleways' – York has more than enough atmosphere to satisfy any number of sensation-seeking paranormalists. And it still does, every week of every year.

THE SUMMER OF BRADBURY
Stephen Bacon

I must have told this story a hundred times over the years, and still I don't fully understand what happened that day. Yet I can still recall with absolute clarity every detail of it, despite the passage of time.

That summer seemed endless. The heatwave lasted throughout all of June, July and August, turning the grass brown and brittle, warping the felt roof of our play-den, fraying the tempers of the townsfolk. To us kids it was a dream come true. The previous winter I'd discovered Ray Bradbury. My mind had been filled with cupolas and orchards, lightning rods and Dust Witches.

Bradbury offered me an escape from the humdrum monotony of the Yorkshire mining village in which I lived. I'd spent rainy school holidays in my bedroom, reading *Dandelion Wine* and *The Illustrated Man* and *Something Wicked This Way Comes*, imagining that I too lived that carefree life of small-town America.

And that summer Renfield actually felt like it could be Green Town, Illinois. It hadn't rained since May. Britain sweltered under record temperatures. A constant aroma of melting road-tar seemed to permeate the air. Brown arid fields surrounded Renfield, transforming the usually-patchwork Yorkshire scenery into a desert-like vista. Zealous newsreaders took great delight in reporting the widespread hosepipe ban. One of our neighbours' dogs had been driven crazy by the merciless heat, and the RSPCA were called into action. Renfield enjoyed a steady whir of lawnmower engines, basked in the heady smell of freshly-cut grass. There was even talk of some towns having to resort to standpipes due to the water shortage.

On the day it happened I was in my room, writing in my notepad with a fountain-pen – a birthday gift from my parents. It was 11am, a Tuesday; the fifth week of the summer holidays. I could hear the radio playing downstairs. The window had been flung open. Blue skies stretched forever. I happened to look up and see Fiona, the twelve-year-old girl from further up the street, sitting on the kerb opposite, chalking on the pavement. I stood and leaned out of the window, shouted her name. She just glanced up and smiled but her eyes looked cheerless.

Dad was at work. Mum was hanging out the washing in the back garden. There was absolutely nothing to indicate this day would be unlike any other.

A few weeks previously, my Uncle Terry had been diagnosed with late-stage emphysema; he wasn't expected to make it beyond Christmas. Since then Mum had shuffled around like she was in a trance. A few times I'd noticed her staring into space; I imagined she was reliving the childhood she'd enjoyed with her only brother. His imminent death felt like a black cloud looming on the horizon. I decided to go outside and talk to Fiona.

She glanced up as I approached, tucking a stray piece of hair behind her ear, wrinkling her nose like she did when one of us was teasing her. But her face looked pale. I thought at first she was outlining a hopscotch grid with the chalk but it was obvious she was just doodling on the pavement.

I sat down beside her. The kerb felt hot through the fabric of my shorts. There wasn't the slightest breeze to disturb the air. An aeroplane droned overhead, its cotton-wool contrail marking a line across the brilliant azure sky.

"Heyup, how's it going?"

She smiled an empty smile. "Not bad." She continued to chalk on the pavement.

This was weird. Fiona was one of our gang. She hung out with us, climbed the same trees as us; sometimes even slept out in the club den we'd built by the reservoir. To see her as listless as this was unsettling. "Owt wrong?" I asked.

She shrugged. "Just belly ache."

I nodded. It was the heat. It sapped the energy, killed your hunger. There wasn't a cloud in the sky. I couldn't imagine it ever raining again.

"Seen the others?"

"Erm – yeah, earlier. They're up at the den. I think Lee's got a new glider."

This brightened my mood. A glider was always a great source of fun. Lee had broken his last one when it had overshot the park fence and landed on the road. Balsa was no match for a car's wheel.

"Wanna head up there?"

She nodded. "Not on bikes, though." She clutched her stomach to illustrate why.

We set off along the track that threaded between the houses. There was an area of waste-ground beyond the estate that extended about a quarter of a mile up the slope towards the reservoir. Our feet raised dust from the dry ground. Lately I'd been mocked for referring to my trainers as *sneakers*, for calling the stream that ran through the middle of the woods as a *creek* – Bradbury's words, which romanticised them beyond their mundane normality. I'd even come to think of the woods as a *jungle*, but had known better than to vocalise that thought. Well that morning I noticed that my *sneakers* were coated in dust. But I trusted it wouldn't slow me down.

We walked in companionable silence for a while. I tried to throw sidelong glances at Fiona. Recently I'd begun to notice aspects of her to which I'd previously been oblivious: her tanned legs seemed that little bit longer, there was shape and definition to her upper body. She looked nice. A small part of me felt embarrassed for harbouring such thoughts, but it was an exhilarating feeling nonetheless.

The walk took about ten minutes, though usually we made the trek on bikes. Whilst I wanted the journey to go slow so I could savour my time alone with Fiona, I was eager to see the state of the reservoir.

All that summer we'd taken great delight in walking up to the peak of the hill and gazing down at the ever-diminishing water level; marvelling as, week by week, more and more of the reservoir's shale bank had been exposed. The valley in which the reservoir was built had originally been a neighbouring village – Bowerton – and had, in the '40s, been purposefully *drowned,* once the council had transferred the inhabitants to a newly-built housing estate in Renfield. The reservoir's expansion had been a necessity, to serve the vast growth that post-war Sheffield had undergone. My grandfather told the story of how the villagers had all gathered one cold morning in March 1946, and watched the dam gates being opened further up the valley, allowing the water to flow into the lower section of the reservoir. By then most of the original buildings had been demolished – except for the church, the primary school, and the majority of the central structure that made up the pub. Apparently the image of the water rising above them was an unforgettable sight.

Sometimes I thought about what lay beneath the water, my imagination conjuring sunken buildings and creepy, weed-filled rooms. The idea that people once lived their lives in a place that was now submerged felt evocative, fertile, terrifying.

I was breathless by the time we reached the brow of the valley. We'd been up three days previously and the level had been lower than I'd ever seen it; the clock-tower of the crumbling church just visible above the water. Now there was more shale exposed as the reservoir's volume had receded even further. The concrete wall at the head of the valley looked ridiculously high. I squinted against the sun and stared out across the reservoir, my eyes drawn instantly to the crumbling structures that protruded above the waterline. As well as the church's clock tower, a section of the school's hall had now been revealed, like the exposed skeleton of some fantastical beast. It looked surreal.

For a few minutes we surveyed the view. I felt infinitely sad, my thoughts turning inexplicably to my Uncle Terry. Fiona's breathing was heavy next to me. Somehow I had the impression she wasn't just breathless from the walk up here. I was conscious of her nearness. I could smell the feminine aroma of her deodorant.

She turned to me, breaking the reverie. "C'mon, let's find the others."

Our den was built further along the ridge, in a copse of trees that overlooked the reservoir. It had originally been an abandoned shed which we'd appropriated for our personal use. Its single glass window was still intact. We'd carefully constructed a screen of bushes around the den in an effort to conceal it from curious eyes. Not many kids played up here. The wire fence that ran around the perimeter of the reservoir was adorned with numerous signs warning of the dangers of deep water.

I tried to make small talk. "Seems a long way up here when we don't have us bikes."

Fiona nodded. She seemed distracted.

I continued. "They're on about riding over to old man Wilson's orchard on Saturday."

She pursed her lips. "I might give it a miss. Apples'll only give me a worse gut-rot."

"Yeah, I s'pose." I hoped she couldn't hear the disappointment in my voice.

"To be honest, I'm thinking of giving the club a miss for a while ..." She glanced at me sharply. "Sometimes them lot can be ... a bit *immature*."

I nodded slowly. Maybe she'd looked more grown-up lately because of those telltale signs of her distancing herself purposefully from us – her jeans had been less grass-stained, she'd sustained fewer cuts and scabs to her legs. It occurred to me that her body-language had become awkward, like she felt self-conscious hanging around with us. Another piece of my heart crumbled.

We'd reached the den, ducking beneath overhanging branches as we approached the door. The dry grass crackled underfoot. Flies buzzed at the periphery of my view. There were two wooden steps leading up to the door and I noticed the padlock fastened across the handle and locking-sash. I reached under the top step and fished the key out from its hiding place. As I gripped the padlock to insert the key I experienced a huge static shock from the metal. My tongue tingled and I felt the tiny hairs on my forearms bristling. The air seemed heavy and damp. I unlocked the door and we entered the den.

It was stifling hot in there. There was a smell of body-odour and stale farts. Lee's glider was lying on the floor next to a stack of *Dandy* and *Beano* comics. There was a pack of Top Trump cards already dealt out into four neat piles.

Fiona dropped down onto one of the beanbags. "Wonder where they are?"

I shrugged, and propped open the door to allow fresh air to circulate with the warmer air inside. "Sure you're all right? You look a bit funny."

"Remember that talk we had at school?" Fiona exhaled loudly. "About ... puberty and stuff? Well soon we'll all start going our separate ways probably. It's just part of growing up."

I didn't know how to reply. This was the last thing I wanted to hear. Our gang felt incredibly important to me. We were a strong unit. As an only child, the gang were the brothers and sister I never had. I loved each member like a sibling. Unconditionally. So to hear Fiona voicing such thoughts left me dismayed.

She continued. "Mum says it happens to lasses earlier than lads so you lot'll probably start to get fed up with the gang next year anyway."

I felt puzzled. Comic books and bikes and climbing trees and playing soldiers on the field – that was my life. It was inconceivable that I'd ever get fed up with it. When I wasn't physically participating in those tasks, I was still thinking about doing them. I felt sure she was wrong.

Just then I heard a frantic chattering of birdsong from outside. I stood at the door and watched as a flock of starlings swarmed into the branches. Their behaviour seemed unnatural. Fiona must have seen my expression because she said, "What's up?"

"Don't know." I moved down the steps onto the ground. The birds had fallen silent once more. I could hear from somewhere distant the jangling chime of an ice-cream van. I guessed it was down by the picnic area that backed onto the reservoir. The air felt muted, like we were insects trapped in a killing jar. I stared at the blistered trees and inhaled the breath of summer, all sweet fruit and dry grass, my view waved on by buzzing flies and skipping butterflies. The contrast between the trees' shadows and the shafts of sunlight filtering through them was startling. I could hear someone swishing through the long grass nearby.

"Sean's here," called Fiona from inside.

He appeared a few seconds later through the bushes, red-faced and panting. His eyebrows rose as he spotted us. "I need the torch. Quick."

He pushed past me and blundered into the den. I felt the heat radiating from him. He began rummaging through the contents of a cardboard box.

"Where's everyone?" I asked.

He looked up as if noticing us for the first time. "Guess what? – we've found a tunnel down there. I need the torch."

Fiona leaned forward on the beanbag. She finally looked enthusiastic. "Where?"

He waved generally in one direction. "The reservoir." He threw a few *Action Man* figures aside and held up a torch. He flicked it on to test the batteries. "C'mon, I'll show you."

A boy-shaped maelstrom had entered our lives, disrupting the calm fabric of our certainty. I glanced at Fiona. The sunlight limned her shape. For the first time I saw the figure of a young woman instead of the tomboy she had been.

We headed out of the den, pausing only to lock the padlock and secrete the key beneath the step. There was a faint breeze stirring the surrounding bushes, giving the impression of something unseen moving through the trees. Sean led the way, explaining as he shuffled ahead. "The water's even lower now. We noticed, soon as we got here." He pointed across the reservoir to the distant bank. "Dec spotted summat. Remember that ladder we saw going into the water? Well it ends at a tunnel in the wall."

We hurried after him. This high in the valley you could see for miles. In the distance I spotted the unmistakeable outline of the Renfield Colliery winding wheel, and the discoloured slag heap beyond it. Until recently my Uncle Terry had worked there. The structure was an imposing sight. Black clouds seemed to be massing in the sky over towards Doncaster. I shivered instinctively, despite the heat.

"There's summat in the tunnel," said Sean. He spoke at the same moment I shivered so I wasn't sure whether it was the environment or his words which had the effect. Fiona blew her hair away from her face like she hadn't heard.

He explained as we walked. They'd gone up to the den to hang out; maybe play cards, throw the glider, read some comics. One of the lads, Dec, had noticed the freshly-exposed tunnel as he'd been messing about with the binoculars. Curious, they'd ventured out to investigate. Mikey had been the first to dare to climb down to the tunnel. The others had waited at the top. Eventually they'd grown impatient and had climbed down, one by one, until only Sean remained. He too had resisted for as long as he could, gathering his courage in the baking sun. He was just about to head on down there himself when he remembered the torch back at the den. That was where we came in.

He told the story through panting breaths, gasps of exertion as we hurried. Yet there was something unspoken beneath the actual words. Maybe I just picked up on the fact that his behaviour suggested fear rather than excitement or anticipation. I think he was relieved to have stumbled across us.

We had reached the part of the fence that had been breached. Sean lifted up a section of the chain-link and we all ducked under. We crossed the grassy bank to where he indicated. As we drew close, I could see the metal frame enclosing the ladder. We'd examined it many times and speculated as to its presence. Now the water level had dropped, it seemed obvious. The ladder descended the reservoir's vertical wall for about thirty feet before ending at the base of a circular tunnel. I suppose it was the service channel, used in the event of a fault. We stood at the top and peered down. I tried to ignore the flat surface of black water lying ten feet below the gaping throat of the tunnel.

"I'll go first," said Sean. He glanced at me. "Then Fiona, then you. There's not enough room for us all together." I nodded.

He clicked on the torch and held it between his teeth. His face was flushed. He gripped the metal handrail and began his descent. I peered over the side and watched him carefully negotiate the slippery rungs until he reached the tunnel. He swung his leg over, beyond my angle of sight, and drew his body across. It appeared the tunnel wasn't that wide.

I glanced at Fiona. "Ready?"

She seemed to hesitate for a second. I could see the indecision in her face, torn between the desire to explore the tunnel and the stomach-ache that was troubling her. On this occasion curiosity won. She stepped over the wall, onto the ladder.

"Fiona." I placed my hand on the railing next to hers. "Be careful."

She nodded and began to move down the ladder. I watched her until she reached the mouth of the tunnel. She stared across at something I couldn't see, then gingerly stepped over to join Sean.

I could hear the birdsong again, the gentle lapping of water against the reservoir's wall, the soughing of wind through the trees. I turned and lowered down onto my haunches, pressing my back against the wall. The heat burned through my T-shirt.

Abruptly I felt like an outsider. Abandoned. I could hear nothing from the tunnel, yet my friends' sudden absence seemed unsettling.

Maybe I was just jittery from becoming attuned to Sean's mood, almost as if the nerves had been passed on to me like a virus. I tried to think about something else but my mind wouldn't allow it.

The air was heavy with moisture. I could taste it. I could feel it on my face, on the tingling hairs on my forearms. The light was strange. Everything had a rather sallow tinge. Those dark clouds were closing in.

Just then I heard the clang of footsteps on the ladder. I spun round and saw Fiona climbing over the wall. There was a look of distaste on her face. She was clutching her stomach. "I don't feel well."

"What's down there?"

She looked at me absently, as if I had just asked her what the currency of Kenya was. Her face was pale, her eyes glazed. "Just dark." She hugged herself. The gesture looked odd in the heat. "I didn't like it."

For a second I wasn't sure what she was going to do. If she had started to walk away then, I think I'd have followed her. Instead she lowered herself to the ground and leaned back against the wall, resting her head on her bent knees.

"I'll just see if they're okay." I waited for her to nod vaguely, then stepped over the wall onto the ladder. My *sneakers* squeaked on the metal rungs. As I climbed down, I was aware of the water lapping below. It sounded like a hungry mouth. The birdsong had fallen silent. Despite the frame encircling the ladder, I felt isolated and vulnerable. My legs shook. My palms were damp.

I reached the tunnel pretty quickly. The air had changed. It was more enclosed. There was a dank aroma that seemed to have attached itself to the ladder. I angled my head and peered into the tunnel. It was only about six feet across, with a flat base coated in silt and mud. The sunlight reached barely more than a few paces inside. I could hear nothing at all, and the darkness was made all the more solid by the bright sunshine that bathed the wall.

"Sean?" The echo of my voice sounded strange. I hesitated, leaning into the tunnel with my feet on the ladder. I could see dead leaves and weeds trapped in the carpet of sludge. My chest felt tight. The skin on the back of my neck prickled. I stepped across into the tunnel, opening my eyes wide to try to become accustomed to the dark.

I sensed that the passage extended back for about a dozen feet or so. In the dim light I could just make out a vague blackness where the tunnel took an abrupt bend to the right. It felt like I was perched inside a mouth, peering into a monstrous constricting throat.

I could just make out the edge of Sean's torch lying half-submerged in the mud. I bent to pick it up. It was so cold it made me recoil. I clicked it on and shone it into the darkness.

Something was standing about ten feet away.

The torch's unsteady beam picked out a pale featureless blur, and I jumped in surprise. In the split-second it took me to realign the beam, my mind conjured a tooth-filled gaping mouth, spindly limbs, matted hair. But my steadying of the beam revealed nothing more than a young boy staring back at me, wide-eyed and grinning.

I held my breath and peered at him. He was dressed in short trousers and a woollen jumper. I could see the knot of a necktie above the V of his shirt. His dark hair was styled in an old-fashioned side-parting. He looked a year or so younger than us. There was some feature of his timid stance that suggested apprehension, and I took a step forward, buoyed by his non-threatening body language.

The torch made his face as pale as marble. He blinked at the glare, and I angled the beam away.

"Hello?" My voice sounded unsteady in the confines of the tunnel. "Where're me mates?"

He didn't speak, just remained peering at me, hunched in that peculiar-looking jumper like he was uncomfortable inside his own skin, let alone his clothes.

What occurred in the next few minutes is difficult for me to explain – not because I don't remember what happened, but rather because a great deal of it took place internally. What I mean is, at that precise moment my head became flooded by thoughts, like a cascade of photographs. I experienced a powerful feeling of elation. I felt my throat tighten. I was on the verge of tears. Everything seemed comfortable and warm and fuzzy. I couldn't see much because of the darkness, yet somehow I knew that beyond the tunnel's bend lay something I desperately wanted. My mind fogged with desire. I thought of comic books and *Victor* annuals, of *Action Man* figures and football cards. I knew this without question. I was giddy. Elated. I simply *had to* go further along the passageway.

The boy's unresponsive face continued to stare back at me.

It was all so unassuming. I was just about to head deeper into the tunnel when something made me hesitate.

In those days my Dad worked at Sheffield Forgemasters, at their Stocksbridge foundry seven miles away. He'd make the journey by motorbike. Occasionally I'd be getting dressed for school as he was returning from his nightshift; I'd hug him as he'd fight to shake off his exhaustion and help Mum get me breakfasted and ready for school before he retired to bed. There was always a distinct smell to his work clothes; a mixture of oil and sweat and his usual Brut aftershave. I remember how comfortable that smell was, how safe it made me feel.

But there was always something lying beneath that smell. Some alien aspect to it that unsettled me. I suppose it must have been from the chemicals that Dad used during the steel manufacturing process, or maybe just the near-toxic industrial air that clung to his clothes whilst he worked. It was certainly not present at other times. But it was mildly unpleasant, like it was doing its best to taint my Dad.

And in that split second as I hesitated in the tunnel, this thought came to me: there was something about the boy that was at odds with his innocent appearance.

I peered a little closer. His black eyes glittered in the beam, he grinned his passive grin. I angled the beam directly at him. There was a green shade to his teeth, up around the gums. His fingernails looked too pointed. Too clean. I studied his clothes, deciding that his appearance looked deliberate, like a book cover or an illustration from a magazine. I thought I could see things squirming in his hair. Insects, earthworms, maybe spiders. I felt suddenly afraid.

It occurred to me then that he had not yet spoken a single word, even though he'd given me the impression that something desirable awaited me further along the tunnel. Had I made this assumption myself? There was no visible indication that this boy would do me harm. Just then I heard laughter and voices in the distance.

"Sean?" I listened but there was no reply, although the voices continued. "Dec!"

I hesitated again, trying to rationalise my thoughts, trying to decide why I shouldn't go and join my friends further along the tunnel. They sounded excited, like they were all having fun, and I yearned to join them.

But this was the summer of Bradbury; a time when the fabric of everyday life was being torn back to reveal dark curiosities beneath; a time when my imagination was being fuelled by a power beyond my childhood comprehension. Recently acquired knowledge had altered the way I'd looked at things. For the first time in my short life I understood that mortality was as fragile as a dew-coated spider's web in October – slender and precious – and that it could be broken at any time. Ray Bradbury's stories had shown me that things were not always as they first appeared. There must always be questions. I had begun to see the world through the eyes of a man who told life's truths through the art of fiction. Uncle Terry's illness had been reflected in the faces of my parents; for the first time it made me realise that they too would one day die. And I'd come to realise that, even though life coursed through our bodies like oxygen in blood, death was waiting to pounce at any minute.

I took a step backwards and gripped the torch like it was a weapon. Now my mind was made up I felt suddenly afraid, that the figure would know my intention and make its move. I kept the beam trained on its grinning face as I edged back through the sludge towards the ladder.

"Listen, I'm going to head back and get Fiona." My voice was soft and placatory, as if I was trying to reassure a snarling dog. I noticed that I'd moved into the arc of sunlight and I reached across and grabbed the metal of the ladder, suddenly fearful of turning my back against the thing that watched in the dark. I clicked off the torch and slid it into the back pocket of my jeans. At the last moment I had the impression of that tall spindly-limbed figure again, but then the darkness rushed in to steal it.

The handrail was hot in the sunlight, such a sharp contrast to the cool interior of the tunnel. For a second I was momentarily blinded, but I scrambled up the ladder, my sneakers making deft clunks on each rung.

At the top, I stepped over the low wall, noting the black water far below. It felt incredibly good to be standing on firm ground. My sneakers were clogged with sludge. I realised my hands were trembling.

Fiona glanced up from where she sat. Her face was pale. She looked startled when she saw my expression. "Where are they?"

I shook my head. The relief at being out of the tunnel suddenly hit me, and I bent and vomited onto the grass. I was aware of Fiona's hand on my back and her nearness brought tears to my eyes. I clutched her desperately, not caring about how pathetic I must have looked.

Lightning flickered in the sky and there was a growl of thunder from across the valley. The breeze was increasing; it flapped the sleeves of my t-shirt, made the trees shudder impatiently behind us.

"C'mon, let's get home," said Fiona. Her hand lingered on my back and I was scared to say anything, to break the spell. "It's gunna rain."

The light had gone weird. A strange sickly colour had tainted the sky, like a yellow caul sealing the valley. I felt dizzy. The lightning strobed again, adding a dimension of melodrama to the proceedings that was not required.

It started to rain then, just sporadic drops at first, but soon they were huge splodges that darkened our t-shirts. We began to hurry. I noticed a weird mark on the back Fiona's jeans and I pointed it out. She stopped and rubbed at it self-consciously, angling her body so that it was hidden. "Are you okay?" I said, studying her face. "Looks like blood."

"I'm fine," she said quickly. "It's nothing."

The rain was heavy now. I could hear it pounding the dry ground around us, shivering the trees into movement. The surface of the reservoir looked like it was being struck by mini-explosions as the rain pelted it. Heavy black clouds had stolen away the blue sky that had been constant for the past three months.

As we hurried along the brow of the reservoir I gazed down upon Renfield, spotting the church spire, a jagged scar of dry-stone walls bordering the school on the far hill, the pub at the central crossroads that bisected our town. The slate roofs of the houses looked drab and grey, glistening in the rain, and I felt my chest ache at the sight. The drab ordinariness of it looked suddenly welcoming, desirable now. My yearning for a life more exotic had been dampened. I longed to be in my bedroom, reading a book and watching the storm through my window.

As if to illustrate a point, lightning flickered in the sky and thunder cracked overhead. It was deafening. We hunched our shoulders and began to hurry.

By the time we arrived home we were dripping wet, our hair plastered flat to our heads by the torrent. Water gushed from overflowing drainpipes, a vast puddle spanned the full length of the main road, its surface peppered by raindrops. My shirt clung to my body as I squelched along our road. I mumbled a hasty goodbye to Fiona, who waved a vague hand and hurried up her drive.

My summer of Bradbury was over.

*

No one ever found out what happened to our friends. Their bodies were never recovered. For a while the story was featured in many of the papers, a tragic tale of four young boys drowned whilst playing in the reservoir. I told my version of what happened but the police dismissed it, instead believing that they'd simply become lost in the service tunnel and had perished as the water level had risen. They ignored what I told them about the strange boy, insisting that I must have been confused in the darkness.

We had a school assembly in memory of Declan, Sean, Mikey and Lee. For a few days Fiona and I were elevated to the status of minor celebrities. I'm ashamed to say there was a small part of me that relished the attention. But I told myself that it was just part of the coping mechanism. For a while afterwards my dreams were stalked by motionless grinning creatures. To this day I have a fear of tunnels, not because of the confinement, but rather from what might lurk in the darkness. Fiona seemed to deal with what had happened by dismissing it as kids' stuff, just a dreadful accident. Her family moved to Barnsley a few months later. I never saw her again.

In the intervening years I've had time to consider that day. I don't mean *understand* what happened – age has allowed me to reconcile what I believed at the time with the rational thought of an adult– but to reflect on how Fiona and I managed to escape. I think there was more than luck involved.

It's clear to me now that Fiona had outgrown our gang. She had changed mentally as well as physically. Perhaps the idea of exploring a filthy, dark tunnel wasn't that appealing to a young girl on the cusp of womanhood.

And in my case, I was saved by Ray Bradbury, whose fiction taught me that death waits nearby for those foolish enough to wander close; a notion fairly alien to most twelve-year-old boys, whose feelings of immortality gradually lessen as they grow older. And poor old Uncle Terry's illness reiterated that fact. He died a few months later, just after Mum's birthday in November. I don't think our family was ever the same after that.

A few years ago I was in Sheffield on business, and I came across a heritage museum on the outskirts of the city centre. It was housed in a building that had once been used as a corn mill on the banks of the River Don. There were sections covering the history of South Yorkshire's industry – a room dedicated to coal-mining, one to the city's steel manufacturing plants and so on – and hundreds of photographs showing how the area had changed since the Victorian times. There were even a few pictures of Renfield from the late '70s, images which evoked powerful memories in me. But it was a section in the corner that I found the most interesting; black and white photographs of Bowerton, the village that was drowned to make way for the reservoir. One in particular caught my eye, dated 1938 – taken outside the primary school, three rows of children starting sullenly at the camera like they were suspicious of what was happening. In particular I noticed their clothes – the short trousers, the woollen pullovers, the neckties of their school uniform. They all had the same short back and sides, the neat parting to one side. Those dark monochrome features offering nothing but a simple reminder of what was now long dead. I shivered as my eyes searched their faces one by one but there was nobody there I recognised.

RADIANT BEINGS

A series of truly bizarre mysteries, not exactly unique to the North of England, but certainly commonplace there – inasmuch as any supernatural phenomena can be commonplace – is that of the so-called 'radiant beings'. In essence these are ghost stories, though they follow none of the normal rules associated with such. They concern fiercely glowing apparitions, often of young people – though they aren't restricted to that – which materialise only briefly and infrequently, and yet are nearly always associated with the murders of children, usually by parents or step-parents.

They particularly figure in the mythologies of the counties of Durham, Cumbria and Northumbria, but Yorkshire has its share too, mainly in the area of the North Riding around Thirsk, where there are written accounts of two separate hauntings perpetrated by radiant beings, though, as there are no certifiable facts attached to either, it may be the case that both accounts actually refer to the same one.

The initial incident allegedly occurred in the early 19th century beside a wooded stream just outside Thirsk, which then, as now, was a pretty little market town. Various witnesses, usually peddlers or farm-workers following the course of the water late at night, were stopped short by the sight of a radiant figure approaching. In each case it appeared to be an archetypical 'white lady': a very young woman clad all in white, yet possessed of a searing brightness, which would drift past them as though totally unaware of their presence.

As so often in these cases, we only have the witnesses' word that this really happened, but the tale was reported so widely that the river was re-christened White Lass Beck. Several years later, sometime in the mid-19th century, a farmer with the unlikely name of John Mealyface was also travelling a wooded riverbank after dark. Whether this was the same riverbank we simply don't know – folklorists have been unable to ascertain further details, except the following. Mealyface was assailed from behind by an explosive light. When he turned, he beheld a male child approaching on horseback, both of them brightly aglow. The apparition rode straight past Mealyface, at which point it faded in the midnight gloom, in the words of the oft-told tale "like a fire or candle doused".

Uncharacteristic of Victorian ghost melodrama, there was no talk of visible murder wounds like slit throats or bullet holes. Likewise, no identifiable features were described, except that one apparition was female and one male. However, this has impressed scholars, whose view holds that reams of detail must be treated with scepticism as witnesses to real shocking events are often too shaken to recall the finer points.

Perhaps predictably, the Thirsk story ends on a more routine note, when we learn that a later excavation on the bank of White Lass Beck uncovered the skeleton of a very young female who had clearly been murdered – though her identity was never established. No information is given as to how the secret grave was traced. Whether it had anything to do with the apparitions on the riverbank we will never know.

Ultimately, the presence of radiant beings at Thirsk can never be more than a good story because there is simply no proof. And yet it's notable that it does fit in with radiant being lore. For example, it is never a necessity that radiant beings reflect or even resemble the murder victims, and in this case radiant beings of different genders appeared, and there are even reports that glowing dogs were sighted in the same place.

Interestingly, these curious phantoms are not native to British culture, but are Germanic in origin.

During the 18th century in Germany, antiquated legal and financial frameworks made it difficult and expensive for unwed mothers or impoverished step-parents to unload their excess children onto the state – hence they sometimes disposed of them. It is no coincidence that fairy tales concerning cruel step-parents – Hansel & Gretel and Cinderella for example – were first written down in Germany around this time, each one emphasising the caring role expected of guardians. Stories about radiant beings, which abound in Germanic tradition, might be another symptom of this. What is more, such parables appear to have arrived in England during the early days of the Industrial Revolution, when so many German immigrants first arrived here looking for work, by far the largest proportion of them settling in the northern counties, like Yorkshire.

RANDOM FLIGHT
Rosalie Parker

Dusk was falling as Patrick slowed the car and pulled into a lay-by. Scots pines swayed in the strengthening wind. He had heard on the radio that a storm was blowing in.

"A close shave," he said out loud, laughing now. "You've still got it, Patrick." He shivered as the car cooled in the chill of the evening. "Better get a move on. 'Time's winged chariot', and all that."

Patrick, dark and good-looking, had celebrated his fortieth birthday a few days before with Annika, a bubbly, bulimic girl, in a Greek restaurant in Leeds. They drank two bottles of champagne and made quite an exhibition of themselves, which none of the other customers seemed to mind. It was the kind of place that provided cheap white china plates for you to smash, for the authentic Greek experience. Annika paid the bill and they rolled out onto the street and back to her flat. She had asked him to move in with her and, after a few days of playing hard to get, that's what he intended to do. But just when everything seemed to be going to plan, her ex husband (who still felt the need to hang around) visited Patrick's rented flat and threatened him with the police, with the result that Patrick had been forced to leave Leeds in a hurry, with little time to think of where to go and what to do next. It was a shame, because as well as being a genuinely nice, intelligent girl (when not throwing up in the bathroom), Annika was an easy touch, always good for a meal out or a trip to the races. They'd had a great time together, without, so far as he was aware, any real commitment on either side.

He'd been working the holiday scam on her and she was falling for it, and he knew she had the money – he'd found her building society book in a drawer in her bedroom. How that thug of an ex-husband of hers had got wind of it and somehow guessed that Patrick would not book the trip to the Seychelles but take Annika's cash and run, he couldn't guess. Perhaps it was just bad luck that she had told the ex about the holiday and that he turned out to be so suspicious and untrusting a person.

So here he was, heading north, somewhere in the Dales on a main road that seemed as twisty and windy as most minor roads further south. Patrick was a city boy, originally from Sheffield, and this was an area unfamiliar to him, but it seemed as good a place as any in which to lie low for a few days, in case Annika's ex made good on his threat.

Night had fallen and he decided to stop at the next town. After another few miles through the steadily increasing rain he drove into Skelton, a village with three pubs ranged around a cobbled square. It would have to do. Patrick chose *The Black Horse* because although the biggest, it was not the best kept pub, and would most likely be cheaper than *The Swan* or *The King's Head*. Money, or the lack of it, would soon become a concern. He parked the Alfa on the cobbles outside the pub, collected his brown leather holdall from the boot, lifted the latch and went inside.

*

The bar was warm, old-fashioned and comfortable, encased in panelled oak, a worn Axminster on the floor. The place seemed full of local farmers and horsey types: there were very few women, and those that were there looked like stable girls, drinking pints – not the right sort for his purposes. Tomorrow he would have to find somewhere more likely.

He struck up a conversation with a wiry little farmer called Bill, from whom he learned that Skelton was a race horse training centre. Bill was, naturally, curious about what he was doing in the village and Patrick gave him the story he'd come up with while unpacking his holdall in the large bedroom above the bar. He straightened his back.

"I'm on leave. I'm a Major in the Yorkshire Regiment. Major Hartley. We've just returned from a tour of Afghanistan. We're being sent back out to Iraq in a few weeks. Thought I'd see some more of my own county – get to know the Dales a bit better."

'Aye, well," said Bill, "they say this is God's Country. I certainly wouldn't live anywhere else."

"Glad to hear it," returned Patrick. "It sure as hell beats the desert."

"I suppose it does. Did you see much in the way of action while you were out there?"

Patrick rubbed the stubble on his chin. "As a matter of fact we did. Had a fire-fight with some insurgents the second week we were there. Two of our lads bought it, but we took out a few more of them. It's a dirty business …"

Bill frowned. "Local lads were they? I don't remember …"

"It's not always reported on the news. Hush, hush, you know. We recruit from all over these days. But they would've been based at Catterick."

193

Bill said he'd have to get back to his farm, as he had a cow about to calf. Rain lashed against the mullioned windows. Patrick bought the farmer a double malt whisky and made him earn it by mining him for local knowledge. Bill, impressed and slightly intimidated by the tall, well-spoken soldier, and made loquacious by the warm, complex whisky, was very forthcoming.

*

The next day, a wet and windy Tuesday, saw Patrick recceing the market square of Gribley, the town closest to Skelton. After some deliberation he picked a large, smart-looking coffee shop, choosing a table from which he could see and be seen from both the door and most of the seating area. On the short drive to the town he had been struck by the quaintness of the landscape: with its quiet roads, dry-stone field walls and substantial stone houses it could still be the 1950s or '60s. He had seen several large flocks of crows – or rooks. Their random peregrinations around the sky made him feel faintly uneasy. In fact the whole place spooked him a little – after what had happened in Leeds he was, he realised, a bit jumpy – outside his comfort zone.

The best way to blow away the cobwebs, he knew from previous experience, was to get down to work. It was still early and he had bought and drunk three cups of coffee before the first likely target came through the door. She was, he guessed, in her early thirties, dressed in good clothes and jewellery, about five feet five, a brunette and nice looking, although wearing a lot of makeup. There was something needy about her – she wanted to be looked at. He looked – she smiled. She picked a table on the other side of the room and Patrick ignored her for a while, then, on his way back from the gents, close to her table, his handkerchief dropped from his pocket. The oldest trick in the book. She picked it up.

"Excuse me!" She had the local Dales accent. "Excuse me! You've dropped your handkerchief."

Their fingers touched as he took it from her. He looked into her eyes.

"Thank you. I'm always losing them."

And before you knew it he was sitting at her table, drinking decaffeinated coffee and listening to her life story – separated – husband with another woman but supporting her financially – a couple of young kids at school – still living in the marital home in a nearby village. Out it tumbled, once he'd spun her the Major Hartley yarn, without him having to put in much effort at all. Her name was Rachel Morton and she was vivacious and a wee bit desperate, with that all too obvious neediness about her that might, he thought, lead to trouble later on.

He asked if he could see her again and they arranged to meet the following evening at an Italian restaurant across the square. He spent the afternoon in the cafes of Fairlees, a small market town about ten miles west of Gribley. Luck was against him, however.

The following lunchtime he bumped into Flick in a pub in Fairlees. Flick was around fifty, he thought, divorced and smart and the owner of a high-end dress shop in the town. He told her that he was ex-army, now working as a researcher for a film production company. He was in the Dales finding locations for their next feature film. As it was a contemporary drama, she might be able to help provide the costumes. They spent the afternoon in bed in her flat, and it was only with some difficulty that Patrick managed to leave in time to meet Rachel at the restaurant in Gribley.

Rachel was late because her babysitter had forgotten to come. She had had to telephone the girl and promise to pay her an extra ten pounds.

"It's impossible to find anyone reliable," she complained. "These teenagers are no good, and Guy is too selfish to help out. He'll only have the kids at weekends." She stroked Patrick's arm. "Perhaps next time you'd better come to mine."

The date progressed well. He presented her with a single red rose – he did it ironically and she liked it – and managed to borrow fifty pounds, extracted as a test of his skill. She spent most of the meal complaining about Guy, her estranged husband, who, he learnt, worked for an investment bank. At the end of the meal Patrick kissed Rachel chastely on the cheek and she invited him to dinner at her house on the following Friday. He got the impression that she would be ringing her husband to tell him about her new boyfriend as soon as he had left.

He spent the next few afternoons with Flick, who had been led to believe that Patrick would be going back home to London in two weeks' time. She invited him to stay at her flat until then. Patrick wasn't entirely sure that it was a good idea, but the financial imperative overrode all else. He settled up at *The Black Bull* and moved himself in.

He found Flick intelligent, undemanding and good company, but he had yet to find the chink in her armour, the vulnerable spot that would lead him to her money. How much money that would turn out to be was difficult to say. Her flat was small but stylish in a minimalist, contemporary way, and her shop very obviously made her a good living. He was sure there was more money somewhere – he could smell it.

Rachel's house was another thing entirely. It was large, detached and cluttered with knick-knacks and ornaments, scented candles and children's toys. Rachel, it seemed, was a compulsive purchaser – shopping her main hobby. When Patrick arrived, her children, Chloe (five) and Jake (three) were still up. After some initial shyness, they clambered all over him, singing nursery rhymes and spouting made-up nonsense. He didn't dislike children; he was indifferent to them, but these two seemed to accept him as a friend. He made a great deal of fuss of them, which appeared to gratify Rachel. She finally put them to bed and served up a rather good casserole and a bottle of wine. Patrick went through the pretence of drinking only one glass, although they both knew that he would be staying the night. (He had told Flick he was working and staying at a hotel in Bradford). Later, in bed, Rachel cried a little, then pulled herself together, and they had an enjoyable time.

Three days later, over lunch, he told Rachel about how he had been diagnosed with Post-Traumatic Stress Disorder and needed to buy himself out of the army, and how his savings were tied up for the next few months. He didn't even have to ask her directly – she offered to lend him £20,000 there and then, more than enough for him to replace the Alfa and have some left over for expenses. That afternoon she took a cheque made out to him from her building society. He couldn't believe it had been that easy.

Driving back to Flick's, after paying the cheque into his bank account, Patrick was again distracted by the odious flocks of crows. There was something about the regimented unpredictability of their flight that got under his skin. He was trying to think of how to get at Flick's money. £20,000 was all well and good, but it wouldn't last forever. He was sure he would be able to extract more from Rachel, but Flick was the bigger challenge. A number of crows broke away from the main flock and swooped low over the road. Patrick flinched and the car swerved. He swore.

"Get a grip, for God's sake!"

He stopped at the tiny village shop and bought a bottle of whisky. The shopkeeper did not bother to hide his curiosity.

"Are you on holiday here?" he enquired. "I've seen you around. Renting a cottage?"

"Just passing through," answered Patrick, pocketing his change. "Visiting a friend."

It seems you couldn't even buy a bottle of whisky without being interrogated. The place was so small that he stood out, that was the problem. He was getting himself noticed, and that was not a good thing at all.

Flick was in the bath. She called out to him:

"Help yourself to some wine. There's a bottle open in the kitchen."

He gulped down a glassful, poured out another, then let himself into the bathroom. Flick was engulfed in a mound of bubbles.

"You look tired Patrick. Are you all right?"

"I'm more than all right. I've had some good news. A little investment of mine has paid off."

She splashed around in the foam. "Oh, goodie! Are we going out for dinner?"

"We are. But I've been thinking, Flick. You could invest too. It would be well worth your while. I could …"

Flick laughed. "Why on earth would I want to do that? The shop's my investment." She sat up, her breasts bobbing invitingly on the choppy bath water. "Go on, out with you. Watch the telly for a bit or read the paper or something while I get ready."

Later, in the Thai restaurant in Fairlees, he tried a different tack.

"Did *you* not want any children, Flick, or was it your ex?"

"We couldn't have any. It was before the days of test tubes and stuff."

"I have a son. Not many people know. He's called Ivan. His mother and I had a brief relationship in the '90s. He's eighteen and at university in Liverpool. He's quite ill, as a matter of fact. Needs an operation. He's on a waiting list. You know what the Health Service is like. He's really sick. If I could find the money I'd pay for him to go private."

"What about this investment of yours? Wouldn't that pay for it?"

"Oh, well … no. That's nowhere near enough. Flick, where would you go if you needed to raise some cash?"

Flick was looking thoughtful.

"I don't know, Patrick. I've never borrowed any money. I had a job and saved like crazy, and I built the shop up from scratch. Do you have any other family you could ask?"

Patrick was silent for a while.

"No. No family to speak of. You couldn't help, could you Flick? I'd pay you back."

She laid down her fork.

"Oh, Patrick. I don't know. How much are we talking about?"

He took a deep breath: "Thirty grand."

"I don't have that sort of money! Leave it with me, though."

And with that she changed the subject.

197

*

The next morning Flick left early on a buying trip to Leeds. Patrick, at a loose end and restless, found an ordnance survey map on Flick's kitchen dresser and went out for a walk. He headed north, through fields, up a steep hill and onto moorland, using the map to guide him. A keen easterly wind was blowing. He found himself striding out along the rough track, perfectly at home in the unaccustomed solitude. The view was stunning, a patchwork of fields, walls and villages, with the heather-clad fells beyond. The better part of him wanted to keep on walking and never go back down there again.

*

Patrick had a date with Rachel in the coffee shop – "their" coffee shop, she had said on the phone – in Gribley. He parked his new Alfa (not brand new, but only a year old) outside. He had bought it from a second-hand dealer in Darlington. The part-exchange deal he had negotiated was not particularly advantageous, but he still had a few thousands to tide him over.

It was obvious that something was wrong. Rachel wouldn't look him in the eye.

"What's up? You can tell your Uncle Patrick."

"Shut up."

"Hey, come on! What've *I* done?"

Rachel burst into hot, angry tears.

"Who is she, that old tart you were with in the Thai in Fairlees? I saw you!"

Patrick laughed easily. "She's no-one. Just someone I had a bit of business with. Come on. Don't upset yourself."

He tried to stroke her hand but she pulled it away.

"I know you've got someone else. It's happened to me before, remember."

"I don't need anyone else. I've got you."

"I'm such a fool. I know nothing about you."

"We're good together, aren't we?"

"That's ... not enough. Not now ... Look Patrick, I'm not playing any games. I want my money back."

Patrick swallowed hard. "Oh ... I might need a little ..."

"I want my money back this week. I should never have lent it to you. Give it back and we'll talk."

Patrick stroked her hand. "I'll see what I can do. It may take longer …"

Rachel finally looked him in the eye.

"I'm pregnant Patrick. It's yours. I don't know what to do about it. I don't expect anything from you."

The colour drained from Patrick's face.

"I'm leaving now," she said. "Call me when you've got my money and we'll talk."

*

Patrick checked that Flick's car was not in its space then let himself into the flat. He packed his holdall (he could do it very quickly), left the key she had given him on the kitchen table and drove straight to Rachel's.

He didn't know if Rachel was inside or not but she wasn't answering the door. He pressed the bell a few more times. It was difficult to work out how he felt about her – Patrick was not often given to introspection. He didn't even know if he believed her about the pregnancy – could she know that quickly? And he thought he'd been careful. After his initial desire to see her and talk her into letting him keep the money, his instincts were telling him not to take any chances: to leave now and get as far away as possible.

He backed the Alfa down the drive. Abruptly, he felt the car lift and then drop back down, as if he had driven over a road-hump or some kind of obstruction. In the rear view mirror he could see a light-coloured bundle lying on the tarmac behind him. It looked about the size of a child. Perched at one end was a shaggy, ink-black crow, pecking where the eyes would be. It *was* a child, he could see now, a child wrapped in some kind of shawl or blanket. One of Rachel's children? What the hell was it doing, lying on the drive? He hadn't seen it. And where was Rachel?

The crow raised its head and cawed. Patrick felt sick. He could see something wet, gelatinous, coating the curved tip of its beak. The bird fixed him with its shiny eye, then returned to its pecking.

Patrick reversed the car round hard. The Alpha screeched off along the village road. Pulling his phone from his jacket he dialled 999 and requested an ambulance. The car rocked from side to side as overhead the crows wheeled and swooped, the flock tracking the progress of the Alfa. There was nothing random about the movement of the flock as it shepherded the car and it's occupant out of the village, out of the dale, onto the motorway and away.

DEATH IN THE HARRYING

*A*ll through the Middle Ages in England, in fact from the 4ᵗʰ century to the 17ᵗʰ, holy places reserved the right to offer sanctuary to fugitives from the law. Any man wanted for a crime could take refuge in a church, and there remain for a total of 30 days while the Church authorities spoke up for him. In the event no agreement was reached, the outlaw could then either face trial or accept exile from the kingdom ... or, in the case of Beverley Minster in East Yorkshire, give up all his worldly possessions and remain for life in the church precincts as a 'frithman', or bonded lay-brother.

This was one rare occasion perhaps when the law of medieval England was weighed in favour of the common man. Not only that, it was a law seemingly protected by unearthly powers – as was discovered in 1069 by the brutal Norman baron, Toustain.

The terrible 'Harrying of the North' was in progress that year. This was King William the Conqueror's psychopathic response when the Anglo-Norse population of Northeast England resisted his rule by supporting Edgar the Atheling, last heir to the House of Wessex. William's policy was quite simply to devastate all the shires of that region – burn villages, trample crops, slaughter livestock and viciously abuse the people – but when he unleashed his army under a 'do as you will' edict, the horror actually went much further than. In fact, it was a near-genocide. Rivers ran red with blood, trees groaned beneath the weight of dangling corpses, and the bones of the murdered and starved were still visible littering the Yorkshire ditches as late 1086.

According to manorial records, some 100,000 people died; that is over four percent of the entire population of England at the time, making this by far the worst assault on the English people by their own rulers in written history.

Trapped in the midst of this darkness, the population of 11ᵗʰ century Yorkshire must have felt God had abandoned them – though the events at Beverley Minster that year would suggest otherwise. Baron Toustain was clearly taking too much pleasure in the Harrying. For no apparent reason other than the sport it gave him, he and his band of cutthroats pursued half the population of Beverley town into the Minster that day, intent on rape and massacre. The terrified townsfolk claimed sanctuary, but Toustain arrogantly disregarded this – and yet, no sooner had he set foot on

Minster ground than he was engulfed in 'a fiery flash from Heaven', which reduced him to a roasted, twisted travesty, his head turned completely around and his limbs burnt to stumps.

The rest of the Normans fled in terror, and even William the Conqueror, a man very quick to claim God was on his side when butchering his enemies, declined to visit the Minster when he heard about the incident, muttering that sanctuary was always to be respected.

No obvious explanation lends itself to the tale, which is attested to in several chronicles of the period. It does genuinely seem as if the brigand and murderer Toustain was blasted by lightning just at the moment he set his foot on sacred ground.

THE RHUBARB FESTIVAL
Simon Clark

The boy disappeared, and for his family and friends life would never be the same again. The ten-year-old had been playing a game of dare with five other children of the same age. One of the friends, Annie Thornhill, speaking thirty years after the tragedy, said, "We dared each other to run through huts where rhubarb is force grown. You see, they keep the plants in the dark to make them grow faster. Those huts are about a hundred feet long; they're open at both ends. We'd rush through in the dark. It made your heart pound like I don't know what. It's always black as midnight inside those places; you can't see anything but a little scrap of light at the other end. I always thought there'd be ghosts in there, or something that would hurt me. Everyone would be screaming. When we got to the other side that's when we'd all start laughing. You know? Sheer relief. It did scare me inside the forcing huts. Not only the dark frightened me. You can hear the rhubarb growing. A strange creaking sound. Once you've heard those plants pushing themselves up out of the dirt it stays with you all your life.

"I remember it all like it was yesterday. Just the thought of what happened turns my stomach, because you see the last time I saw that boy was when he went into the hut with me and my friends. After that? Nothing. Gone."

The mystery of the boy's disappearance has never been explained. All we do know for sure is that six children ran into the farmer's hut one Sunday afternoon three decades ago. Five children emerged at the other end. As for the sixth? The ten-year-old boy? Well – neither hide nor hair of the lad has been seen since that day. Was it a case of abduction? An accident? Or something else entirely?

Murders & Mysteries –
A Secret History of Wakefield

RHUBARB FESITVAL. The signs were everywhere in Wakefield's city centre. A huge TV screen outside the cathedral blazed the news in dazzling colours: RHUBARB FESTIVAL TODAY! COME SEE RUBY RHUBARB! FOOD MARKET. SIZZLING SNACKS. DELI DISHES. AND … **RHUBARB!** The word 'rhubarb' pulsated in crimson letters onscreen. Crowds filled the pedestrian precinct as they browsed stalls that sold rhubarb cocktails, cheese laced with rhubarb, rhubarb relish, rhubarb fudge, and a glorious array of delicacies flavoured with the plant that managed to be both sweet and shudderingly sour.

The man turned to the boy and said, "The theme for the day is clearly rhubarb. Are you hungry?"

The boy shook his head as he held up the cardboard box that contained the radio controlled model helicopter. "This is expensive. You didn't have to buy me it."

"I remember you telling me that you've always wanted a remote control helicopter."

"Once I did."

"Don't you want it?"

"It's great. It says here that it'll fly over a hundred feet up into the air. But haven't you spent all your money?"

"No. I've plenty. And I wanted to get you something nice."

"Ta."

The boy gazed through the cellophane cover at the helicopter and remote control unit embedded in polystyrene. The man hadn't seen the boy smile all day. His expression always remained serious. *But is that really surprising, when all's said and done? After what he's been through?* The boy was aged about ten with spiky, black hair. His blue eyes had a staring quality to them, as if he was preoccupied with some worry or other. The most striking feature was a large brown scab on the side of his face. He'd acquired that riding his bike into Mr Stanley's fence.

The boy studied the helicopter through the cellophane cover. "I do like it. Thanks. Is it alright if I call you Scott?"

"You always have."

"Will you help me fly the helicopter, Scott?"

"Of course, I will. Do you prefer Danny or Daniel now?"

"You decide."

"I'll call you Daniel. Stay close. It's getting really busy near these stalls."

"Coming through, boys and girls. Coming through!"

Scott turned to see a figure dressed in a huge hooped skirt, a frothy black wig, and wearing exaggerated make-up of the kind that pantomime dames adorn their faces with.

"Coming through. Make way. Ta!"

The crowds parted to let the extraordinary figure through.

Daniel stared in amazement. "What's with it, with her?"

"That's Ruby Rhubarb." The man smiled. "She's the physical embodiment of the spirit of rhubarb. That's what it said in the paper anyway."

Ruby Rhubarb moved at a comical trotting pace. She'd soon passed through the mass of festival goers and scuttled away along an empty part of the precinct. The wind blew in from the River Calder, driving scraps of paper, until debris flowed across the pavement like a fast-flowing river itself.

Scott shivered. The wind chilled him to the bone. "I once read something by a local poet. One of the lines was: *Nothing is colder than the creeping black Calder.* I reckon that's true, don't you? Daniel? What's wrong? Why are you staring at me like that?"

"That's where you think I am, don't you? You think I'm in the river. That's why they never found me. Wrong, wrong, wrong!"

"Daniel, I'm sorry. Look, there's a fudge stall. Let me buy you some."

"How can I eat? You don't even know if I have a mouth anymore."

"Daniel, calm down."

"Why don't you buy me rhubarb? After all, that's where you saw me last, isn't it?"

Scott followed the boy to a market stall where rhubarb had been laid out. The red stalks were two feet long and topped with green leaves. To Scott, the blood-red rhubarb always seemed like part of an animal rather than a plant. He never ate rhubarb crumble or pies. He hated the stuff – no mystery why. He associated rhubarb with Daniel's disappearance.

Daniel became agitated. He clutched the box containing the helicopter under one arm as he picked up a piece of rhubarb. He held the stalk so that its broad leaf was above his head. "Remember when it rained, Scott? We'd use rhubarb as umbrellas."

"Daniel, don't be silly, please put that down."

"We'd pinch rhubarb from the hut and walk along the road with the leaves over our heads like this. Rhubarb umbrellas. Do you want me to eat some? Look … Munch, munch." He pretended to bite the crimson stalk.

The rhubarb seller reacted with surprise, together with a good deal of anger, too. "Hey, put that down. Stop laikin' abart wi' it. You'll ruin mi' stock."

"It's not me," Scott protested. "I haven't touched the rhubarb. It's the boy."

"What boy? There's in't any bloody boy. Stop mucking around with that rhubarb."

Daniel laughed… well… the noise sounded closer to a scream. "Oi, mister! You can stick that rhubarb were the sun dunt shine!" Grabbing handfuls, he hurled them into the stallholder's face.

The rhubarb seller thundered, "That's it! I'm calling the police!"

Daniel sped away, laughing. Scott ran alongside him.

"You shouldn't have done that, Daniel. You'll get into trouble." Scott realised he was laughing, too.

When they were safely away, and had vanished back into the crowds, they both paused to catch their breath. Scott patted Daniel on the shoulder, a warm and friendly gesture.

Laughing, he said, "You should have seen that bloke's face. He was so angry I thought his eyes would pop right out."

"Bloody rhubarb," Daniel chuckled. "Crappy rhubarb."

"He couldn't see you, could he?"

"Nah. I'll go back and boot him up the backside. He'll think he's been kicked by an invisible horse."

"Best wait here for a while. We'll go back the other way, so he doesn't see us... or me, rather."

Daniel checked that the helicopter was safe in its box then he asked, "Scott, how old are you now?"

"Forty-two."

"Wow. That's old."

"Yeah, feels old to me as well."

"You talk posher now an' all."

"Do I? I never noticed."

"Well, you do. Have you got a job?"

"I work in local government?"

"Uh?"

"You know – the council? I survey roads."

"Does that mean your job is looking at roads? You get paid for doing that?"

"Yup."

"Hey..." Daniel gave a knowing grin. "You haven't got married, have you?"

"Yes, and I have two children as well."

"Well, keep 'em away from ruddy rhubarb sheds. You don't want the same happening to your kids as what happened to me."

"What did happen to you, Daniel?"

"You said you'd not ask! YOU BLASTED WELL PROMISED!"

"You were my best friend, Daniel. I want to know, because not knowing's like – like having thorns sticking in your skin."

Daniel was in shock. "You said you wouldn't ask why I never came out of the hut."

"Not knowing hurts, Daniel. I can't stand *not knowing* anymore. I keep asking myself why you didn't leave the hut with the rest of us. I can't sleep. I'm drinking too much."

The cold wind blew along the precinct; scraps of paper and fast-food cartons all tumbled in the same direction. At that moment, a loudspeaker attached to a lamppost buzzed before emitting a man's amplified voice. *"Ladies and Gentlemen. What you will hear next is the sound that rhubarb makes when it's growing in the forcing huts. It's dark in there. Completely dark. This, ladies and gentlemen, is that sound."*

The crowds milling around stalls paused to listen. From the loudspeaker came a sound that was somehow unsettling. A loud creaking. Sort of hollow, suggesting that the sound might have come from an underground vault, or an ancient tomb. The creaking would abruptly pause, leaving absolute silence. Then it would come again: *creak, click, snap.* A somehow determined sound – stealthy, relentless and decidedly sinister.

The amplified voice rang out once more: *"You heard it here, ladies and gentlemen, the sound of rhubarb growing in the dark."*

Daniel's blue eyes locked onto the loudspeaker. He began to scratch the brown scab on his face. A drop of blood beaded from his cheek where he'd dislodged part of the hard crust. He didn't seem to notice. He continued to stare at the speaker as it conveyed the eerie, creaking *voice* of the rhubarb.

"Daniel," began Scott gently. "Can't you tell me anything? That Sunday afternoon when the six of us went into the hut? We ran into the darkness, rushing through with the rhubarb growing at either side of us. At the end of the building, like a light at the end of a tunnel, was the opening. What happened in there, Daniel? Why didn't you come out at the other end? What stopped you?"

Daniel became angry. "Do you want another game of dare? Shall we run through one of the huts again? Me and you?"

"Daniel –"

"The same might happen to you, Scott… as what happened to me…" His eyes went wide with horror.

"Daniel. I could drive you to the forcing huts. They're still there in the field by the river. There's a torch in the car. We could look inside and –"

"Here! Take it! I never wanted the bloody helicopter in the first place!"

He hurled the box at Scott. Crouching, Scott picked it up.

"I'm sorry, Daniel. I won't mention it again. Daniel? Uh… no."

The boy ran off along the precinct. Soon the dense crowds had swallowed him.

"Daniel?"

Scott went after the boy. Just then Ruby Rhubarb twirled from behind a cake stall.

"Make way, sir. Coming through. Ta, very much!"

The figure, with its crimson lips, and drawn-on eyelashes that resembled long, black spider legs, pranced in front of Scott. The hooped skirt banged against his knees. For a moment, the striking figure blocked his way. Even when he'd squirmed past between the dame and the cake stall he was instantly confronted by hundreds of people cramming the pavement between lines of yet more stalls selling anything from rhubarb marmalade to mounds of rhubarb tarts. He had to press his lips together hard to stop himself screaming with frustration. *Why won't they let me through? I need to find Daniel.*

Still carrying the model helicopter in its box, he struggled to get through that barrier of human flesh.

"Daniel!"

He could no longer see the boy. The faster he tried to run the more it seemed people got in his way. When a group of drunken lads emerged from a pub to taunt Ruby Rhubarb, and make lewd comments, Scott was actually carried backwards by the gang.

After that, everything became a blur. He vaguely remembered running and shouting, and the way people cast frightened glances at him. Then… well, everything was quiet and he was sitting on a bench near the cathedral. The city centre was empty of shoppers. Stallholders were packing their stock into vans. Only Ruby Rhubarb, in her vast hooped skirt, still trotted along the precinct. The cold wind blew a stream of chip cones, cigarette butts and fast-food wrappers after her, as if she'd been transformed into a latter-day Pied Piper and was leading the rubbish away to the land of no-return.

Scott felt broken. He couldn't raise his head. His throat burned, his eyes were sore. The box had become crumpled, because he'd held it so tightly, crushing it to his chest.

Presently, a female police officer approached.

"Hello, sir. Are you feeling alright?

He didn't look up.

Crouching beside him, she asked in a kind voice what his name was.

"Scott."

"You've been sat here a long time, Scott. Do you feel poorly?"

"No."

"Not had a little drink, have we?"

"No."

"Can you tell me what might be the matter with you, Scott?"

"I've lost my friend."

"Oh."

"He's ten years old. I bought him…" He tapped his finger on the box. "He's only ten. I can't find him."

"Scott, you're telling me that you were here with a child? And he's vanished?"

Feeling so miserable he could barely hold his head up, Scott nodded.

"What's your friend's name?"

"Daniel."

The police officer's expression changed to one of concern. Her eyes scanned the precinct for the boy.

"What's Daniel's second name?"

"Mercer."

"Don't worry, Scott. I'm sure we'll find Daniel. When did you see him last?"

"Thirty years ago."

"Sorry, did you mean thirty *minutes* ago?"

"Thirty years." His heart thudded painfully. "I was with Daniel along with some other friends. We used to play a game of dare. It meant going inside the forcing huts where they grow rhubarb in the dark. We'd go into the hut at one end then run the hundred feet or so until we reached the other doorway. It was so dark in there… you could see nothing but a little glimmer of daylight at the other end. Six of us ran into the hut. Only five came out. Daniel's still in there somewhere."

The policewoman was sympathetic. "You must know that what you've just told me sounds strange, because you also claim that you were here with Daniel at the festival."

"His ghost." He felt surprised now, as if only just beginning to understand what had happened to him today. "It must have been Daniel's ghost. You know, I sort of blotted out it was impossible that he'd come back after all this time, and still look like he did when he was ten, even down to the scab on his cheek – that was there when he disappeared."

"Sir, I think you might be ill. You're very pale."

"Seen a ghost, haven't I?"

"But you do understand that this talk about a ghost will sound odd to people."

"After Daniel vanished, the other children that had been there on that Sunday afternoon were never the same again. We all went a bit odd after that. Annie Thornhill was interviewed about Daniel for a book. Later, she sat in the bath with two bottles of vodka and drank herself to death."

"Listen, Scott. I'd like you to come with me to check some recent video footage of the town centre. I just want to check whether there actually was a boy with you, in case I need to call in my colleagues to conduct a search. Do you understand?"

Scott nodded and soon they were walking together along the precinct.

He felt the need to explain. "I bought Daniel the helicopter. I wanted to make him happy again and see him smile. Because nobody knows what happened to him in that shed. It must have been awful."

Scott followed the police officer into a room above a shop. There she spoke to another woman who sat in front of a bank of TV monitors, showing views of Wakefield. To Scott it all seemed so dreamlike. They showed him CCTV footage from earlier. There were the market stalls. He saw Ruby Rhubarb scuttling through the crowds, the hooped skirt swaying.

"Look, Scott," said the policewoman, "that's you, isn't it?"

"Yes. I'm coming out of the toy shop."

"You're holding the helicopter box. Do you see anyone with you?

Numb, he shook his head.

"Is there a boy, Scott?"

"I'm alone, aren't I?"

"Here's more footage of you walking by the cathedral. Can you see a boy in the picture with you?"

"Daniel Mercer was there. I talked to him."

The CCTV operator turned to Scott in surprise. "Daniel Mercer? I remember my parents talking about him. It was all over the television. He vanished years ago. Nobody ever saw him again."

"Daniel was my friend." Scott felt cold inside as he watched himself onscreen. He walked alone through the crowds. However, his mouth moved. He did seem to be having a conversation.

Later, he sat with his head in his hands, while the police officer made a telephone call from another room. He only caught fragments: "A gentleman... he claims that he was in the company of a boy called Daniel Mercer. The boy disappeared a long time ago. No, the man hasn't been drinking. If anything, he's displaying symptoms of shock: very pale, clammy skin, confusion... yes, an ambulance... restraints? Who reported the assault? A stallholder..."

The cold air hit the man like a slap in the face. He didn't remember climbing out of the car, let alone leaving the CCTV control room and driving to the banks of the River Calder.

"Nothing's as cold as the creeping black Calder." The line from the poem echoed inside of him as he walked across the field in the direction of the forcing hut. The soil hereabouts was black. Completely black. Lines of rhubarb grew in the field, the green leaves contrasting sharply with that blackness of the earth. He could smell the river. Today, its waters were black, too – in fact, just as black as the forcing hut in front of him. This was the very hut where they played their game of dare all those years ago. Six children ran into that hut. Only five emerged. Daniel Mercer had decided to stop inside the building for some reason, or he had been prevented from leaving. Whatever did happen nobody ever saw him again.

The houses where he and his friends once lived could be glimpsed some distance away through a line of trees. The River Calder was perhaps fifty yards away; a broad waterway that had once carried the barges that transported wool to Wakefield's mills. Scott remembered how the water would change colour, depending on what colour all those tons of wool were being dyed on a particular day. Sometimes the river would be green, sometimes blue, and on occasions a vivid crimson.

Scott approached the long, low structure. He stopped dead at the doorway. It was dark in there. The distinctive odour of wet compost filled his nostrils. Straight away, he heard them. The creaks, clicks and snaps of rhubarb plants growing there in the darkness. The long, drawn out creaks could have been the sound of someone slowly… slowly… exerting pressure on a bone until, creaking under the stress, it finally gave way with a snap. The song of the rhubarb wasn't a pleasant one. Scott shivered to the roots of his heart.

"Go on, Scott. I dare you. Run through to the other side."

"Daniel?" Scott turned at the sound of the voice. There was no-one there. In fact, he couldn't see another living soul. The fields were deserted.

"Do it, Scott. A dare's a dare. Don't be such a chicken."

Taking a deep breath, the man lurched through the open doorway with a yell. Straightaway, he glimpsed the rhubarb stems. These were young plants and the stems were pale, almost white. They looked like dozens of deathly, pale fingers poking up from the black soil. Scott loped onwards, shouting, but he didn't shout actual words; this was a violent outpouring of emotion. Darkness engulfed him after a dozen paces. He could see nothing, apart from the smudge of daylight a hundred feet away. At either side of him, rhubarb grew in the darkness. He stopped shouting at this point. All he heard now was his own breathing and the sinister creak of rhubarb as it grew. There was no light in this part of the structure. He moved blindly, leaving the world of daylight entirely. This could be another realm now. A kingdom of darkness. One filled with the menacing creak of plants as they forced themselves upwards, straining to reach the light that wasn't even there.

210

Long ago Daniel Mercer ran, just as Scott ran now. Then what? Why did he stop? What prevented Daniel from leaving the hut with his friends?

Scott glanced to his left. Another figure ran alongside him. This one small... pale... as fragile as a spider's web. And the figure was luminous, allowing Scott to see the boy's face, and that desperate expression he wore.

"Daniel."

"Keep running, Scott! Keep running!"

Scott felt cold and tingly. His eyes watered.

"Daniel?"

"Don't stop!"

"But I did stop, didn't I?" Scott panted. "I was the only who did... but I did stop, and I saw what the man did to you."

Scott came to a halt. He was half way through the hut, surrounded by darkness and the creak of rhubarb striving to reach daylight. In the roof, a small ventilation grill allowed a glimmer of light to fall onto the central pathway.

Daniel Mercer stood there.

Scott whispered, "The man had a wrinkled face; he wore scruffy clothes and a flat cap, and... and I know he did something to you, Daniel. You were too little to stop him. I still don't understand what he did... not fully. But I know that he didn't molest you sexually. It was something else, wasn't it?"

"Scott. Keep going, get out of the hut."

"When adults do bad things to children it's often assumed that there's a sex motive, that it's sexual abuse. That isn't always the case. Adults might commit vicious acts on children for other reasons. Sometimes adults are delusional; they might believe the blood of a child might heal a disease that the adult suffers from, or that the blood of innocent children has a magical power. Is that why he hurt you, Daniel?"

"Go outside, Scott. You don't have to be here anymore."

"I want to stay with you. You were my best friend."

"You've stayed with me in this hut ever since it happened. You have, you know? Inside your head you've never left here."

"Then I didn't abandon you?"

"No. Not emotionally you didn't, but it's time to go now, and let me rest."

The boy remained absolutely still. The words he'd spoken had sounded so mature. His expression was grave and those large blue eyes never left Scott's face.

Scott's own eyes watered. "Did the man kill you and take you away somewhere?"

211

"You were my friend. You stood by me. You didn't leave until you realised that things had reached a point where it was over, and that I wouldn't feel any more pain."

"Daniel –"

"You've got stuff to do with your family without thinking about me all the time." He raised his hand in farewell. "Bye, Scott."

Scott walked through the hut and emerged into daylight. He returned to the car where he sat for a while. At last, he picked up the box, and removed the helicopter and the remote control unit. He returned to the forcing hut where he set the model and the remote control down just inside the doorway. From inside came the clicks and creaks as the rhubarb grew.

"Daniel. I know you liked helicopters. See how high you can make this one go. Knowing you, I bet you can make it fly as high as the moon." He raised his hand to signal good-bye. "Be seeing you, mate."

The man climbed into the car and started its engine. At that moment, an object glided overhead. It flew higher and higher as if gravity could no longer hold it down.

"It's probably just a bird," Scott murmured as he drove in the direction of home.

Very possibly it was a bird. Though, at that instant, he allowed himself to picture a model helicopter soaring into the sky – going up and up, forever and ever. That thought granted him a sense of peace, and that was something he'd not felt in a long, long time.

THE ALIEN

Ilkley Moor, which lies between Ilkley and Keighley in West Yorkshire, is best known as the subject of a popular comic song, On Ilkla Moor Baht 'at, which over the years has become an unofficial anthem for the entire county. However, in real life it is a grimmer place: extensive (about nine square miles, and over 1,000 feet above sea-level), desolate, ridged in some parts, swampy in others, and covered in boulders, mist and the remnants of ancient civilisations.

Various cairns and manmade rock forms give it an eerie atmosphere. The Swastika Stone on Woodhouse Crag, which bears the inscription of a Neolithic swastika, plus the Cow and Calf Rocks and St Margaret's Stones, which all display curious carven images, are regarded as valuable antiquities but also hint at the moor's esoteric past.

And yet it isn't so much tales of the supernatural with which Ilkley Moor is associated, as tales of the extraterrestrial.

The first thing to remember about Ilkley Moor is that it is geographically close to both Menwith Hill airbase and the Leeds-Bradford airport, so though stories about lights in the sky and mysterious objects seen skimming over the heathery hilltops are so numerous as to be almost routine, there may well be mundane explanations for most if not all of them. Perhaps for this reason, the only UFO story that has caused a real stir in the locality involves an incident that occurred on the ground – and not with an unidentified flying object, but with something that may have arrived on the moor by travelling in one.

It was December 1st 1987, and retired Yorkshire police officer, Philip Spencer, was crossing Ilkley Moor to attend a family function. Aware there had recently been reports of UFO sightings over the moor, he had his camera with him. It was a cold winter's afternoon, but visibility, though not excellent, was reasonably good. Spencer was about half way across when he spotted a figure on a low rise just ahead, which appeared to be gesturing at him to go back. Puzzled, Spencer pressed forward. The figure continued to gesture that he retreat, but now he was close enough to see something barely human. It was standing upright, it had a torso, a head and four limbs, but it was unusually short, apparently naked and a greenish-grey in colour.

Spencer shot a photograph of the thing before it turned and fled, vanishing over the nearby ridge. Spencer claims he continued to advance, only to see an object – something along the lines of a typical flying saucer – ascend into the sky a few seconds later, and vanish through the clouds. Bewildered by the experience, he continued on his way, only to then find he had 'lost time', and that he was now in a different part of the moor and in fact heading in a completely different direction.

Thus far, this tale has all the classic ingredients of a so-called 'close encounter', and it fell even more into these realms when later unverified reports leaked out – primarily via UFO investigators – that Spencer afterwards underwent hypnotic regression, during which he recalled abduction and interrogation by alien beings, whose description closely matched the archetypical description of 'the grays', as they are called in ufologist circles.

As with all these stories, it is difficult to get to the truth about what the witness actually claimed to have experienced, let alone what he or she genuinely did experience. However, Spencer had one crucial piece of evidence: the photograph.

Shortly after the incident on the moor, the picture was developed – and caused a minor sensation. It can be seen to this day all over the Internet, where its authenticity is still fiercely debated. It is not absolutely clear what the image depicts, but it would appear to be a vaguely humanoid figure with many distortions, including an overlarge, insect-like head. It was sent for analysis by experts in both the UK and the USA, and though they were able to establish that it did not show any known animal and that whatever the thing was, it stood just over four feet tall, they could not disprove a hoax.

Sceptics have found all sorts of reasons why they disbelieve this tale, but UFO activity continues to be reported on and above the vast barren waste that is Ilkley Moor, and thus far at least, in UK terms certainly, this is the only so-called 'UFO hotspot' where intriguing photographic evidence has been provided.

THE CRACK
Gary Fry

Stacey understood why David behaved the way he did at the moment. When she returned from the campsite shop, the tent was empty and she knew where he'd be. Her husband had never been a big drinker – the habit was hardly conducive to balancing clients' books at the office – but these last few weeks, since the truth had been revealed, he'd visited the pub every other night.

After depositing groceries inside the bright red tent she'd bought for their weekend trip – an attempt to repair their marriage – Stacey headed for the onsite bar, where she was sure she'd find David sinking a pint or several. While passing many other tents, she noticed men looking her way, most with that wild glint in her eye that put her in mind of Tony. Beyond a wall that demarcated the campsite's grounds, she spotted a field scattered with orchids and then felt tears pool in her eyes. But she must put a stop to that.

As suspected, her husband was sitting in one corner of the bar nursing a pint. But he appeared less solemnly disposed to the young woman beside him. Stacey remained in the doorway, out of sight of the two drinkers. With no music playing in the beer lounge, she could hear every word they spoke.

"I'm staying at the far end of the site, close to the boundary wall," David said, his voice slurred from the alcohol he was unaccustomed to. "You can hardly miss it – hell, it's bright bloody red."

If this was a criticism of Stacey, she'd simply have to accept it. After her own recent behaviour, she was hardly in a position to issue rebukes. But what about her husband's behaviour towards this young woman, who was as slim as Stacey if not quite as attractive? Thick makeup clinging to her face seemed to flex as she replied.

"Well, maybe I'll take a walk up there over the weekend. You never know your luck, fella."

The girl – maybe twenty-four or -five – was very common. When she stood coquettishly from the table and moved across the bar to another doorway, she seemed to think her evasiveness was evidence of chastity. But Stacey noticed that her skirt was no longer than an ambitious belt.

Now, pacing towards her husband, Stacey felt roused to action. It wasn't as if her affair had been all her fault. If David had ever shown interest in her, things might have been different. But there was no use pushing that point of view. She'd tried it several times already – back in their five-bedroom detached – and had got nowhere. She should have known better; a man who'd designed his pension plan before hitting his thirties was bound to be a little rigid in outlook.

When David noticed her approaching the table, he looked only slightly guilty. But then the alcohol seemed to kick in, eliminating old habits.

"What do *you* want?" he asked, his voice uncharacteristically dismissive.

But now Stacey focused herself. "I thought we were going on a walk," she said, pointing through the window behind her husband, whose view revealed the majestic North York Moors. Their wild emptiness had appealed to her as a place in which she and her husband could come to terms with problems in their marriage. He'd claimed to prefer somewhere exotic, like the Seyshelles again, or Zanzibar, or maybe even Hawaii. But Stacey knew they could never outdistance the truth.

David said, "I'm not sure I can be bothered taking a walk, to be honest."

"But you … promised," she replied, and realised the inappropriateness of her word a moment too late. His response was as predictable as his mild behaviour during ten years of childless marriage.

"You mean like *you* promised fidelity at our wedding, eh?"

He was being sarcastic, twisting the term of endearment's meaning; he'd rarely used anything similar since they'd met at university. That was just one of the problems, why she'd gone off with Tony…

"But I *want* you to come," she said, emotion rich in her voice. "I want to … reconnect with you. That's why I arranged all this: a quiet weekend away from everything."

The place wasn't *that* quiet. Now in summer season, the campsite was packed, with other couples, large families, and young travellers (like the girl with whom David had just been flirting) filling the grounds with tents and cumbersome caravans. Goathland, the village nearby, was a popular resort, within driving distance of Whitby on the northeast coast but without that town's bustle. There were also plenty of walks to enjoy, and Stacey had used the Internet to choose a relatively short one, just off the popular tracks.

"Oh, you break my heart," her husband snapped back, responding to her plea for decency.

"*Please*, David. Don't make this harder than it has to be."

216

"You should have thought of that before –"

"Yes, I *know*." Now her voice was desperate, pain etched into it. Why could she always predict what he'd say? Why couldn't he sometimes be spontaneous, exciting, even a bit wild? "We've been through this a hundred times. And I'm sorry, okay? I'm sorry, sorry, *sorry*. I don't know how many times you want me to say it. But I'm trying to make amends. So let me ask you one last time…"

By this time, she'd raised her volume, so that even the barman standing idly behind pumps might hear. But she didn't care. In her mind's eye, she saw Tony, holding out a flower for her – Tony who was now dead, as dead as their illicit relationship had been just before she'd ended it and had decided to tell her husband everything.

Stacey said, "…do you want to save our marriage or not? This is our last chance. Come with me or stay here. It's up to you? But just remember one thing: despite what I've done – what I *did* – it won't be *me* ending this. That will be *you*." She hesitated for just one second, before adding, "Unless you come with me now."

David thought for a moment, draining the last of his pint. Then he put down his glass and rose from his seat.

As it turned out, he didn't seem as indifferent as he'd tried to imply.

*

David saw the girl again after returning to their tent to collect something he'd forgotten to pack. At a distance, near the campsite's exit, Stacey watched her husband possibly even wink at her, as he packed the item – Stacey thought it was a bottle of water – into his backpack. She realised that David was an attractive man, and that few women could detect his ponderous character at a glance. As far as she knew, he'd had only one serious relationship – with herself – and that, she truly believed, rendered him vulnerable to temptation.

But what on earth was she thinking? She found her hypocrisy brutal and could now sympathise with David. She wouldn't say anything about the girl, who'd presumably just retreated to her own tent.

When her husband joined her, his eyes a little red from drinking, he said nothing as they exited the campsite and started walking through Goathland, which was already packed with tourists. The village was the setting of a popular TV show, and half was decked out in 1960s paraphernalia, old cars and quaint shops lining a pretty high street. But Stacey and David were headed away from there.

217

Their walk officially began beyond the railway station, a single-platform stop with an old-fashioned ticket office and a bridge from which to observe the arrival of fabulous steam engines. One was leaving as they approached, rousing David from his moribund stupor – he'd always liked trains – and making Stacey hope her planned reunion would come to pass.

She'd grown up in this area, in a small mining village near Middlesbrough but on the North Yorkshire side of the border. She'd met her future husband while studying for a ceramics degree at Newcastle, where he'd been undertaking a Masters in accountancy. She loved the rugged landscapes of the northeast, its purple heather and rich soils. Her parents had often brought her out walking on the moors, a pastime she'd never neglected. She felt free up here, plugged into deeper aspects of existence than were afforded by her modern city lifestyle. The territory was wild, just as a significant part of she was, and sometimes she believed this was what had led to her affair…

But she mustn't think about that. She'd pledged to focus on her marriage. After crossing the railway line, she and her husband advanced up a steep staircase to the top of a hill. Many other people were taking the same route, but Stacey knew from the Internet that the track soon branched off into several different walks. She turned to David, smiling broadly, the landscape already working its magic on her. But her husband simply scowled, a city boy with city habits, perhaps another reason why they had such fundamental difficulties.

"Follow me," she said, but then recalled this was what he'd done last year, after she'd been sneaking out in the evenings to meet her illicit beau. He'd caught them dining together and had grown rightfully angry. Tony had been an out-of-work miner and Stacey had always picked up their restaurant bills, putting it on her credit card without expecting David – who pulled in about eighty-thousand a year – to notice. But he had. He was no fool. A little staid, maybe, but his suspicious mind had proved as keen as his eye for financial detail.

"Go ahead," he replied, his voice cool and acerbic, nodding at the brooding moorland, "lead me along another merry path."

When he was bitter, Stacey found him hard to read, and perversely, she thought this side of his character – perhaps even including the flirtatious chancer she'd witnessed back in the bar – was one she should encourage. It would free him up for … what? Just what did she want from him? What had Tony offered that David couldn't?

She pushed aside her nebulous thoughts and started strolling along a dirt path flanked by withered grass and a bog. She sensed her husband pursuing with barely suppressed anger and mirth.

One of the tacit rules of their marriage involved neither bickering while out in public. Both had been brought up by unimpeachably polite parents and such rules of social engagement went down to the bone. Maybe this was why Stacey had insisted on coming here for a weekend break. It was away from the makeshift policemen of their lives, the family and friends they saw regularly. With nobody else around, they could get to the bottom of what ailed them, really slug it out. But if this was going to happen at all, it would have to be left for later. The path ahead was packed with others: adults, children and giddy pet dogs.

The route led down another hillside to a narrow river snaking alongside several wonderfully secluded houses. Here people picnicked, sunbathed and flung Frisbees, but Stacey and David simply marched ahead, following the map she'd printed at home. This was where they'd split off from the pack, ascending to moorland that had once been excavated for minerals. Disused pits occupied this land, which put Stacey in mind of Tony again.

Despite his rough upbringing and a rougher adulthood back in her native village, he'd been a romantic at heart. One Christmas, Stacey had visited her parents, after she and David had been going through a difficult period, what with his long hours at the office and her lack of success in the ceramics business. She'd gone to the local pub, a place in which she'd learnt to drink as a teenager. And there Tony had been, drinking at the bar. They'd got talking. They'd drunk an awful lot. And by midnight that evening, she was back at his rented terrace and doing things that would shock even her cosmopolitan friends back in Newcastle.

Stacey and Tony had met whenever they could, she driving to Middlesbrough every few weeks. On each occasion, he'd delight her by turning up with a single wild orchid. She'd had no idea where he acquired these flowers, but simply hadn't wanted to know. It was enough that he'd thought about bringing them. David never had.

Although her husband had mapped out their long-term financial security with military precision, he'd rarely done anything as profound as buying her flowers. It wasn't just the simple act of purchasing them that appealed to Stacey, but the underlying sentiment: they implied emotional engagement and spontaneous passion. The truth was that David was rather lapse in that regard.

Perhaps it wasn't possible to have the two qualities in one man. Tony had been unemployed, lacking assets, and had a deeply uncertain future. By contrast, Stacey's husband was highly sought after in his profession and remarkably prosperous. But the first guy had made her heart flutter, and the other often caused it to sink. She simply hadn't been able to help herself. The sex had been incredible. With David, this belt-and-braces act involving double-contraceptive had always struck her more as a business decision – a postponement of family until they were "fiscally prepared to support children" – than an act of passion,

But then, five months after it had started, she'd ended her relationship with Tony. She'd learnt through local gossip (delivered by her mum of all people) that he'd been seeing other women, including some rather lacking in decorum. Stacey wasn't sure whether she'd felt jealous or disappointed, but by that time, after the first flush of excitement had passed and their risqué coupling had lost its edge, she'd chosen to put an end to it. She knew this was selfish, but Tony's lack of means had begun to bother her. It felt unnatural to pay for all the recreational events they enjoyed; that was not something she ever suffered with David. The sex, once carefree and yet dangerous, had become predictable and staid. Even the regular flowers – those solitary orchids, which she suspected he stole from somebody's garden anyway – had lost their symbolic appeal. The relationship had been good while it lasted – no, better than good: *amazing* – but now Stacey had driven this need from her body, perhaps a familiar old story.

But before she'd had chance to tell Tony, and indeed confess to her husband, David had found out…

Snapped away of her reverie, Stacey glanced up and realised that the path along which she'd led them had ascended to rugged moorland. All the other tourists had fallen away, leaving just the two of them, alone with God's good grace. That was when she decided to break the awful, contemplative silence.

Maybe her husband was still feeling the effects of the drinks he'd consumed back at the campsite; he might be tetchy and truth-telling, alcohol's twin toxic legacies. Nevertheless, she had to try. The alternative was returning home with all the subterranean material between them continuing to render their route uncertain, liable to collapse beneath their feet.

"Are you … enjoying yourself?" Stacey asked, turning to observe her husband climbing over the stile she'd just negotiated.

"I can think of worse places," he replied, and if he'd meant the small village in which he'd found his wife with another man, he didn't imply it with his tone. That seemed like progress, at least.

After passing a farmhouse that looked deserted except for several rowdy dogs in pens around the back, they entered a large grassy area with massive undulations. To the left, the land slipped into a valley packed with trees. To the right stood a dry-stone wall, no longer holding back cattle.

"This area has a number of pits, you know," Stacey explained, drawing on what she'd learned from the Internet. "In the 1800s, it was used for unearthing rich minerals deposited over centuries."

This was dangerous territory, but not just because of many muddy potholes along the path. She also meant psychologically; after all, Tony had been an unemployed miner and David knew that. But again he failed to respond negatively. Perhaps the effect of booze was wearing off.

"Better be careful where we stand, then," he said, looking down at the walking boots he'd strapped on back in the tent. "I read a news report recently about abandoned mines sometimes giving way and people getting swallowed alive by the earth."

"Ooh, nasty," Stacey replied, eager to keep her husband talking on such neutral grounds. Every step forward seemed to guarantee their future together. Then she tried pushing the issue a bit harder. "This reminds me of that time on our honeymoon – do you remember? How we scaled that hill in Provence that overlooked a whole vineyard?"

"A vintage memory," David said, and it took Stacey a moment to appreciate his joke. She simply hadn't expected it. But then she laughed with mild unease and spoke again.

"And there was a similar occasion on our second or third anniversary when we –"

"Why did you have an affair, Stacey?"

The question literally stopped her in her tracks. At first, all she could think about doing was buying more time. "I beg your pardon?" she said, a question in response to his question, which she knew that he, a man used to slick office practice, greatly disliked.

Then David, now several paces ahead of her, stopped walking and turned her way, glaring with hard eyes. Over his shoulders, amid fields bereft of other people, Stacey saw wild flowers waving against that stone wall, maybe even orchids…

But that was when her husband spoke again.

"I don't think I've ever asked you directly. That's just like me, isn't it? Emotionally subdued. Solid, predictable but rarely confrontational. The man to approach for practical advice, but no use in a human crisis. Isn't that the way you'd characterise me, Stacey?"

She was shocked, not only because of his bluntness but also by how clinically accurate his understanding of her current perspective was. It was as if he'd reached into her skull and tugged out her secrets. She hadn't realised how much he'd known about her values, but if this was all true, why had he never tried altering his ways? Did he believe that bringing all the money into the household granted him some kind of nuptial immunity?

Feeling angry, Stacey glanced around, at birds flitting from ancient tree to tree, at a frisky rabbit bounding between shadowy holes. The bright sky bore nary a cloud, as if both she and her husband were exposed to a higher judgement. Then, looking back at David, she said with deliberate encryption, "You … you never brought me flowers."

He appeared shocked. "And that's it? You're saying you went off with another man because I never bought you flowers?"

"Stop being so literal. *Think* about it."

"What's to think about?"

"Maybe *that's* the problem, David."

"What is? I don't get you."

"The fact that you need to ask. There's just something … vital missing."

"*Was* something missing … or *is* something missing, Stacey?"

"How do you mean?"

"It's simple. Are you saying that we *still* have a problem, and that the problem is *mine*?"

"No, I didn't mean it like that …"

"How did you mean it, then?"

"I meant … I meant …"

"Come on, Stacey. Be clearer."

She sensed her anger stepping up. She began pacing forwards, unable to prevent herself from undoing all the good work she'd achieved up till now. "God, you can be so infuriating."

"In what way?" he replied, turning to follow her. Soon they were side-by-side, her eyes fixed forwards into the middle distance, his tilted to observe her. "You mean, the way I pull in eighty grand a year and support you in whatever you want to do in life? *That* kind of infuriating, Stacey? Or maybe it's the kind of infuriating that's given us the house of our dreams, any sensible car we desire, and foreign holidays several times a year? Is that what you mean?"

"But *that's* just it, David." The orchids near the wall waved their heads, even though there was no breeze today, no breeze at all. "Everything's so … *instrumental* with you. And sometimes I need more than that. I need you to … to … oh, I don't know."

"Well," he replied, his voice incredulous, "if *you* don't know, how the hell am *I* supposed to?"

In fact, she'd already decided what was missing from his character: she wanted him to do something outrageous for her. She

222

wanted him to take off all his clothes and run across a field packed with bulls to save her from drowning or falling from a tree. She wanted him to occasionally stop focusing on professional activities, and simply show her that he *loved her*. Was that too much to ask? Of course she knew that he cared for her; he was always kind and generous. But sometimes, while involved in a project at work, he could be cranky and dismissive, which made her feel peripheral to his life. To eliminate all the doubt she experienced at such times, which lurked beneath their lives like underground tunnels packed with God-knew-what sly creatures, she'd greatly welcome an act of unambiguous devotion, a paradigm shift in motion. Bringing flowers was just one way of demonstrating such feelings; their pointlessness – decapitated and destined to wither – was their very point. But David would probably consider them dead money, and ultimately that was the real petty, crucial difference: Tony never had.

Stacey had just begun considering the validity of this argument – hadn't she suspected earlier that her late lover had stolen the orchids he'd always brought her? – when she fell flat on her face.

Her husband stopped walking at once and then crouched to help her. When she glanced down, where her feet had tripped, she spotted a large crack in the earth, running across this section of terrain, about a foot wide and twice that deep. It looked as if the earth had broken apart, causing the hill on which they'd been walking to appear dangerous. She recalled David's report earlier about the way mines sometimes rendered the ground unstable and how people could fall to their deaths through occasional holes. But then, the shock of the fall diminished, she laughed out loud, imagining the great absurdity of everything, the fragility of a planet upon which she and her husband had just been bickering like petulant schoolchildren.

Perhaps reading her thoughts, David also started laughing, and when she reached up to accept his support and failed to grab his hands properly, he also tumbled onto the earth, landing almost directly on top of her. It was like their early days again, after they'd just met at university. With only studying to endure, they'd had lots of fun, before the pressures of getting along in life, of keeping up with *mores* and watching that ticking biological clock, had complicated everything. Stacey was a simple person at heart; she thought her husband was, too. But of course he had money to earn, and in any final analysis, that was what Stacey couldn't survive without: security that allowed her freedom; solid ground underfoot.

The bump on the head she'd sustained after tripping over the crack might have triggered these insights. But then she tried pulling David wholly on top of her.

"I'm sorry, my darling," she said, now feeling for his groin through his pants. "But just for once in our lives, do something *dangerous* for me. Screw me on this hill. Go on. I want you to do it. I *need* you to do it."

Her husband looked alarmed at her candour, but a rare glint appeared in his eyes, the like of which she hadn't seen since he'd secured a big deal several years ago, one involving accountancy for a nationwide industrial outfit that had gone into liquidation following a change in government policy. But then his nerve seemed to dissipate.

"No, we can't," he said, gently batting away her roaming hands. "Let's go back to the campsite. We can … get busy that way inside the tent."

"No, not there. I want it here … *here*."

"But people might see."

Stacey stopped for a moment, lifted her head and glanced around. Other than the bobbing heads of those seemingly sentient orchids, nobody was in the area to cause concern.

Then, in a childlike voice she knew David liked – one which convinced her that before long, he'd consent to having a family – she added, "I pwomise to be a gud little girl fowevermore."

Now he pushed her away more forcefully – not hard enough to destroy her reignited feelings for him, but certainly compromising her spontaneous mood.

"Back in the tent, I said," David went on, his voice masterly, promising much but on his own terms. Then he stood and tugged her off the ground, keeping hold of her hand as, slowly and sensibly, they continued strolling back towards picturesque Goathland. But a minute later, he said, "If I'm going to change, I need to feel comfortable while doing so."

And that was fair, wasn't it? *One step at a time*, Stacey reflected, imagining the walk she'd planned to save their marriage as some kind of symbolic process. But if that was true, what role did the disused pits play? And what about her fall just now?

Such thoughts troubled her all the way back to the campsite, but she didn't look back even once. She kept hold of her husband's hand, and even the prospect of receiving a single wild flower, representing acts of passionate abandon, did little to dampen the prospect of returning to her first true lover.

*

224

The sex was good, but not amazing. That was Stacey's first impression after David rolled away from her later that evening.

They'd arrived back at the tent at four pm, and had enjoyed a greasy meal cooked on their gas burner. Then they'd visited the site's bar and downed several resolve-enhancing drinks. While leaving at about nine o'clock, Stacey had spotted the girl her husband had been chatting to earlier, but the girl hadn't seen Stacey. Perhaps she believed David was single, but Stacey had no reason to feel threatened by her ... did she?

Outside it had been dark, and she and her husband had strolled to their tent with only the aid of a distant lamp, fixed to the campsite's reception area. Someone else had obviously left the bar before them; up ahead, a shadowy figure on the fringes of the grounds, where Stacey thought she'd spotted orchids earlier, had shuffled back and forth, as if uncertain about whom he or she was. Stacey couldn't imagine being in such a compromised state, but that had brought back thoughts of Tony and what had eventually become of him.

Perhaps that was why sex with her husband had failed to overwhelm her. She'd tried telling herself that it was because David, demanding a sensible venue after such a delay, had robbed the moment of spontaneity. But the truth was much more grisly. Even while engaged in intercourse, she'd been unable to rid her mind of an image of her former lover, beaten to death one night after a drunken brawl. Maybe the perpetrator, who'd never been identified, had been another cheated spouse, the brutal partner of one of the other women he'd been seeing at the same time as Stacey.

As her husband slept at her side in predictable pyjamas, Stacey found it difficult not to dwell on Tony's demise. He hadn't deserved such a fate. Life had been cruel to him. The only profession for which he'd trained was mining, and nationwide industrial circumstances had eliminated such employment opportunities in the northeast. He'd died an unhappy man, mainly because he'd lacked the means to purchase success. That was the real difference between winners and losers in modern society: a man or a woman might demonstrate romantic inclinations aplenty, but without a marketable ability to attach them to, they amounted to nothing. Stacey's failed ceramics business had been supplemented by David's successful accountancy. That was how life would always be. Stacey needed to eat. And she knew where she was better off.

Snuggling down to embrace her husband – the sex would be better next time, she told herself – she tried falling asleep ... and was awakened maybe hours later by a noise outside.

It sounded like someone creeping covertly towards their bright red tent. The footfalls were abnormal, seeming to shuffle and drag across grass out there. Stacey sat up, nudging David hard enough to modify the pattern of his light snoring, but failing to awaken him. If what she'd begun to suspect was correct, however, she was glad about that. It must be nearly midnight to judge by the moon's crystal wash through the tent's fabric. On the basis of the silence, Stacey believed nobody else on the campsite was awake.

Then that figure – little more than a ragged silhouette in the cold light out there – approached the tent and began stooping with uncertain limbs to its front entrance.

It was the girl; Stacey simply knew it. The one who'd been chatting up her husband earlier, who clearly hadn't realised he was already spoken for. As the newcomer started fumbling at the base of the zippered opening, Stacey was roused like an animal protecting her partner, keeping him safe and keen.

"*Go away*," she hissed, her voice audible enough to an outsider, but not loud enough to wake David. "*Keep your distance from our marriage.*"

And this seemed to work. As if responding directly to her exhortation, the figure began retreating. It straightened up with a perceptible lack of agility – perhaps the girl wasn't as young as she'd appeared at a distance, a thought which cheered and amused Stacey – and then staggered back across the site, those trailing footfalls rarely rising above ground level. The girl might still be drunk; that cheered and amused Stacey even more. Then, lying back down, she detected an unpleasant stench, like spoiled old meat, but told herself that the pan on the gas burner her husband had used earlier would just want washing out.

Moments later, all her defensive / proactive business completed, she fell asleep and dreamed about a crack opening in the ground ... a pair of human eyes glaring up from a pit beneath ... slipshod limbs beginning to move ...

But then Stacey jerked awake.

She found herself in the tent she'd bought especially for this trip, which, to judge by David's early rising, had been a success. Sitting up in the large sleeping bag in which they'd enjoyed such promising acts the previous evening, Stacey noticed her husband crouched at the entrance, having tugged up its zip. Then he looked back at her ... but his face appeared puzzled.

"David?" she said, crawling forwards on all fours and leaving their bedding behind in a disorderly pile. "What is it? What's wrong?"

After he'd turned the rest of his body her way, revealing a gap through the tent's entrance, Stacey noticed other people strolling around the campsite. But then, looking quickly down, she wanted to believe that her husband had been out among them, dressed only in embarrassing pyjamas and not caring a bit about that. She wanted to believe that he'd run towards the site's borders in a singular act of passion, before returning with similar abandon. She wanted to believe that David was changing his character, and that he was doing so just for her.

Because in one hand, she noticed, he held a solitary orchid. And she certainly didn't want to think he'd just collected it from the ground in front of the tent.

THE BOGGART OF BUNTING NOOK

The word 'boggart' almost has comical connotations today. Familiar figures in children's fiction, and possessed of a name more likely to induce sniggers than shivers in the uber-cynical 21st century, it is difficult to imagine how feared these mysterious beings once were in the counties of Northern England.

The word itself stems from the ancient British 'bwg', and has many common derivations: bogle, bugbear, bogey, bogeyman, all with similar meanings – an unknown but evil entity. However, in the folklore of old Yorkshire, the boggart was quite specifically defined. It was a malevolent spirit found in marshes or on bleak moorland, where it would lie in wait for unwitting travellers, so that it could attach itself to them as they passed and then torment their families until such time as it became bored, which could be decades later, if not centuries.

And its manifestations could be varied and terrifying.

One of the best examples is surely the Boggart of Bunting Nook, allegedly the occupant of a stretch of parkland in Sheffield, South Yorkshire. On the face of it, this doesn't seem a likely venue for such a tale, set deep in the heart of a thriving municipal zone. But the Bunting Nook boggart has supposedly lived here since this road ran through wild country on the outskirts of the city, traversing what was then a large area of bog and marsh. Stories about encounters with it date back to a time before the Industrial Revolution, and still continue to this day. Invariably the boggart only appears at night, and has been described as everything from a deformed and braying donkey to a snarling hound, from a towering green mist-form to the black shadow of a man flitting manically back and forth across the path as witnesses approach. Perhaps even more disturbing, numerous disembodied voices have been reported in the vicinity, ranging from eerie, piping laughter to the crying of a baby, the latter of which has been interpreted as a deliberate ploy to lure the unwary into the mist-shrouded trees.

Of course, boggart-free explanations have also been offered, most notably that the whole thing is a hoax perpetrated by local youths amused by these ancient fairy tales. But if that is the case the perpetrators are fairly persistent. Local paranormal groups believe Bunting Nook is genuinely haunted, but they blame more run-of-the-mill ghosts. A spectral bridesmaid said to roam the path – possibly close to the area where a young woman once committed suicide – certainly has the aura of the traditional. While a young boy was beaten to death near Bunting Nook in 1846, and lies buried in a nearby churchyard, and his spectre has also been reported. For all this, it should be noted that written references to the Boggart of Bunting Nook predate both these tragedies.

A prominent Yorkshire-based medium feels there is only one entity here, and that it is something, in his words, "unknowable and unexplainable, because it has never walked this Earth in a corporeal form". He also describes it as a constant presence, as in it does not travel to and from the spirit world using Bunting Nook as a kind of doorway, but dwells here. For this reason, he says, the birds stay away.

That is something even the local press have noticed and queried. Why is birdsong so strangely absent in this otherwise scenic place?

A STORY FROM WHEN
WE HAD NOTHING
Jason Gould

He rolled his thumb over the wheel on his lighter but the flame did not uncurl until he made the action again. He held it out before him: to the right then the left, down then up. Dust lifted in the glow.

He let go of the door he'd been holding open and it banged against its twisted frame. Then he carried forward his oval of unsteady light, and the outbuilding showed itself yard by yard.

In the corner he saw a bucket, a pile of rope, the brown carcass of a tractor engine. A long diagonal crack pulled the wall apart. The brickwork was powdering. Above his head the roof bowed as if a sick animal had been crawling over it and died.

At the far wall he ran his eye along a row of rusted tools suspended from hooks. A pickaxe. A hacksaw. Shears he would not be surprised if the action on which had long since seized.

Not hanging on the wall but standing against it was a spade. The wood of the handle had split. The blade had a stubbly rust, sharp and brown. He crouched and examined it. He did not believe it would take the weight of use.

He pulled down the pickaxe and with that and the spade under his arm he turned back to the door, and the flame in his hand shook itself.

*

Outside it was still dark with no sun. By starlight he looked along the track that ran from the farm and into the trees. It began at the house in a swirl of tyre-marks that led between the outbuilding and the abandoned milking shed and which, further along, edged about an empty pond before it left the perimeter of the farm and curved into the forest. After some distance in the trees it came out on a minor road, a sudden junction, but before that it ran for some miles below the ridge that came gently down from where the heather had been burned at the end of the summer on Lastingham Moor.

He raised his sight higher than the horizon. And in the sky he saw the white and priceless stars, flung into it in their millions.

*

Not much later he went by the thin light of the opening day to the field farthest from the house. He walked along the edge of several fields that had not recently been farmed. They were hardened and overgrown. In a ditch he saw the rusted blade of a circular plough, pushed in when whoever had owned it had given up on the earth.

Where one field joined the neighbouring field he stopped and looked back at the house. It stood wet and without colour in the coming dawn. Above its blank windows and dilapidated roof he saw the woods, and above the woods the rim of the valley in which lay the farm and its surrounding acres. At the very top, above it all, the moorland, roaming endlessly away.

The woods sloping along the valley-side stirred in the breeze like a green lake.

In a secluded corner, shielded by a dry-stone wall, he used the pickaxe to define a square. It was not the time of year to open the ground and after each entry into the earth he had to manoeuvre the blunt tool back and forth to pull it free.

Eventually he had an outline of about six feet along each side and he dropped the pickaxe and used the spade. He hacked and shovelled but disinterred only tiny amounts. He had to work gently to keep the spade from snapping. If it broke he would not get far with his fingers. And it had to be deep enough. He did not want to find in a day or two the things he had to bury pulled to the surface by an animal.

When he had to rest he straightened up and held and rubbed his lower back. The sweat that had risen on his neck dripped between his shoulder blades and he shuddered. His breath lifted out of the hole in grey clouds. In his nostrils and throat the aroma of unpacked soil. In his bones the November cold.

He coughed and spat on the ground. The left-flank of his torso ached where it was bandaged. As he stretched about his task the bandage and the stitching below it pulled.

Under the drifting, bone-white sky he put aside the pain and continued to dig.

*

His name was Frank Edward White, and he'd lived at Black Top Farm less than a fortnight. He still hoped that sometime soon he might be able to leave.

When he'd travelled here, to the northern edge of Yorkshire, he'd left behind in Bradford his entire life. It was a separation he had not wanted but the inevitability of which he understood. He had

231

always held the place in high esteem. He would not be who he was if it had not been for the city of Bradford. From a young age it had forced him to bear witness to the struggle of life.

His father had worked for a money lender, a local loan shark with whom he'd been acquainted some years. Occasionally, Frank had accompanied his father from doorstep to doorstep. They would knock and ask for money, and more often than not be declined. Sometimes, if nobody answered, they'd sit in the car and wait for the curtain behind which the debtor had hidden to be pulled aside, or for a light to be switched on. Then, Frank's father would try again, and if still nothing happened he'd attempt to negotiate through the letterbox.

The young Frank had been inside some desperate dwellings. He'd seen humans living like forgotten animals. He'd seen barely fed infants asleep below patches of damp that seemed almost to breathe in the subdued light. He'd listened to stories of frostbite in unheated flats, eviction orders, husbands on remand. The job someone had been promised never seemed to happen. Benefits cheques failed to arrive. Money kept aside specially (more than was due) had been lifted by an opportunistic thief. He'd seen the tip of a broken bottle held underneath his father's eye, and a woman with flaps of skin where she'd once had breasts suggest that the kid might like to watch, if that's what dad wanted.

The city – its detached nature, its suffering inhabitants – had taught the boy the fundamental truth by which he'd since lived: that life was and would only ever be about survival, and that the key to survival was not love or cunning or a diligent work ethic, it was wealth. If you had that, however acquired, you would never be under threat. The ruined, beseeching face looking up from the pavement, the gnawing cold, the coins in the dirty McDonald's cup – it would never be you.

*

When Frank was about eight or nine he'd suffered terrible nightmares. They happened the evenings after he'd spent the day with his father, prising notes and coins out of desperate hands, and scribbling figures in a little black book. His mother – hearing him sob in his sleep – would rush to comfort him, and promise he would never, ever need to struggle the way those people did.

Frank had different blood in his veins, she said. He was a Prince. Only, for now, the world had forgotten it.

*

He waited in the kitchen for it to be night. He'd arrived back at the farm in the afternoon, and sat on the stool until the light in the window went down. He had not lifted the chairs, the table or any other item in the room back into its rightful position. Everything lay where it had fallen: the saucepans knocked off their hooks above the stove, the cutlery drawers yanked open and their contents scattered, the kettle, one of the few signs of modernity in the room, albeit not the electric kind, tipped on its side in the sink. On the floor potatoes had rolled everywhere. A soup dish had shattered.

The door to the upstairs was ajar, but Frank had not been through it in days. He'd stayed out of the house. He'd been in only to empty the fridge and the larder, the contents of which he'd transferred to the Land Rover in the yard outside, where he'd also been sleeping, sitting upright in the driver's seat, the doors locked, the vehicle facing toward the gate and the track that led into the woods and away from the farm. He'd slept with his hand on the key, the key in the ignition. He started the engine every few hours to check it still worked. More than once he'd started it accidentally when an unidentified noise had disturbed his sleep. His wrist would turn the key before he was fully awake and the motor would fire and the headlights shoot through the trees with a sudden and surprising brightness.

The dark gathered around him now, in the ransacked kitchen, and Frank gazed up through the gloom at the door to the stairs.

He got up, went outside and looked around. Everywhere was silent. The yard and the track. The woods curving along the valley.

For five, maybe ten minutes he stood, watching for any sign of movement. When he was satisfied he took from the boot of the Land Rover the tarpaulin he used to cover the vehicle when it was not in use. It was heavy, the material stiff. He carried it into the kitchen, knelt on the stone floor, and opened it out.

The stairs were lit only by the dusk coming through the tall window at the end of the landing, and they were narrow, and they were steep. The house did not have electricity running to it. They'd brought candles but he did not know where they might be, not now, with the place in turmoil. And he did not want to see too much anyway.

He began to climb, each uncarpeted step, the disturbed sleep of the last few days warping the staircase, shrinking the murky space between the peeling walls.

Halfway, he stopped.

Blood had dried on the top step. It had rolled along the floorboards, and dripped down the stairs.

Frank took a moment to remind himself why he had to continue, why even this – the bodies he would see, when he took the next step, heaped in the evening light – was unavoidable if he was to be rich, if he was to salvage and bring to an end the glorious acquisition he had begun.

*

Frank Edward White had forgotten many bad things he'd done over the years, but he would not forget the moment he pulled a bed sheet over the face of his wife, Judith Melanie White, and over the faces of their two dead girls, Isabelle White, almost nine, and her younger sister, Jane, aged four and three-quarters, before carrying them sideways, each in turn, down the barely lit staircase of a house he did not know, miles from the city he loved, in the dark heart of Yorkshire.

*

Somewhere between the farm and the field the tarpaulin caught on a nail or root and the clump of hair that slid out pulled along behind it in the grass. Frank did not notice until he had the bundle balanced on the edge of the pit, about to ease it in. In the dark he was unable to tell whose head had been nearest the rip in the fabric, whose hair had dragged through the mud, leaving behind its own personal scent.

He tried to inch the package into the ground gently. He had hold of one end. It was sliding in slowly but the further it progressed the more it gathered momentum and the more it seemed to weigh. He lost his grip and it flew through his fingers. The tarpaulin and its contents, and the rope tied around it, tumbled heavily into the grave with a hollow knocking noise like the collapse of a log-pile, and the silence through which Frank had stolen was suddenly and loudly fractured.

He froze. He held his breath.

He listened as the limbs slid into the earth and sank together. He listened until he heard that they had settled. Then he breathed out, and he shovelled the pile of excavated soil back into the hole with the spade and with his feet and at the end, to pack it firm and ensure it was flat, he used the palms of his hands.

When he'd finished he turned immediately and did not look back. He staggered over the fields to the house, where he sat in the Land Rover with the doors locked and his fingers on the key in the ignition. And the spell of disbelief – and the abiding sense of righteousness with which he'd acted – broke and fell apart and he sobbed and said their names, and he was still sobbing, still saying their names hours later when the sun lifted its autumn glow onto the moorland ridge.

*

"Judith. Isabelle. Jane."

He sat in the driver's seat until the day had almost finished. Twice he switched on the engine, twice turned it off. The third time he put the vehicle in gear, let out the clutch and allowed it to roll forward along the track. He stopped at the gate, where the track went into the trees. He did not have a destination in mind. He could not venture anywhere near Bradford. West was a risk he was unable to take. It would have to be north. Through Yorkshire toward Newcastle, maybe Scotland.

But he had nothing. He thought about the situation in which he found himself. How, if he left, he would have no house, no money. Most of all he would have nobody to whom he could turn. No other person – no friend, no brother, no blood – who could help him begin again.

It was not possible for him to leave Black Top Farm until he'd taken back his future.

*

Behind the farmhouse the garden had been left to grow until it had died. If you stood at the kitchen sink you could see the top of the grass outside, its surface flickering on the breeze all the way down to where the woods began five or six hundred yards away, at the ascent to the moor. Also visible from the kitchen was a square of flagstones – somebody's midsummer dream reduced to a slippery lichen-coated island – bearing now a rusted sun lounger and some empty flowerpots, several of which had tipped over and rolled about in the wind. Further away a corrugated iron shed had collapsed. And far off among the weeds a mower was almost entirely submerged.

The only oddity in this forgotten wasteland was the earth. Tiny piles of it, each fairly recent, each carefully removed from the ground and heaped beside an excavation approximating the size of a fruit bowl. They proliferated at random, these little searches, the grass in the vicinity of each pulled up or stamped down, the disturbed soil suggesting that the yellow wilderness was not entirely without its appeal.

Something was under the garden. It had been put there. And somebody wanted it found.

*

Later that day the clouds pulled apart and in the hour before evening the sky hung streaked with violet. Frank was on his hands and knees behind the house, keen to use the last of the light, a trowel in his left hand, a tarnished dessert spoon in his right.

He'd dug, from late afternoon until now, in approximately a dozen places, in addition to the many he'd tried in the days before. Today he'd followed a roughly diagonal route, beginning near the kitchen window and progressing in a north-westerly direction across a sodden patch of uneven earth. It had no logic or design, the pattern he followed. It was entirely random. He was too exhausted to rely on any strategy but luck.

His latest attempt brought into the half-light a shard of terracotta. It had been part of a vase or decorative garden pot. He gazed at it stupidly. It wasn't the first time the tip of the spoon had scratched against a hard surface and he – suddenly energised, hope suddenly renewed – had grabbed at the soil with his fingers, only to feel them close about a stone or piece of slate, or the bone of an animal.

He turned the fragment over in his hand. It had the shape of a skewed diamond. He hung his head, and stayed like that a moment, like statuary in the grass, chiselled in remembrance of somebody lost. Then he crawled forward, further and deeper into the tangled mess, hopeful that the light would last a few more minutes and that he would happen upon a patch of recently disrupted ground, or a polished stone, or a doll, or a pair of sticks in the shape of an X, or any sign that would not be beyond the wit and sympathy of an eight-year-old girl.

*

That night, like every night, Frank sat behind the dashboard of the Land Rover, his hand on the ignition. The big upholstered interior of the 4x4 was the only place he felt safe. But he did not sleep. And if he did doze, if his hand slipped off the key or his left hand lost contact with the shotgun that lay on the passenger seat, he would wake instantly, and the engine would come on, and the headlights would illuminate the forest, and the gun would be secure in his grip.

When it was light Frank drove through the woods, through stripes of sunlight and shade, until he emerged on the moor, and

236

then burnt heather flew by and the wind cracked against the vehicle but the vehicle held itself solid. He braked at the first junction. The signpost said that Lastingham was fifteen miles to the east, and in the west lay villages he hadn't heard of, and further west any number of towns and cities into which he might easily vanish.

Instead of making a decision, he rested his head on the steering wheel and listened to the engine. It was comforting, somehow. It had a warmth and an oiled perfection that reminded him of Bradford.

He turned east, toward Lastingham, and when he arrived it was quiet, its main street empty. He got out of the car and walked toward the doctor's surgery.

The practice had been a house a century earlier, maybe longer, and it had not been modified much in the name of medicine. He looked through the window. The waiting room had nobody in it. Last time he'd been here it had not been pleasant, and coming back made him feel edgy, intimidated. Part of him said he should turn and walk away. The empty wooden chairs in the waiting room, shiny in the early morning sun, put a shudder down his back.

He did not have an appointment and was surprised when he was sent into the consulting room after only five minutes. He remembered, as he took a seat, how the room did not allow into it much air, or light. A clock ticked somewhere within the piles of reference books.

It was a mistake, he thought, returning here. He was considering leaving when Dr Stone, sitting behind his huge desk, said, "You are back. And why is it that you are back?"

"I'm having trouble sleeping," said Frank.

"Anxiety," said Stone. "That's what takes away sleep. I should know. I worry myself silly over the most trifling thing these days. It's my age. But a young man like yourself ..."

"I'm not anxious," said Frank. "I'd know if I was ill."

"Indeed," said Stone. "Do you remember the last conversation we had? About psychological disfigurement. Damage that cannot be seen. Given it any further thought?"

"I'm fine. I just can't seem to get to sleep. And I really need to."

Stone looked up from his notepad. He considered the younger man a moment. Then he said, "How's life on the farm? It can't be easy. Different to what you've been used to. All that land. Harsh winter on the way. And a young family –"

"All I need," said Frank, sitting forward, "is sleep. I've barely slept in days. I just need a few hours. Something mild, that's all."

The elderly doctor returned to his notepad. "It is, of course, entirely within my power to prescribe tablets for a whole host of conditions, physical or mental, real or imaginary. And on this occasion, I shall provide."

"Thank you."

"But you must think about why you lie awake at night," said Stone, tearing a sheet off the pad and holding it across the desk.

As Frank took the prescription, Stone said, "I'll check your stitches. While you're here."

"They're okay."

"Just a quick look. Nothing to worry about."

"No need."

"I'll be the judge of that."

"Really –"

"I insist," said Stone. "You ask me to perform emergency surgery, the first in years, the least you can do is permit me to inspect my handiwork."

Reluctantly, Frank took off his jacket and unbuttoned his shirt. He lifted his arm and twisted to the right. Stone positioned his fingertips along the six-inch ridge of raised flesh on Frank's torso, through which he'd pushed the needle and pulled the thread. He pressed firmly along the torn skin.

"Something really took a piece out of you," he said. "I can count its teeth."

*

Frank dressed, and as he left, as the door closed behind him, he heard Stone say to himself, "Some of the things that live in those cities. Makes you pray for the bomb."

*

In the kitchen, Frank found a knife and sliced one of the sleeping tablets in half. He needed to rest, but did not want to be that deeply subdued he would not be able to wake if necessary.

The pill went down with a handful of water. As he tipped his head back, he glimpsed through the cracked kitchen window the heaps of disinterred earth. It would take months to dig up the entire garden.

"Oh you silly girl," he said. "You silly, silly little girl."

*

Behind the wheel of the Land Rover, Frank closed his eyes, and tried to relax. He ached where the clumsy needlework kept his skin from splitting. He lay the shotgun on his knee.

"No eight-year-old buries treasure without a map," he said to the empty car. "No way."

Soon the tablet began to bring sleep, and with it the hope that on waking he might be clear-headed, focused, and able to deduce exactly where on Black Top Farm his daughter had hidden the tiny glittering objects of his unfettered desire.

*

It was an afternoon of difficult dreams, in which Frank relived recent events. In the first dream, he was leaving Bradford, again ...

It had not happened the way it had been planned, escaping the metropolis. It should have been easy. Instead, the city had clung to Frank, as if it had not wanted to release the man who'd stolen from it and its people for almost thirty years. He was not to be allowed a simple exit.

But he did not know this as he stood, as planned, on the tenth floor of the old Fairfax Mill, a derelict building he'd reconnoitred less than a week earlier. He'd seen it from afar as he and Jimmy had walked the getaway route from *All That Glitters* to where they planned to separate and fade into the West Yorkshire backstreets. He hadn't commented on the ruin as they'd rehearsed their escape, but when he'd returned, alone, he'd looked more closely, and discovered a concealed entrance: a service door located behind a disused electricity generator. To access the door you had to squeeze between the machine and the building itself. If you knew it was there, it was easy to slip inside. If you didn't, it would only be found if you had time to dedicate. And, with police everywhere, Jimmy would not want to wait around.

Frank stood several feet back from the window, covered in shade. Jimmy was striding about in the road below, looking first at the gaping, rain-swept shell of the textile mill, then at the fenced-off wasteland opposite. He was unable to comprehend how and to where the other man had vanished. He was swearing and shouting. He went to the fence and peered through, hoping to spot Frank loping away across the empty plot. He kicked the corrugated iron when he saw nothing.

For almost five minutes – longer than Frank had anticipated – Jimmy paced in circles, afraid to stay for fear he be caught, but unable to drag himself away from the haul Frank carried in his rucksack. Once or twice Frank thought Jimmy had noticed the secret passage but, while he appeared to look right at it, he did not realise it led to anywhere other than a crumbling wall.

At last, Jimmy yelled and drop-kicked the fence again, and gave up. He walked swiftly along the edge of the building toward the main road, punching thin air until he was out of sight.

In the corner, under a blanket, Frank had left a briefcase and change of clothes. Quickly, he swapped his jacket and jeans for a shirt and tie and a business suit.

Squatting, unable to resist, he opened the rucksack, reached inside and lifted up a fistful of diamonds. They seemed to pull the afternoon light toward them. He stared for a moment, transfixed. He let them fall through his fingers. Then, aware of the pressure of time, and the distant wail of sirens, Frank switched the loot into a smaller bag that hung on his waist, tucked it under his shirt and buttoned the suit jacket, and turned and headed for the fire exit in the far wall.

Until recently, the old Fairfax Mill appeared to have functioned as a sweatshop, engaged – it would seem by the tightly installed rows of industrial sewing machines – in the mass production of cheap clothing. Frank walked between the abandoned workbenches. Rolls of cloth lay where they'd been left. Spools of cotton. Templates cut from tissue paper. Boxes from fast food outlets proliferated, piled high, as if each operative had driven their machine with one hand while hurriedly eating with the other.

The stools on which the workforce had sat had been bolted to the floor. Attached to the central leg of each stool was a heavy chain. Welded to each chain was an iron shackle, and further along the chain a second shackle, the first for the left ankle and the second for the right, and barely a hand-span of play between the two. Some of the shackles had turned from iron-grey to dirty-brown, coloured not by rust but by the tightness of the lock that had worried at the skin all through the unending days and nights.

On the wall above the workforce, in lettering three feet high, somebody had painted: NO BREAK! And beneath: INCLUDING SLEEP WITHOUT PERMISSION!

Glass from the shattered windows scratched under Frank's shoes as he made his way to the exit. He glanced down at a pair of leg irons coiled like sinister stockings. The building retained an atmosphere of recent exodus: beads of grease in noodle boxes, flies crawling on pizza crust, walls that still seemed to vibrate from the mechanical din. It had either been evacuated by the owner on the advice of a tipoff, or by the authorities themselves. Either way it still felt warm.

He was not far from the fire door, and the rickety fire escape that led down to the street, when something nearby made a sound. He paused mid-step.

The noise came again, a little louder. Frank turned toward it.

It was coming from behind a row of sewing machines to Frank's right – fifteen, twenty feet away – a part of the room obscured by sunlight falling in through a high window. It sounded like a handful of coins tumbling together.

"Hello?" he said. "Is somebody in here?"

He waited. He was about to continue to the fire exit when the noise happened again, the jangling of silver or copper, a lot louder now, and more prolonged, as if somebody had cupped one hand over the other, only instead of protecting a butterfly or baby sparrow or some other beautiful thing it was money they held, and which they shook about excitedly.

Frank walked to the end of the row. It was happening below the final station, this odd rattle. Somebody was under there.

Slowly, Frank crouched, preparing to bolt if necessary. It was, however, a young girl, barely over the brink of adulthood, kneeling in the filth.

Whoever had cleared the factory had left behind a broken soul. She was wearing pyjama-like overalls, which seemed to be some kind of standard issue, a company moniker on the breast. Out of the sleeves poked wrists like the thin white sticks of an ailing tree. Her hair, cut short, was matted and damaged; if she ever escaped this place her head would need to be shaved, the roots engaged afresh. Her European features had an elegance about them, or a potential elegance had they not been neglected, and in her eyes Frank saw the empty, deserted look often found in people for whom their homeland has only ever been a memory, or the story of a memory, told by others. The girl had naked feet – soles blackened, nails made loose by dirt and disease – and they'd been cuffed together and chained to the factory floor. The radius of her personal freedom was about five feet, Frank estimated, more than he'd seen at the other work stations.

She did not register Frank's presence, even when he said hello and asked if she was in pain. She went on toying with her coins, tipping them awkwardly from hand to hand.

"Is that your money?" asked Frank, trying to get her attention. And it was only then that she froze in her game, seeing the man for the first time, and pulling back into the safety under the workbench.

The girl stared at the stranger. Then she held out her left hand. In its palm, six coins.

241

Frank saw how the ends of her fingers had been taken off by the work, either in an accident or scraped away by exertion, each fragile, off-white bone glinting faintly. And he noticed, on the inside of her left wrist, a tattoo: a string of numbers beginning 701 and ending with an X.

She looked at Frank hopefully. He reached out to take her money but she snatched it away, closing her hand about the coins and holding her clenched fist tightly against her chest.

"Get your own!" screeched the girl whose name began 701 and ended with an X. "Ain't nothing for free in this world!"

"Sorry," said Frank. "I'm sorry." He withdrew his hand. "How long have you been here?"

"That's what makes the world go round," she said. "You'll learn that. You get nothing for nothing. Not in this world. Little Miss Nothing from Nowhere."

Her accent was from the east, perhaps Polish or Russian. She'd picked up fragments of English but it was mimicked rather than spoken with any real comprehension.

"Who did this?"

"An honest wage for a day's work," she babbled. "70143892X. Lucky. Very lucky. Give their right arm to be you. Very lucky."

"I have to go," said Frank, "but later, when I can, I'll call an ambulance." She did not seem to understand. "Help. I'll get help. But I can't now."

"Help you," she said. "We will help you. We will take you to the west. But you owe us. You owe us."

She was becoming anxious, quite agitated. She repeated, "You owe us. You owe us. You must work here to pay."

And then she was offering the coins again, the girl who began 701 and ended with an X, and saying, "I pay! I pay!"

"No need," said Frank, trying to make himself understood. "Not necessary. Help will be free."

She did not comprehend, and she raised her voice almost to a scream.

"I pay! I pay! I owe you!"

Frank made to stand, but before he'd unbent his legs the girl had skittered out from under the bench and leapt at him. She was malnourished, but the momentum sent the pair careering backwards, and they crashed to the floor. His hand shot down instinctively to protect the bag of diamonds.

And then he was underneath her, his back grinding on bits of glass, sunlight blinding his eyes. Somehow, he scrambled backwards and edged out from beneath his deluded attacker.

But in a second she was upon him again.

She had an unexpected strength, summoned as if from a drug or manic need, and he lay helpless as she quickly positioned herself astride his body.

She ripped open his jacket. She tore at his shirt with her red fingertips.

Lifting her palm reverently, and holding it flat like a little girl, she brought forward her small pile of silver.

"I pay," she said. "You take."

Her voice brought Frank back to himself, and he realised he'd been transfixed by the reflection of his own face in her eyes.

But it was too late. The girl who began 701 and finished with an X lowered herself down and drove her teeth into Frank, urgently and with confidence, and he writhed and screamed as she chewed a hole into which she might push all six of her filthy coins.

*

The events of the last few days – the robbery, the aftermath, how they'd fled – swirled through Frank's mind as he slept, but he did not stir, safe as he was, comfortable as he was, surrounded as he was by the thick steel shell of the Land Rover.

*

Next it was Judith who entered Frank's dream, cautiously opening the door to their hotel room, and saying, "My God. What happened?" And Frank staggering in, slumping down, and Judith checking the corridor, left and right, and then quickly closing the door.

When he sat on the bed his blood soaked into it, and Jane, who'd been watching cartoons, began to cry, confused and upset, and Isabelle stared at her father with anger and disappointment.

"I need to get these clothes off," he said to Judith. "Help me."

They pulled off the jacket and peeled the shirt from his chest. His belt was crusty with blood. He'd stemmed the flow with paper towels from a public toilet, but he was still shiny, still red. And at the origin of the red, a long gash curved like a grin.

"Get a towel from the bathroom," he said. "A large one."

After wrapping the bath towel about him they held it in position by looping his belt around his ribcage like a temporary tourniquet. Frank groaned in agony as they buckled it, and Jane, his youngest daughter, hid her face against Isabelle, her elder sister, and Frank swore at the pain – words his children had never heard – and Isabelle said, "We want to go home!"

243

"Soon," said Judith. "Tomorrow."

"Not that farm," said Isabelle. "I don't want to go to that stupid farm. I want to go home. And Jane does, too."

"I knew something bad would happen," said Judith. "You don't turn on your own."

"It was nothing to do with Jimmy," Frank said through his teeth. "It was some crazy woman."

"What woman?"

"It wasn't empty, the old mill. Something got left behind. I don't know what the hell it was."

"You need the hospital," said Judith. "Or a doctor."

"First things first," said Frank. "Put the kids in the car. We leave tonight, not tomorrow. Everything else can wait."

*

They slowed down and halted at a red light on the outer edge of Bradford. In the back seat, Jane sat covered in drying tears, exhausted. Beside her, Isabelle stared gloomily at the window.

"Is this really it?" said Judith.

"We don't come back," said Frank. "Jimmy will be all over the flat. Then the hotels. He won't rest."

"I love this city."

"You'll love the farm."

"I hate the countryside."

"It's only until things settle down. Then we can plan Spain."

The light changed and they drove on, and Judith said, "I'm so sad. I've lost everything."

"Quite the opposite," said Frank. "We have all we need."

And in the back seat, Isabelle listened, miserable for her mother, sad for her sister, and very, very angry at her father.

*

They drove in silence, and the kids fell asleep, and at last their journey came into its final hour. Along the lane parallel to the woods. Below the ridge. Onto the track.

Hard mud cracked like little bones in the night. Their exhaust dispensed its fumes about the forest. And on they went, through the trees to Black Top Farm.

*

And Frank dreamed of Dr Stone, untying the belt from around his chest, peeling back the stiff hotel towel, and saying: "Doesn't look like a dog-bite. Why don't you tell me what really happened?"

In the dream Frank remembered how the door to Dr Stone's consulting room had been left ajar, and how he'd seen all the other patients gathered in the waiting room, the good folk of Lastingham, listening in on the blood-soaked stranger who'd stumbled in from nowhere, asking for his wound to be cleaned and stitched, while his family waited in their big car outside.

"Where did it happen?" the doctor had asked. "The attack …"

"Not around here."

"Some city I'd guess," said Stone. "Manchester or London. Maybe Leeds."

"Somewhere like that."

"You'll need a blood test. And your family. I dread to think what evil might be alive in your system and theirs."

To illustrate the seriousness of the injury, Stone had held a mirror below Frank's armpit. "Look," he said. "Take a look for yourself. No animal did that. No thing that should be walking this earth did that."

As he withdrew the mirror, and stepped away, Stone's attention had been drawn back to the hole in Frank's side. He peered, squinting, his eyesight poor, at the open wound. Then, shaking his head, he said, "Funny, thought I saw something glinting in there. Must be a trick of the light."

He'd turned away then, to pick up an instrument, and said, "No doubt about it, though. That is the bite of a monster. Quite simply, a monster."

At that, Frank heard the whispering begin, out in the waiting room, a concerned, guarded murmur. He felt weak and disoriented, and it hadn't occurred to him to ask if the door might be closed. The doctor seemed oblivious.

Painstakingly slow, and with a tremor in his unpractised hand, Dr Stone pierced the skin, and as the needle went in Frank heard one of the villagers say something that was above a whisper.

One word. One solitary word:

"Monster."

*

The receptionist, in the busy waiting room, had insisted Frank provide his address. He'd had a blood test, she said, and they would need to inform him of the result. Had he not been feeling odd, he would have refused, or written it down. But he was not himself.

Having his wound sewn up had made him not feel right. He felt hot. He could feel his blood rushing in his limbs. And his palms itched. They really, really itched.

"Just up the road," he'd said.

"That's not an address. I need to know where you live, Mr ..." She looked down at her pad. "Mr White."

"The farm."

"Which farm? Yew Tree? Old Brook?"

"Black Top," he said quietly. "Black Top Farm."

But he knew, despite the low pitch of his voice, that the people of Lastingham, sitting behind him with their headaches and their haemorrhoids and their abject fear of monsters, had heard what he'd said.

*

He had not felt well after the doctor had pieced him back together. He'd climbed into bed at Black Top Farm and tried to relax, but it had not been easy. The skin that had been repaired throbbed, as if from inside, as if some inner part had become suddenly alive. His blood pumped hard around his body. And the itching in his palms had intensified.

Beside the bed, in a cereal bowl, the diamonds shimmered and dazzled in the late afternoon sun. They absorbed the orange glow that pushed through the rag-like curtain and bounced it onto the opposite wall.

Frank stared at the kaleidoscope, sliding and shifting on the wallpaper, and his eyes felt heavy. Lulled by the dancing pattern, in love with it no less, Frank's eyes began to close.

When he woke it was after only twenty minutes. Before he opened his eyes, his hand reached out for the bowl. His fingers scrabbled inside. All they made was an awful scratching noise.

It was empty.

*

In the Land Rover, Frank felt a deep sorrow pass through his sleep as he dreamed of the empty cereal bowl. He began to stir, but before he did he dreamed one last dream, and it was a dream of Isabelle.

It was their second night at the farm. Isabelle was in bed. She held a thin blanket up to her chin. The wind was blowing off the moor and the house was creaking. She'd been crying the last two hours. Her father had shouted at her that afternoon, saying some wicked things. But she hadn't told him where she'd hid the

246

diamonds. She firmly believed her family was better off without them.

Frank stood on the landing, talking quietly with Judith.

"She's attention seeking," she said. "She didn't want to leave Bradford. Don't worry. You'll find them."

"This is a big house,' said Frank. "Plus the outbuildings. And how many acres of farmland?"

"You think she might have buried them?"

"Treasure, isn't it."

"Go in and make up with her," said Judith. "She's more likely to confess her hiding place if you're nice to her. Make a game of it."

Frank sighed, and walked into his daughter's bedroom. She refused to look up. After a few minutes of silence, she said, "I can't sleep. I don't like sleeping here. I hate this house." Then: "Tell me a story."

"What story?" he said.

"That's your job."

"What stories does Mum tell you?"

"All kinds. The ones about animals are best."

"Do you want to hear a story about an animal?"

"No," she said, looking out the window at the stars that shone brightly in the absolute dark of this place. "I want a story about the stars."

Instantly, an idea occurred to him, of how he might elicit the information he wanted.

"Do you know where they came from?" he asked. "The stars …"

"No."

"It all began with a Prince," he said. "Listen …"

And Frank began his story, the last he would ever tell his child.

*

This is the story of the Prince, the Stars and the Little Girl, and it happened a long time ago. In fact, it was so long ago, it was before the sky even had stars. Instead, it had only blackness, and under that blackness there lived a Prince …

He was a very handsome Prince, and he was also very rich. But he hadn't always been rich. When he was a boy he'd been poor. He'd lived in a house with a hole in the roof, and at night the cold wind had whistled through the rooms. He would shiver and sob in his bed, and ache from hunger.

But he was a Prince, nonetheless. He knew this because his mother had told him. She'd said, "Son, you are not like the others.

247

You have different blood in your veins. You are a Prince among men. And one day all the world shall be yours."

She had not lied, the boy's mother, and when he was a young man he claimed the riches that were rightfully his.

But, also in the city where the Prince lived, there was a mischievous little girl. And, seeing the Prince's wealth, she decided to play a trick on him.

One day, she entered the Prince's palace, intent on finding his loot. She searched high and low, and soon she found a bag of beautiful diamonds.

The little girl took the diamonds, but the Prince heard her, and he chased her as she fled. She ran into the night, and the Prince followed. He chased her through the city, and when the city ended, he chased her into the desert. She ran and ran.

At last, the little girl could run no more, and the Prince drew near. She was desperate for the Prince not to take back his diamonds, but the little girl had nowhere to hide them.

Then she looked up at the sky. It was black and empty. In those days, the stars did not exist.

The little girl stopped running. She held the diamonds in her hands. Then she flung them as high as she could … and they stuck in the darkness, twinkling and beautiful, the first stars to ever be born.

When the Prince caught up with her he could not understand where the treasure had gone. He did not think to look up …

*

"Then what happened?" asked Isabelle.

"The Prince was sad," said Frank. "Because he could not figure out how to get the diamonds back down from the sky."

"So it wasn't a happy ending?"

"Far from it."

"I don't like that story," said Isabelle. "They both end up with nothing."

"Well," said Frank. "What would you have done? If that little girl was you, where would you have hidden the treasure?"

But Isabelle wasn't falling for it, and she closed her eyes, unprepared to entertain further talk of unhappy Princes.

*

It was almost night when the sleep the tablet had induced fully lifted. Frank stretched in the driver's seat, and rubbed his eyes. He'd slept longer than he'd wanted, but he felt the best he had in days. He had renewed enthusiasm and hope.

Leaving the Land Rover, Frank walked through the yard to the house. It was raining, a drab curtain becoming a downpour. Upstairs, on the landing, he averted his gaze from the blood-sodden floorboards, and entered Isabelle's room.

It did not take long to search her things. They hadn't had space in the car to bring much. She had a few toys, some books. Drawings – crayon renditions of the farm she did not like, and the home they'd left – had been Blu-tacked to the wall. A third illustration depicted a woman, scruffy and feral, baring her teeth as a man, presumably Frank, dragged himself away trailing blood. Beside the figure of Frank, Isabelle had written how brave her father was, how he'd fended off his attacker. She'd also scribbled a short prayer, explaining to God about her father's blood test, and asking if the illness inside him could be taken away.

He turned from the pictures, his eye drawn to the window and, beyond it, the garden, and above the garden the land that sloped up to the moor.

It was onto that ridge – less than seven days before – that the first inhabitant of Lastingham had stepped. And, as the day had set, the horizon had slowly filled. Five or more silhouettes, all along the crest of the valley in jagged outline, looking down at the house.

That had been the arrival, which Frank had watched from the bedroom, before locking and barricading the doors and windows, and hurrying his family up the stairs in a confused mess of questions and tears.

They'd waited until it was fully dark, the good people of Lastingham. They'd loitered up there between the land and the sky, lanterns swaying in the wind like lamps on an ocean. And then, in the absolute black, a sinister wave had broken, and they'd come falling on the farm.

They'd paced about in the grounds outside, duty-bound, bloodlust incarnate circling the house.

None had carried a weapon. They'd come brandishing only their bare hands. And, in their righteousness, they'd been inhumanly strong: snapping bones without effort, opening skulls like bad eggs.

Only Frank had been fortunate enough to survive. He and his family had been cornered by the posse on the landing, and Frank had flipped open the attic hatch and hauled himself up. He'd intended to lift Judith and the girls up behind him, but with no one guarding the top step the village folk had poured upstairs from the kitchen, filling the narrow passage, blocking the light and causing the staircase to creak under their gathered weight.

Frank's fever had not dissipated. The last sight he'd seen, through his dizzied vision, had been Isabelle's legs jerking stiffly as somebody snatched and silenced her from behind, while Jane went running into the bathroom but tripped and fell and was dragged out by her ankles. And, as he sealed the hatch, a heavy hand had lifted Judith by the throat, several feet off the floor, her head pushed back against the beige wallpaper, urine splashing down the inside of her leg as the fingers closed about her neck.

They'd scratched at the attic hatch until after midnight. Eventually, unable to prise it up, they'd returned to the yard, and attempted to burn down the house. Frank had watched from the attic window. Luckily, it had been raining, and every flame had failed to catch.

The next morning, Frank had lowered himself down from the attic, and fled from the farm.

Ten, fifteen miles later, the bloodied soles of his boots slipping about on the pedals, he'd braked, turned the car around, and driven back.

*

The night in the attic had altered Frank. His fever had cooled, his blood reduced to a normal pace. After the villagers had left – climbing reluctantly back up the incline to the moor, the hands that held the lanterns smeared with the blood of monsters – Frank had slumped against the wall, exhausted.

His palms itched like crazy, as if they needed to cling to something. He had no thought aside that of the diamonds. He thought they were the only thing that might help the itching abate.

Momentarily, he remembered the girl in the abandoned sweatshop, chained to her workstation, coveting her coins. He pictured his beautiful gems glinting in their hiding place, cold and ownerless, and he ached.

Sitting in the attic, the sun rising over the moor, his family butchered on the floor below, he'd felt, oddly, as if he was falling in love. But it was not human love. It was a love for the twinkling stones he'd grabbed from inside the smashed counter while the alarm screamed in that shop in Bradford.

Like normal love, it felt good, and it made him feel strong. And like normal love, it was breaking his heart.

*

Frank found no clue to indicate the whereabouts of the diamonds, and as a last resort looked under Isabelle's bed. He found nothing. But as he got to his feet, he noticed a few sheets of writing paper poking out from under the scummy pillow on which his daughter had been made to lay her head.

The paper was daubed in Isabelle's tight, practised handwriting. She'd rewritten Frank's bedtime story, the tale of the Prince. It began the same, but when Frank flicked to the end, he saw that her version had finished with the words: 'Happy ever after!'

Isabelle had called it: 'A Story From When We Had Nothing'.

Frank sat and read. In the middle of the tale, instead of hurling the diamonds into the sky, the little girl had buried them, and to help her retrieve them later, she'd drawn a map.

The map was set out like a constellation of stars, half a dozen dots of yellow crayon on a black background, all swirling around a central star that was bigger than the rest.

Relief coursed through Frank's nervous system, and tears filled his eyes. He flew downstairs, through the kitchen and into the garden.

Holding the map before him, and squinting in the last of the light, he tried to estimate where in the garden the constellation's midpoint might fall. He formulated a rough idea. It wasn't precise, but it reduced the search area to about twenty-five square feet.

He picked up the trowel and dessert spoon and waded into the long grass. His heart hammered as he stepped near the central star. It hammered and hammered. It was that loud he thought all of Yorkshire might hear.

He crouched, and as he did, he noticed a figure step forward onto the edge of the moor. Soon, it was followed by a second, and a third, and then more, and they were all broad and darkly shaped, and they lined up side-by-side on the burnt heather, lanterns swaying.

*

The good people of Lastingham truly believed that a family of monsters had moved into Black Top Farm. They'd arrived on an otherwise indifferent morning, spat out by some awful metropolitan jungle: Father Monster, Mother Monster, and a pair of giggling Girl Monsters.

Father Monster had stumbled into the morning surgery, unsteady on his feet, feverish and shivering and bearing all down his left-hand side the mark of a thing that Dr Stone said should not be breathing the air of our Earth.

251

Word had spread rapidly. Within the day precautionary measures had been decided. It was a sad reflection on modern life that they had to protect their community like this. They had not resorted to the old ways in more than a quarter of a century. But at least five villagers had overheard the diagnosis. Their corner of the world was too special to allow a thing like this to thrive.

A group would be sent by night, it was agreed, over the moor from Lastingham to where the brood had established its nest, the purpose of the nocturnal visit to execute all four of their kind. The group, a selection of random villagers, some old, some young, the former to coach the latter in how to handle a threat of this nature, had succeeded in its aim, and they'd returned safely home a few hours later, hands painted red in the moonlight.

Except one of the diseased had got away. He'd escaped into the top of the house and they hadn't been able to lure him down.

It was that fourth monster, the one that called itself Mr White, that they came for now.

*

Before the figures had finished their descent from the moor, Frank retrieved the shotgun and shells from the Land Rover. He ran into every room and locked the windows. The back door was hanging partly off its hinge from the earlier barrage, but he closed it best he could, shouldering it into its frame. Then he barricaded it with the kitchen table.

He loaded the gun, but it would not be enough and he looked around for a subsidiary weapon. The stools were carved from solid wood. He raised one above his head and brought it down on the edge of the Belfast sink. A leg snapped away, heavy and sharp at the end. He picked it up and swung it back and forth.

He yelled, guttural and raw, arcing the improvised club from left to right and back. He yelled again, and bared his teeth.

When this gang of local killers had called before, he'd been weak, unable to fend them off. Now, though, he felt strong. Like he had new blood, or as if he had behind him an authority with which they could not contend.

He had something worth fighting for, this time, the mud-smeared diamonds stuffed in his pockets.

Walking backwards, so he could watch the door, Frank positioned himself halfway across the room. He stood in the middle of the kitchen, ready with the gun and the stool-leg. First he would shoot bullets into the belly or face of whoever entered. At the end of the bullets he would advance with the piece of broken furniture, and aim for the side of the skull, the tender part.

In the gloom of the kitchen, Frank waited, and it did not take long for the door to begin jumping in its fixture. It leapt with each blow landed from outside. Fists and boots rained down on the panels, a methodical beating, and soon the door split further off its hinge.

Somebody came forward, and the gap that had opened up between door and frame was filled with a bearded mouth.

"I believe," it said, "that in this house resides a monster."

From the yard Frank heard raised voices, heralded by their leader. His grip on both weapons tightened.

Weight was applied to the door, and the space at its edge widened. The table scraped aside.

The man with the beard squeezed inside the house. His eyes hid in the dusk, but he had a steady, confident stature.

He stepped around the upended table, fists balled and heavy at his sides, until he stood across the room from Frank. Behind him, a youngish boy followed. In the semi-light, it was just possible to see that drool had formed on the younger man's chin, tipping out of his mouth, Frank presumed, at the promise of the kill. The boy ran his tongue over his lips.

Outside, others clamoured to be let through, crushing and climbing over each other to get at the abnormality inside.

The bearded man took a step toward Frank. The young boy also drew near, and it was not saliva bubbling over his lips, Frank realised, but blood. In his excitement, or fear, he'd chewed his tongue or bitten down on the tissue inside his mouth. He wiped the back of his hand over his lips and it came away coloured like a bruise.

"You must understand," said the bearded man to Frank, "that the city is built on different soil. It grows a different people."

Others would pour into the house any moment, Frank knew, and fill it like smoke. But he was not afraid. His palms had stopped itching when he'd held the diamonds. And the entry the girl had made in his flesh, which had since been sealed, felt as if it held within it a different heart.

The young boy's jaw churned and churned and blood and spit hung from his lower lip in strings. He said something that was lost in the mess of his mouth, except for the word "monster", which was just legible, and at which the bearded intruder nodded and patted the young acolyte on the back, as if one day he would be fit to fill the older man's shoes.

253

"I'm afraid you're wrong," said Frank. "No monsters here. Just an ordinary bloke trying to scratch out a living."

And he raised the gun and pulled the trigger.

*

It was cold on Lastingham Moor not long after dawn. Frank shivered in his coat. He carried the rucksack, inside of which he had diamonds sufficient in value to live a decent life on mainland Europe for many years. He did not foresee hardship.

Too injured to drive, he limped out of Yorkshire with damage to the left femur and many bruises, below a sunless sky hanging like a roof of dead skin. The landscape was old and empty, with only the occasional tree erupting in the distance from out of the grey nowhere, and now and then a wooden sign or pile of rocks to guide unfamiliar travellers on their way.

Back at Black Top Farm, the last of the exterminators from Lastingham village crawled out from among the dead. It was the young boy, he who'd bled from the mouth, and he dragged his battered body out over the back step and into the rain and the mud of the yard, alive with a tale to tell, a different life ahead of him, and a bite shaped like a grin in the side of his chest.

SOURCES

All of these stories are original to *Terror Tales of Yorkshire*, with the exception of 'The Crawl' by Stephen Laws, which first appeared in *White of the Moon*, 1997, and 'All Things Considered, I'd Rather Be In Hell' by Mark Chadbourn, which first appeared in *Peeping Tom #27*, 1997.

FUTURE TITLES

If you enjoyed *Terror Tales of Yorkshire*, why not seek out the first six volumes in this series: *Terror Tales of the Lake District*, *Terror Tales of the Cotswolds*, *Terror Tales of East Anglia*, *Terror Tales of London*, *Terror Tales of the Seaside* and *Terror Tales of Wales* – available from most good online retailers, including Amazon, or order directly from http://www.grayfriarpress.com/index.html.

In addition, watch out for the next title in this series, *Terror Tales of the Scottish Highlands*. Check regularly for updates with Gray Friar Press and on the editor's own webpage: http://paulfinch-writer.blogspot.co.uk/. Alternatively, follow him on Twitter: @paulfinchauthor.

CPSIA information can be obtained
at www.ICGtesting.com
Printed in the USA
LVOW11s1424261017
553883LV00001B/28/P